Praise for
THE LOVE SEASON

"In a juicy peach of a summer tome, Hilderbrand again alchemizes her three favorite elements—food, love, and Nantucket—with eminently readable results. . . . *The Love Season* is so gratifying."

—*Entertainment Weekly*

"[S]ummer fare that's a cut above the usual beach provisions . . . Hilderbrand, who wrote 2002's *Nantucket Nights*, serves up a mouth-watering menu, keeps the Veuve Clicquot flowing, and tops it all with a dollop of mystery that will have even drowsy sunbathers turning pages until the very satisfying end."

—*People* (four stars)

"Hilderbrand's fifth book is a fulfilling tale of familial excavation and self-exploration. . . . It's a refreshing, resonant summertime treat." —*Publishers Weekly*

"Hilderbrand's sensitive portrayal of a young motherless woman on a journey of self-discovery, and her guilt-ridden godmother's attempt to find the courage to confront the past, is very moving." —*Booklist*

"A good page-turner." —*Library Journal*

"As a storyteller, Hilderbrand ranks among the best, and she has ingeniously constructed this foray into the past around a meal . . . .This is a don't-miss novel."

—*The Star-Ledger* (Newark)

BLUE BISTRO

"A[n] enjoyable beach book."   —*Publishers Weekly*

"Hilderbrand keeps things moving briskly in between sumptuous descriptions of food, drink, and tableware, throwing in an in-depth lesson on the restaurant business for good measure. Fun, stylish, and absorbing vacation reading."   —*Booklist*

SUMMER PEOPLE

"Entertaining . . . Hilderbrand's third Nantucket-set novel effectively juxtaposes the surface calm of the season with the turbulence of the characters' lives."   —*Booklist*

NANTUCKET NIGHTS

"Things get more twisted at every turn with enough lies and betrayals to fuel a whole season of soap operas... readers will be hooked."   —*Publishers Weekly*

"Dips deep into Peyton Place country."

—*Kirkus Reviews*

THE BEACH CLUB

"Surprisingly touching...a work of fiction you're likely to think about long after you've put it down."

—*People*

"A charming, easygoing story about the tangled lives and loves of the summer crew and guests at a hotel and beach club."   —*Boston Globe*

Also by Elin Hilderbrand

The Blue Bistro

Summer People

Nantucket Nights

The Beach Club

The
Love Season

Elin
Hilderbrand

St. Martin's Paperbacks

This is a work of fiction. All of the characters, organizations, and events portrayed in this novel are either products of the author's imagination or are used fictitiously.

Published in the United States by St. Martin's Paperbacks, an imprint of St. Martin's Publishing Group.

THE LOVE SEASON

Copyright © 2006 by Elin Hilderbrand.

All rights reserved.

For information address St. Martin's Publishing Group, 120 Broadway, New York, NY 10271.

www.stmartins.com

Library of Congress Catalog Card Number: 2006040190

ISBN: 978-1-250-62287-7

Our books may be purchased in bulk for promotional, educational, or business use. Please contact your local bookseller or the Macmillan Corporate and Premium Sales Department at 1-800-221-7945, ext. 5442, or by email at MacmillanSpecialMarkets@macmillan.com.

Printed in the United States of America

St. Martin's Press hardcover edition / June 2006
St. Martin's Griffin trade paperback edition / May 2007
St. Martin's Paperbacks edition / June 2015

10 9 8 7 6 5 4

*For Margie Holahan—
a friend for all seasons
XO*

Part One

Provisions

August 19, 2006 • 6:30 A.M.

M arguerite didn't know where to start.

Each and every summer evening for nearly twenty years, she had cooked for a restaurant full of people, yet here she was in her own kitchen on a crystalline morning with a seemingly simple mission—dinner for two that evening at seven thirty—and she didn't know where to start. Her mind spun like the pedals of a bicycle without any brakes. Candace coming here, after all these years. Immediately Marguerite corrected herself. Not Candace. Candace was dead. Renata was coming tonight. The baby.

Marguerite's hands quivered as she brought her coffee mug to her lips. The grandfather clock chimed just as it had every fifteen minutes of its distinguished life—but this time, the sound startled Marguerite. She pictured a monkey inside, with two small cymbals and a voice screeching, *Marguerite! Earth to Marguerite!*

Marguerite chuckled. *I am an old bat,* she thought. *I'll start by writing a list.*

The phone call had come at eleven o'clock the night before. Marguerite was in bed, reading Hemingway. Whereas once Marguerite had been obsessed with food—with heirloom tomatoes and lamb shanks and farmhouse cheeses, and fish still flopping on the counter, and eggs and chocolate and black truffles and foie gras and rare white nectarines—now the only thing that gave her genuine pleasure was reading. The people of Nantucket wondered— oh yes, she knew they wondered—what Marguerite *did* all day, hermited in her house on Quince Street, secreted away from the eyes of the curious. Although there was always something—the laundry, the garden, the articles for the newspaper in Calgary (deadline every other Friday)— the answer was: reading. Marguerite had three books going at any one time. That was the chef in her, the proverbial more-than-one-pot-on-the-stove. She read contemporary fiction in the mornings, though she was very picky. She liked Philip Roth, Penelope Lively, as a rule no one under the age of fifty, for what could they possibly have to say about the world that Marguerite hadn't already learned? In the afternoons, she enriched herself with biographies or books of European history, if they weren't too dense. Her evenings were reserved for the classics, and when the phone rang the night before Marguerite had been reading Hemingway. Hemingway was the perfect choice for late at night because his sentences were clear and easy to understand, though Marguerite stopped every few pages and asked herself, *Is that all he means? Might he mean*

something else? This insecurity was a result of attending
the Culinary Institute instead of a proper university—and
all those years with Porter didn't help. *An education makes
you good company for yourself,* Porter had liked to tell his
students, and Marguerite, when he was trying to convince
her to read something other than *Larousse Gastronomique.*
Wouldn't he be proud of her now.

The phone, much like the muted toll of the clock a few
seconds ago, had scared Marguerite out of her wits. She
gasped, and her book slid off her lap to the floor, where it
lay with its pages folded unnaturally under, like a person
with a broken limb. The phone, a rotary, continued its
cranky, mechanical whine while Marguerite groped her
nightstand for her watch. Eleven o'clock. Marguerite could
name on one hand the phone calls she'd received in the
past twelve months: There was a call or two from the
editorial assistant at the Calgary paper; there was a call
from the Culinary Institute each spring asking for a dona-
tion; there was always a call from Porter on November 3,
her birthday. None of these people would ever think to call
her at eleven o'clock at night—not even Porter, drunk (not
even if he'd split from the nubile young graduate assistant
who had become his late-in-life wife), would dare call Marguerite at this hour. So it was a wrong number. Marguerite
decided to let it ring. She had no answering machine to put
the phone out of its misery; it just rang and rang, as plead-
ing and insistent as a crying baby. Marguerite picked it up,
clearing her throat first. She occasionally went a week
without speaking.

"Hello?"

"Aunt Daisy?" The voice had been light and cheerful;
there was background noise—people talking, jazz music,
the familiar clink and clatter of glasses and plates—was
it *restaurant* noise? It threw Marguerite off. And then

there was the nickname: *Daisy.* Only three people had ever used it.

"Yes?"

"It's Renata." There was an expectant pause. "Renata Knox."

Marguerite's eyes landed across the room, on her desk. Taped to her computer was Renata Knox's e-mail address; Marguerite beheld it every day as she binged guiltily on the Internet for an hour, but she had never sent a single message. Because what could she possibly say? A casual hello would be pointless and anything more, dangerous. Marguerite's eyes skittered from her desk to her dresser. On top of her dresser were two precious framed photographs. She dusted them carefully each week, though she rarely lingered over them anymore. Years ago she had scrutinized them so intensely that they imprinted themselves on her brain. She knew them by heart, the way she knew the streets in the sixth arrondissement, the way she knew the temperament of a soufflé. One picture was of Marguerite and Candace taken at Les Parapluies on the occasion of Renata's christening. In it, Marguerite was holding Renata, her goddaughter. How well she remembered that moment. It had taken a magnum of Veuve Clicquot and several glasses of thirty-year port to get Dan to relinquish his grip on his newborn daughter, and when he did, it was only to Candace so that the baby could nurse. Marguerite sat with Candace on the west banquette as the party thundered around them. Marguerite knew little of babies, or lactation; she fed people every day, but nothing was as captivating as watching Candace feed her daughter. When Candace finished, she eased the baby up over her shoulder until the baby burped. Then Candace passed her over to Marguerite casually, like she was a loaf of bread.

Go see your godmother, Candace said to the baby.

Godmother, Marguerite had thought. The last time she had been inside a church before that very morning was for Candace and Dan's wedding, and before that the Cathedral of Notre-Dame in Paris the year she met Porter, and so her notion of godmother came mostly from fairy tales. Marguerite had gazed down at the baby's tiny pink mouth, which still made the motion of sucking even though the breast was gone, and thought, *I will feed you your first escargot. I will pour your first glass of champagne.*

"Aunt Daisy?" Renata said.

"Yes, dear," Marguerite said. The poor girl probably thought Marguerite was as crazy as the islanders said she was—*self-mutilation, months in a psychiatric hospital, gave up her restaurant*—or worse, she thought Marguerite didn't know who she was. How surprised the child would be to find out that Marguerite thought of her, and of Candace, every day. The memories ran through her veins. *But enough of that!* Marguerite thought. *I have the girl on the phone!* "I'm sorry, darling. You caught me by surprise."

"Were you sleeping?" Renata asked. "It's awfully late."

"No," Marguerite said. "Not sleeping. In bed, reading. Where are you, darling? Are you at school?"

"I don't start back for three more weeks," Renata said.

"Oh, right," Marguerite said. "Silly of me." Already she felt like the conversation was a dog she'd agreed to take for a walk, one that yanked on its chain, urging Marguerite to catch up. It was August now; when Renata went back to college she'd be a . . . sophomore? Marguerite had sent Renata five thousand dollars for her high school graduation the spring before last—an outrageous sum, though who else did Marguerite have to give her money to? Renata had graduated first in her class, and although she'd been accepted at Yale and Stanford, she'd decided on

Columbia, where Porter was still chairman of the art history department. Renata had sent Marguerite a sweet little thank-you note for the money in loopy script with a lot of exclamation points—and Dan had dashed off a note as well on his office stationery. *Once again, Margo, you've done too much. Hope you are well.* Marguerite noticed he had not actually said thank you, but that would have been hoping for too much. After all these years, Dan still hadn't forgiven her. He thought she sent the money out of guilt when really she had sent it out of love.

"Where are you then?" Marguerite asked. In his annual Christmas letter, Dan had written about Renata's infatuation with her literature classes, her work-study job in the admissions office, and her roommate, but he had hinted nothing about her summer plans.

"I'm here on Nantucket," Renata said. "I'm at 21 Federal."

Marguerite suddenly felt very warm; sweat broke out on her forehead and under her arms. And menopause for her had ended sometime during the first Clinton administration.

"You're *here*?" Marguerite said.

"For the weekend. Until Sunday. I'm here with my fiancé."

"Your *what*?"

"His name is Cade," Renata said. "His family has a house on Hulbert Avenue."

Marguerite stroked the fraying satin edge of her summer blanket. Fiancé at age nineteen? And Dan had allowed it? *The boy must be rich,* Marguerite thought sardonically. *Hulbert Avenue.* But even she had a hard time believing that Dan would give Renata away while she was still a teenager. People didn't change that fundamentally. Daniel

Knox would always be the father holding possessively on to his little girl. He had never liked to share her.

Marguerite realized Renata was waiting for an answer. "I see."

"His parents know all about you," Renata said. "They used to eat at the restaurant. They said it was the best place. They said they miss it."

"That's very nice," Marguerite said. She wondered who Cade's parents were. Had they been regulars or once-a-summer people? Would Marguerite recognize their names, their faces? Had they said anything else to Renata about what they knew, or thought they knew?

"I'm dying to come see you," Renata said. "Cade wants to meet you, too, but I told him I want to come by myself."

"Of course, dear," Marguerite said. She straightened in bed so that her posture was as perfect as it had been nearly sixty years ago, ballet class, Madame Verge asking her students to pretend there was a wire that ran from the tops of their heads to the ceiling. *Chins up, mes choux!* Marguerite was so happy she thought she might levitate. Her heart was buoyant. Renata was here on Nantucket; she wanted to see Marguerite. "Come tomorrow night. For dinner. Can you?"

"Of course!" Renata said. "What time would you like me?"

"Seven thirty," Marguerite said. At Les Parapluies, the bar had opened each night at six thirty and dinner was served at seven thirty. Marguerite had run the restaurant on that strict timetable for years without many exceptions, or much of an eye toward profitability.

"I'll be there," Renata said.

"Five Quince Street," Marguerite said. "You'll be able to find it?"

"Yes," said Renata. In the background there was a burst of laughter. "So I'll see you tomorrow night, Aunt Daisy, okay?"

"Okay," Marguerite said. "Good night, dear."

With that, Marguerite had replaced the heavy black receiver in its cradle and thought, *Only for her.*

Marguerite had not cooked a meal in fourteen years.

8:00 A.M.

Marguerite left her house infrequently. Once every two weeks to the A&P for groceries, once a month to the bank and to the post office for stamps. Once each season to stock up at both bookstores. Once a year to the doctor for a checkup and to Don Allen Ford to get her Jeep inspected. When she was out, she always bumped into people she knew, though they were never the people she wished to see, and thus she stuck to a smile, a hello. *Let them think what they want.* And Marguerite, both amused and alarmed by her own indifference, cackled under her breath like a crazy witch.

But when Marguerite stepped out of her house this morning—she had been ready for over an hour, pacing near the door like a thoroughbred bucking at the gate, waiting for the little monkey inside her clock to announce that it was a suitable hour to venture forth—everything seemed transformed. The morning sparkled. Renata was coming. They were to have dinner. A dinner party.

Armed with her list and her pocketbook, Marguerite strolled down Quince Street, inhaling its beauty. The houses were all antiques, with friendship stairs and transom windows, pocket gardens and picket fences. It was, in Marguerite's mind, the loveliest street on the island, although she didn't allow herself to enjoy it often, rarely in summer and certainly never at this hour. She sometimes strolled it on a winter night; she sometimes peered in the windows of the homes that had been deserted for fairer climates. The police once stopped her; a lone policeman, not much more than a teenager himself, started spinning his lights and came poking through the dark with his flashlight just as Marguerite was gazing in the front window of a house down the street. It was a house Marguerite had always loved from the outside; it was very old, with white clapboard and wavy leaded glass, and the people who owned it, Marguerite learned from nosing around, had fine taste in French antiques. The policeman thought she was trying to rob it maybe, though he had seemed nervous to confront her. He'd asked her what she was doing, and she had said, *Just looking.* This answer hadn't satisfied the officer much. *Do you have a home?* he'd asked. And Marguerite had laughed and pointed. *Number Five,* she'd said. *I live at Number Five.* He'd suggested she "get on home," because it was cold; it was, in fact, Christmas. Christmas night, and Marguerite had been wandering her own street, like a transient, like a ghost looking for a place to haunt.

Marguerite reached Centre Street, took a left, then a quick right, and headed down Broad Street, past the bookstore, past the French bistro that had absorbed all of Marguerite's old customers. She was aimed for Dusty Tyler's fish shop. Marguerite's former restaurant, Les Parapluies, had been open for dinner seven nights a week from May through October, and every night but Monday Marguerite had served seafood from Dusty Tyler's shop. Dusty was Marguerite's age, which was to say, not so young anymore. They'd had a close professional relationship, and on top of it they had been friends. Dusty came into the bar nearly every night the year his wife left him, and sometimes he brought his ten-year-old son in for dinner. Dusty had gotten very drunk one night, starting at six thirty with vodka gimlets served up by Lance, Marguerite's moody bartender. He then ordered two bottles of Mersault and drank all but one glass, which he sent to Marguerite back in the kitchen. By the time dinner service was over, the waitresses were complaining about Dusty—he was out-of-bounds, obnoxious, bordering on criminal. *Get him out of here, Margo,* the headwaiter, Francesca, had said. It was a Sunday night, and the fish shop was closed on Mondays. Marguerite overruled the pleas of her staff, which was rare, and allowed Dusty to stay. He stayed long after everyone else went home, sitting at the zinc bar with Marguerite, sipping daintily from a glass of Chartreuse, which he had insisted he wanted. He was so drunk that he'd stopped making any kind of sense. He was babbling, then crying. There had been spittle in his beard, but he'd smelled salty and sweet, like an oyster. Marguerite had thought they would sleep together. She was more than ten years into her relationship with Porter at that point, though Porter spent nine months of the year in Manhattan and—it was well known to everyone—dated other women. It wasn't frustration with Porter, however, that led Marguerite to think of sex with Dusty. Rather, it was a sense of inevitability. They worked together every day; she was his first client every morning; they stood side by side, many times their hips touching as they lifted a bluefin tuna out of crushed ice, as they pried open sea scallops and cherry-stones, as they chopped the heads off shrimp. Dusty was destroyed by the departure of his wife, and Marguerite, with Porter off living his own life in the city, was lonely. It was late on a Sunday night; they were alone in the restaurant; Dusty was drunk. Sex was like a blinking neon sign hanging over the bar.

But for whatever reason, it hadn't happened. Dusty had rested his head on the bar, nudged the glass of Chartreuse aside, and passed out. Marguerite called a taxi from a company where she didn't know anyone, and a young guy wearing an Izod shirt, jeans, and penny loafers had dragged Dusty out to a Cadillac Fleetwood and driven him home. Marguerite felt—well, at first she felt childishly rejected. She wasn't a beauty, more handsome than pretty, her face was wide, her bottom heavier than she wished, though certain men—Porter among them—appreciated her independence, her God-given abilities in the kitchen, and the healthy brown hair that, when it was loose, hung to the small of her back. Dusty had sent sunflowers the next day with just the word *Sorry* scribbled on the card, and on Tuesday, when Marguerite and Dusty returned to their usual song and dance in the back room of the fish shop, she felt an overwhelming relief that nothing had happened between the two of them. They had been friends; they would remain so.

Marguerite felt this relief anew as she turned the corner of North Beach Street, passed the yacht club, where the tennis courts were already in use and the flag was snapping, and spied the door to Dusty's shop with the OPEN sign hanging on a nail.

A bell tinkled as she walked in. The shop was empty. It had been years and years since Marguerite had set foot inside, and there had been changes. He sold smoked bluefish pâté and cocktail sauce, lemons, asparagus, corn on the cob, sun-dried tomato pesto, and fresh pasta. He sold Ben & Jerry's, Nantucket Nectars, frozen loaves of French bread. It was a veritable grocery store; before, it had just been fish. Marguerite inspected the specimens in the refrigerated display case; even the fish had changed. There were soft-shell crabs and swordfish chunks (*"great for kebabs"*); there was unshelled lobster meat selling for $35.99 a pound; there were large shrimp, extra-large shrimp, and jumbo shrimp available with shell or without, cooked or uncooked. But then there were the Dusty staples—the plump, white, day-boat scallops, the fillets of red-purple tuna cut as thick as a paperback novel, the Arctic char and halibut and a whole striped bass that, if Marguerite had to guess, Dusty had caught himself off of Great Point that very morning.

Suddenly Dusty appeared out of the back. He wore a white apron over a blue T-shirt. His hair was silver and his beard was cut close. Marguerite nearly cried out. She would never have imagined that she had missed people or that she missed this man in particular. She was shocked at her own joy. However, her elation and her surprise were nothing compared to Dusty's. At first, she could tell he thought he was hallucinating. For as much of an old salt as Dusty believed himself to be, he had the kind of face that gave everything away.

"Margo?" he said, his voice barely above a whisper.

She smiled and felt a funny kind of gratitude. There were people you knew in your life who would always be the same at base, hence they would always be familiar. Marguerite hadn't seen Dusty Tyler in years, but it might have been yesterday. He looked so much like himself that she could almost taste the ancient desire on her scarred tongue. His blue eyes, his bushy eyebrows, white now.

"Hi," she said. She tried to sound calm, serene, as if all these years she'd been away at some Buddhist retreat, centering herself. Ha! Hardly.

" 'Hi'?" Dusty said. "You disappear for damn near fifteen years and that's all you have to say?"

"I'm sorry." It was silly, but she feared she might cry. She didn't know what to say. Did she have to go all the way back and explain everything? Did she have to tell him what she'd done to herself and why? She had been out of the public eye for so long, she didn't remember how to relate to people. Dusty must have sensed this, because he backed off.

"I won't ask you anything, Margo; I promise," he said. He paused, shaking his head, taking her in. "Except what you'd like."

"Mussels," she said. She stared at the word on her list, to avoid his eyes. "I came for mussels. Enough to get two people off to a good start."

"Two people?" he said.

She blinked.

"You're in luck," he said. "I got some in from Point Judith this morning." He filled a bag with green-black shells the shape of teardrops. "How are you going to prepare these, Margo?"

Marguerite poised her pen above her checkbook and looked at Dusty over the top of her bifocals. "I thought you weren't going to ask me any questions."

"I said that, didn't I?"

"You promised."

He twisted the bag and tied it. Waved away the checkbook. He wasn't going to let her pay. Even with real estate prices where they were, two pounds of mussels cost only about seven dollars. Still, she didn't want to feel like she owed him anything—but the way he was looking at her now, she could tell he wanted an explanation. He expected her to wave away his offer of no questions the way he waved away her checkbook. *Tell me what really happened. You clearly didn't cut your tongue out, like some people were saying. And you don't look crazy, you don't sound crazy, so why have you kept yourself away from us for so long?* A week or two after Marguerite was sprung from the psychiatric hospital, Dusty had stopped by her house with daffodils. He'd knocked. She'd watched him from the upstairs window, but her wounds—the physical and the emotional wounds—were too new. She didn't want him to see.

"I could ask you a few questions, too," Marguerite said, figuring her best defense was an offense. "How's your son?"

"Married. Living in Cohasset, working in the city. He has a little girl of his own."

"You have a granddaughter?"

Dusty handed a snapshot over the refrigerator case. A little girl with brown corkscrew curls sitting on Dusty's lap eating corn on the cob. "Violet, her name is. Violet Augusta Tyler."

"Adorable," Marguerite said, handing the picture back. "You're lucky."

Dusty looked at the picture and grinned before sliding it back into his wallet. "Lucky to have her, I guess. Everything else is much as it's always been."

He said this as if Marguerite was supposed to understand, and she did. He ran his shop; he stopped at Le Languedoc or the Angler's Club for a drink or two or three on the way home; he took his boat to Tuckernuck on the weekends. He was as alone as Marguerite, but it was worse for him because he wanted company. The granddaughter, though. Wonderful.

"Wonderful," Marguerite said, taking the mussels.

"Who is it, Margo?"

"I'd rather not say."

"Not the professor?"

"No. God, no."

"Good. I never liked that guy. He treated you like shit."

Even after all that had happened, Marguerite didn't care

to hear Porter spoken about this way. "He did the best he could. We both did."

"What was his name? Parker?"

"Porter."

Dusty shook his head. "I would have treated you better."

Marguerite flashed back to that night, years earlier. Dusty with his head on the bar, drooling. "Ah, yes," she said.

They stood in silence for a moment, then two; then it became awkward. After fourteen years there were a hundred things they could talk about, a hundred people, but she knew he only wanted to talk about her, which she wasn't willing to do. It was unfair of her to come here, maybe; it was teasing. She shifted the mussels to her other hand and double-checked that her pocketbook was zipped. "Oh, Dusty," she said, in a voice full of regret and apology that she hoped would stand in for the things she couldn't say.

"Oh, Margo," he mimicked, and he grinned. "I want you to know I'm happy you came in. I'm honored."

Marguerite blushed and made a playful attempt at a curtsy. Dusty watched her, she knew, even as she turned and walked out of his shop, setting the little bell tinkling.

"Have a nice dinner!" he called out.

Thank you, she thought.

Marguerite had been in the fish store all of ten minutes, but those ten minutes were the difference between a sleepy summer morning and a full-blown August day on Nantucket. One of the ferries had arrived, disgorging two hundred day-trippers onto the Straight Wharf; families who were renting houses in town flooded the street in

search of coffee and breakfast; couples staying at B and
Bs had finished breakfast and wanted to rent bikes to go
to the beach. Was this the real Nantucket now? People everywhere, spending money? Maybe it was, and who was
Marguerite to judge? She felt privileged to be out on the
street with the masses; it was her own private holiday, the
day of her dinner party.

There was a twinge in Marguerite's heart, like someone tugging on the corner of a blanket, threatening to
throw back the covers and expose it all.

Dusty had let her off easy, she thought. But the girl
might not. She would want to hear the story. And Marguerite would tell her. The girl deserved more than five thousand dollars. She deserved to hear the truth.

8:37 A.M.

The sheets were white and crisp, and the pillows were so
soft it was like sinking her head into whipped cream. The
guest room had its own deck with views of Nantucket
Sound. Last night, she and Cade had stood on the deck
kissing, fondling, and finally making love—standing up,
and very quietly, so that his parents, who were having
after-dinner drinks in the living room with their absurdly
wealthy friends, wouldn't hear.

Once you marry me, Cade had whispered when they
were finished, *all this will be yours.*

Renata had eased her skirt and her underwear back into
place and waited for the blinking red beacon of Brant Point
Lighthouse to appear. She would have laughed or rolled
her eyes, but he was serious. Cade Driscoll wanted to
marry her. He had presented her with a diamond ring
last week at Lespinasse. (The maître d' was in on the plan

in advance: drop the ring in a glass of vintage Dom Pérignon—he didn't realize Renata wasn't old enough to drink.) They set out, cautiously, to inform their families. This meant Cade's parents first—and then, at some point later, Renata's father.

The announcement to the Driscolls had taken place the previous morning, shortly after Cade and Renata arrived on the island. Miles, a drop-dead gorgeous hunk of a man who was spending his summer as the Driscolls' houseboy, had picked up Cade and Renata at the airport, then delivered them to the house on Hulbert Avenue, where the cook, Nicole, a light-skinned black girl with a mole on her neck, had prepared a breakfast buffet on the deck: mimosas, a towering pyramid of fresh fruit, smoked salmon, muffins, and scones (which Mrs. Driscoll wouldn't even look at, being on Atkins), eggs, sausage, grilled tomatoes, coffee with hot frothy milk.

"Welcome to Nantucket!" Suzanne Driscoll said, opening her arms to Renata.

Renata had bristled. She was nervous about announcing the engagement; she was afraid that the Driscolls, Suzanne and Joe (who had early-stage Parkinson's), would notice the ring before Cade was able to tap his silver spoon against his juice glass, and she had to abide another display of the Driscolls' wealth in the form of the house, Vitamin Sea.

Renata tried to view the circumstances through the eyes of her best friend, Action Colpeter, who was cynical about the things that other people found impressive. *House-boy? Cook?* Action would say. *The Driscolls have servants!* Action had traced her ancestors back to slaves in Manassas, Virginia; she was touchy about hired help, including her own retarded brother's personal aide and her parents' cleaning lady. She was touchy about a lot of other things, too. She would be horrified to learn of Renata's engagement; she would pretend to vomit or, because she tended to get carried away with her little dramatizations, she would vomit for real. Faint for real. Die for real. Renata was spared her dearest friend's reaction for three more weeks—Action was working for the summer as a camp counselor in the mountains of West Virginia, where there were no cell phones, no fax, no computers. More crucially for the inner-city kids who attended the camp, there were no TVs, no video games, no Game Boys. In her most recent letter, Action had written: *We are completely cut off from the trappings of modern culture. We might as well be in the Congo jungle. Or on the moon.* She had signed this letter, and every other letter she sent Renata, *Love you like rocks,* which Renata understood to mean a great and rarefied love. Ah, Action. Good thing she wasn't here to see.

Miles had whisked Renata's luggage to her guest quarters; she was presented with a mimosa and encouraged to eat, eat, eat! If either of the Driscolls noticed the whopper of a diamond on Renata's left hand, it was not mentioned until Cade pulled Renata into the sun, placed his arm tightly around her shoulders, and said in his resonant lacrosse-team-captain voice, *I have an announcement to make.*

Suzanne Driscoll had shrieked with delight; Mr. Driscoll, his left hand trembling, made his way over to clap Cade on the back. It was for Mr. Driscoll's sake that Cade had proposed to Renata after only ten months of dating. No one knew how quickly the Parkinson's would progress. Cade was an only child; he was older than Renata, a senior to her freshman when they'd met, and now, with his degree from Columbia in hand, he would start a job with J. P. Morgan the Tuesday after Labor Day. His parents had bought him an apartment on East Seventy-third Street; "a little place," they called it, though compared to Renata's dorm room on West 121st, it was a castle.

Once you marry me, all this will be yours. The castle on Seventy-third Street, the house on Nantucket, the servants, a life of grace and ease. Action would accuse Renata of wanting all this, of finding it impossible to refuse—but what Renata had found impossible to refuse was Cade himself. He was the kindest, fairest person she had ever known; he was principled; he did the right thing; he thought of others; he was a leader in the best sense; he was princely, presidential. A real, true good egg. He adored Renata; he loved her so earnestly and had proposed with such old-fashioned good intentions that Renata overlooked the obvious objections: It was too soon. She was too young.

I'm only nineteen years old, Renata had said when the ring appeared in her drink. She wasn't sure how she wanted her life to unfold, though she and Action had spent many nights talking about it in the minutes before they drifted off to sleep. Renata wanted to finish college, travel, visit museums, drink coffee, forge friendships, make connections, select a career path, a city (maybe New York but maybe not)—and then, once the person of Renata Knox was sufficiently cultivated, she would consider a husband and children.

Renata felt strangely cheated by Cade's proposal. She'd had the misfortune to meet the perfect man at eighteen years of age, and they were to be married. As Renata languished in the guest room bed, she felt surprised that no one in the Driscoll family had seen the shame in this. No one said (as Renata had hoped), *You two should wait a few years. Let your love steep, like tea; let it grow stronger.*

However, Renata was certain her father would put his foot down and that all the current celebrating would be for naught.

Renata wandered downstairs in her bathrobe. It was not quite nine, but already everyone in the house was awake and showered and fed. Renata found Nicole in the kitchen doing the breakfast dishes and Suzanne Driscoll in her tennis clothes leaning against the marble countertop, telling Nicole everything that needed to get done that day. There were lobsters being delivered, but Nicole would have to run up to the farm for corn and tomatoes and salad greens.

When Suzanne saw Renata, she stopped. "And here comes Little Miss Sleepyhead!" This was said with enormous affection, the same tone of voice, Renata noted, that Suzanne used with the family's Siamese cat, Mr. Rogers. Renata heard Action's voice in her head: *There you go, girl. You're the new pet.*

On their third date, Cade had taken Renata to meet his parents. The Driscolls lived on the ninth floor of a building on Park Avenue—the entire ninth floor. Renata had tried to talk herself out of being intimidated—she was smart, her high school's valedictorian; she was worthy of anyone, including Cade—and yet she trembled with inadequacy the whole evening. She had knocked over her glass of wine, staining the tablecloth. Suzanne and Joe had laughed musically, as though nothing could be more charming. Renata got the feeling that it didn't matter who she was or what she was like; if Cade liked her, loved her, married her, the elder Driscolls liked her, loved her, and would overlook her obvious shortcomings. Renata, who had grown up without a mother, had hoped for a real connection with Suzanne; however, her exchanges with the woman were pleasant but artificial, like a bouquet of silk flowers.

"Good morning," Renata said. She felt a stab of guilt as Nicole peeled off her rubber gloves in order to fetch Renata a cup of coffee. "Where's Cade?"

"Sailing with his father," Suzanne said.

Renata's heart sank. "When will he be back? We were supposed to go to the beach."

"Well, you know Joe," Suzanne said, though, of course, Renata didn't know Joe Driscoll, not really. She did know that if Cade had abandoned her, it would only have been to please his father. "They were out the door at seven. We're having lunch at the yacht club at noon. The Robinsons are coming at six for cocktails followed by lobsters on the deck. You do like lobster, don't you?"

"I like lobster," Renata said.

Suzanne sighed as if her day had hung in the balance. "Oh, *good.*"

"But I won't be here for dinner."

Suzanne stared, nonplussed. Was it a bad sign that already Renata enjoyed stymieing her future mother-in-law?

"I'm having dinner with my godmother," Renata said. "Marguerite Beale."

"Of course," Suzanne said. "Marguerite Beale." She said this in a quasi-patronizing way, as if Marguerite Beale were an imaginary friend Renata had invented. "You've spoken to her, then?"

"Last night," Renata said. "After you and Joe left the restaurant, I called her."

"And you're having dinner?"

"That's right."

"Are you going out? Or . . . you'll eat at her house?"

"Her house." Renata sipped her coffee.

"Is she cooking?" Suzanne said. "I hate to sound nosy, but I've heard . . . from friends who have friends who live here year-round, that . . ."

"That what?"

"That she doesn't cook anymore."

Renata set down her coffee cup more forcefully than she meant to and tugged at the sash of her robe. There was a way in which the Driscoll family could not get over themselves. They believed, for example, that they held exclusive rights to the island of Nantucket. And yet how many times had Renata mentioned her own family's history here? Her uncle Porter had been coming since the fifties; he had been Marguerite's lover for seventeen years. Renata's mother, Candace, had worked at the Chamber of Commerce; she and Marguerite had been best friends. Renata's father, Daniel Knox, had owned the Beach Club down the street; he sold it a few months after Candace died, right around the time that Marguerite closed Les Parapluies. Renata herself had been born here and christened here, but the most important fact about Nantucket within the Knox family history was that Candace had died here. Hit by a car, on the road that led to Madequecham Beach. Somehow, Renata felt this gave her the strongest connection to the island; it trumped everyone else. And yet the only tie Renata could claim anymore was Marguerite. Marguerite, her godmother, whom she had been forbidden from seeing her whole life. There had been letters, checks, a distant paper presence. Renata had studied photographs of Marguerite; she had overheard snatches of the old stories. She had only one memory of the woman—a cold day, snow, a grandfather clock, a cup of tea with honey. The tea had burned Renata's tongue. She cried, and arms wrapped around her. She sat on a soft, flowered couch.

"She's cooking," Renata said, though she had no idea if this were true or not, and quite frankly, she didn't care. Pizza was fine, or peanut butter toast. Renata just wanted to talk.

Suzanne sniffed, smoothed her tennis skirt. Her face was at once unbelieving and envious.

"Well," she said. "Aren't you lucky?"

9:14 A.M.

Marguerite smoked the mussels herself. She debearded them and placed them in a smoker that a fellow chef had sent her for Christmas several years ago. She had never used the smoker and remembered thinking when she unwrapped it that she would never use it. But now she had grown old enough to prove herself wrong.

The smoker required a pan of water and wood chips. Marguerite set the contraption up, got it smoking like a wet campfire, and left it on the patio to do its thing. The clock chimed quarter past the hour. Marguerite looked longingly at her sofa, where a collection of Alice Munro stories beckoned to her like a middle-aged siren. Not today. Marguerite checked her list.

> *Call for the meat*
> *Herb Farm*
> *Tart crust*
> *Bread!!!*
> *Pots de crème*
> *Aioli*
> *Polish silver*
> *Champagne!!!*

Back in the day, Marguerite had worked from lists all the time. She had made daily pilgrimages to Dusty's fish shop, and to the Herb Farm for produce; the meat had been delivered. She had prepared stocks, roasted peppers, baked bread, cultivated yogurt, rolled out crusts, whipped up custards, crushed spices. Les Parapluies was unique in that Marguerite had served one four-course menu—starter, salad, entrée, dessert—that changed each day. Porter was driven mad by the simplicity of it. *People want choices,* he'd said. *They want to come in when they're hungry. You're telling the customer what they will eat and when they will eat. You can't run a business that way, Daisy!*

Marguerite triaged her list. *Bread.* If she started it now, the dough would have ten hours to rise. She took a jar of yeast from the fridge and found sugar, salt, and flour in the pantry. The acquaintances Marguerite happened across at the A&P never failed to inspect the contents of her shopping cart—she noticed they did this ever so subtly, skimming their eyes over her groceries the way one ran a white glove over a shelf to check for dust. On any given week, they would find cans of corn, packaged soups, occasionally a hunk of expensive French cheese because the texture pleased her, and basic staples: sugar, salt, flour. But nothing fresh, nothing exotic. There was no pleasure in food for Marguerite anymore. She could taste nothing. She ate only to stay alive.

She missed cooking as profoundly as an amputated limb. It felt odd, sinful, to be back at it; it felt like she was breaking some kind of vow. *Only for her,* she thought. And it was just the one meal. Marguerite bumbled around at first; she moved too fast, wanting to do everything at once. She took three stainless-steel bowls from the cabinet; they clanged together like a primitive musical instrument. The bowls were dusty and needed a rinse, but first, Marguerite thought, she would get warm water for the bread (a hundred degrees, as she'd advised in the column she'd written about bread baking for the Calgary paper). There used to be a rhythm to her process, one step at a time. *Slow down,* she thought. *Think about what you're doing!* She proofed her yeast in the largest of the bowls; then she mixed in sugar, salt, and a cup of flour until she had something the consistency of pancake batter. She started adding flour, working it in, adding flour, working it in, until a baby-soft batch of dough formed under her hands. Marguerite added more flour—the dough was still sticky—and she kneaded, thinking, *This feels wonderful; this is like medicine, I am happy.* She thought, *I want music.* She pushed the play button of her stereo, leaving behind a white, floury smudge. When she dusted the smudge away in three or four days, would she remember this happiness? It would have evaporated, of course, transmogrified into another emotion, depending on how the dinner party went. What Marguerite was thriving on this second was the energy of anticipation. She had always loved it—the preparation, getting ready, every night a big night because at Les Parapluies the evenings when the numbers were the smallest had been the best evenings, the most eventful. The locals came, and the regulars; there was gossip flying from table to table; everyone drank too much.

Ella Fitzgerald. Marguerite felt like singing along, but even shuttered inside her own house she was too shy—what if her neighbors heard, or the mailman? Now that it was summer, he came at irregular hours. So instead, Marguerite let her hands do the singing. She covered the bread dough with plastic wrap and put it in the sun, she pulled out her blender and added the ingredients for the *pots de crème*: eggs, sugar, half a cup of her morning coffee, heavy cream, and eight ounces of melted Schraffenberger chocolate. What could be easier? The food editor of the Calgary paper had sent Marguerite the chocolate in February as a gift, a thank-you—Marguerite had written this very recipe into her column for Valentine's Day and reader response had been enthusiastic. (In the recipe, Marguerite had suggested the reader use "the richest, most decadent block of chocolate available in a fifty-mile radius. Do not—and I repeat—*do not* use Nestlé or Hershey's!") Marguerite hit the blender's puree button and savored the noise of work. She poured the liquid chocolate into ramekins and placed them in the fridge.

Porter had been wrong about the restaurant, wrong about what people would want or wouldn't want. What people wanted was for a trained chef, a real authority, to show them how to eat. Marguerite built her clientele course by course, meal by meal: the freshest, ripest seasonal ingredients, a delicate balance of rich and creamy, bold and spicy, crunchy, salty, succulent. Everything from scratch. The occasional exception was made: Marguerite's attorney, Damian Vix, was allergic to shellfish, one of the selectmen could not abide tomatoes or the spines of romaine lettuce. Vegetarian? Pregnancy cravings? Marguerite catered to many more whims than she liked to admit, and after the first few summers the customers trusted her. They stopped asking for their steaks well-done or mayonnaise on the side. They ate what she served: frog legs, rabbit and white bean stew under flaky pastry, quinoa.

Porter had pressed her to add a seating to double her profits. *Six thirty and nine,* he said. *Everybody's doing it.*

Yes, said Marguerite. *And when I left high school all the other girls were becoming teachers or nurses. University was for boys; culinary school was for Europeans. I don't do what other people do. If people want to eat at Les Parapluies, they will come at seven thirty. In return for this inconvenience, they will get their table for the entire night.*

But the profits, Porter said.

I will not send Francesca out to breathe down some-

body's neck in the name of profits, Marguerite said. *This restaurant is not about profits.*

What? Porter said.

We're in love, Marguerite had said, nodding at the dining room filled with empty chairs. *Them and me.*

The song came to an end. The clock chimed the hour. Ten o'clock. Marguerite retreated to the bedroom to phone the A&P and order the meat. A three-pound tenderloin was the smallest available.

"Fine," Marguerite said. It would be way too much, but Marguerite would wrap the leftovers and send them home for the fiancé on Hulbert Avenue.

There was another startling noise. Marguerite, who had been sitting on the bed next to the phone, jumped to her feet. In the last twelve hours, the noises had come like gunshots. What was that high-pitched ringing? The CD player gone awry? Marguerite hurried out to the living room. The CD player waited silently. The noise was coming from the kitchen. Aha! It was the long-forgotten drone of the stove's timer. The mussels were done.

10:07 A.M.

Renata hadn't counted on being alone, and yet that was exactly what had happened. Cade and his father were sailing and Suzanne was off for tennis, leaving Renata with two blank hours until she was expected at the yacht club. She wanted to go running; it was the coffee, maybe, combined with the antsy-weird feeling of being alone in the house. As Renata climbed the back stairs—she had never stayed in a house that *had* back stairs—to the guest room to change, she found Mr. Rogers weaving deftly between the spindles of the banister. So she was not alone after all.

She dressed in her exercise clothes and gathered her hair into a ponytail. On a scale of one to ten, her guilt was at a six and a half and climbing. Before she embarked on this weekend trip to Nantucket, she had promised her father only one thing: that she would not, under any circumstances, contact Marguerite. But how could Renata resist? She had been dreaming about contacting Marguerite since she and Cade boarded the plane yesterday morning; she had been dreaming of it since the day, ten months earlier, when Cade told her his parents had a house on Nantucket.

Nantucket? she'd said.

You know it?

Know it? she said. *I was born there. My parents' life was there. My godmother is there.*

But Renata didn't really know Nantucket, not the way Cade did, coming every summer of his life.

I'll take you this summer, Cade had said.

That was back in October; they had been dating for two weeks. But even then, Renata had thought, *Yes. Marguerite.*

To Renata, Marguerite was like a shipwreck. She had, somewhere within her hull, a treasure trove of information about Candace, information Renata had never been privy to. And now that Renata was an adult, now that she was a *woman* about to be *married,* she wanted to hear stories about her mother, even silly, inconsequential ones, and who better to tell her than her mother's best friend? The fact that Daniel Knox had forbidden Renata from contacting Marguerite—had, in fact, kept them apart since Candace's death—only fueled Renata's desire to see the woman. There was something her father didn't want her to learn, possibly many somethings. *She's crazy,* Daniel Knox had said. *She's been institutionalized.* But Marguerite hadn't sounded crazy on the phone. She had sounded just the way Renata always imagined—cultivated, elegant, and delighted to hear Renata's voice. As if she couldn't believe it, either: They were finally going to be reunited.

Renata jogged down the back stairs (*Service stairs!* Action's voice cried out), brushing by Mr. Rogers, who was still intent on his acrobatics, and burst out the side door. Beautiful day.

"Hey," a voice said. Renata whipped around. She had thought that she and the cat were the only ones home, but there, among the hydrangeas, was Miles, holding a hose.

"Oh, hi!" Renata said. She had been awed by Miles's good looks when he came to fetch her and Cade at the airport, and once she'd acknowledged this attraction to herself, she was doomed to be tongue-tied in his presence.

"Where're you off to?" he asked.

"Oh . . . ," Renata said. "I'm going running."

"Perfect day for it."

"Yep," Renata said. She bent down and touched her toes; then she lifted her leg to the railing of the porch and touched her toes, hoping for a ballerina-in-a-Degas-painting effect, but she felt like a complete idiot. "What are you doing?"

"Watering," he said, and then in a whispered falsetto he added, "the precious hydrangeas."

"Are you in school?" Renata asked. He looked older than her but younger than Cade. Though maybe not. Cade could already pass for thirty.

"School?" Miles said. "No. I graduated from Colby three years ago."

"So what do you do now?" Renata asked.

"Work my ass off for these people," Miles said. "And in the winter I travel."

"Travel where?"

"You name it."

"Tell me where," Renata said.

"I've been to South Africa, Botswana, Mozambique, Kenya, and Tanzania. I climbed Kilimanjaro twice in one week."

"You did?"

Miles laughed.

"You did not."

"Enjoy your run," Miles said.

Renata set off down the white shell driveway, hoping and praying that Miles wouldn't watch her. She turned around to check. He was staring right at her ass. Renata was mortified and thrilled. She waved. Miles waved back. On a scale from one to ten, her guilt was at an eight.

She headed down the street toward the Beach Club, her father's former business. Daniel Knox had started his career in Manhattan, trading petroleum futures in the 1970s, which, he liked to tell people, was akin to striking oil himself. In five years he had a bleeding ulcer and had made enough money to retire. He took a sabbatical from the business of petroleum futures and moved to Nantucket for the summer to relax. He bought the Beach Club on a whim; he had played tennis with the son of the man who was selling it. At that time, the club was long on history and short on charm. Dan proceeded to renovate, restore, upgrade.

He added a fitness center—the first of its kind on Nantucket—and a hot tub, a sauna, a room for massage. He bought a hundred and twenty beach umbrellas from the company that supplied the most exclusive establishments on the Cap d'Antibes. He built a lunch shack, where families could sign for grilled hamburgers and ice-cream bars. For seventy-five years the members of the Beach Club had packed sandwiches wrapped in plastic; they had suffered with cold-water-only showers; they had lounged on rickety beach chairs and threadbare towels. Many of the members liked things this way; they were reluctant to embrace the improvements and the rate hike that came with them. But Daniel Knox won in the end. Not a single member quit, and, in fact, many had clamored to join. To hear him tell it on a night when he'd had a few scotches (which was what it took to get him to talk about Nantucket at all), he had single-handedly saved the Beach Club.

These endeavors ate up a good chunk of his capital, but he was happy. His bleeding ulcer healed. He had told Renata of the members' attempts to marry him off—to their single niece visiting from Omaha, to a career girl they knew from Boston. He'd endured five hundred blind dates in his estimation—dinners at the Club Car, picnics on Dionis Beach, movies at the Dreamland Theater—all a complete waste of time. The members concluded that he was too picky, or gay. And then one summer he noticed a young woman who would jog past the club every morning. He started saying hello; she would only wave. He began to ask around and heard varying reports: Her name was Candace Harris; she worked for the Chamber of Commerce. Her half brother, Porter Harris, was part-owner of the restaurant Les Parapluies. From someone else Dan heard that Porter was not part-owner at all; he was merely involved with the chef, a woman named Marguerite Beale. Candace hung out at the restaurant every night. She was to be seen with older men, drinking champagne. She was to be seen alone, always alone, or palling around with her brother and the chef. She was training for the New York Marathon or no, not the marathon. She ran for fun. *The best way to see her, man,* someone finally said, *is to go to the restaurant. The food's pretty damn good, too.*

Renata had heard this part of her parents' history plenty of times. Her father went to the restaurant without a reservation, and after a scotch at the bar he insinuated himself at a table with Candace, Marguerite, and Porter. They, having no idea who he was aside from another man in love with Candace, proceeded to punish him by drinking him under the table. He crawled out of the restaurant and claimed he couldn't even think the words *Les Parapluies* without vomiting. Ten days passed before he forced himself to return; when he did, Candace agreed to go out with him. The problem was, the only place she wanted to eat was Les Parapluies. *She* lived *at that restaurant,* Daniel said. *It was her second home.*

As Renata approached the Beach Club, her heart beat wildly. (She was also still thinking of Miles—he *had* been staring at her; she was sure of it.) The club was glorious. The blue, green, and yellow umbrellas were lined up in rows on the beach, and the water glinted in the sun. She spied some children digging with shovels at the shoreline and a solitary figure, swimming. There was a pavilion shading five blue Adirondack chairs and a low shingled building she assumed was the bathhouse. *This could have been mine,* Renata thought, and she pined for it for a minute—a place on Nantucket that would have been hers and not Cade's. She wished that her father could see the club at that moment, with the sun just so, and the water, and the breeze. He would have been forced to admit that he was shortsighted for selling; he would have wanted it back. Renata had heard the possibility of this in his voice in their final conversation before she left. He had been excited for her to see the club. *My old darling,* he said. There was a tone to his voice that sang out, *Those were the good old days,* and this made Renata think that maybe, after all this time, he was healing. But he'd ended the conversation by making her promise not to contact Marguerite. So no. Not healing. Never.

Renata slowed down, then stopped. Then wished for water, the cooling spray of Miles's hose. Cade's parents had been trying to join the Beach Club for years, but they were stuck on the waiting list, a fact that secretly thrilled Renata. She felt a connection to the place, probably more imagined than real. How many years had it been since it was not her but her mother running down this road? Twenty-three years. Renata imagined her father loitering in the parking lot with a clipboard, pretending to check the wind indicator as he waited for Candace to jog by. *Hi,* he would have said. *How are you this morning?* And the mother Renata could barely remember would smile to herself and give a little wave.

Renata loved her father, and she pitied him. His life since Candace died had been comprised of a safe new career—insurance—and his daughter. The career's primary purpose was to provide income for Renata's private high school, her tennis lessons, gymnastics, horses, French, the Broadway shows followed by dinner at One If by Land, Two If by Sea, the vacations to Bermuda and Tahoe and Jackson Hole, with Renata in her own hotel room from the time she was ten because that was, according to her father, the age when she stopped being a little girl and started becoming a young woman. It was around the age of ten, too, when Renata's view of her father changed. When she was a small child, his love had been a blanket, her security, her warmth. But then one day it became a heavy, itchy wool sweater that she was forced to wear in the heat of the summer; she wanted to shrug it off. *Lighten up, Dad,* she'd say. (He'd become "Dad," not "Daddy.") *Back off. Leave me alone.* The light of his interest only intensified; Renata felt like a bug he was torturing under a magnifying glass.

He had taken her to buy her first bra. She was a few months past her eleventh birthday, the other girls in the sixth grade wore bras, and Renata had to have one. *I want a bra*, she said. Her father had looked shocked at this pronouncement, and his eyes flickered over her chest—where, it had to be admitted, not much was happening.

Renata could still remember the trip to Lord & Taylor, the orange carpeting, the fluorescent lights, the soft dinging of the elevators. She and her father walked, not touching, not speaking, to Lingerie.

This is the place? her father asked incredulously, eyeing the mind-boggling array of bras and panties. The bras on display right in front of them were 36 triple-D—beige, black, lacy, and leopard print. Renata wasn't sure this *was* the place; she had never been bra shopping before. She wanted her mother, or any mother at all, and at that moment she hated her father for not remarrying, for not even dating.

They found a saleswoman. GLENDA, her name tag said, like the good witch from *The Wizard of Oz*. She took one look at Dan and Renata—embarrassed father and skinny eleven-year-old daughter who bleated like a lamb, "Bra?"—and whisked Renata into the dressing room while she discreetly snuck over to Juniors to fetch an assortment of training bras. Renata emerged, twenty minutes later, with three bras that fit; she wanted to wear one home. Her father, in the meantime, sat slumped in a folding chair until it was time to pay. On the way out, he started to cry. Renata didn't ask what was wrong; she couldn't bear to hear the answer. His little girl was growing up, and where was Candace?

Where was Candace?

When Renata and Cade started dating, Renata told him the story of bra shopping. *That,* she said, *sums up the way things are between me and my father. He loves me too much. He feels too responsible. He is weighing me down.*

I am weighing him down. I have been his daughter and his wife, you know what I mean?

But you don't mean . . . ? Cade said.

No, Renata had said; then she wondered if her relationship with her father was too nuanced to explain to another human being or simply too nuanced to explain to Cade. She was pretty sure that Cade's relationship with his parents was cut-and-dried; it was normal. *They* took care of *him;* it was a one-way street. Cade didn't feel the need to escape them. What Cade wanted, more than anything in the world, was to be just like them.

Renata gazed out across Nantucket Sound. Her guilt was eating her for breakfast. She blew the Beach Club a kiss, then turned and ran for home.

10:40 A.M.

She was out again, on foot. It was unheard of: Marguerite Beale out of her house, twice in one day. And that was just a start; later she would have to go to the Herb Farm. She would have to *drive.*

But for now, the meat. Picked up, directly, from the butcher at the A&P. And while Marguerite was in the store, she bought olive oil, Dijon mustard, peppercorns, silver polish, toilet paper. It all fit in one bag, and then it was back out into the August sun. Marguerite was wearing a straw hat with a pink satin ribbon that tied under her chin. She felt like Mother Goose. The liquor store was next.

She went to the liquor store on Main Street, steeling herself for interaction; she had known the couple who owned the store for decades. But when she entered, she found a teenager behind the cash register and the rest of the store was deserted.

Marguerite wandered up and down the aisles of wine, murmuring the names under her breath. Chateauneuf-du-Pape, Chassagne-Montrachet, Semillion, Sauvignon, Viognier, Vouvray. She closed her eyes and tried to remember what each wine had tasted like. Wine in the glass, buttery yellow, garnet red, jewel tones. Candace across the table, her shoulders bare, her hair loose from its elastic.

"Can I help you?" the teenager said. He moved right into Marguerite's personal space. He stood close enough that she could see the white tips of his acne; she could smell his chewing gum. Instinctively she backed away. She was browsing the wine the way she browsed for books; she wanted to be left to do so in peace.

"Do you know what you're looking for?" the teenager asked. "Red or white? If it's red, you could go with this one," He held up a bottle of something called ZD. Marguerite had never heard of it, which meant it was from California—or, worse still, from one of the "new" wine regions: Chile, Australia, Oregon, upstate New York. Even fifteen years ago, she had been accused of being a wine snob because she would only serve and only drink wines from France. Burgundy, Bordeaux, the Loire Valley, Champagne. Regal grapes. Meanwhile, here was a child trying to peddle a bottle of . . . merlot.

Marguerite smiled and shook her head. "No, thank you."

"It's good," he said. "I've tried it."

Marguerite raised her eyebrows. The boy might have been seventeen. He sounded quite proud of himself, and he had an eager expression that led Marguerite to believe she would not be able to shake him. Which was too bad. Though maybe, in the interest of time, a good thing.

"I've come for champagne," Marguerite said. "I'd like

two bottles of Veuve Clicquot, La grande Dame. I hope you still carry it."

Her words seemed to frighten the boy. Marguerite found herself wishing for Fergus and Eliza, the proprietors. They used to rub Marguerite the wrong way from time to time—a bit pretentious and very Republican—but they were profoundly competent and knowledgeable wine merchants. And they knew Marguerite—the champagne would have been waiting on the counter before she was fully in the door. But Fergus and Eliza were curiously absent. Marguerite worried for a minute that they had sold the store. It would serve her right to squirrel herself away for so long that when she surfaced there was no longer anyone on Nantucket whom she recognized. It was scary but refreshing, too, to think that she might outlast all the people she was hiding from.

The boy loped over to the wall of champagnes, plucked a bottle from the rack, and squinted at the label. Meanwhile, Marguerite could spy the bottles she wanted without even putting on her bifocals. She sidled up next to the boy and eased the bottles off the shelf.

"Here it is," she said, and because she was in a beneficent mood she lifted a bottle to show him the label. "When you're a bit older and you meet a special someone, you will drive her out to Smith's Point for the sunset with a bottle of this champagne."

The tips of his ears reddened; she'd embarrassed him. "I will?"

She handed him the bottles. "That's all for today."

He met her at the register and scanned the bottles with his little gun. "That will be two hundred and seventy dollars," he said. He shifted his weight as Marguerite wrote out the check. "Um, I don't think I'll be buying that champagne any time soon. It's *expensive*."

Marguerite carefully tore out the check and handed it to him. "Worth every cent, I promise you."

"Uh, okay. Thanks for coming in."

"Thank you," she said. She picked up the brown bag with the bottles in one hand and the groceries in the other. Back out into the sun. The champagne bottles clinked against each other. Should she feel bad that she hadn't selected a Sancerre to drink with the tart and a lusty red to go with the beef? It was grossly unorthodox to drink champagne all the way through a meal, though Marguerite had done it often enough and she'd noticed any person in the restaurant who was brave enough to do it. But really, what would her readers in Calgary think if they knew? Champagne, she might tell them, was for any night you think you might remember for the rest of your life. It was for nights like tonight.

Her hands were full, true. She had a pile of things to do at home: The aioli, the marinade for the beef, and the entire tart awaited, and Marguerite held out hope for a few pages of Alice Munro and a nap. (All this exercise—she would pay for it tomorrow with sore muscles and stiff joints.) But even so, even so, Marguerite did not head straight home. She was out and about in town, which happened exactly never and she had done so much thinking about . . . and if she had really wanted to escape her past, she would have moved away. As it was, she still lived on the same island as her former restaurant, and she wanted to see it.

She lumbered down Main Street and took a left on Water Street, where she walked against the flow of traffic. So many people, tourists with ice-cream cones and baby strollers, shopping bags from Nantucket Looms, the Lion's Paw, Erica Wilson. Across the street, the Dreamland Theater was showing a movie starring Jennifer Lopez. Marguerite harbored a strange, secret fascination with J.Lo, which she nourished during her daily forays into cyberspace. Marguerite surfed the Internet as a way to keep current with the world and to combat the feeling of being a person born into the wrong century; she needed to stay somewhat relevant to life in the new millennium, if only for her Canadian readers. And cyberspace was alluring, as addictive as everyone had promised. Marguerite limited herself to an hour a day, timing herself by the computer's clock, and always at the end of the hour she felt bloated, overstimulated, as though she'd eaten too many chocolate truffles. She gobbled up the high-profile murders, the war in Iraq, partisan politics on Capitol Hill, the courses offered at Columbia University, the shoes of the season at Neiman Marcus, the movie stars, the scandals—and for whatever reason, Marguerite considered news about J.Lo to be the jackpot. Marguerite was mesmerized by the woman—her Latin fireworks, the way she shamelessly opened herself up to public adoration and scorn. *Jennifer Lopez,* Marguerite thought, *is the person on this planet who is most unlike me.* Marguerite had never seen J.Lo in a movie or on TV, and she had no desire to. She was certain she would be disappointed. After a second or two of studying the movie poster (that dazzling smile!) she moved on.

Down the street, still within shouting distance of the movie theater, on the opposite side of Oak Street from the police station, was a shingled building with a charming hand-painted sign of a golden retriever under a big black umbrella. THE UMBRELLA SHOP, the sign said. FINE GIFTS. Marguerite's heart faltered. She ascended three brick steps, opened the door, and stepped in.

* * *

If what the girl wanted was the *whole* story, the unabridged version of her mother's adult life and death and how it intersected with Marguerite's life and how they both ended up on Nantucket—if that was indeed the point of tonight— then Marguerite would have to go all the way back to Paris, 1975. Marguerite was thirty-two years old, and in the nine years since she'd graduated from the Culinary Institute she had been doing what was known in the restaurant business as paying her dues. There had been the special hell of her first two years out when she worked as *garde manger* at Les Trois Canards in northern Virginia. It was French food for American congressmen and lobbyists. The chef, Gerard de Luc, was a classicist in all things, including chauvinism. He hated the mere idea of a woman in his kitchen, but it was the summer of 1967 and he'd lost so many men to Vietnam that, quite frankly, he *had* to hire Marguerite. She had been, if judged by today's standards, egregiously harassed. The rest of the kitchen staff was male except for Gerard's mother, known only as *Mère,* an eighty-year-old woman who made desserts in a cool enclave behind the kitchen. Initially, Marguerite had thought that *Mère*'s presence might help ameliorate Gerard's wrath, his demeaning tirades, and his offensive language. (The worst of it was in French, but there were constant references to the sexual favors he would force Marguerite to perform if every strand of her hair wasn't caught up in the hair net, if the salad greens weren't bone-dry.) But after the second day, Marguerite deduced that *Mère* was deaf. Gerard de Luc was a fascist, an ogre—and a genius. Marguerite hated him, though she had to concede his plates were the most impeccable she had ever seen. He made her instructors at the CIA seem slack. He knew the pedigree of every ingredient that entered his kitchen—which farm the vegetables were grown on, which waters the fish were pulled from. *Fresh!* he would scream. *Clean!* He inspected their knives every morning. Once, when he found Marguerite with a dull blade, he threw her *mise-en-place* into the trash. *Start over,* he said. *With a sharp knife.* Marguerite had been close to tears, but she knew if she cried, she would be fired or ridiculed so horribly that she'd be forced to quit. She imagined the dull blade slicing off Gerard de Luc's testicles. *Yes, Chef,* she said.

Sometimes, staying in a less-than-optimal—or in this case a savage and unsafe—situation was worth it because of what one could learn on the job. In the case of Les Trois Canards, Marguerite became tough; any other woman, one of the cooks told her, would have left the first time Gerard pinched her ass. Marguerite's tolerance for pain was high.

She left Les Trois Canards after two years, feeling seasoned and ready for anything, and so she moved to restaurant Mecca: Manhattan. During the summer of 1969, she worked as *poissonier* at a short-lived venture in Greenwich Village called *Vite,* which served French food done as fast food. It folded after three months, but the *sous chef* liked Marguerite and took her with him down a golden path that led into the kitchen at La Grenouille. Marguerite worked all of the stations on the hot line, covering the other cooks' days off, for three magical years. The job was a dream; again, the staff were mostly Frenchmen, but they were civilized. The kitchen was silent most of the time, and when things were going smoothly Marguerite felt like a gear inside a Swiss watch. But the lifestyle of a chef started to wear on her. She arrived at work at nine in the morning to check deliveries, and many nights she didn't leave until one in the morning. The rest of the staff often went out to disco, but it was all Marguerite could do to get uptown to her studio apartment on East End Avenue, where she crashed on a mattress on the floor. In three years she never found time to assemble her bed frame or shop for a box spring. She never ate at home, she had no friends other than the people she worked with at La Grenouille, and she never dated.

Marguerite left Manhattan in 1972 for a *sous chef* position at Le Ferme, a farmhouse restaurant in the Leatherstocking District of New York. The restaurant was owned by two chefs, a married couple; they hired Marguerite when the woman, Annalee, gave birth to a daughter with Down's syndrome. For the three years that Marguerite worked at Le Ferme, the chefs were largely absent. They gave Marguerite carte blanche with the menu; she did all the ordering, and she ventured out into the community in search of the best local ingredients. It was as ideal a situation as Marguerite could ask for, but Le Ferme was busy only on the weekends; people in that part of New York weren't ready for a restaurant of Le Ferme's caliber. Marguerite even did her own PR work, enticing a critic she knew in the city to come up to review the restaurant— which he did, quite favorably—but it didn't do much to help. The restaurant was sold in 1975, and Marguerite was left to twist in the wind.

She considered returning home to northern Michigan. Marguerite's father had emphysema and probably lung cancer, and Marguerite's mother needed help. Marguerite could live in her old room, bide her time, wait to see if any opportunities arose. But when she called her mother to suggest this, her mother said, "Don't you dare come back here, darling. Don't. You. Dare."

Diana Beale wasn't being cruel; she had just raised Marguerite for something bigger and better than cooking at the country club or the new retirement community. What were the ballet lessons for, the French tutor, the four years of expensive cooking school?

I'm sending you money, Diana Beale said. She didn't explain where the money came from, and Marguerite didn't ask. Marguerite's father had worked his whole life for the state government, and yet all through Marguerite's growing up Diana Beale had magically conjured money with which to spoil Marguerite: weekend trips to Montreal (they had bought the grandfather clock on one trip; Diana Beale spotted it in an antique store and paid for it with cash), silk scarves, trips to the beauty parlor to shape Marguerite's long hair. Diana Beale had wanted Marguerite to feel glamorous even though as a child she'd been plain. She wanted Marguerite to distinguish herself from the girls she grew up with in Cheboygan, who taught school and married men with factory jobs. And so the mystery money. Only then, at the age of thirty-two, did Marguerite suspect her mother had a wealthy lover, had had one for some time.

What should I do with the money? Marguerite asked. She knew it was being given to her for a reason.

Go to Europe, her mother said. *That's where you belong.*

Marguerite could barely remember the person she had been before April 23, 1975, which was the day she stepped into Le Musée du Jeu de Paume in Paris and found Porter fast asleep on a bench in front of Auguste Renoir's *Les Parapluies.* She could remember the facts of her life—the long hours working, the exhaustion that followed her everywhere like a bad smell—but she couldn't recall what had occupied her everyday thoughts. Had she been worried about the stalling of her career? Had she been concerned that at thirty-two she was still unmarried? Had she been lonely? Marguerite couldn't remember. She had walked across the museum's parquet floor—it was noon on a Tuesday, the museum was deserted, and the docent had let her in for free—and she'd found Porter asleep. Snoring softly. He was wearing a striped turtleneck and lovely moss-colored linen trousers; he was in his stocking feet. He was so young then, though already losing his hair. Marguerite took one look at him, at his hands tucked under his chin, at his worn leather watchband, and thought, *I am going to stay right here until he wakes up.*

It only took a minute. Marguerite paced the floor in front of the painting, bringing the heels of her clogs firmly down on the parquet floor. She heard a catch in his breathing. She moved closer to the painting, her feet making solid wooden knocks with each step; she swung the long curtain of her hair in what she hoped was an enticing way. She heard muted noises—him rubbing his eyes, the whisper of linen against linen. When she turned around—she couldn't wait another second—he was sitting up, blinking at her.

I fell asleep, he said, in English, and then he caught himself. *Excusez-moi. J'ai dormi. J'etais fatigué.*

I'm American, Marguerite said.

Thank God, he said. He blinked some more, then plucked a notebook out of a satchel at his feet. *Well, I'm supposed to be writing.*

About this painting? Marguerite said.

Les Parapluies, he said. *I thought I was going to London, but the painting's on loan here for six months so I find myself in Paris on very short notice.*

That makes two of us.

You like it? he asked.

Paris?

The painting.

Oh, Marguerite said. She tilted her head to let him

know she was studying it. She had been in Paris for two weeks and this was the first museum she'd visited, and here only because the Louvre was too intimidating. The little bald man who owned the hostel where she was staying had recommended it. Jeu de Paume. *C'est un petit gout,* he'd said. A little taste. The hostel owner knew Marguerite was a *gourmand;* he saw the treasures she brought home each night from the *boulangerie,* the *fromagerie,* and the green market. Bread, cheese, figs: She ate every night sitting on the floor of her shared room. She was in Paris for the food, not the art, though Marguerite had always loved Renoir and this painting in particular appealed to her. She was attracted to Renoir's women, their beauty, their plump and rosy good health; this painting was alive. The umbrellas— *les parapluies*—gave the scene a jaunty, festive quality, almost celebratory, as people hoisted them into the air.

It's charming, Marguerite said.

A feast for the eyes, Porter said.

When Marguerite entered the gift shop, she was overpowered by the scent of potpourri. *Mistake,* she thought immediately. It was a special corner of hell, standing in a space that used to be her front room, that used to have a fireplace and two armchairs, walls lined with books, and a zinc bar with walnut stools. Now it was . . . wind chimes and painted pottery, ceramic lamps, needlepoint pillows, books of Nantucket photography. Marguerite tried to breathe, but her sinuses were assaulted by the scent of lavender and bayberry. Her groceries and the champagne weighed her down like two bags of bricks.

"Can I help you?" asked an older woman, with tightly curled gray hair. A woman about Marguerite's age, but Marguerite didn't recognize her, thank God.

"Just looking," Marguerite squeaked. She wanted to turn and leave, but the woman smiled at her so pleasantly that Marguerite felt compelled to stay and look around. *It's nobody's fault but your own,* Marguerite reminded herself. *Your restaurant is now one big gingerbread house.*

Porter Harris, his name was. An associate professor of art history at Columbia University, on his spring break from school, working on an article for an obscure art historian journal about Auguste Renoir's portraits from the 1880s—how they were a step away from Impressionism and a step toward the modernist art of Paul Cézanne. Marguerite nodded like she knew exactly what he was talking about. Porter laughed at his own erudition and said, "Let's get out of here, want to?" They went to a nearby café for a beer; Porter was thrilled to find another speaker of English. "I've been staring at the people in Renoir's painting for so long," he said, "I was afraid they would start talking to me."

The beer went right to Marguerite's head as it only could on an empty stomach on a spring afternoon in Paris when she was sitting across from a man she felt inexplicably drawn to.

"Marguerite," he said. "French name?"

"My mother is an avid gardener," she said. "I was named after the daisy."

"How sweet. So what brings you to Paris, Daisy? Vocation or vacation?"

"A bit of both," she said. "I'm a chef."

He perked up immediately. Marguerite had always found it odd that when she first met Porter he was asleep, because his most pronounced trait was that of abundant nervous energy. He was exceptionally skinny, with very long arms and slender, tapered fingers. His legs barely fit under the wrought-iron café table. Marguerite could tell he was the kind of person who loved to eat but would never gain a pound. He lurched forward in his seat, his eyes bulged, and he lit a cigarette.

"Tell me," he said. "Tell me all about it."

Marguerite told. Les Trois Canards, *Mère, vite frites,* La Grenouille. Before she could even brag about her crowning achievement, Le Ferme, he was waving for the check.

I am boredom on a square plate, she thought. *And that is why I am single.*

It would be a lie to say that Marguerite had not entertained any romantic notions about her trip to Paris. She had fantasized about meeting a man, an older man, a married man in the French tradition, with oodles of money and a hankering for young American women to spoil. A man who would take her to dinner: Taillevent, Maxim's, La Tour d'Argent. But what happened was actually better. Porter paid the check, and when they were back on the street he took both of her hands in his and said, "I have a question for you."

"What?"

"Will you make dinner for me?"

She was speechless. *I love this man,* she thought.

"I'm being forward, yes," he said. "But all I've eaten for the past three days is bread, cheese, and fruit. I will buy the groceries, the wine, everything. All you have to do is—"

"You have a kitchen?" she whispered.

"My own apartment," he said. "On the boulevard St.-Germain."

Her eyebrows shot up.

"It's a loaner," he said. "Last minute, through the university. The owners are in New York for two weeks."

"Lead the way," she said.

Now that *was a dinner party,* Marguerite thought. Beef *tartare* with capers on garlic croutons, *moules marineres,* and homemade *frites,* a chicory and endive salad with poached eggs and *lardons,* and crème caramel. They drank two bottles of Saint Emilion and made love in a stranger's bed.

All week she stayed with Porter, and part of the following week, since he didn't have to teach until Friday. Porter was funny, charming, self-deprecating. He didn't walk so much as bounce; he didn't talk so much as bubble over like a shaken-up soda pop. As they zipped through the streets of Paris, he pointed out things Marguerite never would have noticed on her own—a certain doorway, a kind of leaded window, a model of car only manufactured for three months in 1942, under the Nazis. Porter had found himself in Paris on short notice, and yet he knew a tidbit of history about every block in the city. "I read a *lot,*" he said apologetically. "It's the only thing that keeps my feet on the ground." Marguerite liked his talking; she liked his energy, his natural verve, his jitters, his nervous tics; she loved the way he was unafraid to speak his bungled, Americanized French in public. She liked being with someone so zany and unpredictable, so alive. He raced Marguerite up the stairs of Notre-Dame; he bought tickets to a soccer match and patiently explained the strategy while they got drunk on warm white wine in plastic cups; he bought two psychedelic wigs and made Marguerite wear hers when they visited Jim Morrison's grave in Père Lachaise Cemetery.

Every night she cooked for him in the borrowed apartment on the boulevard St.-Germain and he stood behind her, actively watching, drinking a glass of wine, asking her questions, praising her knife skills, fetching ingredients, filling her glass. While the chicken roasted or the sauce simmered, he would waltz her around the kitchen to French music on the radio. Marguerite, at the advanced age of thirty-two, had fallen in love, and even better, she *liked* the man she was in love with.

He made her feel beautiful for the first time ever in her life; he made her feel feminine, sexy. He would tangle his hands in her long hair, nuzzle his face against her stomach. They played a game called One Word. He asked her to describe her mother, her father, her ballet teacher, Madame Verge, in one word. Marguerite wished she had spent more time reading; she wanted to impress him with her choices. (Porter himself used words like *uxorious* and *matutinal* with a wide-eyed innocence. When they visited Shakespeare and Company, Sylvia Beach's bookstore opposite to Notre-Dame on the Ile de la Cité, Marguerite raced to the *First Oxford Collegiate* to look these words up.) In the end, she said *savior* (mother), *diligent* (father), *elegant and uncompromising* (Madame Verge).

"That's cheating," he said. Then he said, "And how would you describe yourself? One word."

She took a long time with that one; she sensed it was some kind of test. *Charming,* she thought. *Witty, talented, lonely, lost, independent, enthralled, enamored, ambitious, strong.* Which word would this man want to hear? Then, suddenly, she thought she knew.

"Free," she said.

*   *   *

Even as she looked back from this great distance, it was nothing short of miraculous—the way that meeting Porter Harris had changed the course of Marguerite's life. But then, as suddenly as it began, it ended: He flew back to New York. Marguerite traveled all the way out to Orly, hoping he would ask her to come back to the States with him, but he didn't, which crushed her. She had his telephone number at home and at his office. He had no way to reach her. She stayed in Paris.

But Paris, in the course of ten days, had changed. The place that had been so mysterious and full of possibility when she arrived was unbearable without Porter. She wondered how long she had to wait before she called him and what she would say if she did. She had given him the word "free," but she wasn't free at all, not anymore. Love held her hostage; it made her a prisoner. She returned to her bed at the hostel; she went back to eating bread, cheese, figs. April turned into May; Paris was warm. Before he left, Porter had given her a copy of *The Sun Also Rises*. She hung out in the Tuileries and read and slept in the afternoon sun.

And then, after two excruciating weeks, the owner of the hostel knocked on the door of her room. A telegram. *DAISY: MEET ME IN NANTUCKET, MEMORIAL DAY.—PH*

Marguerite moved through the shop into the back room, the saleswoman on her trail. This had been the dining room. Eighteen tables: On a crowded night, a Saturday in August when every seat was taken, that meant eighty-four covers. Marguerite closed her eyes. There was Muzak playing, a rendition of "Hooked on a Feeling" on the marimba. But in Marguerite's mind it was laughter, chatter, gossip, whispers, stories told and told again. In Marguerite's mind the room smelled like garlic and rosemary. A spinning card rack stood where the west banquette used to be, next to a display of scented candles, embroidered baby items, wrapping paper.

Porter had found the space; he'd been looking around the island for a place to put an art gallery. He brought Marguerite to the building as soon as he picked her up from the ferry dock. He kept saying, *I want to show you something. You're really going to love it. Really, really, really. I can't wait to show you.* Marguerite was a bundle of nerves. Did Porter know what she would like or not like after only ten days together in what now seemed like a fairy-tale city on the other side of the Atlantic? She was so ecstatic to be back in Porter's presence that she didn't care. On her first ride through town she didn't notice a single detail about Nantucket other than the weather: It was gray and drizzling. Porter pulled his Ford Torino up onto the curb and ran around to open Marguerite's door.

You're going to love this, Daisy, he said. And up the three brick steps they went, hand in hand. Porter pulled out keys and swung the door open.

A narrow room, empty. A bigger room behind it, empty. A lovely exposed brick wall, two big windows.

What is it? Marguerite said.

Your restaurant, he said.

In that moment, Marguerite had many times mused, lay the conundrum of Porter Harris. They had been in each other's presence for less than two weeks and he was making the gesture of a lifetime, offering that space to her. And yet Porter's commitment to her began and ended with the space. The restaurant had, in many ways, taken the place of a marriage, taken the place of children. The space was what Porter had to offer (and, little did she know then, *all* he had to offer). At the time it had seemed a miraculous thing. Marguerite had dreamed of her own restaurant, she was ready, certainly, and she would ask her mother for the down payment. (It was unfathomable, but the building had cost only thirty thousand dollars.) Her life was starting over. That was how Marguerite felt when she'd stood in this room for the first time: She felt like she was being born.

Marguerite returned to the front room. Time to go. She was being self-indulgent; she had to get home. But her conscience prickled; she didn't feel she could leave without purchasing something. A refrigerator magnet quipped, HOW TO LIVE ON AN ISLAND: EXPECT COMPANY. No, no. But then Marguerite saw them by the door, in a brass stand. Umbrellas. She wished they were classic black with wooden handles, like the umbrellas in Renoir's painting. Instead, they were blue and white quarter panels, and on the white it said, NANTUCKET ISLAND, in blue block letters. Marguerite shifted her parcels and plucked one from the stand.

"I'll take it."

The saleswoman beamed. Marguerite pulled out her checkbook. She had no use for an umbrella, as she never left her house in the rain, and she had a visceral aversion to any piece of merchandise that shouted the name of the island. She had lived here for more than thirty years. Why would she need to announce the name of her home on her umbrella? Still, she wrote a check out to the tune of . . . seventeen dollars.

"The Umbrella Shop," Marguerite said. "A curious name. Do you know where it came from?"

The saleswoman folded down the top of the shopping bag and stapled Marguerite's receipt to it. "Quite frankly," she said, "I have no idea."

10:53 A.M.

It was the powers-that-be in the student life office of Columbia University that had brought Renata Knox and Action Colpeter together in Finnerty 205, although Renata suspected another force had been at work: Fate, or the hand of God. The name on the letter Renata received two weeks before she left for Columbia was *Shawna Colpeter*. "Freshman," it said, and it gave a home address of Bleecker Street, New York, New York. Renata pictured *Shawna Colpeter* as a girl raised one of two ways in Greenwich Village. She was either a child of traditional hippies or a child of extraordinarily wealthy hippies. Any which way, Renata was intimidated. The people she knew who grew up in Manhattan went to private school (Trinity, Dalton, Chapin) and they prided themselves on attending fashion shows, rave clubs, charity benefits of which their parents were cochairs. They were grown-ups in teenage bodies; they were cynical, world-weary, impossible to impress. They looked down on suburbia, the Home Depots and Pizza Huts, cheerleaders, beer parties in the woods, driver's licenses. With ten thousand cabs at one's disposal, who needed a driver's license?

When Renata reached Finnerty 205 with her father in tow—hauling boxes and milk crates and all of her hanging clothes in six separate garment bags—Shawna was on her cell phone, crying. Renata was grateful for this for several reasons. First of all, Renata was positive that she, too, would cry when it came time to say good-bye to her father (and *certainly* her father would cry). Second, it showed Renata right off the bat that the person she was going to share a room with for the next nine months had a soft spot somewhere. Third, and most important, it gave Renata a chance to get over her shock at Shawna Colpeter's physical appearance. Shawna Colpeter was black, and although it mattered not one bit, there was still an adjustment to be made in Renata's mind, because Renata had not been thinking black. She had been thinking pale and unwashed and Greenwich-Villagey looking. She had been thinking ennui and devil-may-care; she had been thinking pot smoker; she had been thinking orange glass bong on top of the waist-high refrigerator.

Shawna Colpeter smiled at Renata apologetically and wiped at her eyes.

"My roommate's here," she said into the phone. "Gotta go. Okay? Okay, honey? Love you. Gotta go, Major. Bye-bye." She hung up.

Immediately Renata protested. "Don't mind us."

Daniel dropped the load he was carrying onto the bare mattress that was to be Renata's bed, then he offered Shawna a hand. "Daniel Knox. I'm Renata's father."

She shook his hand, then fished a raggedy tissue from her pocket and loudly blew her nose. "I'm Action Colpeter."

"Action?"

"It's a nickname my parents gave me as a baby. Supposedly, I wore them out."

Another adjustment. Not Shawna but Action, which sounded like a name for an NFL running back. The girl, when she stood up, was six feet tall. She had long, silky black hair that flowed all the way down to her butt. She wore purple plaid capri pants and a matching purple tank top. No shoes. Her toenails were painted purple. She wore no makeup and even then had the most exquisite face Renata had ever seen: high cheekbones, big brown eyes, skin that looked as soft as suede.

"That was my brother on the phone," she said. "My brother, Major. He's ten, but with the mind of a three-year-old. He doesn't understand why I'm leaving home. I explained it, my parents explained it, but he does nothing but cry for me. It's breaking my heart."

Daniel cleared his throat. "I'm going down to get more stuff from the car." He disappeared into the hallway.

Renata didn't know what to say about a ten-year-old brother with the mind of a three-year-old. She could ask what was wrong with him—was it an accident or something he was born with?—but what difference would it make? It was sad information, handed to Renata in the first minute of their acquaintance. Renata decided that since her father was out of the room it would be a good time to explain something herself, in case Action started asking where the rest of her family was.

"My mother is dead," Renata said. "She died when I was little. I don't have any brothers or sisters. It's just me and my dad."

Action flopped backward on her bed. "We're going to be okay," she said to the ceiling. "We're going to be fine."

Renata was too young to understand the reasons why two women clicked or didn't click, though with Action, Renata believed it had something to do with the way they had opened their hearts before they unpacked a suitcase or shelved a book.

They did everything together: classes and parties, late-night pizza and popcorn, attending the football games all the way uptown, writing papers, studying for exams, drinking coffee. Action knew the city inside out. She taught Renata how to ride the subway, how to hail a cab;

she took her to the best secondhand shops, where all the rich Upper West Side ladies unloaded their used-once-or-twice Louis Vuitton suede jackets, Hermés scarves, and vintage Chanel bags. Action gave Renata lifetime passes to the Guggenheim and the Met (her mother was on the board at one and counsel to the other); she instructed Renata never to take pamphlets from people passing them out on the street and never to give panhandlers money. "If you feel compelled to do something," Action said, "buy the poor soul a chocolate milk." Action was so much the teacher and Renata so much the student that Action took to asking, "What *would* you do without me?" Renata didn't know.

Every Sunday, Renata and Action rode the subway downtown to eat Chinese food with Action's family in the brownstone on Bleecker Street. Action's family consisted of her father, Mr. Colpeter, who was an accountant with Price Waterhouse, her mother, Dr. Colpeter, who was a professor at the NYU law school, and her brother, Major, whom Renata had pictured all along as looking like a three-year-old. But in fact, Major was tall and skinny like Action. He wore glasses and he drooled down the front of his Brooks Brothers shirt. (Whenever Renata saw Major he was dressed in a button-down and pressed khakis or gray flannels, as if he had just come from church.) Miss Engel, Major's personal aide, also lived in the house, though she was never around, Sunday being her day off. Her name was constantly invoked as a way to keep Major in line. "Miss Engel would want you to keep your hands to yourself, Major."

The front rooms of the brownstone had been recently redone by a decorator, Action said, because her parents did a lot of entertaining for work. The living room was filled with dark, heavy furniture, brocade drapes, and what looked like some expensive pieces of African tribal art, though when Renata asked about it, Action said it had all been picked out by the ID; her parents had never been to Africa. The dining room had the same formal, foreboding, special-occasion look about it—with a long table, sixteen upholstered chairs, open shelves of Murano glass and Tiffany silver. The back of the house—the kitchen and family room—was a different world. These rooms were lighter, with high ceilings and white wainscoting; every surface was covered with the clutter of busy lives. In the kitchen was a huge green bottle filled with wine corks, a butcher-block countertop that was always littered with cartons of Chinese food, stray packets of duck sauce and spicy mustard, papers, books, pamphlets for NYU Law and the Merce Cunningham dance cooperative. The Colpeters' refrigerator was plastered with various schedules and reminders about Major's life: his medication, his therapy appointments, the monthly lunch menu from his special school. Every week Dr. Colpeter apologized for the mess, and she always reminded them that Mrs. Donegal, the cleaning lady, came on Mondays. "This is as bad as it gets," she said.

Renata grew to love Sundays at the Colpeters' house because it was a whole family—noisy, messy, relaxed—enacting a sacred ritual. They always ate in the den with the football game on TV; always Mr. Colpeter opened a bottle of wine, dropped the cork into the green bottle, and poured liberally for Renata and Action so that Renata had a glow by the time the food arrived. The food was always delivered by a young Chinese man named Elton, who always came into the living room to chat for a minute about the game, his heavy accent obscuring what he was saying, and Mr. Colpeter always tipped him twenty dollars. Always Major insisted on sitting with Action in the plush blue club chair. Renata watched them closely, Action trying to eat her egg rolls while Major wiggled next to her, studying a lo mein noodle, winding it around his tongue. Dr. Colpeter wore sweatpants and T-shirts on Sunday nights; she cheered voraciously for the Jets; she hogged the whole sofa lying facedown after she ate. Renata knew she was one of the most esteemed legal minds in the country, but on Sunday nights she was loose and melancholy as she watched her kids nestled in the armchair.

"Action is more that child's mother than I am," she told Renata once.

Always on the subway home Action complained about the very evening Renata had found so comforting. Action accused her parents of being too absorbed with their careers; she accused them of neglecting Major emotionally.

"Why do you think he wants so much love from me?" she said. "Because he's not getting it from them. They dress him up like a junior executive to make the world think he's normal, instead of letting him be comfortable. Ten years old and that boy does not own a pair of jeans. And then there are the servants." Renata braced herself; she already recognized the tone of Action's voice. "Miss Engel and Mrs. Donegal. One young and Jewish, one old and Irish, but servants just the same. Those women do the work my parents should be doing. The dirty work."

"You're being kind of hard on them," Renata said.

"Please don't take their side against me," Action said. She stood up and grabbed the pole next to the door, as though threatening to step off the train at the wrong station. "I wouldn't be able to bear it."

When Renata got back from her run, she was hot and dying of thirst. She stood inside the refrigerator and poured herself half a glass of fresh-squeezed orange juice cut with half a glass of water. The sweat on her skin dried up and she shivered. She gulped her juice and poured more.

On the marble countertop next to the fridge was a list written out in Suzanne Driscoll's extravagant script. At first, Renata thought it was a list for Nicole—the lobsters, salad greens, and whatnot. But then Renata caught sight of her own name on the list and she snapped it up.

> *Priorities: Pick date! Check Saturdays in May/*
> *June '07.*
> *Place: New York—Pierre or Sherry Neth.*
> *(Nantucket in June? Check yacht club.)*
> *Invites: Driscoll, 400. Knox side?*
> *Call Father Dean at Trinity.*
> *Reception—sit-down? absolutely no chicken!*
> *Band—6-piece min., call BV for booking agent.*
> *Renata—dress: VW? Suki R?*
>
> *Also: flowers—order from K. on Mad.*
> *Cake—Barbara J.'s daughter-in-law, chocolate*
> *rasp, where did she get it?*
> *Favors—Jordan almonds? Bonsai trees?*
> *Honeymoon—call Edgar at RTW Travel,*
> *Tuscany, Cap Jaluca*

"Okay," Renata said. Her breath was still short from the run. This was a list for the *wedding,* her wedding. Suzanne's list for Renata's wedding. A little premature organization from a woman who was, quite clearly, a control freak, right down to the Jordan almonds.

Renata looked around the kitchen. She was in foreign territory. This was nothing like the kitchen in the house where she grew up, which had a linoleum floor, a refrigerator without an ice machine, and a spice rack that Renata had made in her seventh-grade industrial arts class. (How many times had Renata begged her father to remodel? But no—this was how the kitchen had looked when Renata's mother was alive; that was how it would stay.) Nor was the Driscolls' kitchen anything like the Colpeters' kitchen in the Bleecker Street brownstone. The Driscolls' kitchen was a kitchen from a lifestyle magazine: marble countertops, white bead board cabinets with brushed chrome fixtures in the shape of starfish, a gooseneck bar sink in the island, a rainwood bowl filled with ripe fruit, copper pots and pans gleaming on a rack over the island. Renata knew she was supposed to feel impressed, but instead she decided this kitchen lacked soul. It didn't look like a kitchen anyone ever cooked in or ate in. There was no sign that human beings lived here—except for the list.

Something about the Driscolls' kitchen in general—and the list in particular—made Renata angry and uncomfortable. Sick, even, like she might spew the juice she'd drunk too quickly into the bar sink. There was a telephone over by the stainless-steel dishwasher. Renata dialed Cade on his cell.

Three rings. He was sailing. *Can you hear me now?* Renata looked through the glass of the double doors that led to the deck, the lawn, a little beach, the water. Sailboats of all shapes and sizes bobbed on the horizon. Renata might have better luck shouting to him, *Your mother is already planning our wedding! She's calling booking agents! She's arranging for our honeymoon in Tuscany!*

The ringing stopped. It sounded like someone had picked up. But then a crackle, a click. No reception out at sea. Renata hung up and called back. She was shuttled right to Cade's voice mail.

"It's me," she said. Her voice sounded tiny and meek,

like a girl's voice, a girl too young and incompetent to plan her own wedding. A girl without a mother to help her. "I'm at the house. Call me, please."

Because, really, the nerve! Renata hung up. Here, then, was one of life's mysteries revealed. How and when did a woman start resenting her mother-in-law? Right away, like this. Renata crushed the list in her palm. She couldn't throw it away; it was her only evidence.

Renata reached for a banana from the fruit bowl, thinking, *Replace potassium,* but she was so angry, so worried that her wedding might be commandeered by Suzanne Driscoll, that as soon as she picked up the banana she flung it into the cool, quiet atmosphere of the kitchen. It hit a bud vase on the windowsill that held a blossom from the precious hydrangea bushes; the bud vase fell into the porcelain farmer's sink and shattered.

"Shit!" Renata said. She retrieved the banana, peeled it savagely, and ate half of it in one bite, surveying the damage. She was tempted to leave it be and suggest later that Mr. Rogers had knocked the vase over, though of course Mr. Rogers was far too graceful a creature for such an accident. If something had broken while Renata was alone in the house, it would be assumed that Renata was responsible. Thus she did the only reasonable thing and cleaned up the mess—the bud vase was in three large shards and myriad slivers. She threw the shards away with the flower—maybe no one would remember it had even been there—and washed the slivers down the disposal. She had covered her tracks; now all she had to do was eat the evidence.

"Hey."

Renata gasped. Her nipples tightened into hard little pellets. Miles sauntered into the kitchen with Mr. Rogers asleep against his chest. "How was the run?"

"Fine," Renata said, sounding very defensive to her own ears. "Hot." She stuffed the rest of the banana into her mouth. "I'mgngupstshwrnw."

"Excuse me?" Miles said.

Renata finished chewing and swallowed. Her father liked to point out that when she was angry or distracted her manners reverted to those of a barnyard animal.

"I'm going upstairs to shower now," she said.

"Okay," Miles said with a shrug. It was clear he couldn't care less where she went or what she did.

The guest bathroom's shower—unlike the dorms at Columbia where Renata had been living all summer while she worked in the admissions office—featured unlimited hot water at a lavish pressure. It was soothing; Renata tried to calm herself. One of the traits she had inherited from her father was a propensity for flying off the handle. Daniel Knox was famous for it. The sister story to the bra-shopping story was the stolen-bike story. When Renata was nine years old, she forgot to lock up her bike in the shed. She and her father lived in Westchester County, in the town of Dobbs Ferry, which was a safe place, relatively speaking. Safer than Bronxville or Riverdale, though burglars and other derelicts did travel up from the city on the train, plus there was the school for troubled kids, and so the rule with the bike was: Lock it in the shed. The one day that Renata forgot, the one day her pink and white no-speed bike with a banana seat, a woven-plastic basket, and tassels on the handlebars was left leaning innocently against the side of the house, it was stolen. When Daniel Knox discovered this fact the next morning, he sat down on the front steps of their house in his business suit and cried. He bawled. It was the mortifying predecessor to the crying in the department store; this was the first time Renata had seen her father, or any grown man, cry in public. She could picture him still, his hands covering his face, muffling his broken howls, his suit pants hitched up so that Renata could see his dress socks and part of his bare legs above his socks. Her father's reaction was worse than the stolen bike; she didn't care about her bike. At that time, because she was younger, or kinder, than she was during the bra-shopping trip, she clambered into her father's lap and apologized and hugged his neck, trying to console him. He wiped up, of course—it was just a bike, replaceable for less than a hundred dollars—and everything was fine. Renata, over the years and despite her best intentions, had sensed herself about to overreact in the same embarrassing way. The scene downstairs in the kitchen, for example. What if Miles had walked in and seen her throw a banana and break the vase? How to explain that? *I'm angry about Suzanne's list.* It was just a *list,* just a collection of thoughts, of good, generous intentions, which now sat crumpled on the side of the guest bathroom's sink, the words blurring in the shower steam.

And yet something about the list bugged her.

Renata dried off, moisturized, and slipped into her bikini. She wanted to have a swim and lie on the small beach in front of the house until it was time for lunch. But first she sat on the guest room bed—which had, miraculously, been made. (*Made?* Renata thought. She hadn't bothered. *Oh, maid. Nicole.*) Renata yearned for Action, who at that very moment would be doing what? Canoeing down a cold river? Gently dabbing calamine lotion on a camper's mosquito bites? Action would be able to deconstruct Suzanne Driscoll's list; she'd turn it into mincemeat, into dust. She would render it meaningless. Either that or she would become indignant; she would put Renata's outburst to shame with her ranting and raving. *Who does that woman think she is? The Sherry Netherland? Bonsai trees?* Action was unpredictable—at once both passionate and unflappable, always smart, always funny, always exciting. Would Action Colpeter feel comfortable in this house? Would she be *welcome* in this house? Renata seethed with guilt. Her own best friend didn't know about her engagement. Renata had tried to call her the second she got home from Lespinasse, the ring burning on her finger, but when Action's cell phone rang Major had answered. Action's cell phone had been left behind in her parents' brownstone on Bleecker Street. And so Renata was stuck with her guilt. The one person who should know about her engagement—who should have known before everyone else—didn't.

Or no, not the one person. One of two people.

Renata fished her cell phone out of her bag, stared at it for a few long seconds, then dialed her father.

She was so nervous she thought she might gag. This was, most definitely, not in the game plan that she and Cade had devised. They had planned to tell Daniel Knox of their impending nuptials together, in person, in Manhattan—on their turf, either over cocktails at "the little place" that now belonged to Cade on East Seventy-third Street or at a dinner that Cade would pay for, in a restaurant that Cade would select.

It doesn't matter how we tell him, Renata said. *He's going to say no. He'll forbid it.*

Don't be silly, Cade said. *Your father loves you. If you tell him you want to get married, he'll be happy for you.*

Renata was tempted to inform Cade of just how wrong he was, but Cade was a born diplomat. He accepted everyone's point of view, and then, by virtue of his patience and tolerance and goodwill, he inevitably won everyone over to his side. But not this time.

Still, Renata had agreed to wait. She was relieved that telling Daniel would be left until the last possible minute and that Cade would be the one to break the news. Renata couldn't pinpoint what was making her press the issue on her father now. Was it Suzanne's list or a general sense of propriety? Either way, her father needed to know.

Daniel Knox picked up after the first ring. Eleven o'clock on a gorgeous summer Saturday: Renata felt dismayed that he was at home. He would be alone, working, or catching up on *Newsweek,* when he should be at a Yankee game, or playing golf.

"Daddy?"

"Honey?" he said. "Is everything okay?"

"Everything's great!" Renata said. She wished she were wearing clothes. She felt exposed in her bikini. "I'm on Nantucket. At the Driscolls'. It's sunny."

"You're having fun?"

"Yep. I ran down to the Beach Club this morning."

"You did? Oh, geez." He paused. Which, of a hundred things, was he thinking? "I hope you stayed on the bike path. That's why it's there."

"I stayed on the path," she said.

"Okay, good. How was it then? The club, I mean."

"Beautiful."

"Did you go inside? Talk to anyone?"

"No."

"I don't even know if the same people own it," Daniel Knox said.

"I don't know, either," Renata said. She felt like she was spinning; she was dizzy and nauseous. "Daddy? Listen, I have something to tell you."

"You've called Marguerite," he said. His voice oozed disappointment. "Oh, honey. I told you, she's not—"

"No," Renata said, though this was in response to his

digression and not to the accusation, which was true. "I mean, yes, I did call Marguerite, but that's not what—"

"She's not in her right mind," Daniel Knox said. "I don't know how to make you understand. She may sound cogent, but she has serious mental and emotional problems, and I don't want you talking to her. You're not going to try and see her, are you?"

"Tonight," Renata said. "For dinner."

"No," Daniel said. "Oh, honey, no."

"You can't stop me from having dinner with my own godmother," Renata said. "I'm an adult."

"You're my daughter. I would hope you'd respect my wishes."

"Well, I have something else to tell you and you're not going to like it any better."

"Oh, really?" Daniel said. "And what is that?"

"I'm getting married."

Silence.

"To Cade, Daddy. Cade and I are getting married. He proposed and I said yes."

Silence.

"Daddy? Dad? Hello? Say something, please."

There was nothing, save the steady sound of breathing. So he hadn't hung up. He was reeling. Or strategizing. What was the phrase he'd repeated all her life, to anyone who asked him how he did it, raising a daughter alone? *I spend all my spare time trying to stay one step ahead of her.* Everyone always chuckled at this declaration, understanding it to be a comical, fruitless effort on his part. But this silence was unsettling. She had expected shock, anger, an "over my dead body." This would mellow into an insistence that she wait. *Please finish college. Graduate. You're too young. I'll talk to Cade myself. I'll take care of it.*

But the silence. Weird. Dread sat in her stomach like a cold stone. Regret. Should she have waited, adhered to Cade's plan?

"Daddy?"

"Yes?" he said, and now his voice sounded . . . amused. Was that possible? Did he think she was kidding? She fiddled with her ring. That was another reason to tell him in person: He would be confronted by the reality of twelve thousand dollars on her finger. This was not something he could laugh off; he couldn't turn his head and hope it would go away.

"Did you hear me? What I just said? Cade and I are getting married."

"I heard you."

"Well, what do you think?"

He laughed in a way that she could not decipher. He *sounded* genuinely happy, delighted even. Had he spent all his spare time practicing that laugh? Because it threw her off-balance; she felt like she was going to fall.

"I think it's wonderful, darling. Congratulations!"

After she hung up, she sat on the bed as still as a statue. She felt the air on her skin. Another girl would be jumping for joy or, at the very least, wallowing in sweet relief. Renata, however, felt outsmarted, tricked, and yes, betrayed. It wasn't that she wanted her father to keep her from marrying Cade; she had been so sure that he would, so certain that she could predict his very words, that she had never considered the engagement to be real. But now it was real. She wore a real diamond and had what sounded like her father's real blessing.

The phone in the house rang. Cade? She couldn't bear to talk to him. She picked up her monogrammed canvas beach bag—a welcome-to-Nantucket present that Suzanne Driscoll gave to all of her overnight guests—and stuffed it with a striped beach towel, her sunglasses, her book— and, as an afterthought, Suzanne's list. Then she raced downstairs. She had to get out of the house.

When she walked into the kitchen, she found Miles at the counter making a ham sandwich.

"Hey," he said. His favorite syllable. Employable in any situation, Renata now understood.

"Hey," she said. "I'm on my way out."

"Where to?" he said.

"Beach."

"Here?"

"I have no wheels," she said. "So, yes."

"That little beach is crap," he said. "And the water isn't clean. You notice Mr. D. keeps his Contender anchored offshore."

"It's not clean?" Renata said. "Are you sure?" More than anything, she wanted to swim.

"You should come with me," Miles said. "I'm just about to head out. I have the afternoon off."

"Well, I don't," Renata said. "I'm supposed to meet the family at the yacht club in an hour."

Miles rolled his eyes, and even then he was dazzling. Tall, broad shouldered, tan, with brown hair lightened by the sun, blue eyes, and a smile that made you think he was born both happy and lucky. "Blow off lunch," he said. "Cade and Mr. D. won't be there."

"You don't think?"

"Day like this?" Miles said. "Mr. D. will sail all afternoon. He won't have many more days on the water if he gets any worse."

Renata checked the horizon. She wished she was sailing herself, but she hadn't been invited. Cade had hung her

out to dry this morning—but would he really stick her at
lunch with only his mother? Renata could imagine nothing worse, today of all days, than lunch alone with Suzanne
Driscoll.

"Where are you going?" Renata asked.

"The south shore," he said. "Madequecham."

"Made—" Renata tripped over the word; she had never
actually spoken it out loud. Madequecham was the Native
American name for a valley along the south shore, but to
Renata the word meant her mother, dead. She nearly said
this to Miles. *My mother was killed in Madequecham. So
no thanks, I think I'll pass.* Except it was turning out to
be a strange day, unpredictable, and Renata found that a
trip to Madequecham satisfied many, if not all, of her im-
mediate needs. She wanted out of this house. She wanted
to bask in the friendly attention of Miles, however perfunc-
tory, and on a more serious and substantial note, she wanted
to see for herself the place where her mother had been
killed. Was that morbid? Maybe. It was a secret desire,
part and parcel of a larger belief: that somehow once Renata understood her mother's life and death, a fog would
lift. Things that had been obscured from her would become clear.

"Come on," Miles said. He dangled a piece of sliced
ham over the bread in a dainty way, like the queen with
her handkerchief. He was trying to be funny. "I'll have you
back here before Cade even gets home. Say, three o'clock."

"I'd like to go," Renata said apologetically. Strangely,
what was holding her back was a factor she would have
claimed in public not to care about: Suzanne Driscoll's disapproval.

"Whatever," Miles said. "Suit yourself."

Renata was getting a headache. Only eleven o'clock and
already so much pressing down on her. Suzanne and her

list, her father and his bizarre endorsement. They thought they could manipulate her. Well, guess what? They could not. And Cade, perhaps, was the worst perpetrator of all. He had told her they would be going to the beach together today, and yet he'd deserted her. Resolution must have fixed itself on her face, because Miles said, "Do you want me to make you a sandwich?"

"Yes," Renata said. "I'm coming."

11:45 A.M.

Almost noon and still so much to do! And Marguerite was exhausted. She put away the groceries and the champagne. She tucked her new, ridiculous umbrella into the dark recesses of her front closet. She checked on her bread dough—it was puffed and foamy, risen so high that it strained against the plastic wrap. Marguerite floured her hands and punched it down, enjoying the hiss, the release of yeasty stink. She had several things to do before she headed out to the Herb Farm. She would delay that trip for as long as possible, because she was afraid to see Ethan. He fell into the category of people she loved, but the connection between them was too painful. Maybe, like Fergus and Eliza at the liquor store, he would be out, leaving a teenager, a college student, someone Marguerite didn't know, in his place. She could always hope.

But for now, the aioli. Garlic, egg yolks, a wee bit of Dijon mustard. In her Cuisinart she whipped these up to a brilliant, pungent yellow; then she added olive oil in a steady stream. Here was the magic of cooking—an emulsion formed, a rich, garlicky mayonnaise. Salt, pepper, the juice of half a lemon. Marguerite scooped the aioli into a bowl and covered it with plastic.

She barely made it through the marinade for the beef. Her forehead was burning; she felt hot and achy, dried up. She whisked together olive oil, red wine vinegar, sugar, horseradish, Dijon, salt, and pepper and poured it over the tenderloin in a shallow dish. Marguerite's vision started to blotch; amorphous yellow and silver blobs invaded the kitchen.

I can't see, she thought. *Why can't I see?* The grandfather clock struck noon, the little monkey inside having a field day with his cymbals. As the twelve hours crashed around Marguerite like Ming vases hitting the tile floor, she realized what her problem was. She hadn't eaten a thing all day. All that walking on only two cups of coffee. So her symptoms weren't due to brain cancer or Alzheimer's or Lou Gehrig's disease, three things Marguerite feared only remotely, since there was very little to keep her clinging to life—though somehow, the event of tonight's dinner had sparked promise and hope in Marguerite in a way that made her relieved that she wasn't sick, only hungry. She pulled a box of shredded wheat from the pantry and doused it with milk. It was cool and crunchy, pleasing. The clock stopped its racket; Marguerite tried to coerce her vision clear by blinking. She might have sunstroke, despite the valiant efforts of her wide-brimmed hat. She drank a glass of water, slowly made inroads on her cereal. The journey out to the Herb Farm intimidated her; she could sacrifice quality, maybe, and simply return to the A&P for the herbs and goat cheese, the eggs, the asparagus, the *fleurs.* Then she laughed, derisively, at the mere thought.

Forget everything else for now, she thought. *I need to lie down.*

She was so warm that she stripped to her bra and underpants, double-triple-checking the shutters to make certain absolutely no one could see in. (It was the mail-man she was worried about, with his irregular hours.) And even then she felt too odd lying on top of her bed like a laid-out corpse, and so she covered herself with her summer blanket.

Too much walking around in the August sun. That and not enough food, not enough water. And then, too, there was all the thinking she had done about the past. It wasn't healthy, maybe, to go back and float around in those days. In fourteen years she hadn't indulged in the past as much as she had in the last twelve hours. It hadn't seemed productive or wise, because Marguerite had assumed that thinking about the things she had lost would make her unbearably sad. But for some reason today the rules were suspended, the logic reversed. Today she thought about the past—the whole big, honest past—and how she might, tonight, explain it to Renata, and it made her proud in a strange way. Proud to be lying here. Proud that she had survived.

The restaurant had been open for four summers before Marguerite felt the floor stabilize under her feet. She meant this both figuratively and literally. She had spent thousands of dollars getting the restaurant to look the way she wanted it to—which was to say, cozy, tasteful, erudite. She wanted the atmosphere to reflect a cross between Nantucket, whose aesthetics were new to her—the whaling-rich history of the town, the wild, pristine beauty of the moors, the beaches, the sea—and Paris with its sleek sophistication. Marguerite had decided to keep the exposed brick wall at Porter's insistence (this very feature was a major selling point for Manhattan apartments), and she refurbished the fireplace in the bar, installing as a mantelpiece a tremendous piece of driftwood that Porter had found years earlier up at Great Point. (He'd kept it in the backyard of his rental house, much to the chagrin of the house's owners, as he waited for a purpose to reveal itself.) To balance the rustic nature of the driftwood, Marguerite insisted on a zinc bar, the only one on the island. But threatening to throw the whole enterprise off were the floors. They slanted; they sloped; they were tilted, uneven. She had to fix the floors. She couldn't have waitstaff carrying six entrée plates on a tray over their heads walking across this tipsy terrain, and she didn't want people eating their meals in a room that felt like a boat lurched to one side. The floors were made of a rare and expensive wormy chestnut; she was afraid she would damage them if she pulled them up and tried to level the underflooring, and so Marguerite opted for the longer, more arduous process of lifting the building and squaring the foundation.

Marguerite's efforts paid off. The space evolved; it became unique and inviting. She loved the bar; she loved the fireplace and the two armchairs where very lucky (and prompt) customers could hunker down with a cocktail and one of the art history books or Colette novels that Marguerite kept on a set of built-in shelves. She loved the dining room, which she'd painted a deep, rich Chinese red, and she hoped that customers would fight over the three most desirable tables—the two deuces in front of the windows that faced Water Street and, for bigger parties, the west banquette.

However, even with all this in place and precisely to Marguerite's specifications, it took a while for the people of Nantucket to *get it*. At first, Marguerite was viewed as a wash-ashore—some fancy woman chef with a checkered background. Was she French? No, but she peppered her conversation with pretentious little French phrases, and she spoke with some kind of affected accent. Was she from New York? She had worked in the city at La Grenouille—some people pretended to remember her from there, though she had never once set foot in the dining room during service—and she had been educated at the Culinary Institute in Hyde Park, but somehow she didn't quite qualify as a New Yorker. Her only saving grace seemed to be her connection to Porter. Porter Harris was a much-appreciated fixture on the Nantucket social scene; he had rented the same house on Polpis Road since graduating from college in the early sixties. When Porter spoke, people listened because he was charming and convivial, he could single-handedly save a cocktail party, and he was famous for his extravagant taste in art, in food, in women. He liked to tell people that he could look at Botticelli and Rubens all day and move on to Fragonard and the French Rococo all evening. Nothing was too rich or too fine for him. He claimed to have "unearthed a jewel" on a trip to Paris, and that "jewel" was Marguerite. The restaurant Les Parapluies was named after a Renoir painting. (For the first two summers, a good-quality reproduction hung over the bar, but then it came to seem obvious and Marguerite replaced it with a more intriguing piece, also of umbrellas, by local artist Kerry Hallam.) The restaurant served only one fixed menu per day at a price of thirty-two dollars not including wine, and this confounded people. How could one meal possibly be worth it? Porter was instrumental in those early years in filling the room. He lured in other Manhattanites, other academics, intellectuals, theater people on break from Broadway, artists from Sconset with sizable trust funds, and the wealthy people who looked to the aforementioned to set the trends. These people realized after one summer, then two, then three of unforgettable meals that anyone who worried they wouldn't like the food was worrying for no reason. This woman whom no one could figure out wasn't much to look at (or so said the women; the men were more complimentary, seeing in Marguerite's solid frame and long, long hair an earth mother)—but *boy, could she cook!*

It hadn't been easy to win Nantucket over, but at some point during that fourth summer it all came together. The restaurant was full every weekend, Marguerite had a loyal group of regulars who could be counted on at least twice during the week, and the bar was busy from six thirty when it opened (and sometimes a line formed outside, people who wanted to vie for the armchairs) until after midnight. Marguerite's questionable pedigree flipped itself into a mystique; the local press came sniffing, asking for interviews, which she declined, enhancing her mystique. People started recognizing Marguerite on the street; they claimed her as a friend; they announced Les Parapluies as the finest restaurant on the island.

People grew accustomed to her unusual accent (it was a combination of her childhood in Cheboygan and the lilting French-accented English she mimicked from her ballet teacher, Madame Verge, which was later reinforced by so much time in French-speaking kitchens)—but increasing speculation surrounded her relationship with Porter. As the rumors went, he had lured her to Nantucket from Paris and he had bought her the restaurant. (On this last point, Marguerite liked to set the record straight: She bought the restaurant alone; hers was the only name on the deed.) People knew that Porter and Marguerite lived together in the cottage on Polpis Road, and yet summers passed and no ring appeared; no announcement was made. The inquiries and critical glances of the clientele made Marguerite uneasy. The relationship between her and Porter was nobody's business but hers and Porter's.

The summers in the cottage on Polpis Road were good and simple. Marguerite and Porter slept in a rope bed; they used only the outdoor shower, whose nozzle was positioned under a trellis of climbing roses. They ate cold plums and rice pudding for breakfast, and then Marguerite left for work. Porter went to the beach, played tennis at the yacht club, read his impenetrable art history journals in the hammock on the front porch. He stopped in at the restaurant frequently. How many times had Marguerite been working at the stove when he came up behind her and kissed her neck? She had the burns to prove it. When Porter couldn't stop by, he called her—sometimes to tell her who he'd seen in town, what he'd heard, what he'd read in *The Inquirer and Mirror*. Sometimes he used a funny voice or falsetto and tried to make a reservation. They spent an hour or two together at home between prep and service—they tended a small vegetable garden and a plot of daylilies; they listened to French conversation tapes; they made love. They showered together under the roses; Porter washed her hair. They had a glass of wine; they touched glasses. "Cheers," they said. "I love you."

They were lovers. Marguerite adored the word—implying as it did a flexible, European arrangement—and she hated it for the same reason. Despite all the days of their idyllic summers, Porter could not be pinned down. When autumn arrived, Porter went back to Manhattan, back to work, back to school, back to his brownstone on West Eighty-first Street, back to his life of students and research and benefits at the Met, lectures at the Ninety-second Street Y, dinners at other French restaurants—with other women. Marguerite knew he saw other women, she suspected he slept with them, and yet she was terrified to ask, terrified of that conversation and where it might lead. On a spring afternoon in Paris, she had given him the word *free,* and she felt obligated to stick with it. If Porter discovered that freedom was not what she wanted, if he found out that what she craved was to be the opposite of free—married, hitched, bound together—he would leave her. She would lose the beautiful summers; she would lose the only lover she had ever had.

Marguerite's childhood contained one lasting memory, and that was of her ballet lessons with Madame Verge. Marguerite took the lessons in a studio that had been fashioned in Madame Verge's large Victorian house in the center of town. The studio was on the second floor. Walls had been knocked down to create a rectangular room with floor-to-ceiling mirrors, a barre, and a grand piano played by Madame Verge's widowed brother. Marguerite started with the lessons when she was eight. For three years, on Friday afternoons, she ascended the stairs in her black leotard, pink tights, and scuffed pink slippers, every last strand of her hair pinched into a bun. Madame Verge was in her sixties. She had dyed red hair, and her lipstick bled into the wrinkles around her mouth. She was not a beautiful woman, but she *was,* because she was completely herself. She wanted all her girls to look the same, to hold themselves erect, shoulders back, chins up. Feet in one of five positions. She did not tolerate sloppy feet. Marguerite could easily picture herself as a girl in that room on a Friday afternoon—some days were muggy with autumn heat; some days had ice tapping on the windows. She stood with the other girls in front of the mirrored wall, deeply pliéing as Madame Verge's brother played Mozart. She danced. There was a sense of expectation among the girls in Madame Verge's class that they were special. If they kept their chins up, their shoulders back, if they kept their feet disciplined, if their hair was caught up, every strand, neatly, then they would earn something. But what?

Marguerite had assumed it was adoration. They would be darlings; they would be cherished, loved by one man for the rest of their lives; they would become someone's star.

Free, Marguerite had told Porter. But she had been lying, and the lie would cost her dearly.

During the first autumn of Porter's absence, Marguerite traveled to Manhattan to surprise him. She showed up on a Wednesday when she knew he didn't have classes. It was November, chilly, gray; the charms of autumn in the city were rapidly fading. Marguerite had paid a king's ransom on cab fare from LaGuardia; she was dropped in front of Porter's brownstone just before noon. The brownstone was beautiful, well kept, with a black wrought-iron fence and a mighty black door. On the door was a polished brass oval that said: HARRIS. Marguerite rang the bell; there was no answer. She walked to the corner and called the house from a pay phone. No answer. She called Porter's office at the university, but the secretary informed Marguerite that Professor Harris did not teach or meet with students on Wednesdays. Once Marguerite revealed her identity, the secretary disclosed the fact that on Wednesdays Professor Harris played squash and ate lunch at his club. These lunches, the secretary said, *sotto voce,* sometimes included four or five men, sometimes got a bit out of hand, sometimes lasted well into the evening. Marguerite hung up, thinking, *What club?* She hadn't even known Porter belonged to a club. There was no way to locate him. She set about entertaining herself with lunch at a hole-in-the-wall Vietnamese restaurant while reading the *Post,* followed by a substantial wander around the Upper West Side. She was sitting, hunched over and nearly frozen, on the top step of Porter's brownstone when up strolled Himself, in his camel-hair coat and Burberry scarf, his bald pate revealed in the stiff breeze, the tips of his ears red with the cold. Marguerite almost didn't recognize him. He looked older in winter clothes, minus his tan and aura of just-off-the-tennis-court good health. Porter, under the influence of who knew how many martinis, took a bumbling step backward, squinting at Marguerite's form in the gathering dark.

"Daisy?" he said. She stood up, feeling cold, tired, and utterly stupid. He opened his arms and she went to him, but his embrace felt different; it felt brotherly. "What on earth are you doing here? You should have called me."

Of course he was right—she should have called. But she had wanted to take him by surprise; it was a test, of sorts, and she could see right away that he was going to fail or she was or they were.

"I'm sorry," she said.

"You don't have to be sorry," he said. "How long can you stay?" The question contained a tinge of worry; she could hear it, though he did his best to try to make it sound like excited interest.

"Just until tomorrow," she said quickly. In truth, she had packed enough clothes for a week.

His face brightened. He was relieved. He wheeled her toward the front door and held on to her shoulders as they trudged up the stairs. "I have just enough time for a celebratory drink," he said. "But then, unfortunately, I have to make an appearance down at Avery Fisher. I can't possibly get out of it. And I don't have a spare ticket." He squeezed her. "I'm sorry, Daisy. You should have called me."

"I know," she said. She was close to tears, thirty-three years old and as naïve as she had been at eight, with her knobby knees, standing in front of Madame Verge's mirrored wall. She felt she would break into pieces. Did he not remember the one hundred days of their summer? The one hundred nights they had spent sleeping together in the rope bed? They had made love everywhere in that cottage: on the front porch, on the kitchen table. He was always so hungry for her; those were his words. The only thing that kept Marguerite together was the keen interest she felt when the door to his brownstone swung open. This was his home, a part of him she'd never seen.

Porter's house was all she imagined. It was both classic and eclectic, the house of an art history professor—so many books, so many framed prints, and a few original sketches and studies, perfectly lit—and yet scattered throughout were Porter's crazy touches: a vase of peacock feathers, an accordion lying open in its case.

"Do you play the accordion?" Marguerite asked.

"Oh yes," he said. "Very badly."

Marguerite wandered from room to room, picking up *objets,* studying photographs. There were two pictures of her and Porter: one of them in Paris in their wigs at Père Lachaise Cemetery (the picture was blurry; the boy who had taken it had been stoned) and one of them in front of Les Parapluies on its opening night. There were pictures of Porter with other women—but only in groups, and no one face appeared more than any other. Or was Marguerite missing something? She didn't want to appear to be checking too closely. Porter appeared with a drink, a flute of something pink and bubbly.

"I've kept this on hand for a very special occasion," he said, kissing her. "Such as a surprise visit from my sweet Daisy."

She wanted to believe him. But the fact was, things were stilted between them. Porter, who had never in his life run out of things to say, seemed reserved, distracted. Marguerite tried to fill the void, she tried to sparkle, but she couldn't quite capture Porter's attention. She talked about the restaurant—it felt like the only thing they had in common but also sadly irrelevant, here in the city—then she told him she'd been reading Proust (which was a bit of a stretch; she'd gotten through ten pages, then put it down, frustrated)—but even Proust didn't get Porter going. He was somewhere else. As the first glass of champagne went down, followed quickly by a second, Marguerite wondered if they would make love. But Porter remained seated primly on the divan, halfway across the room. And then, he looked at his watch.

"I should get ready," he said.

"Yes," she said. "By all means."

He vanished to another part of the house, his bedroom, she presumed, and she couldn't help but feel crushed that he didn't ask her to join him. They had showered together under the roses; he had washed her hair. Marguerite finished her second glass of champagne and repaired to the kitchen to fill her glass a third time. When she opened the refrigerator, she found a corsage in a plastic box on the bottom shelf.

"Oh," she said. She closed the door.

A while later, Porter emerged in a tuxedo, smelling of aftershave. Now that he was about to make his escape, he seemed more himself. He smiled at her, he took her hands in his, and rubbed them like he was trying to start a fire. "I'm sorry about this," he said. "I really wish I'd had a moment's notice."

"It's my fault," Marguerite said.

"What will you do for dinner?" he said. "There's a bistro down the street that's not half-bad with roast chicken. Do you want me to call right now and see if I can reserve you a seat at the bar?"

"I'll manage," she said.

He kissed her nose, like she was a child. Marguerite

nearly mentioned the corsage, but that would only embarrass them both. He would pick up flowers on the way.

That night, afraid to climb into Porter's stark king-size bed (it was wide and low, covered with a black quilt, headed by eight pillows in sleek silver sheets) and afraid to use one of the guest rooms, Marguerite pretended to sleep on the silk divan. She had purposefully changed into a peignoir and brushed out her hair, but when Porter came home (at one o'clock? Two?) all he did was look at her and chuckle. He kissed her on the forehead like she was Sleeping Beauty while she feigned deep, peaceful breaths.

In the morning, Marguerite knocked timidly on his bedroom door. (It was cracked open, which she took as a good sign.) He stirred, but before he was fully awake, she slid between the silver sheets, which were as cool and smooth as coins.

I want to stay, she thought, though she didn't dare say it. *I want to stay here with you.* They made love. Porter was groggy and sour; he smelled like old booze; his skin tasted ashy from cigarettes; it was far from the golden, salty skin of summer. He wasn't the same man. And yet Marguerite loved him. She was grateful that he responded to her, he touched her, he came alive. They made love; it was the same, though he remained quiet until the end, when a noise escaped from the back of his throat. Might she stay? Did he now remember? But when they were through, Porter rose, crossed the room, shut the bathroom door. She heard the shower. He was meeting a student at ten, he said.

For breakfast, he made eggs, shutting the refrigerator door quickly behind him. While Marguerite ate all alone at a dining-room table that sat twenty at least, he disappeared to make a phone call. Corsage Woman? Marguerite was both too nervous to eat the eggs and starving for them; she had skipped dinner the night before. When Porter reappeared, he was smiling.

"I called you a car," he said. "It will be here in twenty minutes."

What became clear during Marguerite's scant twenty-four hours in Manhattan was that she had broken some kind of unspoken rule. She didn't belong in Porter's New York; there was no niche for her, no crack or opening in which she could make herself comfortable. This wounded her. Once she was back on Nantucket, she grew angry. She hacked at the driftwood mantelpiece with her favorite chef's knife, though this effort ended up harming the knife more than the mantel. She had closed the restaurant for the winter; there weren't enough customers to justify keeping it open. Without the restaurant to worry about and with things as they were with Porter, Marguerite ate too much and she drank. She had bad dreams about Corsage Woman, the woman who sat next to Porter at Avery Fisher Hall. He held her hand, maybe; he bought her a white wine at intermission. She was slender; she wore perfume and a hat. There was no way to find out, no one to ask, except perhaps Porter's secretary. Marguerite gave up on Proust and started to read Salinger. *An education makes you good company for yourself.* Ha! Little had she known when Porter said those words how much time she would be spending alone. She considered taking up with other men—Dusty from the fish store, Damian Vix, her suave and handsome lawyer—but she knew they wouldn't be able to replace Porter. Why this should be so she had no idea. Porter wasn't even handsome. He was too skinny; he was losing his hair; he talked so much he drove people mad. He farted in bed; he used incredibly foul language when he hurt himself; he knew nothing about football like other men did. Many people thought he was gay. (No straight man was that educated about art, about literature, about Paris. No straight man wore pocket handkerchiefs or drank that much champagne or lost at tennis so consistently.) Porter wasn't gay, Marguerite could attest to that, and yet he wasn't a family man. He didn't want children. *What kind of man doesn't want children?* Marguerite asked herself. But it was no use. Marguerite was a country Porter had conquered; he was her colonist. She was oblivious to everyone but him.

Porter, meanwhile, called her every week; he sent her restaurant reviews from *The New York Times;* he sent her one hundred daisies on Valentine's Day. His attentions were just enough to sustain her. She would make up her mind to end the relationship, and then he would write her a funny love poem and go to the trouble to have it delivered by telegram. The message was clear: *It's going to work this way, Daisy.* That was how it went the first winter, the second, the third, and so on. He promised her a trip each spring—to Italy or a return to Paris—but it never worked out. His schedule. The demands on him, he couldn't handle one more thing. *Sorry to disappoint you, Daisy. We still have summer.*

Yes. What got her through was the promise of summer. The summer would never change; it was the love season. Porter rented the cottage on Polpis Road; he wanted Daisy with him every second she could spare. For years it was the same: nights in the rope bed, roses in the outdoor shower, kisses on the back of the neck as she sautéed mushrooms in clarified butter. The first daylily bloom was always a cause for celebration, a glass of wine. "Cheers," they said. "I love you."

* * *

Porter was private about his family, referring to his parents only when he was reminiscing about his childhood; Marguerite assumed they were dead. He did on one occasion mention that his father, Dr. Harris, a urological surgeon, had been married twice and had had a second set of children rather late in life, but Porter never referred to any siblings other than his brother Andre in California. Therefore, on the night that Porter walked into Les Parapluies with a young blond woman on his arm, Marguerite thought, *It's finally happened. He's thrown me over for another woman.*

Marguerite had been in the dining room, lured out of the kitchen by the head waiter, Francesca, who said, "The Dicksons at Table Seven. They have a present for you."

It was the restaurant's fourth summer. Yes, Marguerite was popular, but the phenomenon of gifts for her as the chef was novel, touching, and always surprising. The regulars had started showing up like the Three Wise Men with all kinds of treasures—scarves knit in Peru from the wool of baby alpacas, bottles of ice wine from Finland, a jar of fiery barbecue sauce from a smoke pit in Memphis. And on this day the Dicksons at Table Seven had brought Marguerite a tin of saffron from their trip to Thailand. Marguerite was thanking the Dicksons for the tin—*Such a thoughtful gift, too kind; I so appreciate*—when Porter and the young woman walked in. Porter had told Marguerite when she left the cottage at five thirty that he'd have a surprise for her at dinner that night. She had been hoping for tickets to Paris. Instead, she faced her nightmare: another woman on his arm, here in her restaurant, tonight, without warning. Marguerite turned away and, lest any of the customers perceive her reaction, rushed back into the kitchen.

How dare he! she thought. *And he's* late!

Thirty seconds hence, the kitchen door swung open and in walked the happy couple. The woman had to be fifteen years Porter's junior. *Contemptible,* Marguerite thought, *embarrassing for him, for me, for her.* But the woman was lovely, exquisite, she was as blond and blue-eyed and tan and wholesome looking as a model in an advertisement. She had a face that could sell anything: Limburger cheese, industrial caulking. Marguerite barely managed to tear her eyes away. She searched her prep area for something to do, something to chop, but her kitchen staff had everything under control, as ever.

"Daisy," Porter said. "There's someone I'd like you to meet." He had the trumpet of self-importance in his voice. He'd had a cocktail or two, someplace else. Marguerite busied herself selecting the words she would use when she threw him out.

Marguerite summoned enough courage to raise her eyes to the woman.

"My sister, Candace Harris," Porter said. "Candace, this is Marguerite Beale, the woman solely responsible for my happiness and my burgeoning belly."

Sister. Marguerite was an insecure fool. Before she could straighten out her frame of mind, Candace came swooping in. She put her hands on Marguerite's shoulders and kissed her. "I have been dying to meet you. What Porter told me in private is that he thinks you're pure magic."

"Candace is moving to the island," Porter said. "She has a job with the Chamber of Commerce and she's training for a marathon."

"Really?" Marguerite said. The Chamber of Commerce rubbed Marguerite the wrong way. She had paid the membership fee to join just like everybody else, and yet the Chamber was hesitant to recommend the restaurant to tourists; they felt it was too expensive. And Marguerite's heart wasn't that much warmer toward people who engaged in any kind of regular exercise. They eschewed foie gras, filet of beef, duck confit; they tended to ask for sauces without butter or cream. (How many times had she had been forced to explain? A sauce without butter or cream wasn't a sauce.) Exercisers, and especially marathon runners, ate like little birds. And yet despite these two black marks against the woman right away, Marguerite felt something she could only describe as affection for this Candace person. She was relieved, certainly, by the word "sister," but there was something else, too. It was the kiss, Marguerite decided. Candace had kissed her right on the lips, as though they had known each other all their lives.

Marguerite led Candace to the west banquette while Porter stopped to chat with friends. She pulled a chair out for Candace. As she did this, she noticed a subtle shift in the conversation in the dining room. The decibel level dropped; there was whispering. Marguerite's back burned like the scarlet shell of a lobster from the attention she knew was focused on her and this newcomer. *It's his sister!* Marguerite was tempted to announce. A half sister, she now deduced, from his father's second marriage. Marguerite slipped onto the red silk of the banquette, where she could keep a stern eye on her customers. She held out the tin of saffron.

"Look," she said. "Look what I've been given." She opened the tin to show Candace the dark red strands, a fortune in her palm, dearer than this much caviar, this many shaved truffles; it was for spices like this that Columbus had set out in his ship. "Each strand is handpicked from the center of a crocus flower that only blooms two weeks of the year." She offered the tin to Candace. "Taste."

Candace dipped her finger into the tin, and Marguerite did likewise. The delicate threads smeared and turned a deep golden-orange. This was how Candace and Marguerite began their first meal together: by licking saffron from their fingertips.

Marguerite wasn't really asleep. She was resting with her eyes closed, but her mind was as alert as a sentry, keeping her memories in order. First this, then that. Don't step out of line. Don't digress, wander down another path; don't try to flutter away as you do when you're asleep. And yet, for a second, the sentry looks away, and Marguerite is set free. She sleeps.

And awakens! It might have been an internal alarm that woke her, one saying, *There isn't time for this! The silver! The Herb Farm! The blasted tart! (If you'd wanted to sleep, you should have chosen something easier!)* It might have been the sluicing sound of the mail coming through the slot. But what stunned Marguerite out of sleep was a noise, another blasted noise. It was the phone. Really, the phone again?

Marguerite held the summer blanket against her bare, flushed chest. She took a deep breath. She had a funny feeling about the phone ringing this time; she imagined some kind of memory police on the other end. She would be charged with reeking of nostalgia. She thought it might be Dusty, calling to ask her on a date, or perhaps it was someone Dusty had talked to that morning, a faceless name that would bounce around Marguerite's consciousness like a pinball, knocking against surfaces, trying to elicit recognition. *We heard you're back among the living.* An old customer who wanted to hire her as a personal chef, a reporter from *The Inquirer and Mirror* seeking a scoop on her Lazarus-like return. Marguerite dared the phone to ring as she buttoned her blouse. It did. *Okay,* she thought. *Whoever this is must know I'm here.*

"Hello?" she said.

"Margo?" Pause. "It's Daniel Knox."

Marguerite's insides shifted in an uncomfortable way. Daniel Knox. The memory police indeed. Marguerite tried to decide how surprised she should sound at his voice. He sent a Christmas card every year, and the occasional scrawled note on his office stationery, but not once had he called her. Not once since the funeral. However, the fact of the matter was, Marguerite was not surprised to discover his voice on the other end of the line, not at all. He'd obviously found out Renata was coming to dinner and would try, somehow, to prevent it.

"Margo?"

Right. She had to do a better job on the telephone.

"Hello, Dan."

"Are you well, Margo?"

"Indeed. Very well. And you?"

"Physically, I'm fine."

It was a strange thing to say, provocative; he was cuing Marguerite to ask about his emotional well-being, which she would, momentarily, after she stopped to wonder what a "physically fine" Daniel Knox looked like these days. Marguerite didn't keep his picture around, and the snapshots that arrived at Christmas were only of Renata. She imagined him shaggy and blond gray, an aging golden retriever. He had always reminded Marguerite of a character from the Bible, with his longish hair and his beard. He looked like an apostle, or a shepherd.

"And otherwise?" Marguerite said.

"Well, I've been dealt quite a blow today."

Quite a blow? Was he talking about Marguerite, Renata, the dinner? This dinner should have taken place years ago; it would have, Marguerite was sure, if it weren't for Dan. *The girl wants to find out the truth about her mother. And can we blame her?* Dan had kept Renata away from Marguerite—from Nantucket altogether—for fourteen years. Marguerite couldn't scorn his parenting skills because anyone with one good eye could see he'd done a brilliant job just by the way Renata had turned out, all her accomplishments, and Dan had done it single-handedly. But Marguerite suspected—in fact she was certain—that on the subject of Marguerite, Porter, and Les Parapluies, Daniel Knox had been all but mute. Curt, dismissive, disparaging. *It's nothing a girl your age needs to know.* Except now the girl was becoming a woman and it was difficult to complete that journey without a clear image of one's own mother. There were photographs, of course. And Dan's memories, which would have been idealized for the sake of his daughter. Candace had been presented to Renata as angel food cake—sweet, bland, insubstantial, without any deviling or spice or zing.

"Renata's coming to me tonight," Marguerite said. "Is that what you mean?"

"No," he said. "No, not that. I knew she'd come to you. I knew it the second she said she was off to Nantucket."

"You didn't forbid her?" Marguerite said.

"I advised her against it," Dan said. "I didn't want her to bother you."

"Ha!" Marguerite said, and just like a clean slice through the tip of her finger with a sharp knife, she felt anger. Daniel Knox was a *coward.* He was too much of a coward to tell his own daughter the truth. "You hate me."

"I do not hate you, Margo."

"You do so. You're just not man enough to admit it."

"I do not hate you."

"You do so."

"I do not. And listen to us. We sound like children."

"You resent me," Marguerite said. It felt marvelous to be speaking aloud like this. For years Marguerite had dreamed of confronting Daniel Knox; for years his words had festered, hot and liquid, inside of her. *All you got in the end was her pity. She pitied you, Margo.* With time, however, Marguerite's convictions desiccated like the inside of a gourd; they rattled like old seeds. But now! "You've always resented me. And you're afraid of me. You want Renata to be afraid of me. You told her I was a witch. As a child, to scare her. You told her I was insane."

"I did no such thing."

"Oh, Daniel."

"Oh, Margo," he said. "I admit, it's complicated. What happened, our history. I asked her not to contact you, but she did anyway. So you won. You should be happy."

"Happy?" Marguerite said. Though secretly she thought, *Yes, I am happy.*

"Anyway," he said. "That wasn't why I called. I called because I need your help."

"My help?" Marguerite said. And then she thought, *Of course. He never would have called unless he needed something.*

"Renata phoned me a little while ago," Dan said. "She told me she was coming to you, and then she told me about the boy."

"The boy?"

"You don't know? She says she's getting married."

Ah, yes. The fiancé. Hulbert Avenue. "You just found out?" Marguerite said.

"This morning."

"I wondered when she said 'fiancé.' I wondered about you."

"I can't allow it."

"Well . . ." Marguerite saw where this was headed. Dan wanted Marguerite to be his mouthpiece. *Talk her out of it. Explain how hasty, how naïve, how reckless, she's being.* As if Marguerite had any influence. If she did have influence, would she waste it talking about the fiancé? "She's an adult, Dan."

"She's a teenager."

"Legally, she could go to the Town Building on Monday and get married by a justice of the peace."

There was a heavy sigh on the other end of the line. "I can't allow that to happen, Margo. I will get on a plane to come up there right now. If she marries him, it'll last a year, or five, and then she'll be the ripe old age of twenty-four and maybe she'll have a child or two and then—you know it as well as I do—something will happen that makes her see she missed out on the most exciting time of her life. She'll want to ride elephants in Cambodia or join the Peace Corps or go to culinary school. She'll meet someone else."

"She's in love," Marguerite said. "Some people who fall in love get married." She spoke ironically, thinking of herself and Porter. *Some people fall in love and dance around each other for years and years, until one partner tires, or dances away.*

"If he's knocked her up, I'll kill him," Dan said.

"She didn't sound like she was in that kind of trouble," Marguerite said. "She sounded blissful."

"Nineteen is too young to get married," Dan said. "It should be illegal to get married before you've traveled on

at least three continents, had four lovers, and held down a
serious job. It should be illegal to get married before you've
had your wisdom teeth out, owned your own car, cooked
your first Thanksgiving turkey. She has so many experiences ahead of her. I didn't spend all that time and energy—
fourteen years, Margo, every single day—to stand by and
let her ruin her life this way. Marry some spoiled kid she's
known less than a year. If Candace were here, she'd—"

"Talk her out of it," Marguerite said.

"Flip," Dan said at the same time.

Marguerite cleared her throat. "If Candace were here,
Renata wouldn't be getting married."

"Right," he said softly. "She's getting married to escape me."

"She's getting married because she thinks it will fill the
empty space she has inside of her."

"It won't," Dan said. "That space is there forever."

"I know it as well as you do," Marguerite said.
"Don't I?"

They were both silent for a second, thinking of the
whistling gaps a person leaves behind when she dies, and
how natural it would be for someone young and optimistic like Renata to believe that this hole could be filled with
a substance as magical and exciting as romantic love.

The receiver slipped in Marguerite's hand. The bedroom was hot; she was sweating. She had so much to do,
and yet she couldn't make herself hang up. *You always
made her feel like she owed you something.* Dan blamed
Marguerite for Candace's death and she accepted that
blame; she had tried for years to wash the blood from her
hands. Now he was asking her for help. *Save my daughter.* Marguerite wished she could. But the fact of the matter was, she had one person to save tonight and that was
herself.

"It might work out just fine," Marguerite said. "Plenty of people who get married young stay married. Some do, anyway. You've met the boy?"

"Yes," Dan said. "He's not good enough for her. But he thinks he is. That's what really gets me. He *thinks* he is."

"For you, though," Marguerite said, "nobody would be good enough."

"I'm not going to argue with you, Margo," Dan said. "I'm just going to ask you for your help. Will you help me?"

"I don't think I can."

"Will you try?"

"I'll ask her about him," Marguerite said. "See where she is, how she's feeling, why she wants to make so serious a decision. I would have done that even without this call. I want to know her, Dan. You've kept her from me."

"I wanted to keep her life simple. Knowing a bunch of stuff about the past won't help her, Margo. Her mother is dead. That's a fact she's had to deal with her whole life. How she died, why she died—knowing those things will only confuse her."

"Confuse her?"

"You want to confess everything to make *yourself* feel better," Dan said. "You aren't thinking of Renata."

"Aren't I?"

"No."

"Well, now it sounds like you're arguing with me. I have things to say to the girl and I'm going to say them. After fourteen years, I deserve to have a turn."

"Fine," Dan said. "I'm asking you to think of her. And to be careful. That's all I can do." He was quiet for a moment, and against her wishes Marguerite had a vision of Dan's face, contorted with anger, grabbing the child from her arms. *She pitied you, Margo.* The child had turned back to Marguerite, reached out for her. Those pink over-

alls. Marguerite shook her head. A guttural noise escaped
her throat. Daniel said, "She's coming to you because she
thinks you have the answers. You're like Mata Hari to her,
Margo. She's going to listen to what you say."

"I hope so," Marguerite said. Her voice was very soft,
so soft she knew Dan wouldn't hear. "I hope so."

Dead noon

The wind whipped Renata's hair into her face as she roared
down Milestone Road in Miles's convertible Saab. She
could never have predicted that defiance would be this fun.
Pure defiance! She'd left the Driscoll house without a note,
and she did not bring her cell phone. No one knew where
she was, who she was with, or how to get ahold of her, no
one except for Miles, who was so capable and self-assured
it was making her dizzy. He had grabbed a twelve-pack of
beer from his apartment over the Driscolls' garage, and
now they were driving too fast in the midday sun. Renata
unbuckled her seat belt and eased the seat into recline position. She wore only her bikini and a little skirt. Miles
glanced over at her and she wondered what he was thinking. Did he like what he saw, or did he think she was being obvious and silly? Renata saw his eyes catch on her
diamond ring. She was engaged. Did this make her more
desirable to him or less so? She wanted to believe it made
her more desirable; a girl of nineteen who was already engaged must be the most desirable woman on earth.

It was too loud for conversation, and that was for the
best. If they had talked—about Miles's job, the Driscolls,
Cade—Renata's guilt would seize her like a fever and
make her sick. As it was, they were two actors in a silent
movie. Two kids on a summer day headed for the beach.

Miles hit the brake, hard. Renata gripped the sides of the seat. *Police?* He downshifted, hit his turn signal, and whipped a right so tight that Renata pictured the car tilting, turning on only its right tires. *Screech.* She sat up, readjusted the seat, buckled her seat belt. An airplane took off right over them.

"This is the way to Madequecham?" she said.

"We're picking up a friend."

Renata smiled mildly, as her spirits plopped at her feet. He hadn't said anything about a friend when he invited her, or when they left. It felt like a deception. She had thought they were going alone. This was probably better; Renata could only imagine what Cade and Suzanne Driscoll would say if they found out Renata had disappeared with Miles alone.

Miles headed down the road toward the airport. The planes were so low in the sky, Renata could see their pale underbellies; she could taste the fumes. To her and Miles's left was a massive storage facility, some baseball fields, a lot of construction machines.

"I didn't know anybody lived out here."

"Not everyone on Nantucket is rich," Miles said. "Some of us have to work."

"Right," Renata said. "Sorry."

"No need to be sorry," Miles said. "I can tell you're just an innocent bystander to the great spectacle of the Driscolls' wealth."

"Not so innocent today," Renata said.

"No?" Miles said. He gave her a sneaky sideways look and grabbed her leg with two fingers, right above the knee. She yelped and started laughing. She felt like something was going to happen, and she tried to quell her exhilaration. She turned her diamond ring so that it caught the rays of the sun. *Cade,* she thought. *Cade, Cade, Cade.*

Miles slowed down and turned onto a bumpy dirt road bordered on both sides by scrub pines. A mosquito bit Renata's arm, then her neck.

"Where are we going?" she said. "I'm getting eaten alive."

"Almost there," he said.

Another fifty yards down, he turned into a gravel driveway. There was a small gray-shingled cottage with two dormer windows. The front door was painted a very feminine pink, and the window boxes were planted with spindly pink geraniums. The front lawn had just been mowed; it was shaggy with dried clippings and littered with big-kid toys: two mountain bikes on their sides, a white surfboard, a brilliantly colored box kite. Miles honked the horn. A few seconds later, the pink door opened and a girl came out. Renata thought *girl,* but really she was a woman. She was striking—tall, slender, with long auburn hair cut in angles around her face. She wore a black bikini top and black and pink board shorts. She had a dark green tattoo around her right ankle, silver rings on her toes; a tiny round mirror dangled in her pierced navel. She picked up the surfboard as she walked toward the car. Renata was stunned. He had said *friend* and she had thought male, not female, not a queen bee like this.

"Hey," Queen Bee said, in a sexy-scratchy voice. She was smiling at Miles. Renata felt invisible. This was not better at all. This was awful, a travesty. Ten minutes ago, Renata was perched on a decadent mountaintop, as self-satisfied as she'd ever been in her young life. Then boom, just like that: eclipsed.

Miles turned to Renata. "Can you climb in back?"

"Huh?" Renata said. He was asking her to *move*? "Sure," she said, fumbling with her seat belt, trying to keep dismay from painting itself on her hot cheeks. As she crawled between the seats, her bag snagged on the gear-shift and her tiny skirt hiked up, revealing her backside. She was making an ass of herself quite literally, while Queen Bee waited with an expression somewhere between amused and impatient.

Renata settled into the very cramped backseat. It was so tight that she had to sit on the right side of the seat and put her feet on the left side. There was no seat belt even if she'd wanted one, and to make matters worse, Miles used his backseat as a trash can—there were crumpled Dorito bags, empty CD cases, and lots of sand.

"Here comes the board," Queen Bee said. It seemed she was addressing Renata because suddenly the fin side of the surfboard was shoved into her face. What was she supposed to do with it? There was no room.

"There's no room," Renata squeaked.

"Like this," Miles said, and he balanced one end of the surfboard on top of the windshield and the other end on the back trunk. It sliced right through the backseat, making it impossible for Renata to see Miles, or her own feet. She could turn a few inches to the right to see outside of the car, or she could stare straight ahead at the back of Queen Bee's auburn head. "Now hold on to it."

"Yes, hold on to it," Queen Bee said, as if that were the reason Renata had been invited along: to hold the surf-board.

"I'm Renata," Renata said, thinking that maybe an introduction would make this situation more bearable, but as she spoke, Miles turned the radio up full blast for an old Sublime hip-hop anthem and backed out of the drive-way. Renata's words were left behind, overturned in the yard, like the bikes.

* * *

This was, she thought a minute later when they were back on the Milestone Road rocketing along at unsafe speeds, a bed of her own making. No sooner had she digressed from her proscribed course than punishment was meted out. She should be at the yacht club picking at a BLT while Suzanne Driscoll stopped every other passerby to introduce Renata. ("Cade's new fiancée . . . we're so excited!") She should be with Cade, holding hands, whispering, instead of here, trying to keep a ten-foot surfboard from becoming a projectile missile and decapitating the people in the Audi TT behind them. Up front, Miles and Queen Bee were chatting easily—Renata could hear them talking, though she couldn't make out a single word they said. She ached for Action, who would have handled Queen Bee and Miles in just the right way. For one thing, Action would never have agreed to climb into the backseat. *Where do you think we are, Alabama 1961?* She might even have asked Queen Bee, right off, if she dyed her hair. Action would, however, be proud of Renata for escaping Hulbert Avenue. Vitamin Sea, *bah!* And yet Renata could not cultivate this devil-may-care attitude. Each minute at celestial speed on this road was taking her further and further from where she was supposed to be. She was at Miles's mercy; she was at the mercy of her own idiotic decision. With her free hand she reacquainted herself with the contents of her bag. No money, no phone, no lotion, no bottled water. *No brain,* she thought. *No common fucking sense.* All she had brought was a towel, her sunglasses, her book, and Suzanne's list, which was crumpled into a little ball. Renata was captive, a hostage, stranded with two people she didn't know. What was Miles's last name? She had no idea.

He slammed on the brake again and took another turn at breathtaking speed. Renata held on to the surfboard, but she was no match for the forces at work. *It's going to fall,* she thought. She didn't care. Queen Bee's hair was flying backward, stinging Renata between the eyes. Miles let out a whoop and Queen Bee grabbed the front of the surfboard, her slender arms tensing, revealing taut, toned muscles. Renata was mesmerized by the arms and by the side of Queen Bee's breast, perfectly round and pale and smooth. Renata didn't see the surfboard swing back. It smacked her in the jaw.

Renata yowled. Pain, mixed with rude, rude surprise. Her jaw was broken; it felt like her back teeth had been jarred loose. Renata's vision was blurred by tears. She let them fall. What did those two care if she cried? They wouldn't even notice.

They were driving down another dirt road; each rut and bump stabbed at Renata's jaw.

"Slow down!" she called out. She tasted blood.

Miles sped up; they careened down a road that was ridged like a washboard. Renata panicked. She wanted to escape, but she would never be able to make it back to Vitamin Sea by herself; now she wasn't even sure which direction they had come from. She could hitchhike maybe, pray for some kind person who might deliver her to the Nantucket Yacht Club by twelve thirty. But as they rumbled farther and farther from the main road, Renata's hopes plummeted. The sun burned her shoulders; she hadn't thought to put on lotion. This was awful; this was hell.

And then, for some reason, Miles slowed down. Queen Bee said something; she was pointing. Something on the side of the road. An animal? Renata looked out. A white cross stuck out of the low brush. Renata's jaw pulsed.

"Look," Queen Bee said. "Someone died right there. I think it's so morbid, those crosses, don't you?"

"Stop!" Renata said. She wedged an arm under the surfboard and managed to make contact with Miles's shoulder. "Stop the car!"

He hit the brake. Dust enveloped the car. "What?"

"Stop," Renata said. "I'm getting out."

"What?" he said.

Renata extricated herself from the backseat. Dust coated the inside of her mouth. She hopped down onto the road and walked back to the cross, watching her feet as she went. Her toenails, painted "Shanghai sunset," became filmed with dust.

It was just a white cross, just two pieces of wood nailed together; the paint was peeling. Renata stared at it. Was this it? The marker for her mother? There was a grave in New York, a large, simple granite stone that said: *Candace Harris Knox, 1955–1992, Wife, mother, friend.* Renata's father put flowers on the grave every week; he took a pumpkin in the fall, a wreath at Christmas. But this cross spoke more loudly to Renata. It screamed, *Here!* Here, on a pocked and rutted dirt road, among blueberry bushes, brambles, and Spanish olives. Here is where it happened. Candace was hit, in February of 1992: It was icy; the electric company truck had been going too fast; the driver had been drunk at ten o'clock in the morning. Candace had slipped, or the truck had skidded; it had never been made clear to Renata what had happened. But now at least, she knew where it had happened. If this was indeed a cross for Candace. Renata supposed there might have been other deaths out here; it was impossible to tell if the cross had been there fourteen years or two years, or forty years. There was no writing on it, no hint or clue, except for Renata's intuition. This was it. Would Marguerite know for sure? Would Daniel?

"What are you *doing*?" Miles called out. "Come on; we're going."

"You guys go," Renata said.

"What?" Miles said. "You have to stay with me. If you get lost or whatever, the Driscolls will *kill* me."

"No," Renata said. She sounded preternaturally calm, firm, confident. *This is what I was looking for. Part of it, anyway.* She knelt down in front of the cross. She felt like praying. She had been motherless for so long, it had come to define her. It was like being blind or deaf, or mentally retarded. She was missing something essential, something everyone else in the world had. Growing up there had been no one to braid Renata's hair, no one to bake muffins with, no one to shop for the bra or the nylons or the dress for her confirmation, her prom. There had been no one to read her *A Little Princess* or take her to *The Nutcracker,* no one to buy the Kotex, no one to tell about her first kiss, no one to tell about Cade. There had been no one to rebel against. The mothers of Renata's friends tried to reach out, to fill in. They picked Renata up from riding lessons when Dan worked late; they offered to take her jodhpurs home and launder them. Once, Renata's tenth-grade art teacher took offense to a skirt Renata was wearing. *It's see-through!* she said. But the next day, the teacher came into class with an apologetic look on her face and a brand-new slip in a Macy's bag. *For* you, she said as she handed the bag to Renata. *I'm sorry, I didn't know.* When Renata was little the kids teased her; one girl called her an orphan. Then, once Renata's friends were old enough to understand, they asked nervous questions. *How did it happen? What is it like, just you and your dad?* As they grew even older, they claimed to envy Renata. *My mother is such a pain, such a drain, such a bitch. I don't even talk to her anymore. I wish* she *were dead.* After Renata gave her valedictory speech in front of a hundred graduates and their families, her father alone walked to the podium with a bouquet of roses. He received a deafening round of applause. *So smart, so accomplished, and her mother died when she was little. . . . A beautiful woman,* people whispered when they caught sight of Candace in pictures. *Such a shame.*

The poor girl, Renata imagined Suzanne Driscoll saying. *She has no one to help her plan this wedding.*

Renata's father had given her few details about Candace. Why was that? Was he consumed with his own grief, or was he worried that talk of Candace would upset Renata? Either way, he said very little; all Renata had felt or known for sure was her mother's absence. Renata had never felt as connected to any object as she did to this white cross. It was for her mother, as unlikely as that might seem, out here in the middle of nowhere. *This cross is a part of me, a part of my history.*

In the dusty grass next to her she saw a pair of feet, the silver-ringed toes. Renata looked up; she was crying, she realized.

Queen Bee spoke kindly. "Was this someone you knew?"

"My mother."

"Your *mother*?"

"She was killed out here. Hit by a truck."

"When?"

"A long time ago."

"Oh, geez. I can't believe it."

"Hey!" Miles called out.

Renata stared at the cross, but no words came. She kissed the cross; it pricked her dry lips. *My mother.* They would think she was nuts, but it was true. It was true.

Renata stood up. Queen Bee held out her hand; the mirror in her navel winked in the sun.

"I'm Sallie," she said.

Together they walked back to the car.

12:49 P.M.

The bread dough had risen again. Warm and humid, this was the perfect day for baking bread. Marguerite punched the dough down, then drank a glass of water, took a vitamin, surveyed her list. Just the silver, and . . .

As she had feared. She couldn't procrastinate much longer.

She tied the ribbon of her hat under her chin. *Keys,* she thought. *Where are the keys?* She searched around the house—on the table by the front door? In the soup tureen that served as a junk drawer? On the hook drilled into the wall expressly to hold these very keys? No. She stumbled across a pile of mail on the floor by the front door. She bent to pick it up, thinking, *When was the last time I drove anywhere?* To the doctor in May? It seemed more recent than that. She had a memory of herself in late afternoon, the streets slick from a rain shower. She had been out near the airport—but why? She never had houseguests. Upstairs, five bedrooms waited like bridesmaids. They received attention once every two weeks, when Marguerite dusted. Would the keys be upstairs? Not likely.

Marguerite flipped through the meager envelopes. Did anyone receive less interesting mail than she? Bill for the high-speed Internet, bill for the propane gas, circular from the A&P—and then something thicker, addressed in handwriting: clippings of last month's columns from the Calgary paper. The editor was good about sending them so that Marguerite could appreciate her words in print.

It had kept her alive, that column. When she was released from the psychiatric hospital in Boston after Candace's death, she had to endure something nearly as painful—closing the restaurant. Marguerite had been unable to speak and refused to meet with anyone in person; therefore, her lawyer, Damian Vix, had set up conference calls, on which Marguerite remained mute. The conference calls had made her feel like she was locked with Damian and the gift shop people in a dark closet. The other side had thought—because of her "accident," her "incarceration," her "mental illness"—that they could take advantage of her, but Damian had extorted quite a price. (He negotiated brilliantly, motivated by the memory of a hundred exquisite meals, the bottles of wine Marguerite had saved for him, the shellfish allergy she worked around every time he dined.) At the time, Marguerite had thought money would make her way easier, but she had been wrong. It was, in the end, the newspaper column that had saved her. A call came from out of the blue the very week that Marguerite felt comfortable speaking again. It was the food editor from *The Calgary Daily Press: Someone gave me your number, we'd love to have you write a weekly food column, explain techniques, include recipes. Calgary?* Marguerite had thought. She consulted an atlas. Alberta, Canada? But in the end, how rewarding she found it—thinking about food again and writing about food for a place where she knew no one and no one knew her. Her editor, Joanie Sparks, former housewife, mother of three grown daughters, was officially Marguerite's biggest fan, and the closest thing she'd had to a friend in the past fourteen years. And yet they communicated primarily by yellow Post-it note. Today's note said: *Everyone loved the picnic menu. Hope you are well!*

Someone had given Joanie Sparks Marguerite's name long ago—but Marguerite never discovered who. It was

Porter maybe: One of the daughters could have been a student. Or it was Dusty: He liked to fish in Canada on vacation. Or it was one of the regulars from the restaurant who
wanted to reach out when they heard about Candace's
death. Joanie had never said who passed on Marguerite's
name and Marguerite never asked. Now it would seem
strange to do so, though Marguerite had always wondered.

The grandfather clock struck one, forcefully, like a blow
to the head. Picnic menu, yes. Lobster club sandwiches,
coleslaw with apples, raspberry fizz lemonade. Marguerite
had been late sending the column (she debated for too long
about whether it was reasonable to put lobster on the menu
when her readers were hundreds of miles from the sea)—
and *that* was when she was last in the car. Right? Racing
out to Federal Express like the Little Old Lady from Pas-
adena. It was June, after a thundershower; there had been
little rainbows rising up from the wet road. She had made
it in the nick of time, and this self-generated drama had
left her breathless, flustered. Which meant the keys were
probably . . .

Marguerite's "driveway" consisted of two tasteful brick
strips with grass in between. Her battered 1984 Jeep Wran-
gler, olive green with a soft beige top, was a classic now;
every year some family or other called to see if they could
drive it in the Daffodil Parade. But the Jeep, like Marguerite, was a homebody. She asked very little of it—less than
fifty miles a year—and it kept passing inspection. Marguerite opened the car door. The keys were dangling from
the ignition.

Marguerite eased out of her driveway and puttered
down Quince Street toward the heart of town. The Jeep
had no air-conditioning and it was too hot to drive with
the windows up; already it felt like she had a plastic bag
over her head. She unzipped the windows, thinking that

this was the perfect weather not only for baking bread but also for riding with the top down—but no, she wouldn't go that far. Marguerite didn't want anyone to recognize her. She wore her enormous hat and round sunglasses like an incognito movie star. Even so, she worried someone would recognize the Jeep. When she bought the Jeep, Porter had given her a vanity plate: CHIEF. (He had meant for it to read CHEF, but someone at the DMV misunderstood; hence CHIEF, and since it wasn't inappropriate, it stayed.) When everything else went out the window, so did the vanity plate—now the Jeep was identified by numbers and letters that Marguerite had never bothered to memorize— and yet she still felt that the soft-top olive green Jeep itself was a dead giveaway. *Marguerite Beale, out on the street!*

She felt better once she was out of town, once she was headed down Orange Street toward the main rotary, and even more at ease once she was safely around the rotary and driving out Polpis Road. Wind filled the car and tugged at the brim of her hat. She felt okay. She felt fine.

How to describe Polpis Road, midafternoon, on a hot summer day? It shimmered. It smelled green and sweet in some places, like a freshly picked ear of corn, and green and salt-marshy in other places, like soft mud and decay. Polpis was, quite literally, a long and winding road, with too many turnoffs and places of interest to explore in one lifetime. On the early left was Shimmo—houses in thick woods that became, down the sandy road, houses that fronted the harbor. Shimmo was old money: At the restaurant, Marguerite had often heard people described as "very Shimmo," or "not Shimmo enough." Just past Shimmo on the right was the dirt road that led to Altar Rock, which was, at 104 feet, the highest point on the island. Marguerite swallowed. She had been to Altar Rock only once, with Candace. Suddenly Marguerite felt angry.

Why was it that any memory that mattered led back to Candace or Porter? Why had Marguerite not opened herself to more people? Why had she not made more friends? All of her eggs had gone right into that family's basket; she had put them there herself, and they had broken.

It had been autumn when Marguerite and Candace hiked to Altar Rock, the autumn after they met, perhaps, or the autumn after that. Porter was gone, and Candace came to the restaurant every night by herself. (Had it really been every night, or did it only seem that way?) Candace came late and sat at one of the deuces in front of the window with Marguerite. They ate together; Candace was her guest. That was how their real friendship had started.

"I can't believe my brother leaves you here all winter," Candace said. "And you let him. Why do you let him?"

Marguerite sighed. Sipped her champagne. She had been drinking champagne that night with the aim of getting very drunk because, the previous Sunday, Porter had appeared on the society page of *The New York Times* with another woman on his arm. The photograph was taken at a gala for Columbia's new performing arts center. The caption underneath the picture read: *Professor Porter Harris and friend.* Marguerite had stumbled across the picture on her own; she had been alone, in her newly purchased house on Quince Street, drinking her coffee. Porter's face had jumped out at her from the sea of faces. He was smiling in the picture; he looked positively delighted, smug; he was the cat that ate the canary. He would never have admitted it, but he *wanted* to be on the *Times* social page and had wanted it his whole life—and if he was captured with an attractive escort, so much the better. The woman on Porter's arm—and how many hours had Marguerite wasted scrutinizing that damn picture, cursing the fuzziness of the newsprint, to see precisely *how* Porter was holding the woman's arm—was a brunette. Her hair was in a chignon; she wore a pale, sparkling dress with a plunging neckline. Her face was pleasant enough, though something was off with her mouth, crowded teeth, maybe, or an overbite. Overbite Woman, Marguerite named her. That Sunday the phone rang and rang, but Marguerite didn't answer. It was someone, many someones, calling to tell Marguerite about the picture, or it was Porter himself with an explanation, an apology. Marguerite ignored the phone. She considered calling Porter to tell him she couldn't do it anymore; she didn't want to be treated like a possession he kept in storage and dusted off at the start of every summer. Marguerite took a small comfort in the fact that the woman had not been identified by name. She was "friend," a newspaper euphemism for someone unimportant, someone nobody knew. It could simply have been a woman Porter happened to be standing next to when they were caught by the photographer. But it was humiliating nonetheless; it was a symptom of a larger illness.

Candace had said nothing about the photograph. She had seen it, no doubt, the whole world had seen it, but Candace fell into the category of people who wished to protect Marguerite from it. Now, as they ate dinner five days later, Candace was rallying against Porter in a general way. *Why do you let him go every autumn? Why don't you go to New York? Why don't you leave him?* Marguerite was stumped by these questions; she had never had a friend who cared enough to ask. She was grateful for someone to parse the relationship with, to help her analyze it. But things were complicated by the fact that Candace was Porter's sister. Candace loved to talk about how Porter had refused to indulge her as a child, even though he was fifteen years older. He was, Candace said, stricter and less fun than her parents. Always so self-important with his *art,* his books, his articles for the journals that only a handful of people ever read.

"He takes advantage of you," Candace said.

"Or I take advantage of him," Marguerite said. "I like things this way."

"Do you?"

"No," Marguerite said.

"No, I didn't think so," Candace said, swirling her champagne and studying the glass for legs. (She was charmingly naïve about wine.) "Bastard. He's a bastard; he really is."

"Oh, Candace."

"To not realize what he has in you. Look at this restaurant. The ambience, the food. All Daisy. This place is yours. It's you."

"Some days I wish I had something more," Marguerite said. "Or something different."

"You need to get out of the restaurant for a while," Candace said. "It would take your mind off things. How long has it been since you've been to the beach? Or taken a walk through the moors?"

"Long."

"Tomorrow we'll go together," Candace said. "To see the moors."

And go they did. It was a mercy trip; Marguerite understood that. A feeble attempt to get Marguerite's mind off the photograph she couldn't bring herself to throw away. (It was sandwiched in her copy of Julia Child on her kitchen counter.) But Marguerite knew she had to do something different, no matter how small, and so she laced up a pair of hiking boots that she hadn't worn since her years at Le Ferme. She followed Candace along the winding sand paths that climbed through conservation land to Altar Rock.

"This feels a lot higher than a hundred feet," Marguerite said. "This feels like the Alps." She was breathing heavily, cursing butter and cream, but she plodded along behind Candace to the top. From Altar Rock they gazed out over the moors, which were crimson with poison ivy. Tiny green ponds dotted the moors, and beyond lay the ocean. Marguerite could hear the eerie, distant cries of seagulls.

Candace flung her arm around Marguerite's shoulders. She was not even a little winded; this was nothing but a walk through the park for her. She let out a great yell, a yodel, a howl. "Come on," she said to Marguerite. "It's good for you. Let it all out." When Marguerite regained her breath, she shouted; she bayed. *He's a bastard. He really is.* The words seemed easy and true with Candace at her side. Blood was thicker than water or wine, and yet Candace always sided with Marguerite. As she yelled, Marguerite imagined her anger, her embarrassment, and her longing, floating over the land like mist or smoke and being carried away by the sea. She and Candace howled together until they were hoarse.

A few miles up Polpis Road, Marguerite passed the rose-covered cottage—featured on every third Nantucket postcard—in its second full bloom of the summer. Then Almanack Pond Road, the horse barn, the turnoff for the Wauwinet Inn and Great Point. Marguerite slowed down. She lived so resolutely in town that she had forgotten all this was out here, all this *country.* Sesachacha Pond spread out silvery blue to her left, and directly across the street was the white shell driveway that led to the cottage that Porter had rented for so many years. She would love to turn down that driveway and take a peek. Why not? This day had taken on the quality of the moments before death: her whole life passing before her eyes. She wanted to see if the hammock still hung from the front porch, if the roses still dangled over the outdoor shower, if the daylilies she and Porter planted had survived. But there was no time to waste, plus she didn't know who owned the property anymore. Mr. Dreyfus, who had rented it to Porter, had long been dead; one of his children owned it now, or someone new. The last thing Marguerite needed was to be caught trespassing. She drove on, but not too far. One mailbox, the stone wall, and then she turned right. A dirt path led deep into what guidebooks called the enchanted forest. Not so enchanted, however, because the skinny scrub pines were strangled with underbrush, pricker bushes, and poison ivy and the bumpy path leading through the woods held water, which meant mosquitoes. One could live on Nantucket one's whole life without going to the Herb Farm or even knowing it was there, which had suited Marguerite just fine for the long time that she had avoided it.

Like so much else on this island, the Herb Farm had been Porter's discovery. Every other restaurant provisioned at Bartlett's Farm, a far larger and more sophisticated enterprise, closer to town, and with a farm truck that was a steady presence on Main Street each summer morning. Marguerite held nothing against Bartlett's Farm except that she had never made it her own. She had, from the beginning, woken up in Porter's cottage and walked with an honest-to-goodness wicker basket down the dirt path. The Herb Farm reminded Marguerite of the farms in France; it was like a farm in a child's picture book. There was a white wooden fence that penned in sheep and goats, a chicken coop where a dozen warm eggs cost a dollar, a red barn for the two bay horses, and a greenhouse. Half of the greenhouse did what greenhouses do, while the other half had been fashioned into very primitive retail space. The vegetables were sold from wooden crates, all of them grown organically, before such a process even had a name—corn, tomatoes, lettuces, seventeen kinds of herbs, squash, zucchini, carrots with the bushy tops left on, spring onions, radishes, cucumbers, peppers, strawberries for two short weeks in June, pumpkins after the fifteenth of September. There was chevre made on the premises from the milk of the goats; there was fresh butter. And when Marguerite showed up for the first time in the summer of 1975 there was a ten-year-old boy who had been given the undignified job of cutting zinnias, snapdragons, and bachelor buttons and gathering them into attractive-looking bunches. Ethan Arcain, with his grown-out Beatle hairdo and saucer-sized brown eyes. Marguerite adored the child from the moment she saw him because that was the way she was with people—everything right away, or nothing.

Ethan Arcain worked at the Herb Farm every summer that Les Parapluies was open, and so for a hundred days a year Ethan's face was one of the first Marguerite saw each day. Their relationship wasn't complicated like Marguerite's relationship with Dusty. Ethan was a boy, Marguerite a woman. She thought of him as a little brother, although she was old enough to be his mother. *The son I never had,* she sometimes joked. Ethan's family life was a shambles. Dolores Kimball, who owned the farm in those days, once described Ethan's parents' divorce to Marguerite as a grenade explosion: *Destroyed everyone in the vicinity.* Years later, Ethan's mother remarried and Ethan fell in love with his stepsister and when they were old enough they got married, which people on the island whispered about, because people on the island whispered about everything. Ethan's father, Walter Arcain, worked for the electric company and was a well-known abuser of alcohol.

The one time he had tried to come into the bar at Les Parapluies, Marguerite had asked Lance to see him out to the street.

It was Walter Arcain who had been driving the truck that killed Candace. Ten o'clock in the morning and he was three sheets to the wind, out joyriding the snowy roads of Madequecham for no good reason; there weren't any power lines down that road.

At Candace's funeral, Ethan had sat in one of the back pews—by that time a strong young man in his twenties—and cried bitter tears of guilt, atoning for the actions of his derelict father.

I feel responsible, Ethan had said to Marguerite as he left the church. *Dirty and responsible.*

Marguerite couldn't take anyone's guilt seriously but her own, and therefore she didn't grant him the absolution he was looking for. Now, from a greater distance and a clearer perspective, she felt sorry about that. Ethan eventually bought the Herb Farm from Dolores Kimball; once in a great while, Marguerite saw him in town, and he was always a gentleman, holding open doors for her, touching her arm or her shoulder. But the words unsaid polluted the air between them; she felt it and assumed he did, too.

There was a freckled boy working the register in the greenhouse, a boy about the same age Ethan had been when Marguerite met him. His son? Anything was possible. Marguerite just felt relieved that she didn't have to deal with Ethan head-on; she needed time to get her bearings.

Things in the greenhouse had stayed more or less the same, though the prices had tripled, as had the choices. Marguerite had read in the newspaper that the Herb Farm was supplying not only many Nantucket restaurants now but also several high-end places in Boston and New York. Marguerite was glad for this, she wanted Ethan to succeed, but she was pleased, too, that the trough filled with cool water and bunches of fragrant herbs was right where it had always been. Marguerite picked out bunches of basil and dill, mint and cilantro, and inhaled their scents. This was how Ethan found her, sniffing herbs as if they were her first dozen roses.

"Margo?" he said. The reaction she was getting was universal. Ethan's brown eyes widened as Dusty's had, like he couldn't . . . quite . . . *believe* it. Ethan's face was sunburned and his hair, longer than ever, was tied back in a ponytail.

"Hi," she said, though her voice was so quiet, it was inaudible to her own ears. She took a few steps toward him and opened her arms. He hugged her, she kissed his warm, stubbly cheek, and they parted awkwardly. This was what she had dreaded; the angst of this very second was what had nearly kept her from coming. What to say? There was too much and nothing at all.

"I thought I recognized the Jeep in the parking lot," he said. "But I wouldn't let myself believe it. What are you doing here? I thought—"

"I know," Marguerite said. She self-consciously drew her list out of her skirt pocket, checked it, and bent over to select a bunch of chives, which were crisp and topped with spiky purple flowers. Asparagus, she thought. Chevre, butter, eggs, red peppers, and flowers. If only she could get out of here without explaining. Although deep down she wanted to tell someone, didn't she? She wanted to tell someone about the dinner who would understand. This man. And yet how painful it would be to acknowledge their tragic bond. It would be far more couth, more polite, to ignore it and move on.

"You're cooking," he said. It sounded like an accusation.

"Yes," she said. "A chevre tart with roasted red peppers and an herb crust. You do still have the chevre?"

"Yes. God, of course." He glanced around the green-house, eager to change roles, to be her provisioner. He would recognize some kind of special occasion, but unlike Dusty, he wouldn't ask. He wouldn't want to know.

Ethan rushed to a refrigerated case, right where the chevre and the butter had always been kept; she could have found it herself with ease. He was stopped at the cheese case by another customer, and Marguerite was grateful. She wandered among the wooden crates, picking up toma-toes, peeling back the husks on ears of corn, adding two red peppers to her shopping basket and a bunch of very thin asparagus, a bouquet of zinnias for the table, and seven imperial-looking white and purple gladiolas to put in the stone pitcher that she kept by the front door. She was loaded down with fresh things, beautiful, glorious provi-sions. Could she stop time and stay here, with her basket full, surrounded by organic produce? Could she just die here and call it a happy end?

Ethan appeared at her side with the chevre, just the right amount for her tart. He held the cheese out; his hands, if she weren't mistaken, were trembling. Marguerite cast her eyes around. The woman he had been talking to at the cheese case was now at the counter. The freckled boy scanned her purchases, weighed her produce, and put everything in a used brown paper bag from the A&P. There was no one else in the greenhouse. Marguerite wondered if Ethan was still married to the stepsister. She wondered how marrying someone you were not at all related to could be considered by so many people as incest.

"Thank you," Marguerite said. She, too, could proceed to the checkout and walk across the sunny parking lot to her Jeep, drive home without another word, but for some reason she felt that would be cheating.

And yet she didn't want to knock him over with the force of an out-and-out testimonial. Conversation, she thought. She used to be, if not a master, then at least a journeyman. Able to hold her own with stranger or friend. And Ethan was a friend. What did friends say to one another?

"How *are* you?" she said. "Really, how are you?"

He smiled; his red face creased. He was sun-wrinkled like a farmer, but the hair and the soft eyes and the knowledge of his sensitive soul had always made Marguerite think *poet, philosopher.* "I'm good, Margo. Happy. I'm happy."

"The place looks wonderful."

"It keeps me busy. We're doing all kinds of new things. . . ." He sounded ready to launch into an explanation of heirloom varieties, hydroponics, cold pasteurization, which Marguerite, as a former chef, would appreciate, but he stopped himself. Backed up. "I'm happily married."

"To . . . ?"

"Emily, yes. And the boys are growing up too fast."

"That's one of them over there?" Marguerite asked.

"Yes."

They both looked at the boy, who, now that the greenhouse was empty of customers save for the one his father was talking to, had started reading a book. Marguerite felt proud of him on his father's behalf. Any other kid, it would have been one of those horrible handheld video games.

Ethan cleared his throat. "So you found everything you need? Everything for the tart?"

"Everything for the tart and then some," Marguerite said. She closed her eyes for a second and listened. Was she about to make a colossal mistake? She heard the goats maahing and the refrigerator case humming. She met

Ethan's eyes and lowered her voice. "Renata is coming for dinner tonight."

His expression remained unchanged and Marguerite faltered. Did he not remember Renata? She had been just a little girl, of course. "Renata is Candace's—"

"Yes," he whispered. "I know who she is."

"She's nineteen."

He whistled softly and shook his head.

"I'm sorry," Marguerite said. "I shouldn't have—"

He grabbed her protesting hand. "Don't be sorry," he said. "I figured as much. If you were cooking again, I figured it was the girl. Or Dan. Or Porter."

"The girl," Marguerite repeated. "Renata Knox."

"If I could, I would prostrate myself at her feet," Ethan said. "I would beg her forgiveness."

"You don't have to beg her forgiveness," Marguerite said. "You did nothing wrong."

"Yes, but Walter—"

"Walter, exactly." Marguerite's voice was so firm she startled herself. She glanced at the boy, Ethan's son, but his gaze was glued to the page. "Walter isn't you and you aren't Walter. You never had to carry his load."

"But I did. I do."

"But you do," Marguerite said.

"When I had kids, I promised myself . . ." Here he paused and Marguerite saw him swallow. ". . . that I wouldn't *do* anything that would ever make them feel anything but proud of me."

"Right," Marguerite said. "And they are proud of you, I'm sure. This place is holy, your work is noble, you are a good, good person, and you always have been. Since you were that age." She nodded to the son. "I didn't tell you about Renata to awaken your old, useless guilt. I told you because I knew you would understand about tonight's dinner. How important it is to me. How you will be a part of it."

"I want to be a part of it," he said. "Thank you for coming all the way out here. In my wildest dreams, I never expected to see you today." Ethan took Marguerite by the arm and led her to the counter. "Margo, I'd like you to meet my son Brandon. Brandon, this is Marguerite Beale, an old friend of mine."

Marguerite offered Brandon her hand. "Your father feels no shame in calling me old."

"My apologies," Ethan said. "I meant 'longtime friend.' We've been friends a long time."

Brandon took Marguerite's hand, uneasily glancing between her and his father. Marguerite nearly laughed. She felt unaccountably happy. Relieved. This was almost over; the hard part was through. It would end well. Brandon began to unload Marguerite's purchases, but before he could weigh or scan anything, Ethan said, "It's on the house. All of it."

"Ethan," Marguerite said. "No. I can't let you do that."

"Oh yes, you can," Ethan said. "This is for the best chef on Nantucket and her esteemed guest."

Brandon bagged everything with extreme care as Ethan and Marguerite watched him in silence. Marguerite was grinning; the boy looked so much like his father. When she picked up her bag, Ethan touched her head and Marguerite remembered a priest, long ago, bestowing a blessing. "Now go," he said. "Cook. And enjoy your dinner."

1:14 P.M.

Madequecham Beach was just beautiful enough to improve Renata's attitude. It was a party, a carnival, a scene from *Beach Blanket Bingo*. No wonder her mother had come running down this road. Even in the dead of winter, the beach would have been breathtaking. At the edge of a dirt parking lot was a bluff, and spread out before them the blue, blue ocean and a wide white swath of beach. Renata descended a flight of rickety stairs while holding on to the ass end of Sallie's surfboard. Sallie held the top of the surfboard like a mother dragging an unruly child by the neck. Renata, in addition to watching her step and engineering the descent, was soaking in the action below her: the beautiful young people with their Frisbees and dogs and brilliantly colored beach towels and umbrellas, the radios playing Jimmy Buffett and U2, the beer cans popping open in a sound of serious Saturday celebration. Sallie, meanwhile, was focused only on the waves.

"Hurry up, Renata!" she said. "The surf is screaming my name!"

Renata quickened her step as she felt the surfboard being tugged from her grip. Miles was somewhere behind her. She didn't care where he was. She had left her good sense back on Hulbert Avenue and her heart back at the white cross in the road, and without those two things she felt curiously clean and empty, as though she didn't have a care in the world.

Once they reached the soft, hot sand Renata let go of the surfboard and Sallie raced for the water. Somebody called to her; she waved and pointed at the waves. She stopped suddenly and jogged back to Renata. She handed Renata her sunglasses.

"Hold these," she said. She kissed Renata on the jaw.

"Whoa-ho!" Miles said as he came up behind Renata with the towels and the cooler of beer and sandwiches. "I think she likes you."

She feels sorry for me, Renata thought. Together she

and Miles watched as Sallie lay down on her board and paddled out. Renata slipped Sallie's sunglasses into her bag.

"Is she your girlfriend?" Renata asked.

Miles laughed. "She likes women," he said.

"Really?"

"Really."

Renata felt funny in a way she couldn't name. "Where do you want to sit?" she asked. "Do you know anybody here?"

"A few people," he said. "This is where I hang out when I'm not working. But I don't feel like getting into it all today. Let's just sit here." He plunked the cooler down on a plot of unclaimed sand, several yards away from four girls, tanned and oiled, lined up on a blanket like so many sausages across a grill. Renata stood by as Miles spread out a towel for her; then she slipped out of her skirt and lay down. Miles dug two beers out of the cooler and opened one for her. Renata didn't normally drink in the middle of the day, but she was dying of thirst and today, it was becoming clear, was not a normal day. She took a taste from the sweating bottle and instantly her mood improved. Miles lay down next to her on a second towel. He removed his shirt and every one of Renata's impure thoughts returned. His body was gorgeous—not pretty, like a model or a movie star, but muscular and rugged. Renata's experience with male bodies was limited to Cade, who was lankier than Miles. Cade had long, skinny legs and knobby knees. He had big feet and freakishly long toes that Renata teased him about; as a result, he'd stopped wearing flip-flops. Cade had a farmer's tan. He'd spent the summer with Renata in the city, working at Columbia's business school, and the only time he spent outside was the occasional lunch hour on the steps of Uris Hall and weekend afternoons, when he and Renata ate take-out food in Sheep Meadow, waving away the gnats. It wasn't at all fair to compare Miles to Cade or vice versa, and yet Renata found herself wondering what it would feel like if Miles leaned to his left and then leaned again so that he was lying on top of her. Would his weight feel different? How would he taste if she kissed him? Would sex feel different?

Renata drank her beer with purpose until it was gone. Miles had his eyes closed. Renata raised her head an inch off the towel and became light-headed. She scanned the water beyond the breaking waves for Sallie. There were a lot of people surfing and Renata thought she saw a woman with long hair, but it could just as easily have been a man.

"So," she said. "I'm missing lunch at the yacht club."

Miles didn't open his eyes. "That you are."

"Suzanne will be mad."

"Quite possibly."

"Have you worked for them a long time?"

He opened his eyes and looked at her. Was he annoyed? Was she keeping him awake? She was about to tell him to relax, she would be quiet, when he did half her bidding and leaned to his left, propping himself on one elbow so that he was gazing down at her. He sipped his beer. Renata felt a wave of desire so strong she nearly fainted away. She closed her eyes. *Oh,* she thought. *Oh, oh.* An engaged person should not feel this kind of insane hunger for the houseboy of her fiancé's family. There was something wrong with her.

"Three years," he said. "This is the first summer I've lived with them, though. Suzanne loves it because I'm always around."

"You live there by yourself?"

"No," he said. "I have a roommate."

"Who?" she said.

He licked his lips and twisted his beer into the sand.

"Let me ask you something," he said. "Why do you want to get married?"

"I don't," she said. She sat up and squinted at the water. The surfers were fun to watch once they finally decided a wave was worth pursuing. Renata located the person she thought was Sallie—long hair, bare midriff—and saw her crouch on her board, then stand, shifting her weight, steadying herself with her arms as the board careened along the smooth inside wall of the wave. Then crash. Time to start over. Renata wondered how surfing could possibly be worth all the time spent waiting for a decent wave. Were those seconds of riding just unbelievably rewarding? Was it like the thrill of a first kiss? "I think I'll have another beer," Renata said. "Please."

"Sandwich?" Miles said.

"Not yet."

Miles flipped the top off another beer for Renata and one for himself. Renata's guilt was at a ten; surely it couldn't get any worse than this. She had denied her own fiancé.

"It's not that I don't want to marry *Cade*," she said. She nearly added, *I love Cade,* but at the last minute she changed her mind. "Everybody loves Cade."

"He's a great guy," Miles said. "Very upstanding. Very upwardly mobile. Lots of money."

"That's not why—"

"Oh, I know. That's not why I work for them, either. I work for them because I like Mr. D., and he's sick."

"He's sick," Renata said. "Cade wants to get married before anything happens to him. Before he's too sick to enjoy a wedding."

"Like I said, upstanding fellow."

"He was president of the student body at Columbia,"

Renata said. "And captain of the lacrosse team. He graduated Phi Beta Kappa."

"All very admirable."

"All very admirable," Renata repeated. Cade Driscoll was a catch, and she had spent the past ten months in a daze of pride and disbelief that he had chosen *her,* a lowly, motherless freshman, a relative nobody. And yet now the awe she'd felt had been displaced by something else. She feared him a little bit, his permanence in her life, the *finality* of it all. Marriage. "I guess I'd rather just stay engaged for a while."

"How old are you?" Miles asked.

"Nineteen."

"You're *kidding*," he said. He looked genuinely aghast. "I'm going to have to confiscate that beer."

"How old are you?" Renata asked.

"Twenty-four," he said. He gazed at Renata's chest. "You're getting pretty red."

"No lotion," she said. She pressed her fingers against her skin and the fingerprints turned white. She was frying like bacon.

"Take my shirt," he said. He tossed it to her and it landed in her lap, soft and cool. She put it on. It smelled like a man, but like a man other than her fiancé. Cade wore cologne. This shirt smelled like bleach and sweat and piney soap. Renata felt all muddled; she yearned for clarity. She loved Cade—what woman wouldn't?—but the more she was forced to confront the reality of getting married (Suzanne's damn list, her father saying, *I think it's wonderful, darling. Congratulations!*) the less sure she was that marriage was what she wanted. Telling her father was one thing, but Renata was growing more and more afraid of telling Action. Action would pitch a French fit; she might even threaten to divorce Renata as her best friend, and Renata wouldn't be able to bear that. If she was forced to make a choice between Cade and her father, Cade would win. But if she was forced to pick between Cade and Action, Action would win. What did that say? Renata watched the surfers, keeping her eye on Sallie. *She likes women.* There was an intensity to Renata's relationship with Action that was missing from her relationship with Cade. There was a thrill, an excitement, a passion to their friendship; they were giddy with it half the time and smug the other half. They held hands, many times, walking to the dining hall.

We in love, Action liked to say.

There was a shout from down the beach. "Miles!" Some guys were setting up a volleyball net. A tall, dark man, hairy like a bear, punched the volleyball on top of his fist. "Want to play?"

Miles called out no, but the man didn't seem to hear. He waved his arm like a windmill. Miles shook his head. "No, man, sorry." Then he huffed. "We should have sat farther down," he said. "I'm going to have to go over there. I'll be right back."

"Whatever," Renata said. "Play if you want. You don't have to babysit me." She leaned back and closed her eyes, trying to turn the day back into what she thought it might be when she woke up that morning: a day on Nantucket, a day at the beach. Instead, she pictured the white cross, a piece of her mother up there on the bluff. Renata would ask Marguerite about the cross, first thing.

A few minutes later, Renata felt something land in the sand next to her. She opened her eyes to see Sallie sitting on Miles's towel. Her hair was wet and slick, revealing a small, white ear, which was punched with six identical silver hoops. Renata's father had spent hours of precious breath warning her about the dangers—not the tackiness or flamboyance but the *dangers*—of piercings and tattoos, and in this unique case, Renata had chosen to agree with her father and obey. But the effect of these "dangers" on Sallie was dazzling. There was a city block near Columbia where the residents had pressed colored glass and seashells and silvery stones into the sidewalk—Renata loved to walk that block because it was different; it turned the ordinary cement into a celebration—and Sallie with her earrings and toe rings and mirrored navel and the army green spiral twist of leaves and vines around her right ankle struck Renata in much the same way. She could barely tear her eyes away. Sallie was dripping wet; her eyelashes stuck together in thick clumps.

"How was the surfing?" Renata asked.

"It's wild out there," Sallie said. Her chest heaved; her breasts rose and fell. "It doesn't look that bad from here, but there's a wicked rip. I came in because I'm starving. Did Miles make lunch?"

"Sandwiches," Renata said.

Sallie opened the cooler and dug a sandwich out. "Roadkill," she said. "Another person would have thought to put the sandwiches *on top of* the beer. Ah, men." She said this conspiratorially, and Renata laughed a little, then remembered what Miles had said. *She likes women.* Renata watched Sallie unwrap the sandwich and take a lusty bite.

"Do you want a beer?" Renata asked.

"No, thanks," Sallie said. "I'm going back out in a minute." The offer, though, seemed to train Sallie's attention back on Renata, and Renata couldn't tell if she was flattered by this or worried. "So your mother died on that road back there. That honestly blows my mind. I'm sorry for what I said about the cross before. I hope I didn't offend you."

"No, it's fine—"

"I never thought about those crosses being for real people, you know? I just thought the Department of Public Works stuck them there to keep people from driving too fast. I never thought of them as being for someone's *mother*."

"It's okay," Renata said.

"How old were you?" Sallie asked. "When she died?"

"Five."

"Noooooooo," Sallie said. "Tell me no."

"I was five."

Sallie reached out for Renata's hand and squeezed it. Renata felt grateful and silly. She didn't know what to say. Sallie swallowed the last of the sandwich.

"How do you know Miles?" Sallie asked. "He didn't pick you up at a bar, did he?"

"No," Renata said quickly. "I'm staying with the family Miles works for."

Sallie creased her eyebrows. Her nose seemed to wiggle.

"The Driscolls," Renata said.

"You know, I've never met them."

Renata nearly said, *Consider yourself lucky,* but she checked her swing. They were, after all, her future in-laws. "I . . . date the son. He's my boyfriend. His name is Cade."

Sallie nodded distractedly; her attention was back on the water, with the other surfers. Maybe she was put out by this pronouncement of Renata's heterosexuality. "I assumed you were with Miles."

"I assumed *you* were," Renata said.

At this, Sallie hooted. "That guy?" she said. She nodded down the beach at Miles, who was walking back toward them. "Want to hear something funny?" Sallie called out. "She thought I was your girlfriend."

"Get your ass up," Miles said. "You're sitting on my towel."

"Such a gentleman," Sallie said. She didn't move an inch.

"I mean it," Miles said. "Get up."

"Sit on my board if you're afraid of the sand," Sallie said.

"Never mind," Miles said. He plopped down on the other side of Renata. "So what were you two talking about?"

"None of your business," Sallie said. "Who is that down there?"

"Montrose. Couldn't shake him."

"And what did you two talk about?"

"None of your business."

Sallie looked at Renata and rolled her eyes. *Men.*

"Renata's engaged, you know," Miles said.

"What?" Sallie said. She moved her face so that it hovered directly over Renata's face, blocking out the sun. "I thought you said 'boyfriend.' "

"Well . . . ," Renata said. She realized she had her left hand, her ringed hand, tucked under her butt, and she kept it there.

"I'm trying to talk her out of it," Miles said. "She's only nineteen."

"You're trying to talk me out of it?" Renata said. "Suzanne won't like that."

"Who's Suzanne?" Sallie said.

"The woman I work for," Miles said.

"My future mother-in-law," Renata said. Something about the beer and the pure lawlessness of the afternoon made Renata want to throw Suzanne under the bus. She reached for her bag. "Look what I found this morning," she said. She pulled out the list and did her best to smooth it flat. "Suzanne is trying to plan my wedding without even asking me."

Sallie took the list and read it. Renata hoped she might share her outrage, but instead Sallie got all dreamy eyed.

"Weddings are a sick fantasy of mine," Sallie said. Miles guffawed, but she didn't seem to notice. "I love to think about this kind of stuff. The dress, the flowers, the champagne, a hundred and fifty people standing up when you walk into the church, band or DJ, sit-down or buffet. I've always wanted a big wedding."

"You have got to be kidding me," Miles said.

"Don't you?"

"I haven't given it a second's thought," Miles said.

"Me, either," Renata admitted.

"My parents eloped on Antigua," Sallie said. "They were pregnant with my oldest brother."

"That's romantic," Renata said. "Isn't it?"

"Well, they're still married," Sallie said. "My mother regrets not having a big to-do. She's pinned all her hopes on me, poor woman."

"You'll get married?" Renata said.

"No," Sallie said. "Not in any way that they'd approve of."

There were a few seconds of silence. Staying on this topic was like sitting bare butted on a barnacled rock; Renata wanted to get off. She gently reclaimed the list from Sallie, folded it up, and tucked it back into her bag.

"May I have another beer, please?" she asked.

Miles jumped up. "I'll get it." He opened the cooler and flipped the top off a bottle. "Sandwich?" he said.

"Not yet."

"Look at you, catering to her every need," Sallie said. "How sweet."

"I'm a sweet guy." He sat back down next to Renata, even closer than last time. Meanwhile, Sallie laid a hand on Renata's bicep; her fingers grazed the side of Renata's breast.

"I'm going back out for a beating," Sallie said. "Will you keep an eye on me?"

"Since when do you need a spotter?" Miles said.

"Since today. It's hairier out there than it looks."

"I'll keep an eye out," Renata said, though she had no idea what this entailed. If Sallie did get caught in a rip current, Renata would never be able to save her. All she had wanted from the afternoon was a swim, and yet the waves were pounding the shore so brutally that Renata was afraid to go in, lest she lose her top or get knocked on her ass.

Sallie pointed a finger and smiled. "Don't go getting married while I'm gone," she said, and with that she picked up her board and paddled out.

"Yep," Miles said, once Sallie was past the first set of breaking waves. "She likes you."

Renata sipped her beer. "Shut up."

"What?" he said.

There had been something familiar about it, Renata thought. Miles on one side, Sallie on the other, competing for her attention. It was like all the hours she spent, early on, in the company of Cade and Action—until they realized they didn't like each other that much, they were jealous of each other, they resented each other. Boyfriend, best friend: It didn't work out that well. Renata had spent the last year juggling, compromising, trying to keep them both happy. She sipped her beer and closed her eyes.

"Are you okay?"

"Huh?" Renata said. Miles was on her towel now, or part of his leg was. He had stretched out, and his lower leg and foot were on her towel. And when he spoke, he leaned closer and his right elbow sank into the sand next to her towel and his left hand was on her towel.

"I asked if you were okay."

She nodded, confused. She was lying: She wasn't okay. She felt lost. Cade, Action, her father, Marguerite, her mother, Suzanne. And now Miles, who, if she wasn't hallucinating, was leaning down to *kiss* her. She closed her eyes. Was this happening? He kissed her. He scooted closer and kissed her again, really kissed her, with his tongue. He tasted different from Cade, though she couldn't say how. She didn't have time to think about it; she was too busy worrying about the three hundred witnesses to this treachery—the four girls sunbathing near them, the hairy beast Montrose on the other side of the volleyball net, and most crucially Sallie: What on earth would Sallie think if she saw Renata and Miles kissing only seconds after she had discovered that Renata was engaged? Renata propped herself up on her elbows and did a quick scan—the girls were asleep, the volleyball game was its own spectacle, it had drawn a crowd, and Sallie was indistinguishable from the other surfers. No one had seen them, thank God. Miles took hold of her chin. "Hey," he said. "I'm over here." He kissed her again.

I'm trying to talk her out of it.

Stop! Renata screamed at herself. *Stop right now!* But all she could think was: *I want more. How do I get more?* Miles was turned on, she could tell through his bathing suit that he was hard, and her mind rooted out possibilities: the dunes, the water, his car? Her body was begging for more—she wanted him to reach inside her bikini top and fondle her breast; she wanted him to slip his hand between her legs. *Look what you've done to me.* Wait a minute! *Cade,* she thought. *Cade, Cade, Cade.* Thinking about Cade didn't help. He'd said they would go to the beach together today, but he had vanished without so much as a note. He would expect her to understand; he was sailing with his sick father. How could she argue with that? She couldn't. Cade was, as always, doing the right thing, whereas she, in her anger and confusion, was doing the wrong thing.

Renata broke free for a second, checked around them again. The girls, the volleyball game—on someone's radio, John Mellencamp sang "Jack and Diane." Miles probably kissed girls on this beach all the time. He was a predator; she should escape from him now, while she had the chance. Renata narrowed her eyes and tried to pick Sallie out of the water. If Sallie would only come back, she'd be safe.

"You want to get out of here?" Miles asked.

This was her chance to turn him down, to prove she was pure of soul, worthy of three karats, worthy of Cade, upstanding fellow—but instead, Renata nodded mutely. Miles wrapped a towel around his waist and led her away from the girls and the game, past an older couple, an anomaly in this thirty-and-under crowd, the woman heavyset and topless, lying facedown, reading a novel, the man even heavier in a webbed lawn chair with his binoculars trained on the surfers. They didn't move as Renata and Miles snuck past.

Up a second, smaller staircase, up to the bluff, into the dunes. There was nothing behind them—no road, no houses, nothing but eel grass and bowls of soft, white sand, some with circles of ash where people had lit bonfires, some with empty beer cans and condom wrappers. Renata followed behind Miles, every so often turning around to look at the beach. No one was shouting after them; no one would notice they were gone. Cade was on the other side of the island, possibly still sailing. He would never know.

If you did a bad thing and no one ever found out, Renata asked herself, *was it still a bad thing?*

Just as Miles led her into a deep bowl, deep enough so that they would never be seen and as wide as a king-size bed, Renata's head began to clear. What was she *doing*? Miles unwrapped the towel from his waist and laid it down in the sand. He sat.

"Come here," he said.

She could have run, or claimed she had to pee and *then* run; she could have started to cry, owning up to her guilt— any of these strategies would have worked. But she wasn't strong enough or mature enough to turn down something she wanted so badly. She'd wanted him since the first second she'd seen him at the airport, when his forearms flexed as he lifted their luggage into the back of the Driscolls' Range Rover. And then with the hose. And then making the sandwiches. Now here he was, offering himself up on a platter.

As she stepped down into the bowl, her feet sank into the soft sand. He reached out and pulled her onto the towel. If he had been any bit rougher or more insistent, she would have stopped him. But he kissed her slowly and gently in a way that made her think *love*. This was a trick, of course; she hadn't been kissed by that many men, but she recognized his tenderness as a trick, a lure. He took his shirt off her body and his hands went where she had willed them to go earlier. She was panting; she wanted his bathing suit off; she wanted him right on top of her. He was taking his good old time, going slower and slower to maybe see if he could get her to think *love* again. But who was he kidding? She cried out softly in frustration, *"Oh, come on!"*

He stopped. His bathing suit was uneven around his hips, his cock strained through the nylon. He was sweating. It was blistering hot in the bowl of white sand, blocked from the ocean breeze. By now Renata's bathing suit top was off, discarded, buried somewhere, she didn't care

where. She didn't care! She wanted to scream the words:
I DON'T CARE! About Cade or her father, or even, at that
point, her mother, and the sad little white cross that marked
her demise.

"I'm thinking of you," Miles said. He had his hands by
her ears; he was holding himself above her, shading her,
his knees resting between her open legs. "You're about to
burn your whole house down."

She thought of Sallie kissing her jaw and Cade kissing
her last night on the guest room's deck and Action, who
had kissed her on the mouth and each of the palms the day
she left for the woods of West Virginia. She thought of her
father kissing her good night on the forehead every night
for fourteen years that she could recall. She thought of Suzanne kissing her upon the announcement of her engagement, kissing her with reverence and pride, like a mother
would. Renata did not have a single memory of kissing her
own mother.

"Burn it down," she said.

2:40 *P.M.*

The tart was a new recipe, flagged in a copy of *Bon Appétit*, June 1995, so not really new at all, but new to Marguerite because she had never tried it. She had marked the
page and cataloged the magazine, however. Just in case.

Marguerite turned on different music: Tony Bennett
singing Cole Porter. Happy songs, sad songs, love songs,
lovesick songs. Marguerite whistled and, now that the
mailman had come and gone, she hummed.

The first thing she did was tackle the tart crust. This
was a pastry skill, and pastry skills had never been her
strong suit. She loved to bake bread, but crusts were dif-

ferent from bread. Bread could take a beating, whereas crusts wanted to be handled as little as possible. Bread liked warmth and humidity, whereas crusts liked the cold. The butter had to be cold; the egg had to be cold. Marguerite minced the herbs, relishing the feel of her ten-inch Wusthof in her hands—a knife older than her dinner guest—and the sound of the blade against her cutting board. Dicing, chopping, mincing, all like what they said about riding a bike. Marguerite had always been gifted with a knife; she had cut herself only once, in the early days at Les Trois Canards. Gerard de Luc had been screaming at her in French, something she didn't understand, and Marguerite, who was aiming for a perfectly uniform *brunoise* of carrots, put the knife through her second and third fingertips to the tune of fifteen stitches. After that, she worked to achieve a kind of zen with her knife. When she held it, she blocked everything else out.

The scent of the herbs intensified once they were minced—minty, peppery, pickly. For some reason, this smell got to her. Marguerite started to cry. She wasn't tearing up like she might over an onion but crying. Crying so that she had to leave the herbs in a wet green pile on the cutting board next to the carefully measured flour and salt, crying so that she had to return the butter to the fridge, where it would stay cold, and find a place to sit down. Not the kitchen table, the chairs were too hard; not the bedroom, the bed was too soft. She wandered like Goldilocks through her own house, her eyes blinded by tears, to the sofa in the sitting room where, on any other day, she would have been reading her Alice Munro stories. She settled in a way that felt like collapsing.

Okay, what was it? What was wrong? She was sobbing, gasping, wheezing for air. Classic hysterics. And yet she was curiously detached. Part of her was watching herself cry, thinking, *Go ahead, get it out, get as crazy and as dramatic as you want now, better now than the second the girl walks in; we don't want to send her running back down Quince Street with the news that you actually have lost your mind.* The rational part of Marguerite did the watching. The irrational part of her, the part fully engaged in the sobbing, was feeling all the things she had forbidden herself to feel for the past fourteen years, because she might have wailed like this each and every day. She had been thorough and adamant about stripping her life of all sensory reminders from her old life, like the smell of those herbs, so that she wouldn't be tempted to dwell on what she had lost. It wasn't only her taste buds that had been numbed; it was her heart, too. But now, just for a minute, with snot and tears dripping down her face, she felt.

It was practically legend, the way that Daniel Knox had stormed into their lives. He appeared one night in July, a busy Friday night, around nine thirty. Marguerite, Candace, and Porter had just settled down on the west banquette to dinner. There were still a few tables lingering over dessert; this was usual. What was unusual was the man who approached from the bar, a full drink in his hand, and pulled out the fourth seat, the seat next to Candace, and said, "I know I'm being awfully forward, but—"

Candace looked up and said, "Oh! Hello."

Marguerite and Porter exchanged glances. Candace received a lot of attention from men. Drinks were sent to the table all the time. A few men waited at the bar until Candace rose from dinner; they thought they could trap her there, like an insect in their web. The men were usually older, graying, wealthy; some had accents. They were all full of promises, of ideas; they had a big boat, a big house, a big party the following night. Would Candace join them? Sometimes the answer was yes, and a few nights later Marguerite and Porter would hear about the big boat, the big house, the big party—but most of the time the answer was no. No one had ever been bold enough to approach the table. It was the chef's table, the owner's table. Marguerite ate after everyone was finished for a reason. She wanted a modicum of privacy, at least as much as she afforded her guests. She would never have sat down at one of *their* tables uninvited. The way Candace said, "Oh! Hello," however, made both Marguerite and Porter think that this man with the dark blond hair and the untrimmed beard was someone Candace knew. When the man sat down, Candace fumbled with the introduction.

"This is Marguerite Beale, the chef/owner, and my brother Porter Harris. And Marguerite, Porter, this is—"

"Daniel," he said. "Daniel Knox." They shook hands over and around their drinks.

Candace laughed nervously and said, "And my name is Candace Harris."

"I know," Daniel said.

"You're the man I see when I'm running, right?" she said. "Down at—"

"The Beach Club," Daniel said. "Yes. I own it. I bought it five years ago."

"Aha!" Porter said. He could talk to anyone, given a foothold. "So you're the chap who made all the changes."

"Capital improvements," Daniel said.

"You raised the dues, I hear."

"Had to."

"You must not be very popular," Porter said.

"More popular than one might think," Daniel said. "The place looks a hell of a lot better. You should come see it sometime."

"I'd love to," Porter said.

Francesca approached the table with three appetizer plates. "You have a fourth?" she said. Her voice barely concealed her annoyance; serving Marguerite was her last duty before tipping out.

Marguerite shook her head ever so slightly and tried to send Francesca a distress signal. *We don't know who this man is or where he came from.*

"Oh no," Daniel said. "I wouldn't want to impose."

Candace put a hand on his arm. "Stay," she said. "We'd love it." She looked to Marguerite.

"We'd love it," Marguerite said, though nothing was further from the truth. "A fourth! Francesca, would you ask Lance to bring Mr. Knox another drink. Scotch, is it?"

"Scotch," Daniel said. "But really, I have a full one here—"

"And a bottle of the 1974 Louis Jadot cabernet from the cellar. Two bottles."

"Well," Porter said. "Daisy is pulling out the big guns tonight."

Francesca nodded, then swept away from the table. She was back a second later with another plate of the wild mushroom ravioli and the scotch and the wine.

"More bread?" she asked.

"No, thank you," Marguerite said. She smiled wickedly at Porter and nudged his foot under the table. Together they made sure that Daniel Knox always had a full scotch as well as one waiting, and a full glass of wine. *Drink,* they encouraged him. *Drink!* Daniel Knox talked about the Beach Club; then he talked about living in New York, trading petroleum futures, his retirement at age thirty. Candace seemed interested. She was good at that; she practiced patience all day long at the Chamber of Commerce, fielding phone call after phone call of people asking if there was a bridge to Nantucket. Daniel asked what Candace did for work, she told him, he asked about her running, and she talked about the New York Marathon. *This year for sure.*

By the time the entrées arrived, Daniel Knox was intoxicated. He slurred his words, he stared at his swordfish woefully, and Marguerite knew he was done for. He didn't eat a single bite. Candace chattered along; Porter talked about Nantucket as it was in the fifties when he first started coming there; Marguerite watched over Candace's shoulder as the kitchen was cleaned and closed up for the night. The conversation proceeded as if Daniel Knox weren't there—and a few seconds later, he wasn't. He excused himself for the men's room. Porter chuckled as he filled Daniel's wineglass for the tenth time.

"You two are awful," Candace said; then she smiled.

"Don't I know it," Marguerite said. "I'm sure he's not used to the likes of us."

"He seems like a nice man," Candace said.

"Does he?" Marguerite said.

"Yes!" Candace said, peeved now. "I'm going to check on him."

It took ten days for Daniel to resurface and ask Candace out on a date. He made a hearty campaign for Ship's Inn or the Club Car; he even offered to cook himself, in the small apartment behind the Beach Club where he lived. Candace sweetly declined. *I like to eat at Les Parapluies,* she said. *Sorry. That's what I like.*

And so Marguerite fed Candace and a very reluctant Daniel Knox at the regular seven thirty seating, just like everyone else. Cedar-planked salmon and potatoes Anna. Daniel Knox, despite the fact that he drank almost nothing and did not take his eyes off Candace, cleaned his plate. The following morning, Candace cornered Marguerite in the kitchen.

"Daniel wants to know what you put in our food," she said. "He swears it made him fall in love." Candace kissed Marguerite on both cheeks. "So whatever it was, thank you."

They came in together a lot that summer, though some nights they took sandwiches to the beach, or they went to the movies, or they attended a party thrown by one of the Beach Club members. At first Candace referred to Daniel as "the man I'm dating," and Porter and Marguerite followed her lead. "Daniel Knox," they said, when people asked who he was. "The man Candace is dating." Candace still came to the restaurant without Daniel, though less and less frequently. Marguerite asked, as casually as possible, if things were getting serious. Candace would smile and tilt her head. "Serious?" She was being coy and it drove Marguerite mad. The one time Marguerite tried to talk about it with Porter, they ended up arguing, which almost never happened. It was late at night, they were at Marguerite's house on Quince Street. Marguerite was sitting at her dressing table, unpinning her hair. Porter lay in bed reading a biography of John Singer Sargent.

"Candace is acting strangely," Marguerite said. "When I ask her about Daniel, I can't get a straight answer."

"I think that's probably a good sign," Porter said. "They're falling in love."

"Falling in love is a good thing?" Marguerite asked.

"It was for us," Porter said. He laid his book down on his chest. "Come here."

Marguerite spun on her stool. "I don't think Daniel is right for your sister."

"Because you don't like him."

"I do like him."

"Oh, Daisy, you do not. But then I suspect you wouldn't like anyone Candace dated. You're more protective than a mother."

"I'm not protective."

"Okay, then, you're jealous."

"Jealous? You've *got* to be kidding."

"Right," Porter said. "Why should you be jealous? You have me."

"It's just not like her to be so secretive," Marguerite said. "Your sister and I tell each other everything. And now there's this . . . thing, this big thing, that she won't talk about."

"Probably because she senses that you don't really want to hear about Daniel. Because you don't like Daniel. Because you're jealous."

"Please shut up," Marguerite said. "You're giving me a headache."

"You brought it up," Porter said. "And I'm certain you don't want my advice, but if I were you, I'd get used to the idea of Candace and Daniel together. In fact, I wouldn't be surprised if they got married."

"Oh, for heaven's sake, Porter."

"I heard her call him her boyfriend."

"You did not."

"I did. 'My boyfriend, Daniel Knox.'"

"You're just saying that to annoy me."

"I am not. You have to face the facts, Daisy. She's not going to belong to us forever."

Marguerite had not responded. She'd sat at the dressing table, looking at her reflection in the mirror, lost in thought. Porter called her to bed twice, then gave up and turned off the light.

That conversation had disturbed her deeply, but why?

Why shouldn't Candace and Daniel be happy? Why shouldn't they get married? Was Marguerite being overly protective? *Was* she jealous? Was Candace keeping Marguerite at arm's length, or was Marguerite pushing Candace away by not accepting Daniel? Because the fact of the matter was, Marguerite *didn't* like Daniel. She was afraid of him, and she couldn't stifle a growing sense of resentment.

In the fall, once Porter left, Candace came into the restaurant to eat with Marguerite, and Daniel would plant himself on one of the benches outside the Dreamland Theater across the street, thinking they wouldn't see him among the movie crowds. It was weird, wasn't it? Daniel was stalking Candace. But no, Candace said, he was just waiting there so he could walk her home. Why didn't she just call him, then, when she was finished dinner? Why did Daniel have to be a spy, a silent, unwelcome witness to the most intimate moments of Candace and Marguerite's friendship? Daniel had come into their lives to whisk Candace away. Soon enough, Marguerite thought, she would be gone.

Matters weren't helped by the fact that, in the spring, Porter announced he was taking a trip to Japan. Four years he had promised Marguerite a spring trip, and four years he had backed out. Now he was off to Japan. For work, he said. Research about how the Orient influenced the art of Claude Monet.

Marguerite asked him if he was going alone.

"Alone?" he said, and right then she knew the answer was no. There was a pause. "Actually, no. I'm going with colleagues."

"Colleagues?"

"One colleague. From the department. An expert on Japanese art."

"A woman?"

"Yes, actually," Porter said. "Professor Strickland. A real battle-ax."

A real battle-ax? Marguerite thought. Like Corsage Woman? Like Overbite Woman? She felt helpless with rage; she trembled with jealousy. This was the last straw; he was daring her to confront him. Would she be brave enough? Angry enough? No. She couldn't. She was seething but paralyzed. She confronted Candace instead, over a pot of Darjeeling tea and a plate of macaroons.

"Your brother is off to Kyoto with a woman from his department. Teahouses, he said, pagodas, bridges, gardens. It's like a mystery, he claims, trying to locate Japanese artists who would have been contemporaries of Claude Monet. It all sounds very scholarly, but I'm being an idiot, right? Traveling with one woman alone. He's telling me something without coming right out and telling me."

Candace quietly munched and sipped. She agreed to do some detective work, find out what she could about Professor Strickland. "I'm the first one to condemn my brother," Candace said. "But this could be for real. She could be eighty years old for all we know. I have a hard time believing he would go on vacation with anyone but you. All the way to Japan?"

"It's not like him," Marguerite said.

"Not like him at all," Candace said. "His vacation is Nantucket. It's you. The rest of the year is work, work, work. This trip is work."

"Right," Marguerite said.

* * *

The second part of the conversation took place in the middle of town. Candace called Marguerite from the Chamber and said, "I found out who she is. I'm coming to you."

And Marguerite said, "No, I'm coming to you."

They met on the corner of Centre and India Streets, in front of a guesthouse that was closed for the winter. There was a crust of dirty snow on the curb; the wind was merciless.

"Thirty-five years old," Candace said. "Head coach of the tennis team. Blond. Unmarried."

"Japanese art?" Marguerite said.

"She's not a professor at all, Daisy," Candace said. "She's the tennis coach."

"So he lied," Marguerite said.

"He lied."

"He lied." To Marguerite's knowledge, Porter had never lied to her before. Withheld the truth, perhaps, but never lied.

"I don't know why you stay with him, Daisy," Candace said. "How many years has it been now? Six? Seven? Tell him you're done with him—that'll wake him up. Tell him to go straight to hell."

Marguerite played this out in her mind: *I'm sorry, Porter. It's over.* This was what she should do. Otherwise, she was allowing herself to be stepped on, abused; she was asking for it. Tell him to go straight to hell. *Go to hell, Porter.* She pictured his spidery legs, his tapered fingers; she pictured him asleep in the hammock with an art journal spread open on his chest; she pictured him asleep on the bench, in the Musée du Jeu de Paume. She pictured him practicing his accordion.

"I can't," Marguerite said. "I don't have anybody else."

"You have me," Candace said.

"Yes . . ." Marguerite said tentatively. What she was

thinking was, *You belong to Daniel*. This was now an iron-clad fact. Candace and Daniel were a couple. Whenever Marguerite wanted to get together with Candace, Candace said she had to check. What she meant was that she had to check with Daniel. They had date nights, movies, a TV show they both adored that they couldn't miss, they had their own friends, other couples, dinner parties—a whole social life that did not include Marguerite. *You have me,* Candace said. It was a sweet lie, but a lie just the same. Candace and Porter were both lying to Marguerite, but she didn't dare call them on it. It was beyond her.

"Yes," she said. "I have you."

Porter returned from Japan in very high spirits. He brought Marguerite a pink silk kimono embroidered with butterflies and lotus flowers. It was the most gorgeous thing she had ever set eyes on, and yet when he gave it to her upon his arrival on Nantucket late in May she threw the box across the room; it was the closest she'd come to a tantrum, to addressing the real issue between them. She thought, *It's going to take more than this to win me back*. Porter retrieved the box, smoothed the folds of silk inside. His movements were calm, his face unsurprised, as though he'd been expecting this reaction. He kissed her and wrapped her in his arms. "Next year, Paris," he said. "Next year for sure."

Marguerite blew her nose and blotted her eyes in an attempt to pull herself together. She returned to the kitchen and eyed the pile of chopped herbs warily, like an enemy. She mixed up the dough, rolled it out, and pressed it into her nine-inch fluted tart pan. Marguerite covered the tart with foil, weighed it down with ceramic pie beads, and slid it into the oven. She hated to turn the oven on in the heat of the afternoon, but she had no choice. The monkey in her grandfather clock banged his cymbals together every fifteen minutes, time was slipping away, and the tenderloin had to roast, the bread had to bake and later, once Renata was here, the asparagus.

Marguerite polished her grand old oak table with five leaves that she'd bought at an estate sale in Cobleskill, New York. She left it fully extended for no good reason other than she liked the way it looked, although, as with the five bedrooms upstairs, she found it unsettling to rattle around in a house meant for ten. She brought out china service for herself and Renata, but she couldn't bring herself to set down the tarnished silver.

The tart shell came out; Marguerite cranked the heat on her old, reliable Wolfe stove (the salesman had said it would last forever, and he was correct) and slid in the tenderloin. She fixed herself a cup of tea and carried the mahogany chest that held her silver outside to her small patio.

It was a hot afternoon, but Marguerite's glass-topped table and wrought-iron chairs sat partially in the shade. She loved her garden, small though it was. Along with reading, the garden gave her constant pleasure—her rosebushes, the hydrangeas, her daylilies, each blooming for only one day, then withering. Marguerite snapped off the dead blossoms every morning, though she hadn't that morning, so she did it then, and when she finished, her hands were stained pink, red, orange. She cut a few dahlias to round out the bouquet of zinnias that she'd bought at the Herb Farm.

Finally, she sat down with her tea and her silver. She and Renata each would need a butter knife, a steak knife, a dinner fork, a salad fork, and a spoon for the *pots de crème.* Ten pieces of silver in all and yet, when Marguerite sat down, she remembered about a ladle for the béarnaise, tongs for the asparagus, a serving fork for the meat. She decided to polish it all: 120 pieces. It was soothing work—smearing the utensils with the bruise-colored polish, then wiping them clean with a flour-sack towel. The pieces shone like new dimes. Marguerite looked at her distorted reflection in the bowl of the big serving spoon; she dug the polish out of the crevices of the intricate designs on the handles. The white flour-sack towel became smudged with black, evidence that her efforts were paying off. How satisfying, how symbolic, wiping away the tarnish, the grime from the past. Marguerite cleaned her hands and sipped her tea.

It would be nice to have Ethan and his wife and his boys for dinner, she thought. It would be nice to have Dusty. Or Daniel, Renata, and the fiancé, even the fiancé's parents. It would be nice, in short, to call an end to her house arrest, to her pointlessly austere lifestyle; it would be nice to interact with real people, in person, rather than via a computer screen for an hour each day, rather than reading about made-up lives in stories and novels, rather than visiting with the people she had loved—the people who had both lifted her up and disappointed her—in her mind, her memory. She would never reach out, she knew, but on such a lovely summer afternoon in her garden with a cup of tea and half her silver yet to polish, there was no harm in imagining how nice it would be.

2:41 P.M.

As Renata scavenged through the sand for the components of her bathing suit, she decided that her real mistake wasn't what had happened five minutes ago in the sand, nor was it the events a week ago at Lespinasse. Her real mistake occurred last October when Renata allowed herself to fall in love with Cade Driscoll in the first damn place. Looking back, Renata realized how vulnerable she'd been—six weeks into her freshman year, drinking warmish beer at the Delta Phi house—when she'd met Cade. He had been wearing a beautiful blue button-down shirt with faint blue stripes and his monogram on the pocket; she had instantly turned away, mistaking him for an adult who might confiscate her beer. Renata was feeling unsure of herself; she and Action had been informed that this was a party "honoring" freshman girls, and yet many of the fraternity brothers wore T-shirts that said, FRESHMAN GIRLS: GET 'EM WHILE THEY'RE SKINNY! Cade separated himself from these peers by his sumptuous shirt; he approached Renata and Action and asked them what sounded like substantial questions: Which dorm? Which classes? Which professors? He sipped his beer slowly, thoughtfully, as he listened to their answers. He seemed like an ambassador, a gentleman—he took their plastic cups and refilled them, and when he handed them back he apologized for the quality of the beer.

Is this your party? Renata had asked.

He smiled. He wasn't attractive so much as successful looking. Clean, pleasant, well-heeled, athletic. *Only in the most tangential way,* he said. And then he checked his watch. Renata figured they were boring him to tears while Action (she later confessed) was thinking, *What is a college student doing with a Brietling watch?*

Let's get you out of here, Cade said to them both.

Where are we going to go? Renata asked. They had only arrived at the party ten minutes earlier and Renata was hesitant to leave, despite the pervasive aura that this was a dinner party and girls like Action and Renata were the first course. This, after all, was what she'd dreamed college would be like: a dark room with strobe lighting, Eminem at nearly unbearable decibels, the keg, the swarming boys.

Downtown, Cade said. *There's a band called Green Eggs playing at the Savannah.*

Renata had to beg Action to come along; she was wary of going anywhere with "Watch Boy." In the cab on the way downtown Cade told them he'd grown up in the city.

So did Action, Renata said.

Where? Cade said, leaning over Renata to look at Action.

Downtown, she said. *Bleecker Street.*

High school?

Stuyvesant.

Impressive.

Action snorted. *I gather you went somewhere uptown?* she said. *Let me guess. Collegiate?*

I went to boarding school, actually, he said. *Choate.*

Ah, Action said, as though she should have expected as much.

Renata, sensing the building tension, said, *I like your shirt.*

Thanks, Cade said. *I had a bunch of shirts made when I was in London last semester.*

Renata felt Action's hand press against the side of her thigh. *Right,* Renata thought. Boarding school, London, custom-made shirts. Renata knew Action was sneering, thinking, *privileged, pompous, why are we wasting our time?* But Renata couldn't help being impressed. And he seemed like a nice guy.

Cade paid for the cab ride (twenty-one dollars), he paid for Action and Renata to get into the club (twenty dollars), and he bought them cosmopolitans, which they sloshed all over the dance floor. The band was fantastic; Action and Renata started dancing right away. They screamed along to the music, tossing their hair, feeling their own sexual power. Action got something going with the lead singer; he was leaning down into the crowd toward her, practically devouring his microphone. Renata loved the feeling of slipping out of control; they were both sweating and laughing. Renata spilled a bit of cosmopolitan down her front; she had to go to the bathroom. She turned and saw Cade standing out among the crowd, and she felt a wave of gratitude. Action could say what she wanted, but to Renata, Cade was like a genie who had appeared from a bottle and granted them the three wishes of a good buzz, a great band, enormous fun. He smiled at her and crooked a finger. *Come here.* She went to him and he kissed her. Her stomach dropped away; it felt like a rushing chute down a roller coaster. Cade wanted to leave the bar, he said something about a poker game on the Bowery, he was meeting someone there, and he wanted Renata to come along. Despite the incredible kiss, Renata had no desire to leave the bar, and she knew she would never be able to peel Action away. She would stay with Action.

I'm going to stay, Renata said to Cade.

He had looked at her in a searching way; he was clearly expecting another answer.

Fine, he said. *Can I bring you another drink before I go?*

Sure, Renata said. She looked longingly at the dance floor. Action was still in the front row, going full tilt. Renata wanted to get back out there. *Actually, never mind.*

Cade shrugged, and ever the gentleman, he smiled. *Okay, I'll see you around, I guess.* He turned sideways and disappeared into the crowd.

Renata stood for a moment, looking after him. She felt

guilty, though she didn't know why. Renata fought her way
back to the dance floor, but her heart wasn't in it. It was as
if Cade had taken her good mood with him—or maybe,
she thought, she was only having fun because he was
around.

Someone grabbed Renata's waist from behind. She
turned. It was an older man, with gray hair in a buzz cut
and high, prominent cheekbones. His tie hung loosely at
his neck. When Renata turned, he smirked at her.

Dance?

No, she said, pulling away.

I'll buy you a drink, he said.

No, Renata said. *Thanks.* Somehow she managed to
weave her way up front and grab ahold of Action.

I'm leaving with him, she said.

Who?

Cade.

Watch Boy? Action said. *Shirt Boy?*

Renata nodded.

Action crossed her eyes. *Pathetic,* she said.

Well . . . In the course of only a month, Action and Renata had become such good friends that Renata mistakenly
assumed they were exactly alike. But no, they weren't. Action wanted a man like the lead singer—who had black hair
to his shoulders, who wore a Mexican poncho and a
hammered silver cuff bracelet. Renata wanted Cade with
his tailored shirts. Action thought Cade was typical, ste-
reotypical. Renata would never be able to explain her attraction and especially not here. She squeezed Action's
arm. *You'll be okay getting home?*

I live here, remember?

Renata wended her way back through the frenzy, thinking it could all be for naught; Cade was probably already
gone. She panicked at the thought and pushed, prodded,

poked, until she was free and running for the door. *Please,* she thought. He was right there when she stepped outside— standing on the curb, eating a piece of pizza folded in half.

He didn't seem at all surprised to see her; it was as if he knew she'd follow him anywhere.

Want a bite? he said.

Sex with Miles was over before it began, but that was okay; that was how Renata liked it. She liked it that Miles got so excited he couldn't hold back. He was bigger than Cade, and now, as Renata moved about, she felt a dull ache between her legs. She wanted to find her suit and go for a swim, big waves or no. When Sallie was finished surfing, which Renata hoped was soon, she would make Miles take her back to Hulbert Avenue, where she would shower and nap before scurrying off to Marguerite's house. She could, with luck, avoid Cade until the morning, and by then, she hoped, things would make more sense than they made now.

"Here you go." Miles handed Renata her bathing suit.

"Thanks."

"Do you regret it?" he said.

"No," she said. "Do you?"

"No," he said. "God, no."

She looked at him and saw something in his eyes. Love, or what he mistakenly assumed was love. She smiled at her feet and felt triumphant. She could have him again right now, or tonight in the guest room.

"Hey!"

The voice was faint but insistent, floating up the bluff. "Hey!"

Renata adjusted her bathing suit. Had someone seen them? She looked past Miles to the stairs. A head popped up, the overweight man from the webbed lawn chair. He was huffing and puffing as he climbed the stairs, waving his binoculars. He looked uncomfortable and agitated, like he was suffering from indigestion.

"Vo-tra-mee," he said.

"What?" Miles said.

"Vo-tra-mee," the man said, pointing at the water.

"He's German or something," Miles said. "French."

Renata looked down at the beach. A group was gathering by the waterline—the girls from the blanket, the people from the volleyball game. They were yelling and pointing offshore. Miles scrambled over the dunes and Renata followed, the towel draped over her burning shoulders. Miles raced down the stairs and along the beach back to their stuff. Renata was thinking, vaguely, *Shark, somebody thought they saw a shark,* though what were the chances? Still, she hurried along to see what was happening; she wondered what time it was and if anyone at Vitamin Sea had realized she was gone, if Suzanne was pissed about lunch, if Cade would be able to tell when they made love that she'd been with someone else. She was so wrapped up in her own thoughts that she didn't notice the two men in wet suits carrying a body out of the water. Or, rather, she noticed it but in a way that made it separate from herself, as though she were watching it happen on TV. The men laid the body in the sand and Miles, who had run far ahead, knelt by the body and started mouth-to-mouth. As Renata grew closer she felt her vision narrow; dread closed in. *Noooo!* she thought. *Tell me no.* She recognized the board shorts, the tattoo, the silver rings on the toes.

Renata stumbled to Miles's side, shoving people out of the way. A girl was screaming into a cell phone. "She's dead! She's dead!"

The girl's boyfriend was trying to rip the phone out of her hand. "She is not dead," he said. "Will you please shut up?"

The hairy beast, Montrose, said, "I called nine-one-one. The EMTs will be here in ten minutes, they said. Ten minutes."

Miles started CPR, pumping Sallie's chest, then blowing into her mouth. He was mumbling to himself, counting. Sallie's skin was the color of putty, grayish and goose pimpled. Her hair was plastered to her head; the mirror in her navel was dull.

Queen Bee, Renata thought, *Sallie. A person I've known for an hour. A complete stranger who accompanied me to my mother's cross, who kissed me on the wound she inflicted with her surfboard.* The surfboard—Renata looked down the beach and saw it floating just offshore. She dashed into the water to get it, a gesture that other people might have found very beside the point, but Renata knew Sallie only well enough to know that she would want her surfboard back. This, then, became Renata's rescue mission. She waded out, savoring the cool water on her legs. The waves were as unforgiving as they looked. Twice Renata nearly toppled over as she waded out, farther and farther, in pursuit of the surfboard. The ocean seemed to be teasing her—the surfboard would be inches from her grasp and then the waves would snatch it back. The undertow was fierce; Renata fought to keep her legs planted. If she tried to swim, she would be pulled out to sea. But she wanted the surfboard. She had known Sallie for only an hour or two, maybe, by now. Renata liked her. *Don't go getting married while I'm gone.* Renata's stomach churned on her beer and her guilt. *Will you keep an eye on me? Since when do you need a spotter? Since today. I'll keep an eye out.*

Renata turned back to shore. The other people on the beach were looking at Renata with strange, fearful expressions, but nobody spoke to her. The girls were all crying and the men tried to look both strong and sympathetic; everyone on the beach was touching someone. Renata heard Miles say, "I can't get a pulse. Where are the damned EMTs?"

Renata let a huge wave break over her head. She was knocked down and her face was filled with cold, salty water—in her mouth and her ears, up her nose, stinging her. Miles sounded panicked—and worse, he sounded guilty. If he was guilty, she was guiltier still. *She asked me. And I was up in the dunes.* Renata got to her feet and lunged for the surfboard. She got her fingers on it and a swell brought the ass end into her arms. She clung on tight, thinking she would turn it around, point it toward shore, but it was impossibly heavy; it seemed to want to go the other way—out, to open ocean. Renata was about to let it go when she noticed blood at the top of the board. That was all it took: Renata vomited beer in one gross, powerful stream. It sullied the water. Renata spit. Dear God, no.

Renata heard shouting. She turned to see a force of men and women in black uniforms come charging down the steps to the beach. She pulled the surfboard against her hips as another wave surged, and she managed somehow, to pull herself on top of it. Then she paddled the way she'd seen Sallie do. She got the surfboard pointed toward the beach and propelled herself forward. She rode the next wave all the way in, and then she stood on wobbly legs and dragged the surfboard over to where the EMTs were gathered around Sallie, shouting numbers. They had covered her with a blanket; Renata heard a tall man with a crew cut say, "She's in shock. But she's breathing now. Slap a mask on her and let's get her in. Who is she here with?"

Renata hurried over, lugging the bloody surfboard.

Miles was sitting on his towel, yards away from the action, with his head in his hands.

"Me!" Renata said. "She's here with me!"

The paramedic didn't hear her. "Let's take her in." He spoke into his walkie-talkie and surveyed the beach. Renata grabbed his arm.

"She's here with me," Renata said. "Me and Miles, that guy over there."

"We're taking her to the hospital," the paramedic said. "She received quite a blow to the head. And nearly drowned. Will you gather her personal effects, please, and bring them to the hospital? We'll need you to give us some information."

"Okay," Renata said. Sallie's personal effects consisted of the surfboard and the sunglasses. Renata snatched up her bag and nudged Miles with her foot. "Come on," she said. She ran toward the sound of the sirens.

3:32 P.M.

Check, check, check.

Marguerite's list was dwindling. The tenderloin had been roasted and was resting on the stove top. The tart had been filled with goat cheese and topped with roasted red peppers. The smoked mussels, the aioli, the chocolate *pots de crème,* all in the fridge, waiting. Marguerite had slipped two champagne flutes and her copper bowl into the freezer. She softened the butter she had gotten at the Herb Farm. The asparagus still needed attention, and the baguettes and the béarnaise. Marguerite debated setting up coffee and decided against it, then changed her mind; if they didn't drink it tonight, she'd have it in the morning. The morning: It would come, despite the fact that the day

already seemed as stretched out as a piece of taffy, filled
with as much activity as Marguerite engaged in in a whole
year. She ferreted a wine cooler out from underneath
the kitchen sink. The cooler was filled with cobwebs and
mouse droppings. Marguerite washed it, then washed it
again. The wine cooler was silver, sturdy, and unadorned,
a leftover from the restaurant. There had been twenty
such buckets and twenty iron stands, enough to post at
every table, plus two spares. It was curious, Marguerite
thought, the way some things survived and some did not.

The clock struck the half hour. Marguerite added items
to her list, tasks that would come naturally to another person but that she, in her excitement, might forget. Shower.
Hair, face, outfit. What to wear? The kimono stuck sorely
in her mind like a porcupine quill. The damned kimono.
Still, if she had a spare minute, she might try to find it.
She tidied the kitchen, wiped down the countertops, rinsed
the sink, cleaned the smoker, and returned it to its Styro-
foam braces, closed it up in the box. This was all busywork, but Marguerite found it soothing. It allowed her to
think of other things.

Since the day of Dan and Candace's wedding, there had
been talk of going to Africa. The wedding was held at the
Catholic church, St. Mary's, on Federal Street. Candace
wore a strapless white satin gown with a tulle skirt and ballet slippers that laced up her calves. She was more Grace
Kelly than Grace Kelly. She was captivating. Marguerite had
been coaxed into preceding Candace down the aisle in a
periwinkle dress with matching bolero jacket, despite her
ardent pleas to sit with everyone else.

"I'm more matron than maid," Marguerite had said.
"But I'm not married, so I can't be called matron. And no

one thirty-nine years of age should be called maid. I don't belong in this wedding, Candace."

"I'm not willing to have anyone else."

"I need to be at the restaurant anyway, supervising before the reception."

"I will not have anyone else."

Marguerite had stood at the altar, opposite Dan's roommate from college, holding a cluster of calla lilies while Dan and Candace pledged their eternal love, while they promised to pass this love on to any children they might have, while they swore in front of a hundred-plus people to strive through good and bad, through windfall and famine. Porter had given Candace away, and he sat in the front row next to his brother Andre, in from California. On Andre's other side was Chase, Candace's full brother, whom Marguerite had just met that morning. Porter reveled in the role of patriarch, leaning against the back of the pew with his arm stretched out behind his brother and half brother, his eyes dewy, a proud and resigned smile on his face. Marguerite could picture him like it was yesterday. He'd winked at her and she blushed. In the end, she had felt proud to be standing up there next to Candace, despite the dress that most closely resembled a tablecloth from a Holiday Inn banquet hall; she had felt proud that Candace would not consider asking anyone else to wear the dress, to hold the flowers and Dan's ring, to stand by her side as she wed. Marguerite did not, however, stay for the receiving line. Instead, she negotiated the cobblestones in her inane dyed-to-match heels back to Les Parapluies, where she supervised the prep of the crab and mango canapés and the prosciutto-wrapped Gorgonzola-stuffed figs that would be offered to the wedding guests along with flutes of La Grande Dame.

Marguerite had few memories of the reception. (Had she even sit to eat? Had she changed into her regular clothes? She had no recollection.) The after-reception, however, Marguerite recalled vividly. Everyone had gone home except for Marguerite and Porter, Andre, Chase, the college roommate (whose name was Gregory and who expressed, in no uncertain terms, his wanton desire for Francesca, the headwaiter), and, to Marguerite's surprise, Dan and Candace. They were all gathered around the west banquette with cigarettes and a 1955 bottle of Taylor Fladgate. Marguerite had set a plate of chocolate caramel truffles on the table to a smattering of applause, and then finally she relaxed, amazed that Dan and Candace hadn't beelined to the Roberts House, where they had a suite. They both seemed content to sit and drink and eat and talk, holding hands under the table.

They're married, Marguerite thought. There was nothing left to do but accept it. Daniel Knox would be a permanent part of their lives. He continued to irritate Marguerite—he was forever challenging her within her area of expertise, arguing with her about the quality of American beef or a certain vintage of Chablis, as though he believed he could do a better job of running the restaurant than she did. He had tried his best to sabotage the friendship between Marguerite and Candace. He disliked it when they spent time alone; he teased Marguerite about how often she and Candace touched each other, their kisses, their hugs; he pointed out how Marguerite never failed to choose the seat closest to Candace; he badgered Candace about what the two of them talked about when they were alone—were they talking about him? A hundred times Marguerite could have murdered the man— sardonically she thought all it would have taken was a little rat poison in his polenta—but Candace worked to keep the peace. She gave one hand to Daniel and one to Marguerite. "I love you both," she said. "I want you to love each other." While up at the altar, Marguerite vowed to herself to try her best to get along with Daniel. It was either that or tear Candace in half.

Across the table, Dan was proselytizing to Candace's brothers about how, if he hadn't come along to save the Beach Club, that waterfront would be a chain of garish trophy homes by now.

Candace grabbed Marguerite's hand. "Come with me to the loo," she said. "I need help with my dress."

Thus it was in the cramped, slanted-ceilinged women's bathroom at Les Parapluies, with Marguerite holding seventeen layers of tulle and averting her eyes as Candace peed, that Africa was first mentioned.

"I want to go to Africa."

Marguerite thought she was talking about her honeymoon. As it was, Candace and Dan had decided to wait until winter to take a trip and Marguerite believed discussion was hovering around Hawaii, Tahiti, Bora-Bora. She'd had too much to drink to make the leap across the globe.

"I'm sorry?"

"Dan asked me what I wanted to do," Candace said. "With my life. If I could go anywhere or do anything. And I want to go to Africa."

Marguerite narrowed her eyes. Above the sink, a peach-colored index card was taped to the wall: *Employees must wash hands before returning to work.*

"You mean, like, on safari?" Marguerite said.

"No, no, no. Not on safari."

Marguerite didn't get it. She was uncomfortable thinking of Candace starting a new, married life in Africa.

"It's awfully far away," Marguerite said. "I'd miss you."

"You're coming with me, silly," Candace said.

* * *

In the weeks and months that followed, Candace's vision of them all in Africa crystallized. She wasn't thinking of Isak Dinesen in Kenya, or trekking the Ugandan jungles in search of gorillas, or righting the evils of apartheid in South Africa—she was thinking of deserts, siroccos, sandstorms, of souks and mint tea and the casbah. She was thinking of Bedouins on camels, date palms, nomads in tents, thieves in the medinas. She had been reading *The Sheltering Sky* and begged Marguerite to make *tagines* and couscous.

Night after night after night, so many summer nights strung together like Japanese lanterns through the trees, Candace and Dan and Marguerite and Porter sat at the west banquette and talked and talked and talked until they were too drunk or too tired to form coherent sentences. They talked about Carter and Reagan, Iran, Woody Allen and Pink Floyd, Roy Lichtenstein, Andy Warhol, and the new Musée d'Orsay in Paris. Porter talked about a colleague accused of making a pass at a female student, who turned around and *pressed charges*. Marguerite talked about the bluefin tuna Dusty had caught and how he'd sliced it paper thin and eaten it raw right there on the dock of the Straight Wharf. And always, at the end of the night, like a punch line, like a broken record, Candace talked about Africa. She wanted the four of them to open a French restaurant somewhere in her make-believe North Africa.

"I can see it now," Porter had said, the first time she mentioned it. "A culinary Peace Corps."

"A restaurant in the middle of the desert," Candace said. "I've always dreamed of running barefoot through the Sahara. What would the restaurant be like, Daisy, if it were up to you?"

"If it were up to Reagan, it would be a McDonald's," Dan said. "Talk about cultural imperialism."

"I asked Daisy," Candace said. "So hush. She's the only one of us who would know what she was doing."

Marguerite gazed around Les Parapluies. This was how she loved it best—empty except for the four of them, lit only by candles. The staff had cleaned up and gone home for the evening, but there was still the lingering smell of garlic and rosemary and freshly baked bread. There was still plenty of wine.

"Just like this," Marguerite said. "I would want it to be just like this."

"Except it wouldn't be like this at all, would it?" Candace said. "Because it wouldn't be Nantucket. It wouldn't be thirty miles out to sea; there wouldn't be fog. We'd be surrounded by sand instead of water. It wouldn't be the same at all."

"Spoken like a true Chamber of Commerce employee," Porter said, raising his glass.

"I'm serious," Candace said. She turned to Marguerite with her cheeks flushed and her hair falling into her face. One of her pearl earrings was about to pop out. Marguerite reached for Candace's ear—all she had meant was to gently hold the earlobe and secure the earring in place before it fell and got lost in Candace's blouse or bounced across the wormy chestnut floors and got caught in a crack somewhere—but Candace swatted Marguerite's hand away. Smacked it in anger. Marguerite recoiled, and the energy at the table changed in an instant.

Candace's mouth was set in an ugly line; her eyes were glassy and wild. Marguerite was confused, then frightened. Had Candace had too much to drink?

"No one takes me seriously," Candace said. "Nobody listens when I talk. You treat me like a child. Like a china doll. Like an imbecile!"

Dan and Marguerite reached out for Candace simultaneously, but Candace locked her arms across her chest. Porter chuckled.

"It's not funny!" Candace said. She glared at them all. "You are all so smart and accomplished and that's fine, that's great. I support all of you in your work. But now it's my turn. I want to go to Africa. I mean it about this restaurant. It's a dream I have. You may think it's stupid, but I don't." She turned to Marguerite. "Now reimagine. What will the restaurant look like?"

Marguerite was stunned into silence. She couldn't bring herself to imagine a restaurant different from the one she had, especially one on a continent she had never visited.

"I can't reimagine," Marguerite said. "I want to stay here, where I am. I want everything to stay just as it is."

Yes, it was true: If she could have kept the four of them seated at the west banquette for all eternity—with meals appearing like Sisyphus's boulder—she would have. But then autumn came and Porter returned to Manhattan—to Corsage Woman, Overbite Woman, the blond, unmarried tennis coach. One unfortunate night that fall, Marguerite found herself standing in the restaurant's dark pantry with her lawyer, Damian Vix. Ostensibly, he had been in search of dried porcini for a risotto he wanted to make at home, but they had both had too much to drink and the foray into the dark kitchen and darker pantry was followed by kissing and some lustful groping. *Kid stuff,* Marguerite thought afterward. It gave her none of the satisfaction she'd been hoping for.

In the new year, Nantucket suffered one of the worst winters on record—snowstorms, ice storms, thirty-two hours without power, a record three hundred homes with burst pipes according to the claims man at Congdon &

Coleman Insurance. Marguerite tested out new recipes in her kitchen on Quince Street, Candace was still working at the Chamber of Commerce, as assistant director now, and Dan monitored the weather—the wind gusts, the inches of snow—and he checked on things two or three times a day at the shuttered-up Beach Club. The three of them gathered occasionally, but mostly it was Candace and Marguerite meeting for lunch at the Brotherhood, or hunkering down in front of the fire at Marguerite's house on Quince Street with cheese fondue or pot-au-feu. It was during one of these fireside dinners that Candace proposed the trip: seven nights and eight days in Morocco. They would scout a location for their restaurant.

"Just the two of us," Candace said. "Me and you."

"I couldn't possibly," Marguerite said.

"I already have the tickets," Candace said. "We're going."

"Go with Dan."

"You'd send me to scout a location for a restaurant with *Dan*? You trust him to find the right place?"

Well, no, Marguerite didn't trust him. But Marguerite thought she had made her feelings more than clear: The restaurant idea was delusional.

"Anyway, I don't want to go with Dan," Candace said. "I want to go with you. Girl trip. Best friends and all that. We've never taken a trip together."

"I can't go," Marguerite said.

"Why not?"

"Porter promised me Paris," Marguerite said. "After his trip to Japan last year. He swore on a stack of Bibles."

"A stack of Bibles?" Candace said.

Well, a stack of Marguerite's bibles: *Larousse Gastronomique,* her first-edition M. F. K. Fisher, her Julia Child. At the end of August, before he returned to the city,

Porter had laid his right hand on the cookbooks and said in a solemn voice, "In the spring, Paris."

"It's not going to happen," Candace said. "He'll back out. He'll find some reason."

Marguerite flinched. She stared at the dying embers of the fire and nearly asked Candace to leave. How dare she say such a thing! But perhaps it was tit-for-tat. She thought Marguerite was delusional.

"I'm sorry," Candace said, though her voice couldn't have been less apologetic. "I just can't stand to see you get hurt again. He's my brother. I know him. He promised you Paris to get himself out of a tight spot. But he won't follow through. You should just come to Morocco with me."

"I know him, too," Marguerite said. "He promised me Paris. There's no reason to doubt him."

Candace stared. "No reason to doubt him?"

Marguerite stood up and poked at the fire; it had gone cold.

"Porter is taking me to Paris."

"Okay," Candace said kindly. "Okay." Her tone of voice infuriated Marguerite; it was patronizing. Marguerite had never fought with her friend, though she was ready to now. The only thing that kept her from doing battle was the fear that Candace may be right.

And so, the following week, when Porter phoned, Marguerite pressed him on it.

"Your sister wants me to go with her to Morocco."

"For her restaurant idea?"

"Mmmhmm."

"She's crazy," Porter said. "God love her. Are you going?"

"No," Marguerite said. "I told her we were going to Paris."

Porter laughed.

Marguerite steeled her resolve. She could picture Porter's face when he laughed—his eyes crunching, his head thrown back—but she couldn't tell what this laugh meant.

"Have you checked your schedule?" she asked. "Decided on a week? If we want the Plaza Athenee, we have to book soon."

There was a pause. "Daisy . . ."

She only half-heard the rest of what he said. Something about a paper he was presenting, a week as a guest curator at the Met, a conference they were hosting at Columbia. Marguerite took the phone from her ear and poised it over the cradle, ready to slam it down. She thought of begging, of laying her heart out on the chopping block. It didn't have to be Paris. It could be the Radisson on Route 128 for all she cared. She wanted something from him, something that proved she was more than just his summertime. But in the end, all she could bring herself to do was cut him off in midsentence.

"Never mind; never mind," she said. "Candace will be thrilled. The casbah it is."

As Marguerite formed the bread dough into loaves, laid them down in her oiled baguette pan, as she snipped the tops of the loaves with kitchen shears and rinsed the loaves with water so they would have a sheen to them when they came out of the oven, she could say that the eight days in Morocco with Candace had been the best eight days of her life. It was when everything changed.

They had started out in a town on the coast, seven hours by car from Casablanca. The town was called Essaouira.

It had a long, wide, magnificent crescent of silver sand beach where men in flowing robes offered camel rides for ten dirhams. Candace, who was in for every "authentic" experience she could find, insisted they try it. Marguerite protested, and yet she ended up eight feet off the ground crushed with Candace against the hump of a dromedary named Charlie. Riding a camel, Marguerite soon realized, was like sitting on a rocking chair without any back. Marguerite held on to Candace for dear life as they ricocheted forward and careened back with each of Charlie's steps down the coastline. Candace was shaking with laughter; Marguerite felt her gasping for air. The camel smelled bad, and so, for that matter, did the soft mud-sand at the waterline. Marguerite buried her nose in Candace's hair.

When they dismounted, Candace made the man in the flowing robe take their picture. Marguerite smiled perfunctorily, then said, "I need a drink."

They sat outside at a little café and drank a bottle of very cold Sancerre. They touched glasses.

"To Morocco," Candace said. "To the two of us in Morocco."

Marguerite tried to smile. She tried not to wish she were in Paris.

"Do you wish you were in Paris?" Candace said.

Marguerite looked at her friend. Candace's blue eyes were round with worry.

"You were right," Marguerite said. It was a relief to admit it. "About Porter, about Paris. You couldn't have been more right."

"I didn't want to be right," Candace said. "You know that, don't you?"

"Yes."

"I feel like I twisted your arm to come here," Candace said. "I feel like you'd rather be at home."

"Home?" Marguerite said. Home on Nantucket, where the beaches were frozen tundra, home where she could wallow in the misery of being disappointed again? "Don't be silly."

The heart of Essaouira lay in the souks, a rabbit warren of streets and alleys and passageways within the city's thick, whitewashed walls. Over the course of four days, Candace and Marguerite wandered every which way, getting lost, getting found. Here was the man selling jewelry boxes, lamps, coat racks, coffee tables, and backgammon boards from precious *thuya* wood, which was native to Essaouira. Here was a shop selling the very same items made from punched tin; here was a place selling Berber carpets, here another place selling carpets. Everyone sold carpets! Marguerite sniffed out the food markets. She discovered a whole square devoted to seafood—squid and sea bass, shrimp, prawns, rock lobsters, octopus, sea cucumbers, and a pallet of unidentifiable slugs and snails, creatures with fluorescent fins and prehistoric shells, things Marguerite was sure Dusty Tyler had never seen in all his life. In Morocco, the women did the shopping, all of them in ivory or black burkhas. Most of them kept their faces covered as well; Candace called these women the "only eyes." They peered at Marguerite (who wore an Hermés scarf over her hair, a gift from one of her customers) and she shivered. Marguerite's favorite place of all was the spice market—dozens of tables covered with pyramids of saffron and turmeric, curry powder and cumin, fenugreek, mustard seed, cardamom, paprika, mace, nutmeg.

Who wouldn't open a restaurant if they had access to these spices? Not to mention the olives. And the nuts—the warm, salted almonds sold for twenty-five centimes in a paper cone—and the dates, thirty varieties as chewy and rich as candy.

In the mornings Candace ran, and sometimes she was gone for two hours. The first morning Marguerite grew concerned as she drank six cups of café au lait and polished off three croissants and one sticky date bun while reading the guidebook. She found the hotel manager—a short, trim, and immaculately groomed Arab man—and explained to him, in her all-but-useless kitchen French, that her friend, *une Americaine blonde,* had gone missing. Marguerite worried that Candace had made a wrong turn and gotten lost—that wouldn't be hard to do—or someone had abducted her. She was, obviously, not a Muslim, and unlike Marguerite, she refused to cover her head with anything except for Dan's old Red Sox cap. Someone had stolen her for political reasons or for sexual ones; she was, at that very moment, being forced into a harem.

Just as the hotel manager was beginning to glean Marguerite's meaning, realizing she was talking about *Candace,* whom he himself had given more than one admiring glance, in Candace came, breathless, sweating, and brimming over with all that she'd seen. Fishing boats with strings of multicolored flags, the fortress with cannons up on the hill, a little boy with six dragonflies pierced on the end of a spear.

Marguerite got used to Candace's long absences in the mornings. When Candace returned, they ventured out into the medina to look for a restaurant. The restaurant business was alive and well in Essaouira—there were French restaurants, there were Moroccan restaurants, there was tapas and pizza and gelati, and there was a row of open-air stands along the beach selling fish that Marguerite and Candace picked out before it was grilled in front of their eyes.

They meandered and shopped. Marguerite bought an enamel pot for *tagine* with a conical top and a handcrafted silver platter for fish. Marguerite and Candace always stopped for lunch at one o'clock, gravitating toward the Moroccan places, which were dim, with low ceilings. They sat on the floor on richly colored pillows and, yes, stacks of carpets and ate lamb *kefta,* couscous, and *bisteeya.*

After lunch, they returned to their hotel for silver pots of mint tea, which they drank by the small plunge pool in the courtyard. Men in white pajamas brought the tea, then took it away; they brought the day's papers—the *Herald Tribune* and *Le Monde* as well as the Moroccan paper, which was written in Arabic—they brought fresh towels, warm and cool. There might have been other guests at the hotel, but Marguerite noticed them only peripherally—a glamorous French couple, a British woman and her grown daughter—it felt like Marguerite and Candace were existing in a world created solely for their benefit. Marguerite discovered she was having fun, all of her senses were engaged, she felt alive. She was *glad* she was here with Candace instead of in Paris with Porter, and who could have predicted that? Morocco, Marguerite declared, was heaven on earth! She never wanted to leave.

Several times during their week in Morocco, Marguerite revisited the moment when Candace first walked into the kitchen at Les Parapluies on Porter's arm and kissed Marguerite full on the lips. *What Porter told me in private is that he thinks you're pure magic.* The more time they spent together, alone, in this foreign and exotic country, the more Marguerite began to feel that *Candace* was pure magic. She was not only beautiful; she emitted beauty. Everywhere they traveled in Morocco, the people they met

bowed to Candace as though she were a deity. The baseball hat, which might have been offensive on another
American, was adorably subversive on Candace.

"These American women," one of their taxi drivers
said. "They like everyone to know they are free."

On the fifth day, they traveled to Marrakech. The hotel
in Marrakech was even lusher than their jewel in Essaouira. L'Orangerie, it was called, after the museum in
Paris. The architecture was all arches and intricate tile
work, open courtyards with sumptuous gardens and foun-
tains, little nooks with flowing curtains and silk divans,
bowls of cool water holding floating rose petals. Marguerite
and Candace shared a two-bedroom, two-floor suite with
an outdoor shower and their own dining table on a roof
patio that overlooked Marrakech's famous square, Djemaa
el-Fna. Marrakech had a cosmopolitan feel to it, a kinetic
energy—this was where everything was happening. The
Djemaa el-Fna was mobbed with people every night: jug-
glers, snake charmers, acrobats, pickpockets, musicians,
storytellers, water sellers, street vendors hawking orange
juice, dates, olives, almonds—and tourists snapping it all
up. The call to prayer from the mighty Koutoubia Mosque
came over a loudspeaker every few hours and several times
Marguerite felt like dropping to her knees to pray. Marrakech had done it; she was converted. She started making notes for a menu, half-French, half-Moroccan; she
wanted to attempt a *bisteeya* made with prawns, a *tagine*
of ginger chicken with preserved lemon and olives. She
looked in every doorway for suitable retail space.

And yet as Marguerite's enthusiasm flared, Candace's
flagged. Her stomach was bothering her; she got quiet at
dinner their first night in Marrakech, and the second night
she went to bed at eight o'clock, leaving Marguerite to
wander the chaos of the souks alone. Marguerite slouched

and frowned; shopkeepers didn't give her a second look. Candace missed Dan—Marguerite was sure that was it— she was going to try to call him from the front desk of the hotel. Marguerite was crestfallen. *Girl trip,* she thought. *Best friends and all that.* For the first time in years she felt free of the grasp of Porter Harris—and yet that night, without Candace, she ended up buying Porter a carpet. It was a glorious Rabat-style carpet with deep colors and symbols hidden in the weave, but Marguerite was too gloomy to engage the shopkeeper in a haggle, despite the shopkeeper's prodding. "What price you give me? You give me your best price." Marguerite gave a number only fifty dollars less than the shopkeeper's first price, and he was forced to accept. It was unheard of: a transaction for something so valuable over and done with in thirty seconds. The shopkeeper threw in a free fez, a brimless red velvet hat with a tassel. "You take this, special gift." The hat was too small to fit anyone Marguerite knew; it would fit a baby or a monkey.

The following day, their next-to-last day of the trip, Candace arranged for them to visit a hammam, a traditional bathhouse. She had seemed excited about it when she described it a few days earlier to an ever-skeptical Marguerite. "It's like a spa. An ancient spa." But as they sat at breakfast, Candace picked at her croissant and said she was thinking of canceling.

"I'm just not myself," she said. "I'm sorry. It's something I ate, maybe. Or too much wine every night. Or it's the water."

"Well," said Marguerite. "It's nothing an ancient spa won't be able to cure. Come on. You're the one who wanted authentic experiences. We'll be home in forty-eight hours, and if we miss this, we'll be sorry."

"I thought you said you didn't want to sit in a room with a bunch of naked old women," Candace said. "I thought you said you'd rather eat glass."

Marguerite tilted her head. "Did I say that?"

The hammam was in the medina. It was a low white-washed building with a smoking chimney and a glass-studded dome. A sign on the door said: *AUJOURD'HUI—LES FEMMES*. Marguerite pulled the door open, with Candace shuffling morosely at her heels. Truth be told, Marguerite was nervous. She wasn't used to working outside her comfort zone. She had no experience with ancient Moroccan women-only communal bathhouses, where, no doubt, there were rituals one was supposed to follow, rules one was supposed to know, gestures to be made. She wished for Porter, who was worldly enough to finesse any situation, or for the old Candace, Candace as she'd been only the day before yesterday—ready to throw herself into any experience headfirst with daring gusto.

There was a desk, ornately carved and inlaid, and a woman behind the desk in an ivory burkha. She was only eyes. Marguerite was wearing the Hermés scarf, Candace the baseball hat.

We don't know what we're doing, Marguerite wanted to say. *Please help us.* But instead, she just smiled in a way that she hoped conveyed this sentiment.

"Deux?" the woman said.

"Oui," Marguerite said. She reached into her money belt, which was hidden under her blouse, and pulled out a wad of dirham. Candace slumped against the beautiful desk. She was pale, listless, chewing a stick of gum because, along with her other symptoms, she couldn't rid her mouth of a funky, metallic taste. The only-eyes woman plucked three bills from Marguerite's cache, then paused and said.

"Avec massage?"

"Oui," Marguerite said. "Avec massage, s'il vous plaît."

The woman extracted two more bills. Was it costing three dollars, a hundred dollars? Marguerite had no idea. The only-eyes woman slid two plush towels across the desk and pointed down the hall.

The hallway had marble floors, thick stone walls, arched windows with translucent glass. The windows were on the interior wall, which led Marguerite to believe there was a courtyard. The overall aura of the hallway, however, reminded Marguerite of a convent: It was hushed, forbidding; their footsteps echoed. At the end of the hallway was a set of heavy arched double doors. Marguerite pulled one side open and stepped through, holding the door for Candace. *I'm not doing this without you.*

They entered a cavernous room with a high, domed ceiling. The floor was composed of tiny pewter-colored tiles; there were platforms at different levels around a turquoise pool. Women lay on mats around the pool in various stages of undress. There were naked teenagers; there were women older and heavier than Marguerite in underpants but no bras. There was one very blond girl who looked Western—she was American, maybe, or Swedish—wearing a bikini. Along the wall were pegs where the women had hung their clothes.

Okay, Marguerite thought, *this is it.* She looked at Candace, who gave her a wan smile.

"Here we are," Candace said, and in her voice Marguerite was relieved to hear the playful tease of a dare: *You go first.*

Marguerite stepped out of her shoes. Okay. She peeled

off her socks. She stared at the wall as she unbuttoned her
blouse. Her initial instinct had been correct. This was not
the place for her. She hated the thought of all these women,
and especially Candace, seeing her naked. She was too vo-
luptuous, a Rubens, Porter called her, but that was him
being kind. Her breasts hung heavily when she stripped to
her bra. She thought of Damian Vix ushering her forward
into the dark pantry. He had swept her hair aside so he
could kiss her neck; then his hands had gone to her breasts.
He had pressed against her and moaned. Marguerite
laughed. If she had endured the embarrassment of being
groped by her attorney in a pantry, she could endure this.
She took her bra off next, then her slacks, but left on her
underpants.

Candace had stripped completely, and she'd let her hair
out of its rubber band. Her body was a museum piece:
healthy American woman. Strong legs, small, shapely ass,
flat stomach, and breasts a bit larger than Marguerite would
have guessed.

"Nobody is swimming," Candace said, and she giggled.

"Right," Marguerite said. She was baffled. What was
the point of lying around an indoor pool, naked, with other
women? How did this make a person feel anything but
anxious? She watched the Swedish girl exit through a door
marked with an arrow. Marguerite nodded her head. *Follow her.*

They entered *la chambre froide,* the cold room, which
was an elongated room with three domes in the ceiling.
There was a pool in this room also, but the Swede bypassed
it and so did Marguerite and Candace. The room itself
was not particularly cold, but it was empty and inhospi-
table. The next room was noticeably warmer and more
ornate—there were carved wooden pillars around the
outside of the pool, and niches where women reclined

like odalisques. *Like Ingres,* Marguerite thought. *Porter would love this.* There were attendants in this room with buckets and scrub brushes, loofahs and combs. Someone was having her hair washed; someone was getting a massage; someone was rubbing herself down with what looked like wet cement. Marguerite wondered if they should stop—they had, after all, paid for massages—but the Swede kept going and Marguerite decided to follow her.

They ended up in the warmest room of all; *LA CHAMBRE CHAUDE,* the sign said. The hot room. The room was filled with steam. It was a sauna. Candace breathed the steam in appreciatively and sat down on a tile bench. Marguerite sat next to her. The Swede popped into what looked like a very hot shower. The sound of water was loud and since they were the only three people in the room, Marguerite felt okay to speak.

"How do you feel?" she asked.

Candace gazed at Marguerite and started to cry. Because of the heat and the steam, however, it looked like she was melting.

Marguerite reached out. It might have been awkward, an embrace with both of them naked, but to Marguerite it felt natural, elemental; it felt like they had been friends since the beginning of time, like they were the first two women put on earth. Eve and her best friend. Candace cried with her head resting on Marguerite's shoulder, her hair grazing Marguerite's breast. It was absurdly hot, their bodies were being poached like eggs, and yet Marguerite couldn't bring herself to move. She knew she would never have Candace closer than she was right that second. Marguerite wanted to touch Candace, but she wasn't sure where. The knee? The face? Before she could decide, Candace reached for Marguerite's trembling hand and placed it on her taut, smooth stomach.

"I'm pregnant," she said.

Marguerite prepped the asparagus by chopping off the woody ends and peeling the skins. She drizzled it with olive oil and sprinkled it with *fleur de sel* and freshly ground pepper. Nearly two decades later and a hemisphere away, it was astounding how well she remembered those minutes in the hammam. Her best friend was pregnant. Marguerite had found she didn't know how to respond. She should have been ecstatic. But she felt offended by the news. Betrayed.

You're pregnant, Marguerite said. *Pregnant. I can't believe it.*

Candace blotted her eyes with her towel. *I thought I was sick.*

You're pregnant, Marguerite said.

Pregnant, Candace said with finality.

They returned to the center room. An attendant asked them, *Massage?* In a daze, Marguerite remembered to nod. They were led to mats and instructed to lie down. Marguerite had never been massaged by anyone other than Porter and she was anxious about a massage out in the open, in public, so she closed her eyes. The attendant's hands were both firm and soft; it felt wonderful.

Marguerite let her mind wander. A baby. She should have been relieved. She had thought perhaps Candace was homesick, missing Dan—or sick of Marguerite. But a baby. It was the best news a person had to give. It would be, Marguerite told herself, more of Candace to love.

And yet, as the hour wore on, as Marguerite peeked at

Candace—on her stomach with an attendant kneading her shoulders, and later in the pool, her hair caked with greasy clay, her hair rinsed by the same attendant and smoothed with a comb—Marguerite experienced a jealousy that left her breathless. Candace's body would bear a child, and as Marguerite glanced about the room she guessed that most, if not all, of the bodies surrounding hers had borne children. They were, in some unspoken way, more of a woman than Marguerite would ever be. She thought back to her eight/nine/ten-year-old self in leotards and tights in front of the mirror of Madame Verge's studio. The reason she had never graduated to toe shoes, the reason she quit Madame Verge altogether, was that with adolescence came the cruel understanding that she was not pretty, she was not graceful, she would not dance the *pas de deux,* she would never be someone's star. Promises would go unfulfilled. She would not marry and she would never reproduce. The real shame of her body was that it contained some kind of an end. She would die.

Marguerite decided not to wash her hair—it was far too long and it took hours to dry—though the attendant seemed to enjoy touching it, admiring its length and its thickness. Marguerite waited by the side of the pool, dangling her feet in the water, until Candace was finished, and then they walked, wrapped in their towels, back to the room where they had gotten undressed.

Marguerite made what felt like a Herculean effort to be upbeat. *Success?* she said.

Success, Candace said. She beamed. *I'm so glad we came.*

They drank mint tea and ate dainty silver dishes of watermelon sherbet in the courtyard of the hammam. Candace talked, gaily, about names. She liked Natalie and Theodore.

What names do you like? Candace asked.

Inside, Marguerite was dissolving. Candace was married to Dan; she would bear Dan's child. She would form her own family. Marguerite could feel Candace separating herself, breaking away.

Names? Marguerite said. *Oh dear, I don't know. Adelaide? Maurice?*

Candace hooted. *Maurice?* she said.

Candace was right across the table, laughing, and yet to Marguerite she had already started to vanish.

They boarded the plane the following evening. While rummaging through her carry-on bag for her book, Marguerite found the notes for her half-French, half-Moroccan menu. She read the pages through, wistfully, then tucked them away. There would be no restaurant in Africa.

4:06 P.M.

Patient's full name.

Renata peeled her sunburned thighs off the vinyl waiting-room chair and eyed Miles. He wasn't doing well. His hands were shaking so badly that Renata had had to drive the Saab to the hospital while he clumsily grappled with the surfboard. (Renata had stopped, for just a second, at the white cross in the road and said a little prayer—for Sallie, for her mother, for herself.) Now she was filling out the admittance form, even though Sallie was already upstairs, hooked up to oxygen and an IV, awaiting someone's decision as to whether or not she should be medevaced to Boston. It was unclear as to whether that decision would be made by the doctors here or by her parents. Renata felt, absurdly, like she knew Sallie's parents: She could picture them standing on a beach in Antigua with a black preacher, Sallie's mother with flowers in her hair, wearing a white flowing sundress to hide her burgeoning belly. Renata could picture this, but she didn't know where the parents lived, and Miles had shrugged when she asked him. They had called Sallie's house, but none of the roommates answered, so they left a message, which felt woefully inadequate.

Patient's full name.

"Sallie," Miles said. "With an *i-e*. Her last name is Myers. But I don't know how she spells it."

Renata wrote: *Sallie Myers.*

Address.

Miles exhaled. "She lives on Mary Ann Drive. I don't know which number."

"Do you know *anything*?" Renata asked impatiently.

"Do you?" he snapped.

Renata wrote: _____ *Mary Ann Drive, Nantucket.*

Phone number. Miles started reciting numbers. Home and cell. He had them memorized.

"You're sure she's not your girlfriend?" Renata said. She meant this to be funny, but Miles didn't crack a smile. He had let Renata wear his shirt into the hospital since she had agreed to take care of all the official stuff like talking to the doctors and filling out the forms, and he, in turn, had plucked a zippered tracksuit jacket out of the abyss of his car's backseat. The jacket was wrinkled and covered with crumbs; it smelled like old beer. He had it zippered all the way up under his chin. His teeth were chattering. The air-conditioning was cranked up. Renata herself was freezing, in no small part because her entire body was red and splotched with sunburn; however, you didn't see *her* shivering.

Miles didn't answer Renata. His blue eyes were glazed over. Renata gathered this was the worst thing that had ever happened to him. He wasn't used to accidents, to bad luck, to tragedy. He hadn't lived with it, maybe, the way Renata had.

She scanned her eyes down the form. "Age?" she said. "Date of birth?"

"No idea."

When they'd arrived at the hospital, Renata explained to the admitting nurse that they were friends of the young woman who'd had the surfing accident at Madequecham Beach. The nurse slid them the clipboard with the form and Renata had stared at it, wide-eyed, like it was a test she hadn't studied for.

"Just do the best you can," the admitting nurse had said.

"Occupation?" Renata said. "Place of employment?"

"She's a bartender at the Chicken Box," Miles mumbled.

"Really?" Renata said. She had pictured Sallie owning something, a surf shop maybe; she had pictured Sallie as the manager of a hotel or as one of the charming, witty guides on a tour bus. She had envisioned Sallie in a starched white shirt, with pearls replacing her six silver hoops, as the sommelier at a restaurant like 21 Federal.

Renata wrote in: *Bartender.*

She wrote in: *The Chicken Box,* wishing for something that sounded more dignified.

"Phone number of the Chicken Box?"

Miles rattled it off from memory. Renata gave him a look.

"I go there a lot," he said. "That's how I know her."

"Does she have a boss?" Renata said. "Maybe we should call her boss."

"Why?"

"We have to call someone," Renata said. Her voice was

so loud that the admitting nurse looked up from her desk. A few chairs down, a woman was breast-feeding a fever-ish infant. Past the row of chairs was the large automatic sliding door of the emergency room, and on the other side of the door was bright sunlight, fresh air, the real world. It was after four o'clock. Renata felt a strong pull of respon-sibility to be here, and just as strong a desire to find some-one who knew more about Sallie than they did, someone who could take charge, make decisions. But for the time being, Sallie belonged to them. Renata had promised to keep an eye on Sallie in the water and had failed misera-bly, but Renata was not going to fail now. She was going to handle this. "Listen. We're going to call her boss. Maybe he knows how to reach her parents."

"Maybe," Miles said.

Renata could see Miles was going to be absolutely no help. How had she ever found him attractive enough to sleep with? Only an hour later, it was a mystery. "Do you know the boss's name?"

"Pierre."

"Pierre what?"

"I don't know. People just call him Pierre. That's his name. If you call the Chicken Box, there's only one Pierre."

"Fine," Renata said. She had no money; she was at the mercy of the admitting nurse—who, much to Renata's grateful surprise, offered to dial the number for her.

The phone rang and rang. Finally, someone answered. A man. There was loud rock music in the background.

"Hello?" Renata said. "Is this Pierre?"

"What?"

Renata cleared her throat. "Is this Pierre? May I please speak to Pierre?"

"He's not here."

Renata sighed. She had a vision of Sallie upstairs,

plugged into ten machines, with only Renata to advocate on her behalf. Renata said, "Is there another way to reach him?"

"His cell phone."

"Great," Renata said. She reached over Admitting Nurse's desk in search of a pen. "Can you give me the number, please?"

"Who is this?"

"My name is Renata Knox," she said. "I'm a friend of Sallie, the bartender."

"Do you know Pierre?"

"No," Renata said. "I'm calling because—"

"I can't give you the number."

"But I'm calling because Sallie—"

"Doesn't matter. He doesn't want his number passed out. There are too many psycho chicks in this world."

"I'm calling about Sallie Myers? The bartender?" Renata said. "You know her?"

"I know her, but—"

"She had a surfing accident," Renata said. "She's in the hospital."

"She is?"

"She is."

"But she's okay, right? She's supposed to be in tonight at seven. It's *Saturday* night."

"I promise you, she won't be coming in. She's in the hospital. She's unconscious."

"Dude."

"When you see Pierre, will you tell him?" Renata asked. "Will you tell him to come to the hospital? In fact, will you call him on his cell phone and ask him to come right now, this second? We need his help."

"Sallie's not going to die or anything, is she?"

"No," Renata said. Renata didn't care if she had to

donate a lung herself; Sallie was not going to die. "But it's serious, okay? Tell Pierre to come; tell him it's serious."

"Okay," the man said. "Dude."

Renata hung up. She thanked the admitting nurse and returned to her chair. Miles didn't look the least bit curious about her conversation. He looked like he might need to be admitted any second himself. He had lost his tan, and the shivering had turned into convulsions.

Renata picked up the clipboard and delivered the sparsely filled-out form to the admitting nurse, who checked it over while sucking on her lower lip.

"No date of birth?" she said.

"Sorry," Renata said. She lowered her voice. "I don't know Sallie very well. I just met her today."

The admitting nurse's mouth formed an O. Her face was sympathetic, though, and Renata felt like she might be able to confess: *I told her I'd keep an eye on her. But I didn't. I was up in the dunes cheating on my fiancé.*

"We called the house where she lives and left a message, but her roommates weren't home. So that's why I just called her boss. I thought maybe he would know more than we do."

At that second, Admitting Nurse's phone rang. She held up a finger to Renata and answered the call, speaking in such a low murmur, it was impossible to hear. Renata turned her back so as not to seem too interested. The skin on her chest was throbbing, but the tops of her thighs had taken the worst of it—they were red and shiny and very hot to the touch. How was she going to explain this hideous sunburn to Cade? How was she going to explain any of this? She raised her head to see a very tall, very dark-skinned black man walk through the automatic door.

Pierre, she thought.

He stopped, surveyed the room, took in the woman

breast-feeding, Renata at the desk, and the admitting nurse. Pierre wore tiny rimless glasses that seemed like toy glasses on his wide face. He pushed the glasses up with a long finger and surveyed the scene suspiciously, like maybe this was all a hoax. But then he saw Miles and his shoulders jumped in recognition. He jogged over. Miles, miraculously, stood up and shook Pierre's hand.

"What happened?" Pierre said. His voice had the lilt of a flowery accent. From the Caribbean, Renata thought.

"Hit in the head with her board," Miles said. "She went down and it took a while for someone to find her. She was under for almost three minutes, they think. But she's breathing now. Unconscious, though, and they said maybe brain damage." At this, Miles teared up. Pierre put a hand on his shoulder.

"Hey, man, it's okay." "Okay" sounded like "okee."

Renata joined them. "Hi," she said. "I'm Renata. I'm the one who called you."

Pierre and Renata shook hands. Renata watched their two clasped hands, one huge and dark, one skinny and sunburned. Her qualms subsided a bit. Pierre seemed very capable.

"They need her date of birth, her age, stuff like that," Renata said. "And do you know how to reach her parents?"

"I have it all in my files," he said. "At the bar. I have her tax information and her emergency contact. I'll go get it."

"Thank God," Renata said. "Thank God you came."

"Don't thank me. I love the girl." He said this simply and sincerely, and Renata was helpless to do anything but nod along in agreement. One hour she had known the woman and she had felt Sallie's pull.

"Excuse me!"

The three of them turned. Admitting Nurse had come

out from behind her desk and was approaching in what looked like an official way. Her face said nothing good. "I have something to tell you."

She's dead, Renata thought. The floor under her feet moved and she fell toward the chairs. Pierre caught her arm.

"Whoa!" he said.

"Ms. Myers is being helicoptered to Boston," the admitting nurse said. "She needs help we aren't equipped to give her here."

"Where in Boston?" Pierre said.

"Mass General."

"Okee," he said. He pulled out his keys. "I'm going to get the information. Her emergency contact. Okee? I'll be back in five."

Miles sank into a chair. "Boston?" he said.

Admitting Nurse repeated herself, using different words. "The care is much better there . . . the equipment more sophisticated . . . not even in the same league . . ."

Renata followed Pierre out the automatic door, but whereas he headed into the parking lot and climbed into a Toyota Land Cruiser, Renata just stood on the hot sidewalk and turned, slowly, in circles.

She heard the helicopter before she saw it—a great roar followed by a hammering. It sounded like machine-gun fire. And then, several seconds later, Renata saw it rising, straight up, as though it were being pulled by an invisible hand. It hovered above the hospital for a few seconds, long enough for Renata to think, *Sallie.* And then, like a dog following a scent, the helicopter dipped its nose and flew away.

Even with Sallie gone, Renata was hesitant to leave. If she stayed at the hospital, there might be something else she could do. Miles sat slumped in the chair like he was planning on making it his permanent home.

"What should we do?" Renata asked.

"Once Pierre comes back, we'll call her parents," he said. "That's all we can do."

"We could go to Boston. We can be there when she wakes up," Renata said.

"Are you kidding?" Miles said. "Why would you want to do that? You don't even know her."

Renata took the seat next to his and lowered her voice. "She asked me to keep an eye on her," she said. "And I didn't."

Miles crossed his arms over his chest. "Even if you had seen her go down, there was nothing you could have done. You weren't going to be able to find her any faster than the guys who were out there did."

This sounded like an easy answer, but Renata was grateful for it. "You don't think?"

"There was nothing we could have done," Miles said. "And there's nothing we can do now except call her parents."

"Right."

"You should go," he said. "I'll wait for Pierre."

"Go where?" Renata said.

"Back to the house."

"I'll just wait for you," she said.

"I'm not going back there," he said.

"What does that mean?"

"It means I quit."

"What?" Renata said.

Miles had his chin tucked to his chest and wouldn't meet her eyes. "Just go home," he said. "Please."

"How?" Renata said.

"Call your boyfriend," Miles said. Renata had already realized that her love affair with Miles was over, but his words stung nonetheless.

"Fine," Renata said. "Do you have money for the phone?"

He wiggled a finger into the tiny Velcro pocket inside his bathing suit and produced fifty cents. He told her the number of the house.

Renata didn't want to call the house, she was afraid to talk to Cade, she wanted to quit, like Miles, but she had no choice in the matter. She located a bank of phones and made the call.

An unfamiliar voice answered the phone. "Driscoll residence."

Renata paused. Who was it? Then she thought, *Nicole.* "May I please speak to Cade?" Renata said. "This is Renata calling."

Ten minutes later, Cade pulled up to the emergency room entrance in the family's Range Rover. Renata had spent those minutes trying to piece together a plausible story, but in the end she decided to just tell him the truth, minus the part where she had sex with Miles. Cade got out and opened the passenger door for Renata, though he didn't speak to her or touch her. She hadn't seen him since the night before—it seemed like years. She was startled by how handsome he was, how upright with his military-school bearing, his perfect posture. He had taken a shower. His hair was damp and freshly combed, and he was wearing one of his beautifully tailored shirts, blue, with a white windowpane pattern. His mouth was a grim line. Renata felt like she had skipped school and now had to face the truant officer, the principal, her father. She was afraid that once she started to speak, she would never stop. *I'm sorry, I'm sorry, I'm sorry.*

He pulled out of the hospital parking lot, the only sound

in the car the ticking of the turn signal. Cade's window was down; the air felt good. Renata tried to imagine what Action might say in this situation. *What are you feeling sorry for? He doesn't* own *your ass!*

In her nervousness, Renata selected exactly the wrong words. "I'm starving."

Cade turned to her with a look on his face like he just could not believe it.

He's not the boss of you, Renate heard Action say. *Why is he all of a sudden acting like he's the boss of you?*

"Well, I am," Renata said. "I haven't eaten anything all day."

"You ate a banana," he said. His voice was barely above a whisper.

"True," she said. "I ate a banana." She wondered how he knew this. Did Suzanne *count* her bananas? Did she hunt through the trash for the peel? Was there closed-circuit TV footage that showed Renata throwing the banana and breaking the bud vase? On the road, they passed a group of bikers wearing fluorescent yellow T-shirts. Cade slowed down, then stopped at the intersection so the bikers could pass. Ever the gentleman. He took a left when Renata suspected that home was to the right.

"Where are we going?" she said.

"For a drive," he said. "I'd like you to explain yourself."

Now Renata was the one with the incredulous face. Explain herself? He spoke like he was indeed her father, like he did indeed own her ass. She had to give him something, some reason for her absence, some excuse. She'd had a plan a minute ago, but that was before he pulled up and she had to confront the disappointment on his face. What had her plan been? To tell him the truth? Was she nuts?

"I don't know what you mean," she said.

"That's bullshit!" he shouted. The veins in his forehead

were popping. Renata had never seen him this angry before, and certainly not at her. In fact, in the ten months of their dating, they'd had only one argument. There was a night when Cade's parents had asked them for Sunday dinner at the apartment on Park Avenue—Cade's aunt and uncle were visiting from California—but Renata decided to go with Action to her parents' house for Chinese food instead. Cade had pleaded, and when Renata turned him down he was exasperated and disappointed; a long conversation about Renata's priorities ensued. But there hadn't been any shouting. "You never showed up at lunch! You left my mother *stranded* at the yacht club."

Renata nearly laughed. It was impossible to strand Suzanne Driscoll; the woman had three thousand friends.

"So when we got back from our sail, my mother went on and on about how you'd stood her up, how you never showed and never phoned to explain. But she was worried, too, and so we all went home to figure out *where Renata was,* and Nicole informed us that she passed you and Miles on the road in Miles's Saab. She told us it looked like you were going to the *beach.*" He smacked his hands against the inside of the steering wheel so violently that Renata feared the air bag would explode. "How do you think it made me feel to know that my girlfriend, my *fiancée,* blew off lunch with my mother so she could gallivant around the island with the *help*?"

The help? Renata could hear Action's voice loud and clear. *The Driscolls have servants. They have slaves.*

"You went sailing," Renata said. Her voice was calm and even. How this was possible she had no idea, but she was grateful. "I figured you'd be gone all day."

"Not all day," he said. "We were back at two. Two thirty."

"You didn't tell me you were going," she said. "You didn't leave me a note. You just took off."

"Well, I'm sorry," he said, though he didn't sound at all sorry. Renata let the words hang in the air of the car so he could hear his insincerity. "It was important to my father."

"What about what was important to me?" Renata said. "You brought me to Nantucket and then you left me to fend for myself."

"We spent yesterday together," Cade said. "All day yesterday. And it's not like I *abandoned* you. My mother said she'd take you to lunch."

"You said we were going to the beach. I was looking forward to it. I didn't want to have lunch with your mother."

"Nice," Cade said.

"Well, I'm sorry, but it's true. You should have told me you were going sailing."

"I didn't know until this morning."

"You could have left me a note."

Cade snapped his fingers fiercely, like a magician breaking a spell. "It's not going to work, Renata."

"What?"

"You're trying to make it seem like *I* did something wrong. *I* did not do anything wrong. You are the one who disappeared."

They were quiet for a while as they rolled down the street. The story of Renata's day filled her until she thought she would burst. Cade prided himself on being reasonable, tolerant, on being able to place himself in other people's shoes. That was what he did best. That was why she loved him. And yet she knew there was no way to explain her afternoon to Cade so that he'd understand.

"Why did you go with Miles?" Cade asked. He swallowed; his Adam's apple bobbed in his throat. Another man would have been jealous, but Cade had skipped over jealous and gone right to hurt. He was hurt.

"I wanted to go to the beach," she said. "He was going. He invited me to join him. He said we'd be back by three. But things happened."

"What kind of 'things'?" Cade said.

"We picked up a girl. Sallie Myers. She's a friend of his. She came to the beach with us and she went surfing."

"What did you and Miles do?" Cade asked.

"Sat on the beach and watched her."

"Is that his shirt you're wearing?"

"Yes."

"Why are you wearing his shirt?"

"Because I was getting sunburned. I forgot to put on lotion."

"That wasn't too smart."

"I know," Renata said. She nearly said, *Nothing happened between me and Miles.* But Renata couldn't bring herself to lie. Only when Cade out-and-out accused her would she out-and-out deny it. She sighed. The sunburn hurt, she felt like she had a fever, she was suffering from guilt at a ten, she was hungry, her throat was dry and sore from vomiting, and she was tired. She had a headache. "Sallie got hit in the head with her board. She went under. It took a few minutes to find her. When they brought her out, she wasn't breathing. The paramedics came. They took her to the hospital. They asked Miles and me to follow with Sallie's stuff. We didn't know how to reach her parents. I called her boss and he showed up. Then they sent her in a helicopter to Mass General in Boston. Miles decided to stay at the hospital until everything was settled. I should have stayed, too, but I didn't. I called you. End of story."

"Is it?" he said.

"No," she said. "Actually, it's not. There's something else I have to tell you."

He took his eyes off the road to look at her.

"We went to Madequecham Beach. And on the road that leads to the beach, we saw a white cross. It was a cross for my mother."

Cade knit his eyebrows. "What?"

"There was a white cross on the side of the road. Marking where someone had died. My mother was killed in Madequecham. The cross was for my mother."

"Are you sure about that?" Cade said.

"I'm sure."

"Did the cross say anything?" Cade asked. "Did it have your mother's *name* on it?"

"No, but it was for her."

"How do you know?"

"I could tell," Renata said. "I could feel it."

"Oh, honey," he said. "Okay. I'm sorry."

Was he sorry? His sympathy sounded forced to Renata, just as it did every time she brought up her mother's death. Like when she told him the story of her high school graduation, her father walking up to the podium with an armful of American Beauty roses to thunderous applause. *Everyone felt sorry for me, because I had no mother,* Renata said. *Why do you look at it that way?* Cade said. *They clapped because they were proud, and impressed.* He didn't get it. He could cluck and apologize all he wanted, but he didn't understand what it was like to be her and he never would. Even now, he couldn't get that patronizing look off his face, as though Renata had told him she believed in UFOs, or Santa Claus. She was prepared to hate him at that moment. *Hate* him. She was ready to put down her window and throw her twelve-thousand-dollar diamond ring into the high brush at the side of the road, to spit the truth in Cade's direction: *I had sex with Miles in the sand dunes. He was bigger than you.* But then, in an instant, Cade turned back into his usual, princely self.

"You look tired," he said. He turned the car around. "Let's get you home."

Renata closed her eyes.

When they reached Vitamin Sea, Renata expected both of the elder Driscolls to be stationed on the front porch exuding their disapproval, their suspicion, their disgust. But the house was quiet. Cade pulled into the white shell driveway, right alongside Suzanne Driscoll's precious hydrangea bushes, the ones Miles had been watering that morning. Suddenly Renata felt contrite. The day had gotten away from her; it had turned into something she couldn't control. She had acted irresponsibly, immaturely, immorally. There was no other way to look at it.

"I'm sorry," she said. "I am so, so sorry."

Cade took the key out of the ignition. He sighed in that way he had, like he understood the rest of the world would fall short of his expectations, but that he was full of grace and willing to forgive. He was, maybe, willing to forgive her.

"My parents are . . . confused by your behavior today. So I'm going to suggest something."

"Yes," Renata said. "Anything." She would apologize to Suzanne Driscoll, beg her forgiveness, and cry doing it. Because along with everything else, Miles was going to quit. That, somehow, was Renata's fault.

"I'm going to suggest that you call Marguerite and cancel dinner. My mother wants you here. The Robinsons are coming and she went to all this trouble with the lobsters and stuff."

Renata was silent. She couldn't believe Cade would suggest such a thing. He didn't realize how important the dinner with Marguerite was. He didn't realize that Renata, at base, knew exactly nothing about her dead mother and this was her one opportunity to find out. He didn't get it. He didn't care about Renata's mother; he cared only about his own mother, who had made it clear without saying a word that she didn't want Renata to eat at Marguerite's.

"No," Renata said.

"Go see her tomorrow," Cade said. "We're not leaving until four."

"No," Renata said.

"I wouldn't ask you unless it was a really important dinner."

"My dinner is important, too," Renata said. "Very important." *More important,* she thought.

"I just don't know what my parents will think. You've been gone all day and you're disappearing again tonight. You're supposed to be joining this family."

"I'm not *disappearing,*" Renata said. "Your mother knows about my dinner with Marguerite."

"She does," Cade said. "But she still wants you to eat with us."

"Can't you say something to her?" Renata said.

"I did my best to smooth things over this afternoon," Cade said, and his meaning was clear.

Renata trained her eye on Cade's right knee, knobby as it was, and covered with fine blond hairs. This was the knee she was going to spend the rest of her life with.

"I won't ask you anything else about Miles," Cade said. "Quite frankly, I don't want to know. I'm not going to bring it up and I won't allow my parents to bring it up."

"Thank you," Renata said. "I'd appreciate that."

"But I'd like you to cancel dinner."

She stared at him. He had a faint white mask where his sunglasses had been. He was negotiating, playing diplomat. *I slept with him,* she thought. *He was bigger than you.*

"You can go tomorrow, first thing. You can stay all day. But please cancel for tonight. My mother wants you home, and so do I. I feel like I haven't seen you."

At that moment, Renata heard a door slam. She looked up. Nicole was descending the stairs from the apartment over the garage. *Tattletale!* Renata thought. *Snitch!* Nicole glared at Cade and Renata. Cade waved lamely; Renata lowered her eyes. Once Nicole entered the house, Renata got out of the car. She should have known it from that first night with Cade at the dance club; she should have known it from the way he'd drawn her out onto the street, away from the music, and her dearest friend, without a word. She should have understood that things always—always, *always*—went the way Cade Driscoll wanted them to.

It was not quite five o'clock, and yet Suzanne Driscoll was showered, dressed in Lilly Pulitzer pants and a pink silk shell, drinking a glass of white wine. She was lounging across the sofa with Mr. Rogers in her lap. Renata heard banging in the kitchen: Nicole, the little narc, preparing dinner.

"Oh, there you are, dear," Suzanne said. "We were beginning to wonder what had become of you."

"I'm sorry I missed lunch," Renata said sullenly.

"Don't give it a second's thought," Suzanne said, smiling. Suzanne Driscoll had red hair that she combed back over her head; the ends turned up under her ears. Every time Renata saw her, the hair always looked exactly the same. "I'll just bet you had fun with Miles. He is such a doll."

Renata studied Suzanne for signs of sarcasm but found none, which meant Suzanne was more slippery than Renata ever could have imagined. Before Renata could respond with an, "Oh yes, I had *lots* of fun," Cade spoke up.

"Renata's going to call Marguerite and cancel, Mom. She's going to eat here tonight with us."

Suzanne Driscoll squealed in such a grating way that Mr. Rogers jumped off her lap and left the room.

"Oh, good," Suzanne said. "Good, good, good. The Robinsons are coming at six for cocktails. They are dear friends and they really want to meet you. What can I get you? How about a big glass of ice water? How about some crackers and cold grapes? How about some aloe for your skin? If you go upstairs right now, you'll have time for a nap."

I will not play into this woman's hands, Renata thought, but she found she was too tired to rebel, too hungry and thirsty and sore to stand her ground. Too guilty to do anything but nod yes.

5:00 P.M.

The stove's timer buzzed again, making awful music in concert with the monkey in the clock as he announced the hour. Five o'clock. *Quitting time,* Marguerite thought, though this notion was from some long-ago life—five o'clock had been quitting time for her father. He was always home, without fail, at five fifteen and Diana Beale had dinner on the table by five thirty. Later, after culinary school, Marguerite would view this early dinner as middle-class, provincial, midwestern. For most of her professional life, five o'clock was the hour when she returned to work—after a full morning of prep and an all-too-short afternoon break, a glass of wine with Porter, lying in the unmade rope bed.

The timer insisted. Marguerite took the bread out of the oven and checked it off her list. She considered preparing the béarnaise and letting it sit in a warm-water bath until dinnertime, but she never would have done that at the restaurant and she wouldn't do it now. Marguerite set out the polished silver and then she moved the place settings across from each other. She wanted to look Renata in the eye.

So now the table was set, the china and water glasses buffed to a gleaming shine, the zinnias and dahlias crowded cheerfully in a crystal vase. The gladiolas were in the stone pitcher by the door. Marguerite had located cocktail napkins in a kitchen drawer that she hadn't opened in ages. The napkins had, at one time, been red with white polka dots, though the red was faded to pinkish-gray and they curled up slightly at the edges like burnt toast, but they would do. Marguerite changed the CD to, of all people, Derek and the Dominos, because "Bell Bottom Blues" had been Candace's favorite song. It was her anthem. Marguerite would tell Renata this.

All day Marguerite had been aware of time pressing down on her, and yet she suddenly found herself with two unclaimed hours. She wandered through her house. She had dusted on Wednesday and vacuumed on Thursday. The house looked fine. There was time for a few pages of the Theodore Roosevelt biography, her afternoon reading, there was time for the Internet, but Marguerite would never be able to concentrate on either. Renata, her goddaughter, was coming here for dinner. Marguerite had had the whole day to digest this fact, but still it struck her as unbelievable. In the bedroom, Marguerite picked up the photograph of Candace and herself and baby Renata, four weeks old, newly christened.

Marguerite didn't often pray. On those occasions when she'd found herself at church—Candace's wedding, Renata's christening, Candace's funeral—she'd bowed her head along with everyone else, and when required she moved her lips, spoke the words she'd memorized as a child. But she didn't feel anything. Marguerite was certain God existed and just as certain that God knew she existed, but for sixty-three years they had ignored each other. Marguerite had had no use for faith until the day Candace was killed, at which point Marguerite found her spiritual reserve empty. There was nothing to draw on, and rather than being angry at God for not appearing in her time of need the way he seemed to for so many others, rather than hating him for not providing her with a tool to make her way easier, Marguerite accepted his absence as her due.

Once Candace was gone, Marguerite frequently spoke out loud as she moved through her days alone. *Would you look at the bloom on that Jacques Randall? Elizabeth Taylor in rehab again! A wholly unsatisfying ending on the last story by Mr. Salinger, anyone would agree.* Marguerite assumed this was a symptom of her "insanity," a consequence of her decision not to allow anyone into her day-to-day life, but every once in a while she recognized her mumblings as prayer. She was talking to Candace.

As Marguerite gazed at the photograph, she echoed the words she'd said on the altar the afternoon Renata was baptized. *"Will you, Marguerite, as godmother, do the best that you can to . . ."* The priest went on to say something about guiding the child in the ways of the Lord, something about seeking truth, goodness, humility, grace, something about maintaining faith. Marguerite had agreed to do all these things, but only because she was relieved by the gentle phrasing of the question: *Will you do the best that you can?*

Yes, she thought. *I will do the best I can.*

Candace was pregnant through the summer. Her breasts swelled first; then her belly popped. Her hair grew at an amazing rate; at one point, it was nearly as long as Marguerite's. Her left hand became numb with carpal tunnel; she suffered from debilitating heartburn when she lay down; she had to pee every twenty minutes. And yet still she worked, climbing the steep stairs to the Chamber of Commerce office each day; still she ran—five, six, seven miles—even though people would stop in their cars, roll down the windows, and tell her to get on home.

One day at noon, she showed up at Les Parapluies and found Marguerite elbow deep in prep work: roasting peppers, reducing stock, marinating tuna steaks. Candace kissed Marguerite on both cheeks and demanded lunch.

"This is not a diner," Marguerite grumbled. "You know I don't make lunch. Half the time, I don't even eat lunch."

"You don't have to make lunch for me," Candace said. "But what about the baby?"

Candace came in almost every day for ten weeks. She was used to bringing soda crackers to work, carrot sticks, a hard-boiled egg, which she ate at her desk, but it wasn't matching her voracious appetite. Marguerite made quiches, Caesar salads, *croque monsieurs* like the ones she'd eaten in Paris; she made gazpacho, BLTs, tuna salad. She began to feel like a part of the pregnancy. She liked having Candace in her kitchen while she cooked. She liked having Candace to herself. They talked, really talked, and it was almost like the old days, before Dan. Candace expressed her concerns about the baby.

"I can't become somebody's mother," Candace said. "I don't know what I'm doing."

"Who does?" Marguerite said.

"I don't have the warm, fuzzy maternal feelings that other women have," Candace said.

"They'll come," Marguerite said. "When the baby's born."

"I don't even like babies," Candace said. "I think other people's babies are boring."

"They say it's different when it's your own," Marguerite said.

"How do you know so much?" Candace said.

Marguerite laced her fingers through Candace's and said, "You're going to be a wonderful mother."

"You think?"

Candace had given up alcohol and she was easily tired, but still Candace and Dan came to the restaurant to have dinner with Porter and Marguerite two or three times a week. Marguerite insisted on it.

"You're coming in tonight?" Marguerite would ask at lunch.

"Oh," Candace would say. "I don't know. I'm so tired."

"You should come while you can," Marguerite said. "Once the baby arrives, things will be different."

In the end, Candace always agreed. "Okay, we'll come. Nine o'clock. See you then."

Candace's belly was impressive—perfectly round and hard as a rock. Customers of the restaurant couldn't help themselves from stopping by the west banquette. "Boy," one said. "The way you're carrying, it's definitely a boy." The interruptions came so frequently, it annoyed them all.

"No one has any sense of boundaries," Dan complained. "Everyone has something to say to a pregnant woman."

"I know they're excited for us," Candace said. "But I feel like public property."

Candace drank mineral water while Dan and Porter and Marguerite carried on with cocktails and wine—two bottles, three bottles, four, followed by a glass of port or a cordial. The three of them drank more heavily, perhaps, while Candace was pregnant. There were dozens of conversations about Reagan, who might succeed Reagan, did the Democrats have a chance, and if they were to have a chance they needed to run somebody who would make a better showing than Walter Mondale did the last time around.

One night, Candace stopped conversation with a hoot. "Baby's kicking," she said.

Marguerite reached over and laid her hand on the smooth sphere of Candace's belly. The instinct to do this was perfectly natural, she thought. She, who would never have a child, wanted to know what it felt like, if only from the outside. She sensed the light but insistent tapping—*tap, tap, tap,* like the baby was trying to send her some kind of coded message. Without thinking, Marguerite moved her hand in a circle, as though Candace were a crystal ball.

Dan snorted. "That's my wife you're fondling," he said. "I will ask you kindly to remove your hand."

Marguerite lifted her hand. She looked at Candace. Always, when Marguerite and Dan bickered, Candace was the peacemaker. But now she just gazed into her lap. Marguerite's face burned with shame. "I feed that child," she said.

"Oh, Marguerite and her fabulous cooking," Dan said. "Where would we be without it?"

There was a terrible silence at the table. Marguerite looked to Porter. Confrontation made him cringe, but she couldn't believe he would let Dan talk to her that way. Porter glanced at her in a way that let her know he was embarrassed for her; then he tried to smooth things over by hoisting the last third of the bottle of Sauternes.

"Maybe we need some more wine," he said. "How 'bout it? Daisy?"

"I'm all done," Marguerite said. She threw her napkin onto her plate and stood up. "I have things to do in the kitchen. Good night." She addressed the centerpiece of hydrangeas because she couldn't bear to meet anyone's eyes.

The following morning Candace came into the kitchen looking as plain as Marguerite had ever seen her. Her hair was lank and unwashed; there were bruise-colored crescents under her eyes.

"Croque monsieur?" Marguerite asked, doing her best to smile. "Or is it a tuna fish day?"

Candace twisted a strand of hair around her finger. "I'm not hungry," she said. "I just wanted to apologize for last night."

"It's my fault," Marguerite said. "What I did was inappropriate." She said this, though she didn't quite believe it. Her touch had been innocent, curious. Had she crossed a line? Was she no longer able to touch her best friend? It pained her to think so.

"I have to stop coming in at night," Candace said. "It's too much for me. I'm too tired."

"No!" Marguerite said. "You can't stop coming." She heard the desperation in her voice and suddenly she saw herself the way other people must see her: As a woman terrified of being abandoned, of being left alone. She, who had prided herself on strength, on independence; she, who had chosen the word *free*. What was happening to her? "I mean, fine," Marguerite said. "Fine, yes. By all means, stay home."

Candace walked to the sink where Marguerite was seasoning a striped bass and put her hand on Marguerite's back. "There's going to be enough baby for all of us."

"It's you, though," Marguerite said. "There's not enough you for all of us."

The clock chimed the half hour. *Shower,* Marguerite thought. Hair, face, outfit. These were the only unchecked items left oh her list, and for some reason this made her apprehensive. She went to the refrigerator and eyed the champagne. Candace had always insisted on a dressing drink, and now Marguerite knew why. All those years with Porter, and Marguerite had never felt a nervous anticipation as keen as this very moment. She took one of the bottles out, popped the cork, poured herself three fingers in a jelly jar.

She took a sip. She couldn't taste it in any kind of proper way, though there was a cold, fizzy crispness that brought back memories of Porter's arched eyebrows, his bulging eyes, the feel of the zinc bar under her bare elbows, the sound of forks scraping plates, laughter, voices (Candace's voice sifting through all the rest), Marguerite closing her eyes at any point during the dinner service and knowing that she was responsible for everything that happened in that restaurant. *She* was God. Then, incongruously, Marguerite thought of the pimpled boy in the wine shop that morning, his discomfort with the price of the champagne, with the whole idea of the champagne, and she laughed.

Right, she thought. *Shower.*

*   *   *

It was as she was stepping out of the shower that the phone rang. The bathroom door was closed, the overhead fan humming, and despite her promise to herself to be moderate, Marguerite had slugged back the champagne all at once, like a shot of tequila. It went straight to her head. She heard the phone, but even after the day she'd had, she couldn't quite identify the sound. She cracked open the door. It was indeed the phone.

Before the shower, she had located the pink silk kimono that Porter brought her from Kyoto; it had been at the far edge of her closet, the very last thing, beyond her five embroidered chef's jackets, which were pressed and vacuum-packed in dry cleaner's plastic. *Wallflower,* Marguerite thought as she wrapped herself up in the kimono. She stepped into the bedroom. The room was dim, though the sun had not set; there was liquid gold light slanting through her bedroom windows. The phone rang, and rang again. Marguerite was so preoccupied by the sight and feel of herself in the kimono (as though whoever was on the phone could see her) and with the circumstances under which Porter had given it to her (it was the consolation prize—he had taken a trip with the blond, unmarried tennis coach instead of her; he had lied *and* cheated) that she never considered who might be calling. She supposed, if pressed, she would have said it was Dan again, with another petition. Or Ethan, wishing her luck.

"Hello?" she said.

"Aunt Daisy?"

"Yes, darling, hello. How are you? Had a good day, I hope?" Marguerite was thinking, *She needs directions, after all. Would she be walking or taking a cab? Or would someone from the house on Hulbert Avenue be dropping her?* Marguerite was just about to ask when she realized a reasonable amount of time had passed and Renata hadn't answered. There was breathing on the other end, labored breathing, which Marguerite identified as weeping. Weeping, but no words.

"Are you all right?" Marguerite asked. "Darling?"

"Aunt Daisy?" Renata said.

The girl's voice was so despondent, so transparently on a mission to deliver bad news, that it was all Marguerite could do to find the edge of her bed.

"Yes?"

"I can't come," Renata said.

"You're not coming?" Marguerite said. She felt ambushed and stunned, like the victim of a surprise attack. How stupid she was! How daft! Because never once this whole day had it occurred to Marguerite that Renata might cancel.

"My boyfriend's parents," Renata said. "They want me here. They're being weird about it. And I'm in no position to argue with them because I did an awful thing today."

Awful thing? Marguerite knew she was supposed to ask about the awful thing, but her mind struggled like a weak flame. She was thinking about the boyfriend's parents, former customers who missed her restaurant. These people were asking Renata to forgo dinner with her own godmother who, because of a set of complex circumstances, Renata hadn't seen in fourteen years. The boyfriend's parents didn't understand the situation, its importance. Awful thing? Nothing could be so bad that it warranted the boyfriend's parents taking Renata from her. However, Marguerite said nothing. *Not coming,* she thought. The term "crushing blow" came to mind, the term "heartbreak." How would Marguerite be able to step into the other room and see the table set for two people, one across from the other? How would she deal with all the food she'd prepared?

Her mind was running amok now. It was the champagne; she should never have allowed herself. God knows if she let herself do whatever her heart desired she would drink a bottle, or two, every night, and turn herself into a drunk. She would give herself cirrhosis of the liver. Marguerite squeezed the phone's receiver. She was in a conversation, she reminded herself; she had a responsibility to the person on the other end of the line to move the conversation, however unpleasant, forward.

"Awful thing?" Marguerite said.

"I ran away."

"You ran away?"

"I went to the beach without telling anyone where I was going. I went with this . . . *guy* who works here."

The way she said "guy" seemed significant. But how to respond?

"We went to Madequecham," Renata said.

Marguerite hissed involuntarily, like a balloon losing air. Madequecham. The poor girl.

"You saw the cross?" Marguerite said.

Renata started weeping again. "Yes." She snuffled. There was a pause, the sound of a tissue being pulled from a box. "It's for her, right?"

"It's for her. Your mother." Marguerite had made the cross herself. She bought the wood at Marine Home Center, painted it with three coats of heavy-duty white primer, nailed it together. She had done this as busywork, really, the whole time in a numbed daze, three days after Candace's death and the day before her funeral. Marguerite had softened the ground with a thermos of boiling water and pounded the cross into the sandy mud with her kitchen mallet. And then she drove away. She had thought she might visit the marker like a grave, lay down flowers each week or some such, but she had never once gone back to see it.

"I knew it was for her," Renata said. "I saw it and I knew."

Good, Marguerite thought. She wasn't exactly sure why she had put the cross there. At least not until this very second.

"I'm sorry you can't come," Marguerite said. "Deeply sorry." *Devastated*, she thought. *Stupefied*. She felt like crying herself, like throwing a childish tantrum. She nearly listed the efforts she had made on behalf of the meal, but that would be selfish and rude. And yet she couldn't help herself from wondering if the situation could be salvaged or manipulated. "Would it help at all if I spoke to the boy's parents?"

"Oh no," Renata said. "God, no. I wouldn't want to drag you into all this."

"Are you sure, darling? Because I could explain—"

"Thank you, Aunt Daisy, for offering, but *no*." The "no" was so emphatic, it wounded Marguerite's ego. Maybe the boyfriend's parents were an excuse, then. Maybe Renata simply didn't want to come. Maybe the boyfriend's parents or someone else had made a comment about Marguerite; maybe they'd perpetuated the worst of the rumors.

"Okay," Marguerite said. She felt ashamed for pressing the issue. This was rejection, another broken promise. She should be used to it by now.

"They said I'll have time for a visit tomorrow," Renata said. "I could come for lunch, maybe? Or breakfast?"

"Breakfast?" Marguerite said. A person less rigid than she would snap up this opportunity and start thinking about eggs, or crepes filled with fresh peaches. But Marguerite couldn't help feeling that something would be lost from their conversation if it took place in the bright, unforgiving sunlight of morning. An intimacy would be sacrificed; Marguerite felt that the confessions she had to make would only come across properly with candlelight, with wine, with nothing to stop them from talking but sleep. Marguerite felt annoyed, and resistant to changing her plans like this. After all the work she'd done, the way she'd choreographed the evening in her mind, she didn't want to accommodate. The girl would have to learn, eventually, that she couldn't go about disappointing people like this. But in the end, Marguerite decided, she wasn't willing to turn the girl away altogether. So eggs it would be. Crepes with fresh peaches.

"Breakfast is fine. Or lunch." They could have cold tenderloin sandwiches, asparagus salad.

"Breakfast," Renata said. "I'm coming over as soon as I wake up."

Marguerite surprised herself. She was able to laugh. "We'll see you in the morning, then."

"Thank you, Aunt Daisy," Renata said. "Thank you for understanding."

"Anything for you, darling." Marguerite said, and she meant it.

The sun set. Marguerite's windows shone pink, then darkened. Even here, in the heart of town, she could hear crickets. She did not turn on any lights and she did not get dressed. She sat on her bed through two chimes of the stodgy, unforgiving old clock and then she moved through her house as nimbly as if she'd lived in it all these years as a blind woman. She let the tenderloin sit, and the bread; she didn't have the heart to wrap everything up and put it away just yet. She took one of the chilled flutes from the freezer, filled it with champagne, and carried both the flute and the bottle to the dining-room table. There she lit the candles. The light was such that she could see herself in the dark window opposite, a woman drinking alone. She raised her glass to her reflection.

Part Two

The Dinner Party

S uzanne Driscoll said, "The Robinsons just pulled in."
She and Renata were standing at the bottom of the staircase, a few steps to the right of the open front door. Suzanne touched her hair, her earrings, and then, reassured that she looked perfect, she inspected Renata. "My God, what is that mark on your chin? You look like you've been in a prize fight."

Renata's hand flew to her jaw. She had noticed it herself only a few minutes ago: a garish purple bruise where the surfboard had smacked her. The spot throbbed with dull pain, as did the sunburn across her nose and cheeks. Suzanne had given her a tube of aloe mask, and she had applied it liberally, then lain down for twenty minutes of dreamless sleep. When Renata washed the mask off, her face felt fragile, like if she smiled, it would crumble and fall apart in chunks. There was no way to explain the bruise without explaining about Sallie, so Renata said nothing. She was hurt that this was what Suzanne had chosen to notice, because she had tried to make an effort with her appearance: She wore a white T-shirt with a scoop neck and a short pink skirt. She wore pink thong sandals embossed with the letter *R*. And yet now Renata felt that what she was missing was the bag for over her head.

Attention was drawn from Renata's wound with the appearance of the Robinson family in the Driscolls' foyer. Renata had thought the Robinsons would be a couple, but there were three of them; they had brought along a daughter who was about Cade and Renata's age. Someone Renata, no doubt, would be expected to make friends with. Joe Driscoll came out to the foyer to greet the Robinsons, as did Cade. Everyone kissed, shook hands, thumped backs, grasped arms, and then Renata was ushered forth— Suzanne placed a light but insistent hand on her lower back and moved her forward into the center of a circle they'd all unconsciously made.

"And this," Suzanne said, "is the future Mrs. Cade Driscoll."

Renata tried to smile, though being introduced in this way offended her. She had been reduced to an announcement in *Town & Country*. Her face felt like plastic. She held out her hand. Mr. Robinson who was tall and balding, wearing Ben Franklin spectacles and a bow tie, was the first to take it.

"Pleasure to meet you. Kent Robinson."

"Renata Knox," Renata said, because for all the pomp and circumstance of the introduction, Suzanne had neglected to mention her name.

Mrs. Robinson, a short-haired brunette who was as thin

and made up as Renata's future mother-in-law and as cheerful with the same kind of questionable sincerity, hugged Renata quickly but fiercely, kissed her burning cheek, and said, "Oh, Suzanne, you are so lucky!"

"Aren't I?" Suzanne said. She beamed as if standing before her were not a sunburned, bruised, delinquent, vase-breaking, list-stealing, lying, cheating Renata but someone else entirely. "And Renata," Suzanne said in the fetching voice she reserved for the cat, "this is Kent and Kathy's daughter, Claire. Claire and Cade went to Choate together. They are old, old friends."

Renata smiled at the Robinsons' daughter, trying to remember that first impressions were just that. Look how things had turned around with Sallie. But Claire Robinson had failed even more miserably with her appearance than Renata had. She wore a long peasant skirt and a man's white T-shirt, and a pair of leather sandals that had been mended with white medical tape. She had long, dark hair on its way to becoming dreadlocks, and the whitest skin Renata had ever seen—as white as a geisha under layers of powder—so that the freckles on her nose and cheeks looked like the black beans in vanilla ice cream. Renata looked at her and thought, *Ragamuffin, waif*—she reminded Renata of a street urchin from a Dickens novel—though her blue eyes were bright and overexcited. Renata wondered if she was on drugs.

"Hi," Renata said. And in case Claire had missed the earlier introduction, she added, "I'm Renata."

Claire was staring at Renata in a way that bordered on rude. Then she offered a limp, moist hand. "It's nice to meet you. I couldn't believe it when I heard Cade was engaged."

"Right," Renata said. "We're kind of young."

"Claire and Cade went to Choate together," Suzanne said again. She took a sharp breath. "Let's go to the big room and get a drink."

They repaired to the big room in three groups: Mr. Robinson, Joe Driscoll, and Cade led the way, slowly, accommodating Joe's occasional stutter step. (He was using a cane tonight because the sailing had worn him out.) Suzanne, Mrs. Robinson, and Claire followed behind, and Renata, feeling like a Sunset Boulevard streetwalker with her short, tight skirt and ugly bruise, brought up the rear. At least she thought she brought up the rear, but then she sensed a light, whispery presence behind her—Mr. Rogers, perhaps? She turned and was startled to find Nicole, dressed in black pants, a black shirt and black apron, quietly shutting the door and tucking away Mrs. Robinson's turquoise wrap. Renata felt angry at Nicole—she was a snitch—and yet this anger was mixed with an odd sense of kinship. Nicole was a black woman, as was Renata's best friend, whom she missed keenly, especially in these strange and compromised circumstances, and Nicole worked for the Driscolls, as did Miles, whom Renata still considered vaguely, though she might never see him again, to be her lover. On the strength of these two imagined connections, Renata felt it was okay to linger until she and Nicole were in step next to each other. She wasn't sure what to say, but she wanted to let Nicole know that she, Renata, wasn't like the rest of these people. As the future Mrs. Cade Driscoll (God, it made her shiver just to think it) she was as much Suzanne's pawn, Suzanne's servant, as Nicole was.

"You've worked hard today," Renata said. "I hope you're off soon?"

Nicole didn't deign to meet Renata's eye. "Miles was

supposed to spell me at six. He phoned to say he wasn't coming." Nicole had a light and crisp British accent. It surprised Renata until she realized that this was the first time she had heard Nicole speak more than two words. The loveliness of her voice was poisoned by the disgusted look she shot Renata. "But you, I'm sure, know *all about that.*" She quickened her step and Renata hurried to keep up.

"His friend Sallie, you know," Renata said. "She had a surfing accident and went to the hospital."

Nicole dismissed this with a wave of her hand. "I have to fetch drinks," she said.

Even as mentally anguished and physically battered as Renata was, she had to admit there was no room as perfect for entertaining on a balmy summer evening as the Driscolls' living room. The room was lit only by candles and by a soft fluorescent light over the wet bar. The white couches had been connected to create a semicircle facing the out-of-doors. The coffee table had been cleared of Suzanne's collection of porcelain eggs and her copies of *Travel + Leisure* and was now laden with platters of food—bluefish pâté, crackers, grapes, cheese straws, nuts, olives. The glass doors had been flung wide open to the night. The deck was festooned with tiki torches; the teak table had been covered with a red checkered cloth and set with butter-warmers and lobster crackers, cocktail forks and plastic bibs. Just seeing the table costumed like this made Renata pine for the dinner she was not having with Marguerite. The white cross! Beyond the deck, Renata could see the moon shining on the water; she could smell the water; she could hear the water lapping against the side of

Joe Driscoll's boat. *Once you marry me,* Cade had said, with the promise of a game show host, *all this will be yours.*

Renata tried to decide which of the two groups to join. She would be most comfortable with Cade at her side, though the second she had called Marguerite to cancel she had filled with a fury that could only be directed at him. She had thrown him several frosty looks since descending from her room (where, earlier, he'd knocked timidly, no doubt looking for sex, and Renata had told him brusquely and without opening the door that she was busy getting ready and to please go away)—but Cade didn't look as apologetic or as distraught as he should have. He seemed oblivious to her, and he had done nothing to acknowledge the sacrifice she made so that she could have lobsters with the Robinsons. Renata also felt put out by Claire Robinson's presence, primarily because it hadn't been mentioned and thus felt like something secret, something the Driscolls were trying to pull over on her. If an old friend of Cade's from boarding school was coming for dinner, why wouldn't anyone have mentioned it? And yet Cade didn't seem interested in Claire Robinson; Renata didn't remember seeing them even greeting each other. At this moment, Cade was talking to Kent Robinson about his new job at J. P. Morgan while Joe Driscoll leaned on his cane with one hand and tried to discreet away his other hand, which shook violently.

Renata, unable to place herself comfortably with the gentlemen, stood with Suzanne, Mrs. Robinson, and Claire. Suzanne and Mrs. Robinson were as thin as blades and Renata could imagine them working a crowded room, alternately smoothing and cutting. They were talking about a third woman, a friend of theirs maybe, but maybe not, who had breast cancer. The cancer had metastasized; the woman was the mother of three small children.

"In the end, I can't help but feel it's her own fault," Mrs. Robinson said. "All it would have taken was a yearly mammogram!"

At this, Claire gasped. "I can't believe you just said that. Really, Mother!"

"Those poor children," Suzanne said.

It was Renata's least favorite kind of story—those poor, motherless children. Just as she thought, *I can't be a part of this,* and made the slightest movement toward the men, Nicole appeared holding a tray of drinks.

"White wine spritzers," she said. She smiled warmly at the women and especially at Renata. Renata couldn't decide if Nicole had forgiven her or if she was being grossly insincere. Was there, Renata wondered, a genuine person in the room, including herself? She took a glass from the tray.

"Thank you," she said.

Mrs. Robinson also took a glass, though Claire and Suzanne declined. Claire asked for a hot chai ("if it's not too much trouble"), which Nicole assured her it wasn't. Renata noticed a very full glass of white wine resting on a side table just below Suzanne's fingertips, which, now that other guests had drinks, she felt free to pick up.

"Cheers," Suzanne said. "Here's to the end of the summer. And to Cade's engagement. And to being together."

The three of them clinked glasses while Claire stood among them, beaming, and cheerfully mimed as though she had a glass. Renata drank down quite a bit of her fruity, fizzy wine punch, hoping Nicole hadn't poisoned it. She glanced at Cade, who was drinking a Stella, still deep in conversation with Kent Robinson about his future on the buy-back desk. Joe Driscoll had availed himself of the sofa—he couldn't lean on his cane and hold a drink—and he smiled benignly at Cade and Kent's conversation, though he wasn't really a part of it any longer. Renata considered joining him. If there *was* a decent person in the room, it was probably Joe Driscoll. She could ask him about the sailing.

"We're lucky to have Renata with us tonight," Suzanne said. "She originally made other plans."

"Really?" Mrs. Robinson said. She smiled as though she couldn't imagine such a thing.

"I was supposed to have dinner with my godmother," Renata said. "Marguerite Beale."

"Marguerite Beale?" Mrs. Robinson said. "Marguerite *Beale*? The chef? From Les Parapluies?"

Suzanne smirked and nudged her friend's elbow. All of a sudden she seemed about to burst with pride and excitement, as if she'd just announced that Renata was related to the queen of England. "Her godmother."

"But why?" Mrs. Robinson said. "How?"

"She was my mother's best friend," Renata said. "Candace Harris Knox?"

"Renata lost her mother when she was terribly young," Suzanne said, clucking. "Joe and I used to go to the restaurant all the time, of course."

"Of course," Mrs. Robinson said. "So did we. God, that seems like ages ago."

"I think I remember your mother," Suzanne said. "Though maybe not. I only ever caught glimpses of Marguerite Beale. She used to sit down to eat with friends after everyone else went home, or moved into the bar. I have to admit, I wasn't really part of her crowd."

"Nor was I," Mrs. Robinson said. She sounded sad about this for a moment; then she cleared her throat. "So,

Marguerite Beale. She's better then? You heard the strangest stories, right after the restaurant closed."

"Yes," Suzanne murmured. She sipped her wine and touched Renata's arm. "You must know all about it. Marguerite's trouble?"

Renata's face burned; her jaw pulsed. She sipped her drink and resolved to say nothing, to give nothing away. She glanced at Claire, who was staring at her again.

"It was rather like Vincent van Gogh cutting off his ear," Mrs. Robinson said. She tittered nervously. "At least that was what one heard. I'm sure she's better now; I'm sure she's just fine. Your godmother! That's simply extraordinary."

To keep from slapping Mrs. Robinson or telling her to fuck off, which was what the Action-voice in Renata's head was advising her to do, Renata made a move for the food on the coffee table. She had eaten nothing but the damned banana all day. She slathered a cracker with bluefish pâté and shoved it in her mouth. She could hear Suzanne and Mrs. Robinson whispering behind her. She heard Claire say in an aggravated whisper, "Mother, please! You're a terrible gossip!" Cade appeared at Renata's elbow.

"Are you okay?" he said.

Vincent van Gogh? she thought. She hated Mrs. Robinson. But before Renata could express this sentiment to Cade, Nicole appeared with a tray of fresh drinks.

"Renata?" Nicole said.

Renata slammed back the rest of her spritzer, placed the empty glass on Nicole's tray, and took another.

"Thank you," she said to Nicole. "I think you're the only person in the room who knows my name."

"Oh, come on," Cade said. "I know your name."

She glared at him. Nicole walked away. The four adults

mingled in a group and then strolled out to the deck. Joe Driscoll leaned on his wife; he was moving without his cane.

Renata took a pull of her wine spritzer. She was feeling more dangerous every second.

"What's wrong?" Cade said. "Tell me."

Burn it down, she thought. But she was too afraid. If she told Cade about what had happened with Miles, he might forgive her. That was her fear. If she told him and he forgave her, she would never be free; she would always be indebted to him.

"Nothing's wrong," she said. She picked up a handful of mixed nuts. "I'm just hungry."

"Are you sure?" he said. He was asking her, but his voice was revved up with a false playfulness; he sounded like he was acting. And then Renata realized why: Claire Robinson was standing a few steps behind them, alone, chuckling to herself over the witticisms needlepointed on Suzanne's throw pillows. *LORD, DO NOT LEAD ME INTO TEMPTATION. I CAN FIND IT JUST FINE BY MYSELF.* She was listening to every word they said, and now that the adults were outside it was rude not to include her in the conversation. Cade, with his brilliant breeding, should know that.

Renata turned, forced her stiff face into a smile. "So you and Cade went to Choate together," she said to Claire. "That's exciting. I never met anybody that Cade went to Choate with." This wasn't strictly true. There was a girl at Columbia who had graduated from Choate a year behind Cade. She wore black capes and a lot of eye shadow. She had dyed her hair white, and when she saw Cade and Renata on campus she wolf-whistled and yelled out, "Cay—dee! Cay—dee, bay-bay!" The girl, her name was

Esther, scared Renata; Renata wondered if Claire knew her; maybe they were friends.

"Yeah," Claire said, twisting her dirty hair. "We've known each other a long time."

"A long time," Cade echoed. "My dad and Mr. Robinson went to business school together. And Claire and I grew up here together summers."

Claire smiled at Cade over the top of her mug of tea. "All those JYC dances."

"Right," Cade said.

Renata bent over for another cracker. She was picking up an awkward vibe. Claire had a crush on Cade; she'd probably suffered from it her whole life.

There was a burst of laughter from outside. Renata, Cade, and Claire looked out at the two couples. Suzanne and Joe were arm-in-arm, as were the Robinsons, all of them gazing at the water. From here, they looked like nice people. How difficult would it be to just play along with this fantasy—to indulge Cade and Claire as they reminisced and used acronyms she didn't understand, to drink more wine, to eat lobster drenched in lemon butter, to laugh and chat and revel in being one of the most privileged people on earth out on the deck of Vitamin Sea? Could Renata make herself do it? Could she pretend she was someone else entirely?

"So where did you go to college, then?" Renata asked.

"Bennington," Claire said, and this sounded right to Renata. There seemed to be a lawlessness to Claire, starting with a blatant disregard for how to dress for this dinner party. Claire wasn't wearing a bra; her nipples poked right through the threadbare white T-shirt. Action probably would have loved the girl, and Renata tried to love her, too—she was the exact opposite of her mother and Suzanne.

But there was something about Claire that irritated Renata, a cool knowingness, a sense of superiority. She moved around the house with confidence, even a sense of ownership—as though, someday, it would all be *hers*. "Vermont's a long way from New York City," Claire said. "So I barely saw Cade at all during college. Except for the semester in London, spring before last."

"You went to London, too?" Renata said. By Cade's account, the semester abroad had been overrated, yet he went because *that was what one did.* One attended the London School of Economics and bought a closetful of hand-tailored shirts. Renata supposed that, being a married woman, a semester abroad would be out of the question for her, though she and Action were desperate to go to Barcelona. They wanted to stroll the *Rambles* at midnight, drink sangria, learn to flamenco dance. It would be so much better than Cade and Claire stuck in cold, fussy London. "That's a coincidence. Both of you there at the same time."

Cade and Claire just stared at Renata like she had two heads. She gingerly touched her bruise; it reminded her of Sallie.

"Claire and I went to London together, actually," Cade said.

"Huh?" Renata said. There was some meaning to be extracted from the way he said "actually." Renata looked at them, side by side now, as though they were standing at a front door, about to welcome Renata into their home. Then she got it. They had dated, been lovers. Really? It struck Renata as funny and sweet—almost. A part of her recognized how much they had in common: Their parents were friends; they had all that shared history. Cade could play the flaming liberal when he wanted; had he been anti-establishment when he was with Claire? Renata could picture him holding Claire in his arms. She was tiny, doll-like, featherlight; he could pick her up with one hand. Had he liked that? Had he touched her nipples? Had he kissed her nose, with freckles so dark and distinct he could count them?

Renata twisted her ring to the inside of her hand; for the umpteenth time today it made her feel ashamed. And to make matters worse, Claire was staring at her again. What *was* her problem? Renata recalled the childhood retort: *Take a picture, it lasts larger.*

"I have to go to the ladies' room," Claire said. She disappeared into the front of the house.

Cade took Renata's arm a bit more forcefully than was necessary.

Somewhere in the house, the phone rang. Renata wrested her arm free and snarfed another handful of nuts. Manners of a barnyard animal, but she didn't care. Nicole rushed from the kitchen to the deck with a significant glance at Renata. Even Nicole knew about Cade and Claire; that was why she had suddenly been so friendly. It was amusing to see Renata made a fool of. Nicole fetched Suzanne from the deck and Suzanne sailed past, leaving Joe to plop in a teak chair.

"Renata," Cade said. "Listen to me."

"You dated her?"

"Renata—"

"She's your ex?"

He sighed. "Yes. We were together, off and on, for a long time. Since we were freshmen in high school."

Renata did the math. "Seven years?"

He nodded. "We broke up after London. But Renata—"

"But what?" Renata said; then she held up her hand. "On second thought, don't say anything. Don't explain. Please." She felt like Cade had just handed her something precious—a legitimate reason to be angry. She could be angry because at no time during the ten months of their courtship had Cade mentioned his seven-year relationship with Claire Robinson. There had been occasional references to a "girlfriend in high school"; Renata thought there had been more than one. She could be angry because she had been tricked into giving up dinner with Marguerite so that she could stay here and suffer through lobsters with Cade, his ex-girlfriend, and his ex-girlfriend's parents. She could even be angry on Claire's behalf; this couldn't be pleasant for her, either.

There were murmurs about the phone call. Who was it? Was it Miles? Had Sallie died? Renata nixed this last thought; she wouldn't be able to bear it.

"You've got quite a bruise on your chin," Cade said. "Miles didn't . . . *hit* you, did he?"

"Go to hell," Renata said.

"I was going to explain it all when I came upstairs earlier," he said. "But you told me to go away."

"Please," Renata said. "Don't."

"Don't what?"

"Don't pursue this. I am not willing to talk about it right now."

Suzanne approached, holding a fresh glass of wine. Renata doubted she needed it; her eyes were bright and wild, and she seemed unhinged. Her always-perfect hair was mussed, which was to say a thick strand fell across her forehead, into her eyes.

"Renata?" she said.

Renata raised her eyebrows, a gesture that hurt, physically, because of her face.

"That was your father on the phone."

Renata's heart plummeted and skipped at the same time, like a stone scudding across the road.

"He's here, on Nantucket!" Suzanne said. "He's joining us for dinner!"

7:18 P.M.

Everyone was in a hubbub about Daniel Knox's arrival. Suzanne had given Nicole instructions to set another place at the table—thank God she'd had the foresight to order extra lobsters—and then make up the west guest room.

"He won't have much sun in the morning," Suzanne said. "But if we give him enough wine, he'll be grateful for that."

Cade was pacing. "We're going to have to tell him as soon as he gets here," he said to Renata quietly. "Maybe I should run out to the airport to get him myself; that way I could tell him alone. I should have asked him for your hand. People still do that, you know. If I hadn't been so sure he would say no—"

"He knows already," Renata said flatly. "I told him."

"What?" Cade said. "You told him when?"

"This morning," she said. "While you were sailing. I called him and told him."

"I thought we were going to wait," Cade said.

"I couldn't just have him not *knowing*. He's my father."

"So that's why he's here, then," Cade said. "He came to take you back."

"You may find this hard to believe," Renata said, "but I am an adult woman. A human being with my own free will. I'm not an object that can be handed over or taken back."

"I never implied you were," Cade said.

"You imply it all the time," Renata said. "Just because we're engaged doesn't mean you own me."

Claire appeared from the powder room. Her face looked dewy, like she had splashed it with water. "I finally figured it out," she said. "Where I've seen you before. It was today, at the beach. You were at Madequecham, right? You were there with Miles? When they pulled that girl out of the water?"

Now it was Renata's turn to stare. Claire had been at Madequecham? Claire had seen Renata there?

"Renata was there with Miles," Cade said quickly, as though he sensed Renata might deny it. "He kidnapped her for the afternoon."

"Lucky you," Claire said. "I've always thought Miles was hot."

"So what's the deal with that chick, anyway?" Cade said. "Is she going to be okay?"

"Yeah," Claire said, turning to Renata. "Did you *know* her?"

"My sunburn is bothering me," Renata said. "I may run up and put on some more aloe before Daddy gets here."

Outside, she heard Kent Robinson ask, "So what's this fellow Knox's business, anyway?"

"Insurance," Joe Driscoll said. "Or reinsurance."

"I'll be down in a few minutes," Renata said.

Once she was upstairs, she had to remind herself to breathe. She turned on the light in her room and threw all of her belongings into her duffel bag. She started whispering to Action, *I am getting out of here. You could not pay me enough money to stay.* She threw her damp bathing suit in, and the aloe mask, though she decided to leave behind the monogrammed beach bag, Miles's shirt, and Suzanne's list. Renata inhaled, exhaled. Her father, Claire, Sallie. On the one hand Renata couldn't believe the way things were turning out, and on the other hand it made all the sense in the world. She was going to get caught, but it hardly mattered. No one could tell her what to do.

She heard the Driscolls and the Robinsons below her on the deck. Suzanne said, "I've never had this happen before, at the last minute like this. He said he'd get a hotel—"

"But really," Mrs. Robinson said. "It's August! What was he thinking? We have extra room, Suzanne, if—"

"Oh, we have *room*," Suzanne said.

Renata did not hear Cade or Claire. They were, no doubt, huddled in the living room, where Claire was describing Renata's treachery. *And then she followed Miles up into the dunes. They were gone for a while.* Renata looked long and hard at her engagement ring. Three karats, twelve thousand dollars. She had owned it now for seven days, but not for a second had it felt like it was hers. The ring came off easily. Renata left it on top of the dresser.

Renata checked the hallway. Clear. She hitched the strap of her duffel bag up over her shoulder and took off down the hall toward the back staircase. A light was on in one of the bedrooms. Renata stopped and peered in. She was so nervous, so giddy with her crime-movie escape tactics that she nearly laughed. Nicole was in the room, making up the bed. She snapped out the fitted sheet and it billowed. Renata watched her for a second, studying her face. It was grim, disgusted, and melancholy. Renata felt like she had X-ray vision; everything that had once been hidden in this house was now crystal clear. Nicole and Miles shared the apartment above the garage. *I have a roommate.* But he never said who it was. Miles and Nicole were sleeping together. *I'm sorry,* Renata thought. *I am truly sorry.* She snuck past, her bag bumping against her hip. At least she knew the kitchen was empty. She

tiptoed down the back stairs (*The Driscolls have servants,*
Action's voice said; *they have slaves*) and out the side
door. Renata's sunburned skin puckered in the night air.
She was standing in gravel by a row of trash cans next to
the tall hedge that shielded Vitamin Sea from the western
neighbors. Renata waited in the near dark until she
heard the Range Rover start up and saw the headlights
looping round.

Now, she thought. *Now!*

She heard a sound. Mr. Rogers was at the side door,
mewing. He wanted to come with her, maybe.

"Good-bye," Renata whispered.

And she ran.

7:33 P.M.

Four glasses of champagne and nothing to eat—no wonder
the room seemed off-kilter—and yet Marguerite couldn't
bring herself to move. She poured another glass of champagne, already dreading the headache she would have in
the morning. She should go get the mussels from the
fridge, the aioli. She should tear off a hunk of bread; it
might act like a sponge. The problem with having no
sense of taste was that food held zero appeal and eating
fine, beautiful food was an exercise in frustration. Marguerite would know, intellectually, that the mussels tasted
like the ocean and that the aioli was heady with garlic and
Dijon, and yet in her mouth it would be mush. She didn't
dwell on the loss of this sense much anymore—after fourteen years it was a fact of life—though she often wondered what it felt like to be blind, or deaf. Was it as
disheartening to imagine a painting by Brueghel or Ver-
meer, or a sunset on a winter's night, or your own child's

face, but be trapped in darkness, even with your eyes wide open? Was it as ungratifying to remember the exultant tones of the "Hallelujah Chorus" on Christmas Eve, or a guitar riff of Eric Clapton, or the sound of your lover's voice, but be wrapped in baffling silence?

The grandfather clock went through its half-hour spiel. Seven thirty: the very moment this whole tumultuous day had been about. *Can I feel sorry for myself now?* Marguerite wondered.

There was a knock at the door. Surely not. But yes, Marguerite heard it: three short, insistent raps. She looked in the direction of the front hall but was too petrified to move. She sat perfectly still, like a frightened rabbit, well aware that if someone looked through the proper window at the proper angle, she would be fully visible.

Another knock, four raps, more insistent. Marguerite didn't fear someone trying to hurt her as much as someone trying to help her. She rose slowly, got her bearings with the room, eyed a path from her seat at the dining-room table to the front door. She cursed herself for not getting dressed; she was still wearing the kimono. She thought about all the brilliant minds who had written about drinking—Hemingway a master among them with his wine bags made from the skin of animals and the simple repetition "He was really very drunk." And yet no one had ever captured the essence of four glasses of champagne on an empty stomach. The way the blood buzzed, the way the eyes simultaneously widened and narrowed, but most of all the way one's perception of the world changed. Everything seemed strange, funny, outrageous; the situation at hand became blurred, softened—and yet so clear! Someone was knocking on the door and Marguerite, drunk, or nearly so, rose to answer it.

There had been many, many nights of serious drinking

at the restaurant. The cocktails, the champagne, the wine, the port, the cordials—it was astounding, really, how much the customers drank, how much Marguerite herself had consumed on a nightly basis. Lots of times she had stumbled home, leaning on Porter, singing to the empty streets. Lots of times her judgment had been compromised—she had said things that were indiscreet, unwise, and possibly even cruel; she had done things she regretted (the episode in the pantry with Damian Vix came to mind), and yet she kept on drinking. She loved it to this day; she thought it was one of God's marvelous gifts to the world—the sense of possibility alcohol inspired. As her hand turned the doorknob, she conceded that she had been lucky; alcohol had never gotten the best of her the way it had, say, Walter Arcain. She had never tipped back whiskey at ten in the morning and then hit an unsuspecting jogger from behind while driving erratically over the speed limit on icy roads. The mere thought sobered Marguerite so that when she swung open the door, heedless of who it might be—hell, it could be the mailman with his irregular hours—she was frowning.

"Aunt Daisy?"

Marguerite heard the words before she focused on the face. *She came after all,* Marguerite thought, and then checked to see if it was true. Renata Knox, her godchild, stood before her—red in the face, panting, sweating, with a plummy bruise to the left of her chin. Her white-blond hair was in a ponytail, she wore a white shirt and a pink skirt, and slicing through her small breasts was the strap of an unwieldy duffel bag. It looked like she had run in her sandals all the way from Hulbert Avenue; it looked like she was trying to escape the Devil himself—and yet she was utterly beautiful to Marguerite. She was Candace.

"Darling!" Marguerite said.

"Can I come in?" Renata asked. "I'm kind of on the lam."

"Yes," Marguerite said. "Yes, of course." She ushered Renata into her hallway, still not quite believing it. Was this really happening? She came anyway? Marguerite shut the door, and when Renata kept a steady, worried gaze on the door, Marguerite locked it.

"Thank you," Renata said.

"Thank *you*," Marguerite said.

Marguerite pulled the second champagne flute from the freezer and filled it to the top. Meanwhile, Renata dropped her heavy bag.

"Is it all right if I stay the night?" she asked.

"Of course!" Marguerite said. She was so happy for herself, and for whichever of the upstairs bedrooms that would finally be used, that it took her a moment to realize something must have gone terribly wrong at the house on Hulbert Avenue. Marguerite handed the champagne to Renata, who accepted it gratefully. "Go right ahead and drink. You look like you need it. We'll have a proper cheers in a minute." Marguerite had planned to serve the hors d'oeuvres in the sitting room, but it suddenly seemed too stuffy; the grandfather clock would watch over them like an armed guard. So, the kitchen table. Marguerite fetched the polka-dotted cocktail napkins, the toothpicks, the mussels, the aioli. She decided to stay in her kimono. She didn't want to leave Renata for even a minute; she might disappear as quickly and unexpectedly as she had come.

"Sit, please, sit!"

Renata collapsed in a kitchen chair. Her face was still a bright alarm. Sunburn. She impaled a mussel on a toothpick and zigzagged it heavily through the aioli.

"Can you tell me what happened?" Marguerite said, settling in a chair herself. This was supposed to be an evening when Marguerite did the talking, and she had worried about how she would negotiate the requisite small-talk-to-start. Now there was no need.

Renata didn't seem keen on explaining right away. She was too busy feasting. She brought the mussels successfully to her mouth a third of the time—otherwise, dollops of aioli landed on the table, which she didn't notice, or on the front of her white shirt, which she did. She swabbed those drops with her cocktail napkin, leaving behind pale smudges.

"Sorry," Renata said. "I'm starving."

"Eat!" Marguerite said. "Eat!"

"These are delicious," Renata said. "They're divine."

She finished her glass of champagne, burped quietly under her breath, and tried to relax. She was safe, for the time being, though her whereabouts wouldn't be a secret for long. Someone would come sniffing around shortly, but Renata wasn't leaving. They couldn't make her.

"Darling?" Marguerite said.

Renata had seen pictures of Aunt Daisy in her parents' wedding album. In these pictures, she wore a purple dress; her hair was in an enormous braided bun that sat on top of her head like a hat. There were different pictures of Marguerite in the back of the album, pictures taken during the reception. In one photograph, Marguerite's hair was down—it was long and wavy, kinked from the braiding—she had changed into a black turtleneck and black pants; she was holding a cigarette in one hand, a glass of red wine in the other. Renata's parents were also in the photograph, her uncle Porter, her uncle Chase, and one of the restaurant's waitresses. It looked like a photograph from a Parisian café—everyone was half-smiling and sexy and smoky. Marguerite, though she wasn't pretty like Renata's mother, appeared very glamorous in these pictures, and that was the image Renata had clung to. Her godmother, a famous chef with sophisticated sensibilities, her mother's best friend.

The Marguerite sitting next to Renata now had a short, shaggy haircut (truth be told, it looked like she'd cut it herself) and she seemed much older than she had in the pictures. She was wearing a pink silk kimono, an article of clothing that intrigued Renata; it was exactly the kind of thing Action would have picked out of a vintage shop and boldly made her own. The kimono looked like it had history, character; if Suzanne Driscoll owned such a kimono she would have stored it in the attic, pulling it out only for costume parties, Halloween. But here was Marguerite wearing it to dinner. Despite the haircut and the aging, Marguerite had style. And more important, most important, the thing Renata had counted on, was that she exuded generosity, tolerance, acceptance. Renata felt she could confide everything, just from the way Marguerite had said, *Can you tell me what happened?* Just from the way she said, *Darling?*

"Well," Renata said. "I ran away. Again."

Marguerite nodded, and gave a little smile. "So I see."

Renata wondered what kind of scene was enacting itself back at Vitamin Sea. Had her father arrived yet? Had anyone noticed she was missing? How long would it be until the phone rang? By leaving, Renata hoped she had made herself clear: She wasn't going to marry Cade. She wasn't going to conform to Cade's idea of her, or the Driscolls' idea, or her father's idea. She was going down another road entirely.

"I cheated on my fiancé today," Renata said. "I had sex with someone else."

Marguerite's eyebrows arched. The secret smile faded. Renata felt a wave of regret. Did Marguerite disapprove? Renata felt guilty about Miles, but mostly because she had been up in the dunes with him when Sallie had her accident. The act of sex bothered her less—though there were Cade's feelings to consider, and now Nicole's. The sex had seemed predestined, somehow, the inevitable result of the bizarre circumstances she found herself in today.

"If I tell you about it," Renata said, "you won't judge me, will you?"

"No," Marguerite said. "Heavens, no." She sipped her champagne, nibbled a mussel, and nodded her head. "Go ahead," she said. "I'm listening."

The clock ticked; it ding-donged out quarter till the hour, then the eight strokes of the hour. The number of mussels diminished as the number of used toothpicks piled up on the side of the platter. When the mussels were gone, Marguerite brought Renata a hunk of bread to wipe up the aioli. The girl remembered her manners from time to time, placing her hands daintily in her lap—then, as she got swept away by her own storytelling, she would forget them, downing her champagne in thirsty gulps, polishing the inside of the aioli bowl to a shine. Meanwhile, Marguerite tried to predict the girl's needs—more champagne, more bread, a fresh napkin—while trying to keep track of the tale she was spinning. Renata started with the engagement only a week earlier—a diamond ring in a glass of vintage Dom Perignon at Lespinasse. Impossible to say no to, Marguerite had to agree. Then Renata moved on to the house on Hulbert Avenue, and the boy's parents, Suzanne and Joe Driscoll. Did Marguerite remember them? Marguerite couldn't say that she did. Renata described the mother, Suzanne, very carefully: the red hair swept back and curled under the ears, the big blue eyes, the skinny forearms jangling with gold bracelets. Marguerite didn't remember anyone like this—or rather, she remembered too many people like this, so many years in the business, so many nights in the summer, it was impossible to keep track. Marguerite felt like she was letting Renata down by not recalling the couple who were to be her in-laws, but then Renata smiled wickedly and it became clear she was glad Marguerite didn't remember them.

"How about the Robinsons?" Renata said. "She's short with dark hair, weighs about eighty pounds. His first name is Kent; he wears half spectacles."

"No, darling. I'm sorry. If I saw them, maybe . . ."

Again, the look of someone who had just won a secret point.

Marguerite heard about Renata's jog to the Beach Club, the discovery of Suzanne's wedding list, the conversation in which Renata told her father of her engagement, followed by the decision to go with this boy, Miles, to Madequecham Beach.

"I can see how that would be hard to resist," Marguerite said.

"You don't even know," Renata said.

And then there was a change in Renata's tone. Her voice grew somber; the words came more slowly. Marguerite heard about a girl named Sallie, decorated like a Christmas tree with tattoos and piercings. Sallie had a surfboard in the car; it got loose and smacked Renata in the jaw, hence the bruise. Renata disliked Sallie. But then came the discovery of the cross Marguerite had fashioned so long ago (she could remember pounding it into the ground with a mallet meant for tenderizing meat, her bare hands freezing) and Sallie was there, next to Renata as Renata knelt before the cross and kissed it. Next Marguerite heard about heavy surf, Sallie handing Renata her sunglasses, Sallie kissing Renata on the jaw. Marguerite heard about the volleyball game, sandwiches smushed by beer bottles, Sallie and Miles sitting on either side of Renata, making her feel, somehow, like she had to choose sides. Marguerite heard the girl Sallie's words, *Will you keep an eye on me?* And, *Don't go getting married while I'm gone.*

"I said I'd keep an eye on her," Renata said. "But as soon as she was back in the water I disappeared into the dunes with Miles."

Marguerite nodded.

"And she went down. Hit her head on her board and went under and when they found her, when they brought her out, she wasn't breathing."

"Oh," Marguerite said.

"It was like I caused the accident," Renata said. "I said I would watch her and then I didn't, I was off doing this other horrible thing, and I feel . . . not only like I was negligent, but like it happened because of me."

"You feel responsible," Marguerite said. "Guilty."

"God, yes," Renata said.

Marguerite stood up to slide the asparagus into the oven. Guilt, responsibility—these were topics Marguerite knew intimately. She should be able to offer some words—*things just happen; we don't have any control; we can't blame ourselves for the fate that befalls others*—but Marguerite didn't believe these words to be true. Guilt lived in this house with her; it was as constant as the clock.

"I understand the way you must be feeling," Marguerite said. She cut two pieces of tart and set them down on the table.

Renata blinked her eyes; tears fell. Marguerite replenished their champagne and touched Renata's hand.

"Is the girl all right?" Marguerite said. "She went to the hospital?"

"She went to the hospital here," Renata said. "Then they flew her to Boston in a helicopter. I don't know if she's all right. I have no way of knowing."

Marguerite sniffed the air, as if she *were* a witch, or an intuitive person, capable of divining things.

"She's all right," Marguerite said. "I can feel it."

"Really?" Renata said.

For a second, Marguerite felt cruel. The conversation with Dan seemed like aeons ago, but she did recall his words: *You're like Mata Hari to her, Margo. She's going to listen to what you say.*

"Really," Marguerite said. "But if it makes you feel better, we can call someone. We can call the hospital in Boston and ask."

Renata searched Marguerite's face. More tears threatened to fall and Marguerite panicked. She wasn't prepared for any of this. But then Renata's features settled and she picked up her fork. She gazed at the tart. "This looks delicious," she said. She took a bite, then eyed the dark glass doors that led to Marguerite's garden, as though she expected the bogeyman to appear.

She started talking again—about Cade demanding that Renata stay for dinner, about the Robinsons, their daughter, Claire, the ex-girlfriend no one had mentioned to Renata, about the shared semester at the London School of Economics.

"The semester before he met me," Renata said. "And he never said a word."

Marguerite forked a bite of tart. The pastry was flaky, the cheese creamy, and although she registered no flavor at all, she could tell the tart was a success. Renata devoured hers, then pressed the pastry crumbs into the back of her fork. Marguerite cut her another piece, a small piece, because there was more food to come.

"Oh, thank you, Aunt Daisy," Renata said. "Thank you just for listening. It has been the weirdest day. Nothing was as I expected it to be."

"Indeed not," Marguerite said. She marveled at Renata's story. And Marguerite thought *her* day had been extraordinary—because she left the house, visited old friends, stopped by her former place of business, because she drove to the country side of the island and back, because she had telephone conversations, because she polished silver and drank tea, because she looked at old photographs, because she sacrificed her Alice Munro stories in favor of the old, useless stories of her own life, because she cooked a meal for the first time since Candace's death. Ha! That was nothing.

"I'm glad you escaped," Marguerite said, only a little ashamed at herself for lauding the girl for leaving a dinner party without any excuse, warning, or word of good-bye. Marguerite was being horribly selfish. "You're safe here."

"I haven't told you the real reason I left," Renata said.

"You haven't?"

"No."

"Okay," Marguerite said. The champagne had officially gone to her head. She had lost her wits, or was about to. *Water,* she thought. She fetched a tall glass of ice water for herself, and one for Renata, who simply stared at it. "What is the real reason you left?"

"My father is here."

Marguerite hiccupped, then covered her mouth and closed the top of her kimono with her other hand. "Here where?"

"On Nantucket. He flew in tonight. When I snuck out, Cade was leaving to pick him up at the airport."

Marguerite let her eyes flutter closed. She remembered Dan's promise to show up if he thought that was what it would take to save his daughter. *But look, Dan,* Marguerite thought as she gazed at Renata—bruised from the surfboard, sunburned, her two ringless hands pushing her corn silk hair back from her forehead—*she saved herself.*

"Daddy will call," Renata said. "Once he realizes I'm gone. He'll come here."

"Yes," Marguerite said. How it panicked her, knowing she didn't have much time, knowing she still had a story of her own to tell. "I'm afraid you're right."

8:11 P.M.

Claire Robinson was the first one to notice Renata's absence. She figured Renata was upstairs in her bedroom, pouting like a child, because no one, it seemed, had told her that Cade and Claire had been a couple for seven years. Either that or she was hiding, afraid Claire would tell Cade about her frolic with Miles in the dunes. Claire chuckled; this was just too good. She had battled her parents about coming tonight—how could they possibly ask her to share a meal with Cade and his new fiancée? But when Claire saw Renata, a bell sounded. It took her a while to be sure— but sure she now was—Renata was the same girl that everyone playing volleyball at Madequecham that afternoon had watched Miles lure into the dunes. Eric Montrose had pointed it out. "There goes Miles with another Betty. Young one this time."

Claire tiptoed up the stairs, grinning with the stupid

pleasure it gave her to be privy to this scandalous information.

To the left, Claire spied the dark doorway of Cade's room, a room she knew intimately. How many nights had she sneaked up and slept with Cade, both of them naked and salt-encrusted from a late-night swim, arms and legs and hair entwined until one of them woke up to the sound of the early ferry's horn or the cry of seagulls. Claire sighed. She had thought, for certain, that she and Cade would be married. Now she was headed to graduate school at Yale to study Emily Dickinson, and she should be grateful she hadn't married Cade Driscoll. Hell, if Miles had looked at *her* twice, she would have followed him into the dunes herself. She might even tell Renata this; they would conspire. *Don't worry, I won't tell a soul.*

Claire tapped on the guest room door. Light spilled out from the bottom of the door, but Claire heard no noise. Maybe Renata had fallen asleep; Claire noticed the way she had been pounding back the drinks. Claire knocked again. Nothing. She cracked the door. "Renata?" Claire hated to admit how much she loved the name; it was a poetic name, both harmonic and sensual. It meant "reborn."

Claire peeked into the room. It was empty. The bed was made, though a bit rumpled; there was a head-shaped indentation in the soft, white pillow. One of Suzanne Driscoll's canvas beach bags lay on its side on the floor among a scattering of sand. Inside the bag, Claire found a damp beach towel and a piece of folded-up paper. Did she dare? She checked the bathroom, empty, and the deck, deserted. Renata must have slipped downstairs.

Carefully Claire smoothed out the paper. It was a list, written out in Suzanne's hand. Wedding stuff. Claire sniffed. The list was silly—flowers, cake, party favors—and yet Claire felt a pang of . . . what? Regret? Jealousy?

She reminded herself of her disastrous reunion with Cade in London: He admitted that he felt nothing for Claire anymore, nothing but a great fondness, a brotherly love. Claire was quick to agree. *Of course. I feel the same way.* This wasn't true, but at least she'd escaped with her pride.

Claire laid the list on top of the dresser. As she did so, she gasped. Sitting there all by itself like someone's forgotten child was Renata's engagement ring. The stone was huge, square, in a Tiffany setting; the stone must have been close to three karats. Claire turned the ring in the light. The diamond was clear, flawless. Claire's hands were trembling. Did she dare? Why not? It was obvious at that moment, though perhaps only to Claire, that Renata was gone for good.

Claire slipped the ring onto her finger. It fit perfectly.

The ride from the airport to Hulbert Avenue was a quarter hour of hell for Daniel Knox, forced as he was to listen to Cade, a kid with a shirt and a watch and a car more expensive than Daniel's own, make a twenty-point case about why he should be allowed to marry Renata. Daniel said very little during this presentation, figuring silence was the best way to put Cade on edge. Daniel had given his "blessing" to Renata that morning, in a panic. Never in fourteen years of raising his daughter had he used reverse psychology, but for some reason the announcement of her engagement cried out for it. If Daniel said yes when she expected him to say no, it would frighten her. And it must have worked, because clearly Renata had said nothing to Cade about Daniel's cheerful response. Despite the tedium of listening to Cade describe how he would care for Renata, Daniel felt triumphant. He knew his daughter better than these people.

It was very dark, and Nantucket, out of town, had few streetlights, but Dan peered through the window nonetheless. It was a singular experience, returning to the place where your life had once been. He had *lived* here—alone at first, running the Beach Club, then he lived here with Candace, and then with Candace and Renata. He knew the streets, cobblestone, paved, dirt, and sand; he knew the smells of bayberry and of low tide on a still, hot day; he knew the sounds of the ferry horns and the clanging bell at the end of the jetty. This had once been his home, but now he was very much the visitor.

Cade hit the turn signal and pulled into a white shell driveway. The house loomed in front of them—it was huge, bedecked, terraced, landscaped, a castle of a place, and every light in the house was on; it was as bright as a Broadway stage. Dan couldn't help thinking that this looked suspiciously like new construction; they had probably bought the lot and then torn down the fine old summer cottage that stood here in order to build this monstrosity. *VITAMIN SEA,* the quarterboard said.

"So I hope, Mr. Knox, that Renata and I have your blessing," Cade said. "I know she's young, but we wouldn't be getting married until the spring."

"Spring?" Daniel said, to show he was listening.

"Yes, sir. After school is out."

Daniel Knox said nothing else, though he was dying to utilize his "one shouldn't get married until one's traveled on three continents" speech. He was cognizant of the fact that he had shown up without warning and would be relying on Cade's family and their good graces for a place to sleep tonight. And dinner—Daniel wasn't particularly hungry, but he'd gathered from something Cade said walking from the terminal to the parking lot that there was a dinner party in progress. Lobsters or some such, with family friends, and that was what had, miraculously, kept Renata from going to Marguerite.

A woman with red hair and the tight face of someone who'd had plastic surgery appeared in the door, waving a glass of wine.

"Welcome!" she called out. "Welcome, welcome!"

"My mother," Cade whispered.

Uh-huh. Dan felt a familiar disappointment. Why was it that women his own age went to so much trouble to beautify that they ended up erasing any natural beauty they might have possessed in the first place? It was one of the things that had kept Dan from dating again after Candace's death: the way women tried so hard. Cade's mother, for example. Clearly a pretty woman, if you could get past the fact that she was fifteen pounds underweight, had suffered a chemical peel, colored her hair, wore too much makeup and too much jewelry. Women like this made Daniel long for Candace, who had looked her most beautiful first thing in the morning when she woke up, or after she got home from a run—when she was sweaty, sticky, and the picture of all-natural glowing good health. Candace would never have done these things to herself. Her idea of glamour was a shower and a clean dress.

Daniel Knox ascended the stairs and shook hands with the woman, Cade's mother. She planted a wet kiss on his cheek, which seemed awfully familiar, though she was probably under the impression they were soon to be family—and what, really, was more familiar than showing up unannounced?

"I'm Daniel," he said. "It's nice to meet you."

"Suzanne," she said in an exaggerated way, as though she weren't trying to tell him her name so much as sling it at him. *Sha-zaam!* "I'm so glad you could come."

"I'm sorry it was last-minute," Daniel said. He had no good reason to offer these people for why he'd shown up out of the blue, and he was counting on them being too polite to ask.

"Come in; come in," Suzanne said. "Your timing is perfect. Nicole is just putting dinner on. And you must meet our dear friends the Robinsons. They've been so charmed by Renata that to meet you is just icing on the cake."

"Icing," Daniel repeated. He was ushered into the foyer, where there was a black-and-white parquet floor and a Robert Stark painting hanging on the wall—the lone sailboat with the flame red sail; every house on Nantucket must have that painting. There was a curving staircase to the left; down the stairs came a pale milkmaid of a girl with messy dark hair. She smiled at Daniel.

"Hello!" she said.

"Claire, this is Daniel Knox, Renata's father. Daniel, this is Claire Robinson, a dear friend of the family. Claire and Cade went to Choate together."

"I see," Daniel said. He extended a hand to the girl, then began to wonder after the whereabouts of his own daughter. It didn't surprise him that she'd skipped the airport run; Cade had obviously seen that as an opportunity for a man-to-man chat. However, now that Daniel was in this enormous house with perfect strangers, he wanted to set eyes on his own flesh and blood. Renata was not going to be happy to see him; she would be decidedly unhappy, angry, mortified. That was the risk he had taken.

They moved into the living room, which was decorated in seventeen shades of white. Suzanne asked what he was drinking.

"Scotch," he said. "Straight up."

"You and my husband will get along just fine," Suzanne said. She did not make the drink herself but called a young black woman in from the deck and asked her to make it. "Mr. Knox would like a scotch straight up."

The woman nodded. Daniel grew warm around the neck. He hated to see people accept orders on his behalf.

"And how is dinner coming along?" Suzanne asked.

"All set, ma'am."

"Okay, then, please bring Mr. Knox's drink out to the deck. Cade? Claire? We're ready to sit."

"Yes, Mother," Cade said.

They moved out to the deck. It was a stunning evening, warm but breezy, with a black velvet sky and a clear crescent moon. And to be on the water like this, with Nantucket Sound spread out before them like a kingdom—well, overdone house aside, Daniel Knox was impressed. He introduced himself to the father, Joe Driscoll, who did not stand to shake hands but merely nodded and said jovially, "So glad you could join us!" His hands were clasped in his lap, one hand was rattling around like a Mexican jumping bean, and it was then Daniel remembered that Renata had mentioned that Joe Driscoll was sick. Parkinson's. Daniel bowed to him.

"Thank you for having me."

Next, Daniel met the elder Robinsons, Kent and Kathy.

"We hear you used to own the Beach Club," Kathy said.

"Years ago."

"We've been languishing on the wait-list for what seems like forever," Kathy said.

"Same here," Joe Driscoll said. "It's quite the exclusive place."

"We belong to every club on the island," Kent Robinson

said. "Except for that one. So naturally that's the only one my wife cares about."

"Mmmmm," Daniel said. They were talking like he was somehow responsible for their exclusion from the club. "I don't have a thing to do with it anymore. I sold it in '92, the year my wife died."

The group nodded mutely, Joe Driscoll tipped back the ice in his drink with his good hand and they all listened to the clink of it in his glass. Suzanne came out, waving her wine. "Okay, everybody sit! Kathy, you're next to Daniel, and Kent, you come over by me. Claire, you're right there, and Cade—"

Daniel watched the Robinsons sit. Joe Driscoll stayed where he was, turning in his chair and raising an arm with his empty glass toward the young black woman, who whisked it away to be refilled. Claire sat, and Suzanne. Only Daniel and Cade remained standing, presumably wondering the same thing. The table was laden with a feast: A shallow bowl at each place held a two-pound lobster; there was a platter with twenty ears of steamed corn, an enormous bowl of green salad, Parker House rolls. But there was no Renata.

Daniel shot Cade a questioning look. Cade said, "She went upstairs to put some aloe on her face. She got quite a sunburn at the beach today."

"Who?" Suzanne said.

"Renata."

Suzanne glanced around the table as if double-checking each person's identity. "My word," she said. "Renata!"

"She's upstairs?" Daniel said.

"She wanted to fix her face," Cade said. "But that was a while ago. Maybe she fell asleep."

Claire coughed into her napkin.

"I'll go get her," Cade said.

"I'll go get her," Daniel said. "If she's hiding from any-one, it's me."

"Hiding?" Suzanne said. "Don't be ridiculous. You both sit. Nicole will go up and get Renata, won't you, Nicole?"

"Certainly," Nicole said.

"Wonderful," Suzanne said. "Thank you. The rest of us should start before everything gets cold." She lifted her wineglass and waited with a pointed gaze until Daniel and Cade took their places. "Cheers, everyone!"

Nicole trudged up the back stairs. She felt cranky and venomous, like a snake ready to strike. She had worked nearly fourteen hours today, she had not had a moment to take her dinner break, and she was pretty certain that, de-spite all the beautiful promises he had made in order to lure her to Nantucket from South Africa, Miles was leav-ing her. It would be unfair to say this was all Renata's fault. Things between Nicole and Miles had been strained all summer—he constantly asked her to take his shifts so he could hang out at the Chicken Box or go to the beach with the lesbian surfer girl. Since one of them was responsible round-the-clock for meeting Suzanne Driscoll's needs and desires, there was no time to be alone together, no time for sex except the wee hours (when, quite frankly, Nicole was too tired), no time to enjoy each other's company or even plan their winter escape—a three-month kayaking trip to Irian Jaya. No, it wasn't Renata's fault, though Nicole sus-pected they had slept together. Nicole heard it in Miles's voice that afternoon when he'd called to say he wasn't coming back. Miles had wanted Nicole to pack his stuff up and leave it hidden in the bushes at the end of the driveway;

he wanted Nicole to tell Suzanne he was quitting. Nicole was incredulous. *I am not going to do your dirty work. Come pack your things yourself. Come tell Suzanne to her face, like a man.* But he claimed he couldn't—he told her the whole sob story about the lesbian surfer girl hit in the head with her board, nearly drowned, and then he confessed that the real reason he couldn't return to Vitamin Sea was because of a bad judgment call he'd made in regard to Renata. He'd kidnapped her for the afternoon; he'd convinced her to skip lunch with the madame. *And you know what Suzanne will think,* he'd said. Oh yes. It was what Nicole thought herself, it was what Cade thought, it was what everyone thought when they heard that Miles and Renata had slipped away together for the afternoon. Bad judgment indeed. Nicole had hung up on him, mid-sentence. She would never again trust an American.

Nicole knocked on the guest room door with authority, as though she were a dormitory proctor, or the police. "Renata?" she said. "Please open up, Renata. I'm afraid your absence has been detected downstairs." She knocked again, with such force the door rattled in its frame. Renata had had . . . three wine spritzers? She was probably passed out facedown, drooling all over the linens. Nicole knocked once more for propriety's sake, then opened the door. Simply telling Suzanne that Renata wasn't answering wouldn't be good enough; Suzanne liked tasks completed.

Nicole was no detective, but she was able to put two and two together and draw a conclusion in a matter of seconds—the room was empty; the duffel bag that, only that morning, looked as though it had exploded everywhere was gone; the much-celebrated engagement ring sparkled on top of the dresser. On the floor lay Miles's shirt, his white polo with the small rip in the collar. Nicole picked it up. Sure enough. *The little bitch,* Nicole thought. *Gone with Miles.* Nicole hissed with anger. What a day. The worst of her life.

They didn't sit down to their proper dinner until nearly nine o'clock, and by that time they had emptied both bottles of champagne. Marguerite suggested a trip to the basement for a third bottle, and Renata, because she was younger and more sure-footed, led the way down the stairs. The basement wasn't as scary as she imagined. There was a washer and dryer, a folded-up card table, a basic box of tools, and a wall rack that must have held five hundred bottles of wine.

"My secret cache," Marguerite said. "What I took from the restaurant when it closed."

"Geez," Renata said. Marguerite slid a bottle of 1990 Pommery off the shelves, and they went back upstairs.

They decided to be brave and eat in the dining room, where the table was set and waiting. Marguerite pulled all the shutters on the front of the house closed and yanked the curtains firmly across.

"No one can see in," she said.

Renata settled into a chair while Marguerite served pieces of rosy tenderloin ladled with béarnaise, crispy asparagus, and slabs of homemade bread served with the butter from Ethan's farm. Marguerite filled their flutes to the top and set the bottle of Pommery in the wine cooler. She eased herself down across from Renata and raised her glass. Derek and the Dominos played in the background. Yes: This was what Marguerite had been dreaming of when she woke up this morning.

"Salud," she said.

Their flutes clinked like a tiny bell. The clock struck nine.

"I feel so at home here," Renata said. "Nothing at all like I felt on Hulbert Avenue. I feel so peculiarly at home."

"I'm glad," Marguerite said.

"Will you tell me about my mother?"

"Yes," Marguerite said.

"I don't have anyone else to ask," Renata said. "Dad won't talk about it."

Marguerite cut a small piece of meat. "Have you thought to ask your uncle Porter?" This was something she'd been wondering. Porter had been there for nearly all of it; he could have shed a lot of light.

"Caitlin doesn't let him see us," Renata said. "She doesn't like my dad, I guess, and she doesn't like Uncle Chase. She has no use for anybody in Porter's family."

"That's too bad," Marguerite said. She wished she could say she was surprised, but Porter had gone against all good sense when he decided to marry Caitlin. "Surely you see him at school?"

"Never," Renata said. "He only teaches graduate students now, and every time I stop by they say he's busy."

"Right," Marguerite said. She cleared her throat. "Well, let's see. Your mother."

As Marguerite talked, Renata ate slowly. She laid her knife and fork down while she was asking a question; otherwise she savored every bite of the meat, the rich, lemony sauce, the asparagus, the chewy bread, thick with butter. When the clock struck the quarter hour, the half hour, the hour, Renata straightened, arched her back, stretched her legs under the table. Marguerite poured what seemed like an endless stream of champagne into Renata's glass, which she didn't need. She was very drunk—and yet, instead of impeding Renata's concentration, it enhanced it. Renata absorbed every word: Marguerite and Porter meeting at the Musée du Jeu de Paume under Renoir's *Les Parapluies,* Marguerite's first minutes on Nantucket when Porter brought her to the new restaurant, the wormy chestnut floors, the driftwood mantelpiece, the prix-fixe menu, the night Porter first brought in Candace, the kiss, the tin of saffron. The walk with Candace through the moors after Porter's picture appeared in *The New York Times* with another woman, the dinners when Candace and Marguerite sat by the fireplace in the very next room talking until well after midnight, the night in July when Daniel Knox first set foot in Les Parapluies and made it clear he wasn't leaving until Candace agreed to go out with him. Their first meal alone together, Marguerite said, was one that she cooked them: cedar-planked salmon and potatoes Anna.

"I'll bet your father never told you that," Marguerite said.

"Never," Renata said. "Do you think he even remembers?"

"He remembers," Marguerite said. "He swore I put something in the food that made him fall in love."

Renata smiled. She was wallowing in this talk like a pig in mud; she was sucking it in like a dog with his snout stuck out a car window. Her parents together, her parents in love—it was Renata's own history she was hearing about.

"Your father thought I was back in the kitchen stirring potions in my cauldron, my uncut hair graying in its braid. Even before your mother died, he never fully trusted me."

Renata kept quiet; she sensed this was probably true. She marveled that it was growing so late and no one from Vitamin Sea had called—not her father, not Cade.

"No one has called," she said.

"I unplugged the phone," Marguerite said.

"And no one has come by."

"Not yet," Marguerite said. She sipped her water and took a rejuvenating breath. She enjoyed telling Renata about the good times: the restaurant open, Marguerite and Porter together, Candace alive. Was she making herself clear? Could the child see her mother as Marguerite saw her—showered after a long day of exercise and sun, in one of the cocktail dresses that left her shoulder bare. Her blond hair freed of its elastic and spilling down her back. Her easy manner, like the best women of that time, full of simplicity and grace.

"She desperately wanted to go to Africa," Marguerite said. "She wanted to open a restaurant in the Sahara."

"She did?"

"We went to Morocco together, your mother and I."

"You did?" In her mind, Renata heard the metallic rain of coins falling from a slot machine. Jackpot. This was something she never would have known about her mother if she weren't sitting right here. Her mother had been to Morocco. She had gone running through the medina in a Boston Red Sox cap; the men who owned the carpet shops, the men who carved *thuya* wood, the men who served conical dishes filled with *tagine,* the men who drove the taxis, the men who pressed juice out of oranges on the Djemaa el-Fna, they had called after Renata's mother in wonder. It was her blond hair, her smile, her sweet and awkward French—the whole country fell in love with her.

"Your mother was one of those people," Marguerite said. "Everyone was drawn to her—friends, perfect strangers. She could do no wrong; she could get away with anything. I can't tell you how many times I wished I could be like that. I wanted to . . . *be* Candace." Marguerite arranged her silverware carefully at an angle on the side of her plate and folded her napkin. She had never admitted this to anyone; she hadn't even thought it all the way through in her own mind—but yes, it was true. When Marguerite stood in front of Madame Verge's mirror she thought she would grow up to be like Candace. Marguerite smiled. "I'm going to guess you take after your mother."

Renata's first instinct was to deny it. Her father loved her unconditionally, of course, and Action and Cade. She attracted people easily—like Miles and Sallie. Renata wasn't sure what all these people saw in her; she wasn't sure who they thought she was—she didn't even know herself yet. Her mother had had a magnetism, something natural she emitted from her heart: love, maybe, patience, understanding. Whereas Renata felt like she was constantly giving pieces of herself away, she was engaged in a juggling act to keep everyone in her life happy. *Yes, I'm being careful; yes, you're my best friend; yes, I love you the most.*

Renata shook her head. *No, not me. I'm not like that.* "Whatever happened with the restaurant in Africa?"

"Nothing happened," Marguerite said. "While we were in Morocco, your mother discovered she was pregnant."

"With me?"

"With you."

"So I ruined her dream, then?"

"No, no, darling. It would never have worked out anyway, for a million reasons. It wasn't meant to be."

"You could still do it," Renata said.

Marguerite laughed. "That time has come and gone."

"No, really," Renata said. "You could open a restaurant over there like you and Mom wanted. You could leave this place for a while." Renata's voice sounded concerned and Marguerite wondered if it contained any pity. The last thing she wanted was for the child to pity her.

"Leave?" Marguerite said, as though the thought had never occurred to her. It had, of course. Sell her house and move to Paris. Or Calgary. Start over someplace new, like she was nineteen instead of sixty-three. "I'll have to think about that."

Marguerite cleared away the dinner plates and left Renata in the dining room to enjoy the champagne, the flowers, the ticking of the old clock. All this information at once, it was a lot for a person to process; Renata could use a few minutes of quiet. As Marguerite rinsed the dishes she pondered the girl's words. Out of the mouths of babes. *You could still do it.* Marguerite thought about the night Candace first mentioned the restaurant. She remembered Candace's anger with her, her frustration. *I want you to reimagine.* She could reimagine now, with ease: A restaurant with walls of canvas, swathed like the head of a Bedouin. A place in the middle of the desert that would be hard to reach, where some nights it would be just Marguerite alone, enjoying enough romantic atmosphere for fifty people. She would wait those nights for the ghost who left footprints in the sand.

Before she set out dessert, Marguerite retreated to her bedroom to fetch the photographs from her dresser. There were only the two that Marguerite had to show, though there were hundreds of others—pictures from the restaurant opening, benefit nights, pictures from Candace's wedding, from Morocco—that Marguerite kept in a wooden wine crate in the storage space of the smallest of the five upstairs bedrooms. Maybe one day down the road she would have the courage to pull that box out and sift through it, but for now there were just these two pictures. Marguerite set them down in front of Renata. Renata picked up the christening picture first and squinted. Admittedly, there wasn't much light in the dining room, but Marguerite didn't want to spoil the atmosphere by making it brighter.

"That's me?" Renata said. "The baby?"

"That's your christening party."

"It was at the restaurant?"

"Of course. You're my godchild. The one and only."

Renata gazed at it with the most heartbreakingly earnest expression Marguerite had ever seen.

"You don't have pictures of Candace at your house?" Marguerite asked.

"Oh, we do," Renata said. "Just not this one."

"Right," Marguerite said. The girl's life had more holes than Swiss cheese. But here was a hole Marguerite could fill. Renata, Marguerite, and Candace at the party following Renata's christening. "It was probably the most glamorous christening party any child ever had. We had foie gras, black truffles, champagne, thirty-year port, Cuban cigars, caviar—"

"Really?" Renata said. "For me?"

"Really. For you." Daniel had insisted on footing the bill for everything, though Marguerite had given a case of champagne and Porter had, somehow, conjured up the cigars. "It was a big deal, your arrival in the world."

"I love this picture," Renata said.

"Yes, so do I." Marguerite studied it, trying to see with fresh eyes. Both she and Candace looked so proud, so awestruck, that they might have been the baby's parents: mother and godmother.

The other photograph was black-and-white. It was taken one long-ago autumn; it was just Candace and Marguerite sitting at one of the deuces facing Water Street. Neither of them was looking at the camera; they had plates of food in front of them, but they weren't eating. Marguerite was

saying something, and Candace's head was bent close to
the table, listening. Marguerite doesn't remember the moment the photo was taken or even the night; it was snapped
by one of the photographers from *The Inquirer and Mirror*. It ran the week of October 3, 1980, on the Seen on the
Scene page. Marguerite had been furious; she'd called
the newspaper and threatened to sue, though the editor
of the paper had laughed and said, *The picture's completely
innocuous, Margo, a slice of life, and it's a damn attractive shot of you both, I might add.* The caption under the
picture read: *Chef Marguerite Beale engages in tête-à-
tête with friend Candace Harris at French hot spot Les
Parapluies.* Marguerite never quite came around to the
editor's point of view—to her the picture was an invasion
of privacy; it reminded her uncomfortably of the picture
of Porter with Overbite Woman in *The New York Times*.
It put Marguerite and Candace's intimacy on display—
however, it was this very thing that eventually endeared
the picture to her, and she asked that the editor send her
a print.

"Dessert?" she said. She spoke the word brightly, though
inside she panicked. Dessert, no matter how sweet, meant
the end. Marguerite would have to tell about the end.

"I'd love some," Renata said.

Marguerite disappeared into the kitchen.

9:30 P.M.

The young black woman came out onto the deck with her
eyebrows knit together and her mouth pressed into a flat
line. Even in the night air, lit only by candles and tiki
torches, Daniel could tell she was a few shades paler than
she'd been when she left. Daniel stood up and the table

grew quiet. They had just been talking about the Opera House Cup sailing race, and an old boat they all remembered called *Christmas*.

"Renata?" Daniel said. "She's asleep?"

"She's gone," Nicole said.

Cade whipped around in his chair. "What?"

"The guest room was empty," Nicole said. "Her things are gone."

The Robinsons were quiet, except for Claire, who coughed into her napkin, in order to keep from laughing. She wasn't sure why but she found this very funny. All except for Cade, who looked like he was fourteen years old again, dropped off for his first day of boarding school, abandoned by his parents, separated from his friends. He had been so forlorn that first day, whereas Claire had felt free at last.

Suzanne laughed, too, but shrilly. "That's ridiculous," she said. "Where did she go?"

Nicole felt like Suzanne was daring her to come right out and say it: *She left with Miles.* But Nicole couldn't stand to think the words, much less speak them out loud to a tableful of people, and furthermore, she hated being the center of attention. *Don't shoot the messenger,* she wanted to say, though she knew they would anyway. That was why she'd left the ring right where it was, on top of the dresser. There was no use bringing down all the bad news at once; they could find the ring themselves when they went upstairs to investigate.

"You're sure her stuff is gone?" Cade said.

"I'm sure."

"I know where she is," Daniel said.

"Where?" Cade said.

"Where?" Nicole asked, forgetting herself. Then she thought, *You don't know where she is. You're only her father.*

"She's with her godmother," Daniel said. "Marguerite Beale."

"No," Cade said. "She called Marguerite to cancel."

"That's where she is," Daniel said. "Trust me." Faces around the table seemed unconvinced, or uncaring, but what these people didn't understand was the allure Marguerite held. Daniel had kept Renata away from her for fourteen years. He didn't want Renata to have to hear Marguerite's side of the story, her teary admissions, her apologies. But Renata had sought it out on her own. In a way, Daniel felt proud of her. She hadn't been taken in by these people; she hadn't been hypnotized by their wealth; she had kept her eye on what was important to her—seeing Marguerite, and learning about her mother.

Suzanne exhaled loudly and cradled her pink cheeks in her hands. She looked completely deflated. Daniel thought he might feel gratified by this, but instead he was ashamed. He very calmly sat back down. The poor woman had put a lot of work into tonight's dinner party and Renata had poked a hole in it. Despite Daniel's overwhelming desire to see his daughter, he wasn't willing to shred the evening further; he would salvage what he could. Renata wasn't going anywhere; she was safe. Daniel buttered a Parker House roll and took a bite.

Cade glared at him. "I'm going over there to get her."

Daniel swallowed the bite of roll and sipped his scotch. "Leave her be, son."

"What do you know about leaving her be?" Cade said. "She left because you showed up. I'm sure that's why she left."

"I'm sure you're right," Daniel said.

And because she doesn't want to marry Cade, Claire thought.

And because she had sex with Miles, Nicole thought.

She was swept along by his beautiful promises. Just the way Nicole had been last winter when she was working as a breakfast waitress on the harbor front in Capetown. Miles had suckered her in with promises of love and money. Nicole was encouraged, however, by the confidence of the father's words. Maybe Renata did go to whatshername Beale's house. Hadn't she been talking about it with Suzanne that morning in the kitchen? Nicole sensed a filament of hope. Maybe Renata didn't go with Miles after all. For the first time all day, Nicole felt relieved. She felt almost happy.

"Let's just eat," Joe Driscoll said in a voice that would not be argued with. He held the end of an ear of corn with one hand and his butter knife with the other. Neither hand was shaking.

Cade noticed this, but he was too agitated to let it register. He threw his napkin onto his plate. "I'm going up to see for myself," he said.

"Cade," Suzanne said. "Listen to your father, please. Eat your dinner."

The Robinsons returned to their dinner plates; Kathy Robinson murmured something complimentary about the salad dressing. Joe Driscoll buttered his corn. Claire Robinson sipped her tea, which had grown cold. She knew, as did Nicole, who slipped into the kitchen, as did Daniel Knox, as did the others deep down in their hearts, what Cade was going to find.

9:42 P.M.

Nine thirty was Lights-Out at Camp Stoneface and had been all summer. The twelve girls in Action Colpeter's cabin were doing their nighttime-whisper thing, which

sometimes lasted until midnight if Action didn't lay down
the law. However, tonight, for some reason, Action was
antsy, eager to wash her hands of Camp Stoneface and the
million and one rules she hand to enforce. What she
wanted more than anything was to be *alone,* so she could
think.

"I'm going to be right outside on the stoop," Action announced to her campers. "So do not attempt any funny
business." Such as drawing with indelible marker on the
girl who fell asleep first, such as telling stories, real or
made up, about doing drugs or having abortions.

Action took her flashlight and her pen and notebook and
sat on the top step right outside the cabin door. If they
thought they were escaping tonight to raid the mess hall
for stale potato chips or to make mooning noises through
the screens of the boys' cabin, they were mistaken. Action
started a letter to Renata. *Hola, bitch-ola!* But this sounded
too cavalier. The truth was, Action was worried about
Renata. Action had been born with nearly perfect instincts,
and her instincts about Renata this second rang out:
Doomsday.

Action heard a noise coming from the grass nearby.
Even after eight weeks in the thick woods of all-but-
forgotten West Virginia, Action was still freaked out by
the wildlife—the bullfrogs, the owls, the bats, the mosquitoes. Action had grown up on Bleecker Street; her experience with wildlife had been limited to the freaks she'd seen
on Christopher Street and in Alphabet City. The noise in
the grass sounded suspiciously like a bullfrog. It made a
buzzing, thrumming sound at regular intervals. Action
shined her flashlight in the frog's direction; if she kept her
eye on it, it wouldn't land on her—*plop!*—wet and slimy.
She was wearing jeans and running shoes. She could step
on it or nudge it away. The noise persisted. Action climbed

down off the steps and hunted through the grass for the frog.

Her flashlight caught a glint of something silver. What was this? Action bent down, peering at the thing that was making the noise as if it were as unlikely as a moonstone. Ha! She snapped it up, triumphant. It was a cell phone, the ringer set to vibrate.

Eight weeks ago, discovering a cell phone in the grass would have made Action livid. Cell phones—and all other treasures from the world of IT—were strictly *verboten* at Camp Stoneface. Action and her fellow counselors took great joy in stripping campers of their cell phones, Game Boys, iPods, and laptops. But now, in the third week of August, discovering a cell phone in the grass, at night, while she was alone, was like a sign from the Virgin Mary herself. Action was supposed to call somebody.

She flipped the phone open. It was a Nokia, sleek and cool in her palm. And—would wonders never cease?—she got a signal.

Action felt a flash of guilt. *Hypocrite!* she screamed at herself in her mind. She hadn't even let twelve-year-old Tanya, who was the youngest and best-behaved child at the camp, call her mother on her mother's fortieth birthday. However, Action's presiding sentiment was that enough was enough and she had had enough of West Virginia unplugged. If she had to sing "Take Me Home, Country Roads," one more time, she would have a Tourette's-like outburst. *"Blue Ridge Mountains, Shenandoah River."* No, sorry.

One call, she thought. *I'll only make one call.* The call should rightly go to her brother, Major. Action received a letter from him every single day, written out in Miss Engel's neat block script. He wrote about how he went to Strawberry Fields, ate ice cream, watched some kid fly a kite that looked like a parrot. It was hot, he wanted to go on vacation to the ocean the way they did when Action was at home, but Mom had work and Dad had work. *I miss you, Action. I love you miss you love you.* He always signed his own name, and this was what hurt Action the worst. His name in wobbly capitals, a smiley face drawn into the *O.* Action had never gone eight weeks without seeing him, and what she missed the most was him needing her. Of course, she had twelve needy cases evading sleep inside the cabin, but it wasn't the same.

Action should have called Major—woken him up if he was asleep—but she didn't. She'd had a Doomsday instinct about Renata all day long in the front of her mind. Action was worried that something terrible had happened—she'd gotten hurt, or she died. The girl never looked both ways before she crossed the street; she was constantly getting her foot stuck in the gap between the subway car and the station platform; in nearly every way, Renata Knox acted like a person who didn't have a mother. However, that was one of many things that Action loved about her. Renata was her best friend, the sister she never had; she was special. Their friendship couldn't be explained any easier than one could explain peanut butter and jelly. Why? Just because.

Action dialed Renata's cell phone number, praying she wasn't sleeping over at Watch Boy's new apartment on Seventy-third Street. The phone rang. Action stepped away from her cabin and closer to the bordering woods, despite the hoots of owls. She didn't want her girls to hear. The phone rang four, five, six times; then Renata's voice mail picked up. *Hi! You've reached the voice mail of Renata Knox.* Action grinned stupidly. Voice mail was still the old girl's voice, which Action hadn't heard in eight weeks. *I can't answer my phone right now—*

Because I'm being held up at gunpoint, Action thought. But suddenly that didn't feel right. *Because I'm cuddling up with Watch Boy.* Yep, that was probably more like it.

Action cleared her throat; then after the beep, she whispered, "Hi, it's me." Action had never had a friend whom she could say those three words to. Before she met Renata, Action had never imagined having a *Hi, it's me,* friend; she never realized how important it was—to be recognized by another person, known instinctively, whether she was calling from down the street or the Tibetan Himalayas, whether she was calling from the woods of West Virginia or the D train. Action hoped that for the rest of their lives they would be each other's *Hi, it's me.* "I found a cell phone in the grass and I decided to break the first commandment of Camp Stoneface and call. I've been thinking of you all day. I hope you're all right. I have a funny vibe, like something is happening. Maybe you joined the circus today, maybe you found religion, but something is happening; I can feel it. Don't call me back. I'm about to turn this phone over to the authorities where it rightly belongs. So . . . write me a letter. Tell me you're all right. I'll be wait—" Action was cut off by the second beep. Renata always accused her of leaving the world's longest messages. Action thought to call back, to finish, but she had promised herself only one phone call.

I love you, she thought. *Love you like rocks.*

10:10 *P.M.*

In Room 477 of the Trauma Unit of Massachusetts General Hospital, Sallie Myers opened her eyes.

Ohhhkay, she thought. *Very strange.*

She registered *hospital,* herself pinned to a bed, stuck

in both arms and attached to machines that blinked and beeped; she noted a white curtain to her right, shielding her from someone else, or someone else from her. She tried not to panic, though she had no idea why she might be in a hospital. *Think back,* she told herself. *Slowly. Carefully.* But there was nothing.

She was afraid to move; she was afraid she would try and find herself unable. So she remained still, except for her eyes, which roamed the room, and thus it was that she discovered a figure huddled in a chair off to the left, at the edge of her field of vision. She turned her head. Her neck was stiff, but it worked. It was . . . *Miles* in the chair. He was asleep, snoring.

Ohhhhhkay, she thought. What did she do to deserve waking up in a hospital room with Miles? Miles, Miles. She was still drawing a blank.

A minute passed, or maybe not a full minute but fifty or sixty beeps of the machine, which might have been counting the beats of her heart. Her heart was beating. Sallie figured she might as well try her arms. She turned her wrist. The right one moved just fine, but her left side felt fuzzy and not quite attached, like it was a prosthetic arm. Sallie gazed down. It was her arm. She touched it with her right hand. She could feel her own touch but she couldn't make the arm move.

At that second, some people walked in. There was a gasp from one of the people—a woman, Sallie's mother. Sallie's father followed right behind, and then a dark person, who towered over Sallie's parents like they were little children. Pierre. Pierre was here? Sallie couldn't recall ever seeing Pierre anywhere but at the bar.

Sallie's mother rushed to the side of the bed and took hold of Sallie's leaden arm. "You're awake!" she said. "The nurses told us it sounded like you were awake. They can tell from the way they monitor the machines out there."

Sallie's father clapped his hands in a rallying way. He was the head football coach at the University of Rhode Island. "I knew you'd snap out of it."

Pierre approached next, timidly. He was out of his element, away from the noise and the beer and the grime of the bar, away from his back office with the black leather couches and his computer where he played Tetris while the kids out front got smashed and slam-danced. "Hello, gorgeous," he said.

Sallie turned her attention back to her mother, her beautiful mother, who taught classical music at Moses Brown, who wore bifocals when she read a grocery list, who had fretted and worried so much over Sallie's three older brothers that she had been content to just let Sallie be. Bartending? *Fine.* Surfing? *Good for you.* A pontoon boat down the Amazon River? *You only live once.* Sallie's eyes filled with tears. She'd had a dream that her mother had died. In the dream, Sallie was driving down a dusty road and she spotted a white cross in the brush. She stopped, checked it out. The cross was for her mother. Sallie had screamed when she saw the cross, *Wait! Mom, wait! I'm getting married!*

"Honey?" Sallie's mother said. "How do you feel?"

"Confused," Sallie said. The cross hadn't been a dream. It was real. But how? Sallie's mother stood right in front of her. "What am I doing here?"

"You had a surfing accident on Nantucket," her father said. "You hit your head. They say you were underwater for a while."

"Just a little while," her mother said.

"And where am I now?"

"At Mass General. In Boston," her mother said. "Pierre called us. And your friend . . ." She nodded at the chair where Miles slept. ". . . was here when we arrived."

"Miles," Sallie said. It all came back to her like something that fell from the sky and landed in her lap. Miles picking her up at the house with the girl, Renata, who was the cutest, sweetest thing Sallie had ever seen. So innocent, so young, so clean. It was *her* mother the cross was for. She had knelt before it. Kissed it.

"The doctors say they expect you to be fine," Sallie's mother said. "You may feel stiff and numb for a while, but there's been no brain damage."

"Thank God for that!" Sallie's father said.

"You're going to be fine, doll," Pierre said.

"Did Renata come?" Sallie asked. "Did she come to the hospital with Miles?"

"Who?" Sallie's mother asked.

Sallie watched Miles snoring in the chair. *Wake him up!* she wanted to say. *Ask him if Renata came!* But Sallie knew the answer was no. After all, why would she?

10:25 P.M.

Ethan Arcain couldn't sleep. His wife, Emily, was dozing heavily beside him, her breathing deep and regular. His boys were asleep in their respective rooms; the house Ethan had built himself was solid and quiet. Out their open bedroom window Ethan could hear the occasional bleat of one of the goats. He and Emily had eaten grilled steaks for dinner with a fresh corn salsa and heirloom tomatoes drizzled with pesto. Such were the feasts when one lived on a vegetable farm. Ethan had drunk too much—he and Emily split a bottle of Shiraz from the Barossa Valley—

and then he'd opened a second bottle to drink alone, despite Emily's warning eyebrows.

He hadn't been able to tell Emily about Marguerite coming to the farm that afternoon, despite Brandon announcing, "Dad introduced me to an old friend of his today."

Emily had been pulsing basil and garlic and pine nuts in the Cuisinart. "Oh yeah, who was it?"

Brandon conveniently chose that moment to leave the kitchen. "Nobody," Ethan said. "Someone who used to come to the farm back in Dolores's day, when I was just a kid."

"Someone you had a crush on?" Emily said.

"Oh God, no," Ethan said. "Nothing like that."

He hadn't been able to tell Emily, and then he drank too much and now both things weighed on his mind. He had lived on Nantucket his whole life; lots of people knew his history: his parents' brutal split, his father's drinking. And yet no one brought home the guilt and the shame of being Walter Arcain's son like Marguerite.

You never had to carry his load, Marguerite said. But he did. Despite the fact that he had worked hard to create a decent, peaceful, productive life, he did.

It had happened during the first week of February. Ethan had graduated the year before from Penn State with a degree in agriculture; he had confessed to his mother that he was in love with her new husband's oldest daughter, Emily; he was working as a waiter at the Jared Coffin House to make money. He had a deal all worked out with Dolores Kimball; he was going to buy the farm from her when she retired. Everything was moving forward—not quickly, maybe, but in the right direction. And then, just before service for the weekly Rotary luncheon, Ethan's mother came into the dining room to say that Walter had killed someone and not just someone but Candace Harris Knox. She was jogging out in Madequecham; Walter was driving the company truck, drunk out of his mind.

To a young man who had helped put vegetables and flowers on the table at Les Parapluies since he was ten years old, Candace Harris Knox was a living legend. She was much older than Ethan but captivating nonetheless. The blond hair, the way she could run for miles without ever looking tired, the successful husband, the adorable young daughter. Candace was royalty on the island; she was a goddess among women, Ethan knew it just from the way she carried herself, just from the genuine ring of her laugh. And Walter Arcain, Ethan's father, had run her down like she was a frightened rabbit.

Ethan pulled the quilt up under his chin. He was freezing, and a headache was starting from the wine. When he rolled over, he checked the red numbers of the digital clock. Ten thirty. He figured Marguerite's dinner with Renata must be nearly over.

10:41 P.M.

Cade Driscoll was nothing if not disciplined. He was nothing if not obedient. And so, in the end, he suffered through the world's longest dinner—through lobster cracking, corn munching, and people talking just to cover up the obvious awkwardness of Renata's desertion. Then he endured dessert—blueberry pie with ice cream, coffee, and port. He sent mental pleas to his mother: *Let the Robinsons go home! Set them free!* But his mother seemed to feel that the longer the Robinsons stayed, the less likely it was that they would remember the night as a disaster. Finally, finally, at nearly eleven o' clock, Kent Robinson stood up and offered to get his wife's wrap. Good-byes were said. Claire kissed Cade on the mouth and said, "She wasn't good enough for you, anyway." As if she knew something Cade didn't.

As soon as the Robinsons' car pulled out of the driveway, Joe Driscoll excused himself for bed. When he shook Daniel Knox's hand he said, "Any chance you'll be up for sailing tomorrow?"

"Let's see how things go."

"Yes, yes," Joe said. "Let's." He grabbed Cade's elbow before going up, but he said nothing. Suzanne, in a moment of mercy, set her wineglass on the lowboy and said, "I'll worry about cleaning up in the morning. Good night, all." And she followed Joe up the stairs.

Once his parents were gone, Cade turned to Daniel Knox. "How about you?"

"I'm a night owl," Daniel said. "I may sit on the deck for a while."

"Okay," Cade said. "Good night, then." He marched up the stairs, as if dutifully going to bed.

He had sneaked out of dinner, just for a minute, pretending to use the bathroom, and he'd called Marguerite's house, but he got no answer—the phone rang and rang. Then he called Renata's cell phone. Voice mail. He hung up without leaving a message. He wanted to believe Renata's disappearance had nothing to do with *him* per se. It was just a nineteen-year-old girl doing as she wished without thinking her actions through. She was upset with Cade for making her cancel dinner, and the whole thought of her father showing up freaked her out. So she bolted.

Cade pushed open the door to the guest room, thinking maybe she had left him a note. He turned on the light.

He was looking for a piece of paper—and that was what drew his eyes to the list. He snapped it up, but seeing that it was just something in his mother's handwriting, he balled it up and threw it on the floor. He looked out on the deck, the deck where only the night before he and Renata had made love while his parents entertained friends below them. But the deck was deserted. Ditto the bathroom. It wasn't until Cade was ready to leave the guest room—and, quite possibly, make a surreptitious run over to Quince Street—that he noticed the ring. It was right on top of the dresser, as obvious as the nose on his face, so maybe he had seen it a minute ago and just not admitted it to himself.

He picked up the ring, squeezed it in his palm, and sat on the bed. *Renata*. He thought he might cry for the first time since who knew when. People had said he was crazy to propose to a nineteen-year-old girl. *She's too young*— his own parents had warned him of that—*she hasn't had time to get started, much less be finished.* And then there was Claire's parting shot: *She wasn't good enough for you, anyway.* Claire was jealous—either that or she suspected Renata had been indiscreet with Miles, which was, Cade had to admit to himself, entirely possible. Even so, Cade loved Renata fiercely. Yes, she was young, but she was going to grow into an amazing woman, and he wanted to be there for that.

He rocked back and forth on the bed. She didn't want him. Cade had the urge to knock on his parents' bedroom door and, like a three-year-old, crawl into their bed, have his mother smooth his hair, have his father chuck him under the chin. But his parents weren't like that; they weren't nurturing. They had given him every possible advantage and they expected him, now, to make his own way. He would have better luck seeking comfort from Daniel Knox.

Yes, Cade thought, he would go down, pour himself a scotch, and confide in the man who might have been his father-in-law. Daniel knew Renata better than anyone. Maybe he could tell Cade something that would make him understand.

Cade walked down the hall, past the west guest room, in case Daniel had come upstairs. But the door to the west guest room was open; the room was dark and empty. Cade stumbled down the back stairs into the kitchen—it had been cleaned by somebody, Nicole probably—and into the living room. Empty. Cade walked out onto the deck. The table had been cleared, the tiki torches extinguished. The deck was deserted. Cade gazed out at the small front lawn, and down farther to the beach.

"Daniel?" Cade whispered into the darkness.

But he was gone.

11:00 P.M.

At eleven o' clock, with the old clock's grand recital of the hour, its eleven ominous bongs, Marguerite brought out dessert. Two *pots de crème,* topped with freshly whipped cream and garnished with raspberries. Renata was fading; Marguerite could see it in the way her pretty shoulders were sagging now, her eyes staring blankly at her own reflection in the dark window. Marguerite set the ramekins down with a flourish. This was it. There was no more champagne to pour. Nothing left to do but tell her. Marguerite's heart hammered away. For years she had imagined this moment, the great confession. Many times Marguerite had considered going to a priest. She would sit in the little booth, face-to-face with the padre, and confess her sins—then allow the priest to touch her head and grant her absolution. But it would have made no difference. Marguerite knew that God forgave her; his forgiveness didn't matter. Forgiveness from the girl in front of her, Candace's child, that did matter.

Marguerite had imagined this moment, yes, but she still couldn't believe it was about to happen. Her chest felt tight, like someone was squeezing her windpipe. Heart, lungs—her body was trying to stop her.

"I'd like to talk to you about your mother's death," she said.

"You don't have to tell me," Renata said. "You don't have to say anything else."

"I'd like to anyway. Okay?"

"Okay."

"A couple of years after you were born, your parents bought the house in Dobbs Ferry. They wanted a place to spend the winter. Your father thought maybe Colorado, but your mother wanted to be close to the city. She loved New York, and Porter was there. She wanted to put you in a good school; she wanted to be able to take you to the museums and the zoo. It made sense."

Renata nodded.

"They bought the house when you were four."

Renata swirled her whipped cream and chocolate together, like a child mixing paints. She had yet to take a bite.

Marguerite paused. Her task was impossible. She could speak the words, relay the facts—but she would never be able to convey the emotion. Candace had spent months preparing Marguerite for the news—saying that she and Dan were looking at houses off-island, saying they'd found a house in a town they liked, Dobbs Ferry, New York, less than four hours away. Marguerite never responded to these announcements; she pretended not to hear. She was being childish and unfair—they were all adults, Candace and Dan were free to do as they liked, they had Renata to think of, and Nantucket in the winter had few options for the parents of small children. The warning shots grew nearer. One day Candace had the gall to suggest that Marguerite join a book group or a church.

You need to get out more, she said. *You need to make more friends.*

What she was saying was that she couldn't carry the load by herself. She was going to be leaving. But Marguerite, stubbornly, would hear none of it.

You can't leave, Marguerite said. She picked Renata up, kissed her cheeks, and said, *You are not leaving.*

But leave they did, in the autumn, a scant three weeks after Porter returned to Manhattan. In the final days, Candace called Marguerite at the restaurant kitchen every few hours.

I'm worried about you.

Dobbs Ferry isn't that far, you know.

We'll be back for Columbus Day. And then at Thanksgiving, you'll come to us. I can't possibly do the dinner without you.

We're leaving nearly everything at the club. Because we'll be back the first of May. Maybe April fifteenth.

On the day that Candace left, Marguerite saw them off at the ferry. It was six thirty in the morning but as dark as midnight. Dan stayed in the car—Renata was sound asleep in the back—but Candace and Marguerite stood outside until the last minute, their breath escaping like plumes of smoke in the cold.

It's not like we'll never see each other again, Candace said.

Right. Marguerite should have been used to it, sixteen years Porter had been leaving her in much the same way, and yet at that moment she felt finally and completely forsaken.

"Your mother leaving was painful," Marguerite said.

Candace had phoned every day during Renata's nap and Marguerite—despite her claims that she would be fine, that she was very, very busy—came to rely on those phone calls. After she hung up with Candace, she poured her first glass of wine.

"I traveled down to the new house for Thanksgiving like your mother wanted. We cooked three geese."

"Geese?"

"Your uncle Porter took the train up from the city. It was a very big deal. That was the only time in seventeen years that I ever celebrated the holidays with him."

Marguerite closed her eyes for a second and was gone again. Three geese stuffed with apples and onions, served with a Roquefort sauce, stuffing with chestnuts, potato gratin, curried carrots, brussel sprouts with bacon and chives—Marguerite made everything herself, from scratch, while Candace did her best to help. Porter, bald and with a belly, did his old stint of lingering in the kitchen all day, drinking champagne, shaving off pieces of the exotic cheeses he'd brought in from the city, providing a running commentary on the Macy's parade, which played on TV for Renata, who stacked blocks on the linoleum floor.

At the dinner table, they all took their usual spots: Marguerite next to Candace, across from Porter. It was a careful imitation of their dinners at Les Parapluies, though Marguerite keenly felt the difference—the strange house, the evanescence of the occasion—in three short days, she would be back on Nantucket alone, and Porter, Dan,

and Candace would return to the lives they had made
without her.

Later, though, Porter cornered her in the kitchen as she
finished the dessert dishes—Dan was in the den watching
football; Candace was upstairs putting Renata to bed. He
pushed Marguerite's hair aside and kissed her neck, just
like he used to all those years ago in the restaurant. She
nearly broke the crystal fruit compote.

I have something for you, he said. *Call it an early
Christmas present.*

Marguerite rinsed her hands and dried them on a dish
towel. Christmas used to mean pearls or a box from Tiffany's, though in the last few years Porter's ardor had mel-
lowed or matured and he sent an amaryllis and great
bottles of wine that he picked up at one of the auctions he
attended in New York.

Marguerite turned to him, smiling but not happy. Porter sensed her misery, she knew, and he would do anything short of performing a circus act to get her to snap
out of it.

He handed her an envelope. So not the amaryllis or vintage Bordeaux after all. Marguerite's hands were warm
and loose from the dishwater, too loose—she fumbled with
the envelope. Inside were two plane tickets to Paris. It was
like a joke, a story, something unreal, but when she looked
at Porter his eyes were shining. She grabbed his ears and
shrieked like a teenager.

"Just after the first of the year, your uncle took me back
to Paris," Marguerite said to Renata. "Finally. After nearly
seventeen years."

"How was it?" Renata said. "Was it like you remembered?"

"No," Marguerite said. "Not at all as I remembered."

* * *

Marguerite had convinced herself that Paris was the answer to her prayers, the key to her happiness; her expectations were dangerously high. There was, after all, no way to re-create their earlier time in Paris: Too much had happened; they were different people. Marguerite was nearly fifty years old, and Porter was beyond fifty. They were professionals; they were seasoned; they had money and tastes now. Instead of being caught up in the throes of fresh love, they were comfortable together; they were, Marguerite thought, a pair of old shoes. And yet she held out for romance—a promise from Porter, a proposal. She believed the trip to Paris was a sign that he was finished with his bachelor life in New York; he was done with his string of other women; the sparkle had worn off; the effort wearied him; he was ready for something lasting, something meaningful. Marguerite had won out in the end for her perseverance. She would finally belong to someone; she would finally be safe.

No, it wasn't the same, though still they walked, hand in hand. Marguerite had compiled a list of places she wanted to visit—this *fromagerie* in the sixth, this chocolatier, this home-goods store for hand-loomed linens, this wine shop, this purveyor of fennel-studded salami, which they ate on slender *ficelles,* this butcher for roasted *bleu de Bresse*. It was January and bitterly cold. They bundled up in long wool coats, cashmere scarves, fur hats, leather gloves, boots lined with shearling. Despite the temperature, Marguerite insisted they visit the Tuilieries, though the gardens were brown and gray, dead and dormant—and afterward Le Musée du Jeu de Paume. The museum was smaller than either of them remembered; it was overheated; the bench where Porter had fallen asleep was gone, replaced by a red circular sofa. They revisited the Cathedral of Notre-Dame. When they opened the door, the draft licked at the flame of five hundred lit prayer candles. Marguerite paid three francs to light one herself. *Please,* she thought. At Shakespeare and Company, Marguerite lingered among the Colette novels and picked one out for Candace while Porter, to her astonishment, bought something off the American bestseller list, a thriller penned by a twenty-five-year-old woman.

"All my students are reading it," he said.

They were staying in a suite at the Plaza Athenee—it was all red brocade and gold tassels; it had two huge marble bathrooms. It was sumptuous and decadent, though a far cry from showering together under the roses. One afternoon, while Porter worked out in the new fitness center, Marguerite lounged in the bubble bath and thought, *I should feel happy. Why aren't I happy?* Something was missing from this trip. An intimacy, a connection. When she got out of the tub, she called Candace.

"Why are you calling me?" Candace said, though she sounded happy and excited to hear from Marguerite. "You're supposed to be strolling the Champs-Elysées."

"Oh, you know," Marguerite said. "I just called to say hello."

"Just hello?" Candace said. "This must be costing you a fortune. Is everything okay? How's Porter?"

What could Marguerite say? Suddenly, with Candace on the phone, her worries seemed silly, insubstantial. Porter had brought her to Paris; they were staying in a palace; Porter was sweet, attentive, indulgent. He hadn't so much as called his secretary. She couldn't possibly complain.

"Everything's great," she said.

Each night, they dressed for dinner—Porter in a tuxedo, Marguerite in long velvet skirts or the silk pantsuit

Candace had sent her from Saks. They went to the legends: Taillvent, Maxim's, La Tour d'Argent. The service was intimidating; the food was artwork; the candlelight was flattering to Porter's face as Marguerite hoped it was to hers. She worried that they might run out of things to talk about, but Porter was as manic and charming as ever; he was so filled with funny stories that Marguerite was surprised he didn't burst from them. And yet she couldn't combat the feeling that he felt it was his job to keep her amused.

One night, at a bistro that had been written up in *Bon Appétit,* they drank three bottles of wine and when they got in the cab they spoke to the driver in fluent French. When they reached the hotel, they were laughing and feeling extremely pleased with themselves. Porter looked at Marguerite seriously, tenderly; he seemed to recognize her for the first time during the trip and maybe in years. They were standing outside the door to their suite; Porter had the old-fashioned iron key poised above the lock.

"Ah, Daisy," he said. He paused for a long time, searching her face. Marguerite felt something coming, something big and important. She wanted him to speak, though she was afraid to prompt him; she was afraid to breathe.

"This is the life," he said.

This is the life? Marguerite nodded stupidly. Porter unlocked the door on his third try; then he shed his tuxedo and called her to bed. They made love. Porter fell asleep shortly thereafter, leaving Marguerite to brush her teeth alone among so many square feet of marble and turn off the lights.

As she climbed into bed she realized she felt like crying. She was too old for this kind of rushing emotion, this kind of searing disappointment, and yet the sorrow persisted; it lay down and embraced her.

"A few weeks after your uncle Porter and I returned from Paris, something happened that took me by surprise. Porter called to say that he had fallen in love with his graduate assistant. Caitlin. She was twenty-four years old. Now, I knew he dated other women in New York. It was a source of enormous heartache for me. He took other women to plays and dances and benefits and restaurants. Once, he took a woman to Japan. He wasn't exactly open about this, but I knew it and he knew that I knew. I never learned a single woman's name except for the woman he took to Japan; that was a favor he granted me. I presumed they weren't important enough to be named. He told me he loved me; he used to say I hung the moon. But he would not commit. I thought maybe when we were in Paris . . . but no. Paris was good-bye. He already belonged to somebody else; every hour he spent with me, he was thinking of this other person. This girl. But I didn't know that. Until."

Until the phone call. Marguerite sensed something wrong immediately. Porter's voice, always booming and upbeat, had been resigned and sorrowful. *You're the greatest friend I have in all the world, Daisy,* he'd said. *And I'm afraid I'm about to hurt you very badly.*

Marguerite had listened, without comprehending a word he said. Back in September, he'd fallen in love with his graduate assistant, twenty-four-year-old Caitlin Veckey from Orlando, Florida. She was red haired and freckled, fresh faced, naïve, she was young enough to have grown up in the shadow of Disney and Epcot. Marguerite imagined her as a cartoon character, a two-dimensional, Technicolor fairy like Tinkerbell. It was all wrong. If Marguerite was going to lose Porter, finally, after so many years, she wanted it to be to a worthier opponent—a sultry, dark beauty who spoke seven languages fluently, a sophisticate, someone with European sensibilities. Or even one of the women Marguerite had imagined Porter with over the years: Corsage Woman, Overbite Woman, Japan Woman. An aging ballerina or show jumper with a degree from Vassar and a trust fund, a closetful of shoes. But it was not to be. Porter had been stolen away by a child, a Lolita. He was in over his head, he said, in love beyond reason, and the only way he could make things right—with the university, certainly, but also in his own heart—was to marry Caitlin.

I'm getting married, Daisy, he said.

She thought of Paris and felt deeply betrayed, embarrassed even. All the usual signs had been absent. There had been no mysterious phone calls, no suspect gifts purchased that she knew of. There was the book he'd bought, and the way he'd worked out religiously at the hotel's fitness center. Twice he'd skipped dessert and he had passed up the Cuban cigars. *Are you getting healthy on me?* she'd asked him, teasing. Now she saw.

Marguerite held the receiver long after Porter hung up, staring out her bedroom window. Snow was falling, blanketing Quince Street. She remembered back to the first moment she saw him, she remembered the quiet sounds of him waking up on that bench in the Jeu de Paume, the way he'd blinked his eyes rapidly, unable to place himself for a moment. She remembered his worn leather watchband, and the first time his long, tapered fingers touched her hair. That was a Porter Harris this Caitlin person would never know, never understand.

"Your uncle Porter called to say he was marrying Caitlin," Marguerite said. "He called to say our relationship was over."

"You must have been devastated," Renata said.

It was like learning of her own death; she'd always known it was coming, but so soon? In this ridiculous way? She was shocked, incredulous; her ego was like an egg found cracked in the carton; she was angry, insulted—and worried for Porter's sake. He'd been tricked by beauty and youth, by sex. He didn't know what he was doing. The end of a seventeen-year relationship seemed too fantastical to Marguerite to be taken seriously. Porter said it was over, he said he was getting married to this young girl from Florida, and he promised he would never bring the girl to Nantucket, meaning he would never return himself. So Marguerite would never see him again. It couldn't just end, she reasoned; their relationship couldn't go from a rich and layered creation to *nothing*. Her way of life, her identity, her whole world, was threatening to shift, to tilt, to dump her into cold, unfamiliar water. She and Porter were no longer together? It was impossible. So yes, *devastated* was a fair choice of words. But the hurt was located in distant parts of her—her brain, her reason, her nerves. (Her hands shook for hours; she remembered that.) Her heart cried out for one person, the way a hurt child called out for her mother, and that person was Candace.

"I called your mother to tell her what happened," Marguerite said. "The weather was bad, it was snowing, it was horrible weather for traveling, and yet I asked her to come up. She wanted me to come to Dobbs Ferry, but I couldn't move. I was immobilized."

I want to come, Daisy, she said. *Believe me, I do. But Dan is in Beaver Creek looking at a second property and so I'd have to bring Renata—*

By all means, bring her.

I'm worried about traveling with her in this weather. Have you looked at the TV? It's awful. Is it snowing there?

Snowing, yes. Quietly piling up outside.

Okay, Marguerite said. *It's okay. I'm okay.*

Are you?

No, she said, and she dissolved into tears. *Of course not. Daisy, don't cry.*

Do you understand what's happened? Marguerite asked. *You cannot reasonably tell me not to cry.*

Okay, I'm sorry. There was a long pause, the sound of shuffling papers, the sound of Candace's sighing. *Okay, we'll come. We're coming.*

Marguerite should have backed down at that point; she should have listened to the reluctance in Candace's voice. What did another day or two days or a week matter? It was blizzarding. Asking anyone to travel in that weather was absurdly selfish, cruel even. And yet those words, *we'll come, we're coming,* were the words Marguerite craved. She needed to know there was someone in the world who would do anything for her. That person had never been Porter.

"That night, your mother was on my doorstep, holding you in her arms."

"I came here?"

"I remember it like it was yesterday. You were wearing pink corduroy overalls."

Marguerite had been pacing her house for hours when the knock finally came. She opened the door and found Candace and Renata, bundled in parkas, dusted with snow. As soon as she saw them she felt ashamed. She had guilted her best friend into traveling three hundred miles through a blizzard with a child. Candace had caught a flight from White Plains to Providence, where she hired a car to take her to Hyannis, where she caught the freight boat, which was the only boat going. And yet, in her gracious way, she made it sound like an adventure.

It's a miracle, Candace said. *But here we are.*

"I remember being embarrassed that I didn't have dinner ready. All that jangling around the house, I could have been making a stew. Instead, we ordered a pizza, but the pizza place refused to deliver, so your mother trudged down Broad Street to get it. All those years I had cared for her, but she had turned into a real mother hen. She set the table, whipped up a salad, made me a cup of tea—I wanted wine, of course, but she said no, alcohol would only make things worse—and she stared us down until we'd eaten a proper dinner, you and me."

Renata smiled.

"Your mother brought a prescription of Valium with her, thank God. She gave me two, tucked me into bed, and I fell asleep. I woke up at four in the morning and made a pot of coffee. Your mother woke up, too, and sat with me in the dark kitchen, but neither of us spoke. We didn't know what to say. It was like we'd known all along the sky was going to fall and then it fell and we pretended to be taken by surprise. Then Candace's face brightened like she'd had some inspiration, like she'd devised some foolproof way to get Porter back, to make everything right again. But she did the strangest thing. She insisted on cutting my hair. My hair hadn't been cut since I was a child. Candace said, *'Time for a new look.'* Or a new outlook. Something like that. She'd cut her own hair that winter—it was short and she wore a bandanna to push it off her face. She wouldn't let me say no. We pulled a chair over by the kitchen sink and your mother wrapped me up in an old shower curtain."

Marguerite sat in the makeshift salon chair. As Candace wet her hair, massaged her scalp, combed the length, and snipped the ends, holding them up between two fingers, something dawned on Marguerite. Something transpired. Marguerite could barely breathe; the truth was so obvious and yet so startling. *This* was what she wanted, all she wanted, Candace here, her warmth, her voice in Marguerite's ear. Marguerite filled with longing. It wasn't Porter's love she sought, and it hadn't been, maybe, for years. Marguerite wanted Candace; she loved Candace. With Candace fussing and clucking around her, with Candace touching her, Marguerite experienced a new realm of emotion. It was terrifying but glorious, too.

"When she was finished, your mother blew my hair dry and styled it, and when she handed me the mirror I started to cry."

Candace's face had fallen apart. *You hate it.*

"I was crying; then I was laughing," Marguerite said. "I put down the mirror and I took your mother's hands and I told her that I loved her."

I love you, too, Candace said. *You're the greatest friend I have.*

The greatest friend I have. Marguerite faltered. Those had been Porter's exact words and Marguerite thought, *These are the words the Harrises use when they are leaving you.*

I don't care about Porter, Marguerite said. *I loved the man dearly at one time, and we were intimate. Yes, we were.*

You're better off without him, Candace said. *I've been wanting to say that since I arrived. You* will *be better off.*

It doesn't matter, Marguerite said. *Because when I heard, when Porter told me, my heart cried out for you. You are the one person I cannot bear to lose. I love you. You are the one that I love. Do you hear what I'm saying? Do you hear?*

Confusion flickered across Candace's face. Marguerite saw it, though it only lasted a second. Did Candace understand what Marguerite was saying?

You're the best person I know, Candace said. *I can't believe what my brother has done to you.*

Say you love me, Marguerite said. *Please say it.*

Of course I love you. Daisy, yes.

I want you to love me, Marguerite said. *I don't know where this can lead. I don't know what I'm asking. . . .*

Candace's hands were cold. Marguerite remembered that. She remembered the cold hands; her friend was frightened. Marguerite dropped the hands, and as soon as she did so Candace turned away.

I think I hear Renata, she said, though the house was silent.

You don't want me, Marguerite said.

I don't even know what those words mean, Candace said. *What are you asking me for? You're upset about Porter. He hurt you. You asked me to come and here I am. What else do you want me to say?*

You don't feel the same way that I do, Marguerite said.

What way is that? Candace said. *Are you saying you're in love with me?*

Marguerite looked at herself in the mirror. The short hair now. She was a stranger to herself. What *was* she saying? Did she want to take Candace to bed, do things neither of them could imagine? Did love fall into categories, or was it a continuum? Were there right ways to love and wrong ways, or was there just love and its object?

I can't help the way I feel, Marguerite said.

You don't know how you feel. Right? Porter hurt you. You're confused. Aren't you confused?

I don't feel confused, Marguerite said. *I'm as sure about this as I've been about anything in my whole life. Since the second I met you, when you kissed me. I thought you were Porter's lover, but you kissed me.*

I kissed you, Candace said quickly, *because I knew we were going to be friends.*

Friends, yes. But more than friends. The hundreds of dinners, their mingled laughter, the walk through the moors, the winter evenings by the fire, the trip to Morocco. Candace there, that was all Marguerite had ever wanted.

It's been since the second I met you, Marguerite said. *This feeling.*

You're upset, Daisy. You don't know what you're saying.

You don't feel the same way, Marguerite said. *I'm an idiot to think you would. You have Dan. Dan and Renata. You belong to them.*

Yes, Candace said. *That's right. But you're my best friend and you have been for a long time. Things don't have to change between us just because Porter's gone. Don't make them change, Daisy. Please. Do not.*

Marguerite didn't know what to say. Things had already changed. Marguerite had crossed a boundary; she'd handed herself over, a gift to someone who didn't know what to do with it. No, not a gift, a burden. A woman nobody wanted. The girl in the mirror with the knobby knees.

"It was a big mess," Marguerite said now, to Renata. "The messiest mess. I said things to your mother I should never have said. I loved her so immensely—and I wanted her to love me. She tried her best, but things were different for her. So she found herself stuck in this house with her best friend and this huge, unwieldy confession. Your mother would have done anything for me—she'd proved that just by showing up—but there was no way I could make her feel as I felt. There was no way. She tried to pretend everything was okay, that everything could go back as it was before, but we both knew it was impossible."

Yes, Candace tried. She wiped Marguerite's face gently with a dish towel, like Marguerite was the five-year-old. Then she gave Marguerite a long and beautiful hug. Looking back, Marguerite could see there was a good-bye in the hug, but she didn't understand it then. She didn't understand. Renata had started crying upstairs, and Candace went to her.

She needs me, Candace said.

Fourteen years spent thinking about it and yet there was no way to convey to Renata what had happened that morning. Marguerite said, "Here is the thing you need to know about your mother. Everyone loved her, everyone was drawn to her, but no one more than me. I loved Candace with my whole being. Do you have someone like that? The fiancé, maybe?"

"I thought I loved Cade," Renata said. "I do love Cade. But it's not like you described. Not with my whole being. I don't even know who my whole being is."

"You're so young," Marguerite said.

"I love my roommate, Action," Renata said. "My best friend. I know it's not the same. We've only known each other a year. But still, I feel like I would die without her."

Marguerite could see the girl trying to process what she'd just heard, trying to relate. Marguerite wasn't sure, however, if Renata was intuiting what Marguerite was telling her. *I loved your mother too much, and the love destroyed her.*

Marguerite looked down at her dessert. It was beautiful enough for a magazine shoot, and yet she couldn't bring herself to eat a single bite. "Your mother brought you downstairs and she made the three of us breakfast. Tea and toast. Cinnamon toast, cut into squares. She did all this but she didn't speak, except to soothe you. She didn't speak to me; we didn't speak to each other. What to say? Then, once we were finished eating and the dishes were washed, dried, and put away, she started talking about a run."

You can't run, Marguerite said. *Look outside. The weather.*

Candace had stared, said nothing, disappeared upstairs. She came down bundled in workout clothes.

Is it okay if I take the Jeep? she said.

Where are you going?

I need air, she said. *I need to clear my head. I feel like you, like I . . .*

What?

I need to get out of the house for a while. Is it okay if I take the Jeep?

Candace . . .

Please, Daisy? You'll watch Renata? If not, I'll take her with me. . . .

You can't take her with you. It's too cold. You shouldn't be going at all. I'll bet the roads are a sheet of ice.

I have to get out, Candace said. *I need to get out of this house!* She was yelling now. Renata was scared, hugging her around the knees. What else could Marguerite have said?

Okay, yes, the Jeep. Take it. The keys are on the hook by the door. Renata will be fine. I'll take care of her. We'll have fun. And you'll . . . be careful? It's not the car I'm worried about, it's you. . . .

"But Candace didn't answer; she was halfway out the door. She couldn't wait to leave. She wanted to escape me."

Renata nodded.

"I helped you crayon in a coloring book, I got down on my hands and knees and played with blocks, and when Candace still didn't return I put you down in front of *Sesame Street,* where you fell asleep. I made myself a cup of tea. I swept up the hair trimmings; I started a stew."

"Were you worried about her?" Renata asked.

"I tried to tell myself I was being silly. Your mother used to run for hours."

"I remember being here," Renata said. "That must be what I remember. I drank tea with honey and burned my tongue. You sang to me in French, or we read in French. I remember the pattern of flowers on the sofa."

"Yes," Marguerite said.

When Renata woke from her nap, she was crying. Her hair was tangled. She was thirsty. Marguerite fixed her a small cup of tea and added honey. Together they sat on the sofa and read from *Babar.* When the phone rang the first time, Marguerite ignored it.

Renata set her spoon down in her empty ramekin. *Ching!* Marguerite flinched.

"The roads were covered with ice. Walter Arcain was drunk; he was out on the very same road you were on today, joyriding, doing doughnuts, going way too fast. He claimed he didn't see Candace at all; he claimed he felt a thump, he thought he'd hit a deer. He stopped the truck and found Candace underneath."

Renata's breath caught. Her mother. "It was his fault," Renata said. "He went to jail."

"For ten years," Marguerite said. "And yes, technically, it was his fault. But it was my fault that Candace was here in the first place. I guilted her into coming. And then the things I said that last morning . . . undid her. She was not herself when she left here. I had scared her; I had created a rift, a horrible awkwardness. I had pushed our friendship beyond its limit. Your mother would have been thinking that it was all Porter's fault; he had hurt me, made me needy; he had left me for her to sweep up; she would have been screaming at him in her mind. She would have wondered if the Valium was a mistake; she would have chastised herself for bringing it. I guarantee you she was thinking of these things, some, if not all, of them. She didn't hear Walter Arcain's truck; she didn't sense the rumble on the road. She was preoccupied, muddled, distracted. By me." Marguerite put her hand to her forehead. It was hot and damp, like she had a fever. "I should never have let her leave the house. But she wanted to get away from me. She said she needed air. She wanted to go." Marguerite searched for words that would soften the blow, but if the girl had been listening, she would see the truth, plain as day. "I have always felt responsible for your mother's death, Renata."

Renata blinked. Marguerite hadn't been driving the electric company truck, she wasn't the one who was drunk at ten in the morning, and yet Renata could see why Marguerite blamed herself. *She was here because I guilted her into coming. I abused our friendship. I upset her. She left the house upset. . . . God,* Renata thought. *Yes.* Marguerite had admitted to Candace what few people would ever be honest enough to say, even to themselves. *I love you more. I need you more.* Was it wrong to love someone too much, to love them in a way you knew they could never return? Was it possible to kill someone by loving them? Clearly, Renata's father thought so, and that was why she'd been forbidden to see Marguerite, banned from this house, from hearing this story. Was Renata supposed to feel angry at Marguerite? Was she supposed to hate her, to shun her, to judge her the way Daniel had? Maybe she was; maybe she should. But strangely, Renata didn't feel angry. She felt relieved that there was someone else in the world as confused, as guilty, as flawed, as Renata herself was. That very day she had taken her eyes off of Sallie; she had cheated on Cade, then deserted him. Was it possible to kill someone by not loving them? Renata's head swam.

"I don't know what to say," she admitted.

"I'm sure not."

"What if she wasn't thinking about you?" Renata said. "What if it was just an accident? What if Walter Arcain ran her down on purpose? Or what if it's all part of some predestined plan that we can't control? It might not have had anything to do with you. Have you considered that?"

"No," Marguerite said.

"In which case, all you'd be guilty of is telling her you loved her before you left. I wish I had told her I loved her before she left."

Marguerite twirled the stem of her empty champagne flute. If anyone could have kept Candace from going running that morning, it was the little girl in pink overalls. Renata had wrapped her arms around her mother's legs and refused to let go until Candace bent down, kissed her, and gently pried her arms away. *You stay with Aunt Daisy,* she said. *I'll be back in a little while.*

At that moment, Marguerite understood why Renata had skipped out on Hulbert Avenue, why she ran all that way with a heavy bag, in her sandals. She had come not to hear Marguerite's confessions but for another reason altogether. *I feel so peculiarly at home.* Home: The last place she felt her mother's touch.

"You did," Marguerite said. "You did."

* * *

She could have stopped there, maybe. It was late, nearly the start of a new day, but Marguerite was determined to finish.

"You've heard people say I'm crazy," Marguerite said. "Your father, and other people?"

Renata wanted to deny it, but the words were too fresh in her mind. *Not stable,* her father had said. *Rather like Vincent van Gogh,* Mrs. Robinson had said. And then there were all the things Renata had picked up in the past: *She lost it, complete mental breakdown, miracle she didn't kill herself, no one in her right mind would have . . .*

Renata shrugged.

What words did Marguerite have left at her disposal to describe the days after Candace died?

Daniel flew in from Colorado. Marguerite picked him up at the airport, and during the twenty-minute ride in the dark car, she tried to explain what had happened.

This whole thing with Porter, she said, *took me by surprise. . . .*

You made her feel like she had to come here, Daniel said. *With my daughter. In the middle of a goddamned blizzard. Who does that?*

Marguerite didn't answer. They were in the Jeep, with the wind whining through the zippered windows like an angry mosquito. Even with the heat turned up full blast, it was freezing. Marguerite's face was frozen, her fingers were frozen to the steering wheel. Her heart was frozen.

Daniel repeated himself in a louder voice. *Who does that, Margo? Who asks her best friend and her godchild, age five, to travel in a blizzard?*

I'm sorry, Marguerite said.

You're sorry? Daniel said. He spat out a mouthful of air, incredulous. *You spent all these years making her feel like she owed you something, but what you got in the end was her pity. She pitied you, Margo.*

The words were awful to hear. But how could Marguerite deny them? *You're right,* she said. *She pitied me. And I frightened her.* Here, she swallowed. If he were going to condemn her, he should condemn her for all of it. Someone should know what Marguerite had done, and a part of her held out hope that Daniel would understand. And so she told him about how she'd confessed her love, how confused Candace was by the confession, how addled. *She was desperate to get out of the house,* Marguerite said. *There was no stopping her.*

That's twisted, Daniel said. *It's sick. You made her sick. You make me sick.*

There was nothing sick about it, Marguerite said. *It was a revelation to me—how I felt, how important she was to me. I wanted her to know.*

Revelation? Daniel said. *Revelation? She's* dead, *Margo. My wife. Renata's mother. Candace is dead. Because of you.*

Yes, Marguerite said. It was almost a relief, hearing it spoken out loud. Marguerite blamed herself, others who learned the whole story or part of the story would blame her silently, but Daniel was angry enough to blame her openly. It was like a slap in the face—it hurt, but she deserved it.

When they reached the house on Quince Street, Dan snatched Renata away from the babysitter and marched upstairs, returning with Candace's suitcase.

Every last thing that belonged to her, he said. *Put it in here. You will keep nothing for yourself.* He bundled up Renata and hurried her out the door. Marguerite believed she would never see the girl again.

She had lost everyone who mattered, making it that much easier to give up. After the funeral, she saw no one, spoke to no one—not Porter, not Dusty, not Ethan. . . . She decided immediately that she would close the restaurant, but that didn't seem like enough of a sacrifice.

"After your mother died," Marguerite said, "I considered suicide. I did more than consider it. I tried it on like it was a dress, imagining how I would do it, and when. Eating the Valium was too much like falling asleep. I wanted to drive my Jeep into the ocean, or throw myself off the ferry with a weighted suitcase chained to my leg. I wanted to set myself on fire, like the women in India. I felt so *guilty,* so monstrous, so bereft, so empty. And then at some point it came to me that dying would be too easy. So I set out to destroy the part of myself that I valued the most."

"Which was?" Renata was almost afraid to ask.

"My sense of taste." Marguerite brought a spoonful of creamy chocolate to her mouth. "I can taste nothing. This could be pureed peas for all I know."

"So how . . . ?"

"I branded my tongue." She had been very scientific about maiming herself; she had been meticulous. She made a fire of hickory, which burns hotter than other woods, and she set one of her prized French utensils among the embers until it glowed pinkish white. "I burned my taste buds so profoundly that I knew I would never taste a thing again."

"Didn't it hurt?" Renata asked.

Hurt? Marguerite hadn't been concerned about the pain; nothing could hurt more than . . . But there had been nights in the past fourteen years when she'd awoken, terrified of glowing metal, of the hiss, the stink.

"When it happened, my tongue swelled up. I can remember it filling my mouth, suffocating me. I nearly lost consciousness, and if I had, I probably would have died. But I got to a phone, dialed the police. I couldn't speak, but they found me anyway, took me to the hospital." Insidious pain, yes, she remembered it now, but also a kind of numbness, the numbness of something newly dead. "A day later, stories were everywhere. Some people said I'd cut my tongue out with a knife; others said I went into convulsions and swallowed my tongue. Everyone said I had lost my mind. Some believed Candace and I were lovers; others thought I'd done it because of Porter. Self-mortification, they called it at the hospital. They weren't willing to release me. They said I was a danger to myself. I spent three months in a psychiatric hospital in Boston. Posttraumatic stress disorder—that's what they would call it now. Eventually, the doctors realized I was sane. My lawyer helped a lot; he fought to get me released. But even once I returned home, I couldn't go back out into the world. I sold the restaurant and made a fortune, but I knew I was destined to spend my days alone and dreadfully misunderstood. And I was right. My life"—here Marguerite lifted a hand—"is very small. And very quiet. But that is my choice. I am not insane. Some days, believe me, I wish I were."

Renata didn't know how to respond, but like everything with Marguerite, this seemed to be okay. Silence seemed preferable; it seemed correct. And so, they sat—for a few minutes, fifteen minutes, twenty; Renata wasn't sure. Renata was tired, but her mind wouldn't rest. She had heard the whole story for the first time and yet what she found was that she knew it already. Inside, she'd known it all along.

The clock struck midnight. Marguerite snapped to attention; Renata realized that for a second or two she'd drifted off to sleep.

"We should go to bed," Renata said. She stood up and collected the dessert dishes.

"Leave them in the sink," Marguerite said. "I'll do them in the morning." Marguerite blew the candles out and inhaled the smell of them, extinguished. *Dinner over,* she thought. But before Marguerite could feel anything resembling relief or sadness or peace, there was a knock at the door. This time there was no mistaking it for something else; there was no wondering if it was a figment of her imagination. The knock was strong, authoritative. Renata heard it, too. Her eyes grew round; the dishes wobbled in her hands.

"We should hardly be surprised," Marguerite whispered, ushering Renata into the kitchen. "We knew someone would come looking for you."

Right, Renata thought. Still, she felt hunted down. "What should we do?" she said.

"What would you like to do?" Marguerite asked. "We can answer, or we can pretend to be asleep and hope whoever it is gives up and comes back in the morning."

"Pretend to be asleep," Renata said.

"All right." Marguerite flipped off the kitchen light. There was no way anyone could see in the kitchen windows unless he scaled a solid eight-foot fence onto the garden patio. Marguerite reached out for Renata's hand. "Let's wait for a minute. Then we'll sneak you upstairs."

Renata could barely nod. She squeezed Marguerite's bony fingers. There was a second barrage of knocks.

"Is there any way we could check . . . ?" Renata said.

"And see who it is?" Marguerite said. "Certainly. I'll go." Marguerite crept into the dark hallway, telling herself she was not afraid. This was her house; Renata was her guest. She tiptoed down the hall and into the sitting room. She peered out the window, terrified that when she did so another face would be staring back at hers. But what she saw was Daniel Knox, sitting on the top step, his head in his hands. He had a small travel suitcase on the step next to him.

Marguerite hurried back to the kitchen. "It's your father."

"He's alone?"

"He's alone. He's brought a suitcase. Perhaps you should come take a look."

Renata followed Marguerite to the window. They pulled the curtain back, and both gazed upon Daniel sitting there. Marguerite's heart lurched. She tried to forget that the last time he stood on the step it was to take his daughter away; it was to pass his terrible judgment. *She pitied you, Margo.* The words she would never forget. He had meant them—and worse still, they were true. But Marguerite found it hard to conjure the old pain. So much time had passed. So much time.

Renata bit her bottom lip. She tried to erase the sight of her father on a different front step, crying because someone in the world had been cruel or thoughtless enough to steal his little girl's bicycle. All he'd ever wanted to do was protect her. He'd come to Nantucket tonight because of her phone call. He had heard it as a cry for help—and now Renata could see that's exactly what it was.

"Shall we let him in?" Renata said. "Would it be okay with you?"

"Of course," Marguerite said.

Together, they opened the door.

August 20, 2006 • *12:22 A.M.*

Cade Driscoll pulled up in front of the house on Quince Street in his family's Range Rover. Once he was parked and settled, however, he just sat in his car like a spy,

Renata's engagement ring clenched in his hand. On the first floor, the shutters had been pulled, though Cade could see thin strips of light around the edges of the windows. A light went on upstairs. Through the curtains, Cade discerned shadowy figures. Renata? Daniel? The godmother? He waited, watching, hoping that Renata would peer out and see him. *Come down,* he thought. *Come down and talk to me.* But eventually the light upstairs went off. A light came on downstairs, on the right side of the house, and Cade watched with renewed interest, but then that light went out and Cade sensed that was it for the night. They were all going to sleep. He would be well advised to do the same.

Cade opened his palm and studied the engagement ring. He hadn't told Renata this, but he had bought the ring at an estate sale at Christie's; the ring, initially, had belonged to someone else. What kind of woman, Cade had no idea; what kind of marriage it represented, he couldn't begin to guess. He placed the ring in the car's ashtray. Monday, when he was back in Manhattan, he would sell it on consignment.

He resumed his stakeout of the dark house. Like the ring, Number Five Quince Street contained a story, a secret history. The same could be said, no doubt, for every house on Quince Street and for every bright apartment window in Manhattan, for every igloo, Quonset hut, cottage, split-level, bungalow, and grass shack across the world. They all held stories and secrets, just as the Driscoll house on Hulbert Avenue held the story of today. Or part of the story.

The rest, Cade feared, he would never know.

1:05 A.M.

Marguerite lay in bed, used up, spent, as tired as she'd ever been in her life, and yet she couldn't sleep. There was excitement and, yes, anxiety, about not one but two of her upstairs guest rooms occupied, about Renata and Daniel asleep above her head. In a hundred years she never could have predicted that she would have them both in her house again. To have them show up unannounced and know they would be welcome to stay the night, like they were family.

Marguerite had expected Daniel to be officious, gruff, angry, annoyed, impatient, disgruntled, demanding—but if she and Porter were playing their old game and she had only one word to describe Daniel, it would be "contrite." He was as contrite as a little boy who had put a baseball through her window.

"I'm sorry," he said when Marguerite and Renata opened the door. "I'm sorry. I'm so sorry." The apologies came in a stream and Marguerite couldn't tell if he was sorry for showing up on her doorstep at midnight with his overnight bag, or sorry for coming to Nantucket to meddle in his daughter's affairs, or sorry for keeping Marguerite and Renata away from each other for fourteen years, or sorry for his punishing words so long ago or sorry for feeling threatened by Marguerite since the day he showed up at Les Parapluies without a reservation, when he pulled out a chair and took a seat in their lives, uninvited. Possibly all of those things. Marguerite allowed Dan to embrace her and kiss her cheek, and then she stood aside and watched as father and daughter confronted each other. Renata crossed her arms over her chest and gave Daniel a withering look.

"Oh, Daddy!" she said. Then she grimaced. "Don't tell me what happened over there. Please don't tell me. I really don't want to know."

"I'd rather not think about it myself," Daniel said. He sighed. "I'm not trying to control your life, honey."

Renata hugged him; Marguerite saw her tug on his earlobe. "Yes, you are," she said. "Of course you are."

"Would you like a drink, Daniel?" Marguerite asked. "I have scotch."

"No, thanks, Margo," he said. "I've had plenty to drink already tonight." He sniffed the air. "Smells like I missed quite a meal."

"You did," Renata said. She shifted her feet. "Can we talk about everything in the morning? I'm too tired to do it now. I'm just too tired."

"Yes," Daniel said. Marguerite noticed him peer into the sitting room. In the morning he would want to see the house; he would want to see what was the same, what was different. He would look for signs of Candace. It was fruitless to hope he might bestow a kind of forgiveness, but she would hope anyway.

"Yes," Marguerite agreed. "You, my dear, have had quite a day. Let me show you upstairs."

Marguerite led the way with Renata at her heels. Daniel, who had been left to carry the bags, loitered at the bottom of the stairs. He was snooping around already, reading something that he found on one of the bottom steps, something Marguerite hadn't even realized she'd left there—her columns from the Calgary newspaper.

"Dad?" Renata said impatiently.

He raised his face and sought out Marguerite's eyes. "Do you enjoy working with Joanie?" he said.

Marguerite raised one eyebrow, a trick she hadn't used in years and years. "You know Joanie Sparks?" she said. "You know the food editor of *The Calgary Daily Press*?"

"Do you remember my best man, Gregory?"

Marguerite nodded. How would she ever explain that she'd been thinking of Gregory just today, and the relentless way he'd pursued poor Francesca?

"Joanie is his sister," Dan said. "I dated her a million years ago. In high school."

"*You* gave her my name then?" Marguerite said. "You suggested I write the column?"

He shrugged, returned his attention to the clippings for a second, then set them down. He picked up his overnight case and Renata's lumpy bag and ascended the stairs with a benign, noncommittal smile on his face. "I did," he said. "And not only that but I read the column every week. Online."

"You do?" Marguerite said.

"You *do*?" Renata said.

"It's a wonderful column," Daniel said.

Forgiveness, Marguerite thought. It had been there all along.

"Well," she said, trying not to smile. "Thank you."

The grandfather clock eked out another hour. The announcement was mercifully short: two o'clock.

Sleep! Marguerite commanded herself. *Now!*

She closed her eyes. In the morning, she would make a second meal, breakfast. She and Daniel and Renata would drink coffee on the patio, read the Sunday *New York Times,* which Marguerite had had delivered every week since the year she met Porter. They would say things and leave many things unsaid. And then—either together or separately—Renata and Daniel would leave to go back to New York. They would resume their lives, and Marguerite would resume hers.

She was not optimistic enough to believe that, from this day on, she would see them often, or soon, though she hoped her status improved from a mere name on the Christmas card list. She hoped Renata would write—or e-mail! She hoped both Renata and Daniel would think of Nantucket on a bright, hot summer day and know they were welcome there anytime, without warning. For them, her door was open.

If nothing else, Marguerite told herself, she would be left with the memory of this day. It would be a comfort and a blessing to think back on it.

There was, after all, nothing like living in the past.